Weapons Of Old

Kent Wayne

The Unbound Realm

Weapons of Old

The Unbound Realms, Book 2

First published as an ebook on March 29, 2023

First print edition published September 12, 2025

This is a work of fiction. Names, characters, places, and incidents are either products of the author's imagination or are used fictitiously. Any resemblance to actual events, locales, or persons, living or dead, is entirely coincidental.

ISBN (print): 978-1-959476-05-4

Interior design by Jeremy C. Rowley

Printed in the United States of America

Published by:

Kings Entertainment Press LLC

"This is a story as old as time. Some would say older. One door closes, another one opens."

—The last words written by the Prophesied Traveler

A Door into Evermoor introduces Jon Dough, an unenthusiastic teen who's facing a moderately cushy yet deterministic future. He just started college. His parents are upper-middle class in San Francisco (yes, I agree—that's blindingly rich to the rest of the world). He's set up for a degree and a comfy job, but he's plagued by a sense of existential lack. On paper, the boxes are checked. He just has to stay in his lane and avoid any egregious mistakes.

Through a synchronistic twist of fate, he encounters a Marine recruiter named Chris Atriya (yep, a reincarnation of the guy in the *Echo* series) who—as his BFF dog-buddy/Gribbles/Wolven-king/Gyrax later explains—is an "Eternal Archetype." Jon signs a magical, existential contract, which triggers a deluge of visions from a fantasy-world called Evermoor. He bumbles into a high-level wizard named Alijyar SyCajister before he and his dog (Gribbles/Gyrax) pass through a portal into Evermoor.

Jon meets Rennarean Arteris, supposedly the last of the Wayfarer Advance (a loosely organized body of wandering fighter/mages who were dedicated to exploring the breadth of Evermoor, uncovering hidden knowledge, and bettering society by sharing their insights). Ren gives him an overview of Evermoor's recent history. During the Bright Age, a magical network (roughly analogous to the internet) known as the Velic Tessellate came into being. It allowed for instant communication, exchange of energy, and in some cases, physical transport. Unfortunately, civility broke down to the point of no return. (Like most of you, I sincerely hope that doesn't happen to us.) The populace's hate manifested as a magical curse called the Crimson Reft. The Reft spread throughout the Tessellate, infecting the masses with murderous anger.

It destabilized society to the point where the Crimson Reft became the Crimson Wars.

The Wars were a period of chaos, death, and suffering. Folks become desperate and appointed a temporary protector: a fearmonger named Lyderea Fairdyle (it may be a little late for this, but I pronounce "Lyderea" Lie-DEE-ree-uh in my head.) Lyderea didn't want to relinquish power, so she declared herself the White Veiled Queen, with total control of the powerful Tessellate.

Rebels banded together, into an alliance known as the Juric Unity, but they failed to overthrow her at Sidehelm Pass. The Kings of Erendor—key components of the Unity's army—sat back and watched, instead of charging Lyderea's forces with their soldiers. They had secretly betrayed the Unity and sided with the White Veiled Queen. In an ironic twist of double-betrayal, Lyderea turned on the Kings and laid a curse on them all. She rendered them into spectral haunts, doomed to wander Sidehelm Keep. They're now known to all as the Watchers of Erendor, because they sat back and watched the decisive battle.

Lyderea halted the Wars, but now folks suffer under her rule. The Eldritch Protectorate (Lyderea's Queendom) stretches across nine-tenths of Evermoor's surface.

Jon and Ren find Jon's dog Gribbles (Gribbles went missing after he walked into the portal) who is now revealed to be Gyrax Aclasian, king of the Wolven (humanoid dog-warriors). They join up with Lucknar Hap (a master thief) and Elier Finn (a High Taire Duelist) then journey to Naversé and visit Ren's mentor: Terrelly Jindow, a former Wayfarer who fought at Sidehelm.

Terrelly is riddled with chronic wounds. He is bitter, jaded, and stuck in the Evermoor equivalent of palliative care. Terrelly throws cold water on Ren and Gyri's desire to vanquish Lyderea. At the end of the meeting, Ren gives Jon the lower half of Ailura Qartesi, a magical revolver called the Avalon Clapfire.

The party of four set off for Elerica. On the road, they encounter Eralindíany Aihladi (Erany is the shortened version), a half-Elf princess from Delán, which is an Elven kingdom that Lyderea invaded and destroyed. Jon becomes infatuated with Erany.

Throughout his journeys, Jon learns more about the structure of magic. Everyone has an innate store of magical energy. It's contained in their aura, organized throughout their loci (spherical reservoirs) and their meridians (long-running channels). There are three tiers of magic. Most mages use traditional magic, which goes by a variety of implicitly known nicknames (arcanix, hedge magic, faeweave, and others). Traditional magic relies on preestablished patterns of thought. While it's precise, it's the least potent. Primal Magic is more powerful, but it's based on emotions, and the results aren't as predictable. Laiddinic powers can be interpreted as magic, but they're more akin to an existential bending of reality. God-mode, so to speak. Also, it is possible to "Shift" one's senses. That's a term that refers to opening one's perception to magical energy.

Ren tells Jon about *The Turning of Evermoor* (an ancient tome that holds prophetic weight) which details the arrival of the Prophesied Traveler, a savior figure who hails from another dimension. The Prophesied Traveler will be able to wield Laiddinic powers. He will defeat Lyderea and reach the Unbound Realm (a mythical place that is the endpoint of reality. Not everyone believes in it), where he will be granted the ability to manipulate reality without constraint. Paradoxically, the Unbound Realm can only be reached by one who has been there. Jon fits the bill in that he comes from another dimension. (Also, later on, he heals a member of their party through Laiddinic powers.)

On the way to Elerica, the party meets Nyanti Eldara, a high-powered Witch. Nyanti informs them that Elerica (also called the Witchcraft City) fell to a trio of Sytishí Whisper Folk (high-level Elven renegade mages), and an accompanying army of warlike Iguar (synonymous with Goblins). They took Elerica by surprise and drove out the populace.

Jon and his friends (now including Nyanti) retake Elerica. During the fighting, they're ambushed by Sytishí, but Arganti Knifelock, Lyderea Fairdyle's Nightkeeper Captain (Nightkeepers are Protectorate agents who wear magical blindfolds that enhance their abilities), saves them through his magical simulacra (an arcane double that can interact with matter).

Lyné Anir, the Sygress of Elerica, informs Jon and Erany they must go to Earth to retrieve the upper half of Ailura Qartesi and complete the revolver. Afterward, they must return to Evermoor, then Erany must retrieve the Rosecraft Blade: a magical sword located on the mountain known as Yom Dagur.

With the Sygresss's help, Jon and Erany travel to Earth. They complete the revolver and return to Evermoor. During their Earth-side adventure, Jon and Erany develop a romantic relationship. They finally kiss while riding a magically charged horse through a Taylor Swift concert.

After their return, they receive a message from Gyrax. Erany realizes that they've been gone for two days, but over a year has passed on Evermoor. During that time, commoners have rebelled against Lyderea, and deadlocked her forces at Algulis Devari. Gyrax wants to meet Jon and Erany at Glimmersend City.

Thus far, Jon has been thrown into the fantasy-world deep end. He's learned a few moves, been in some fights, and used Laiddinic powers when he healed Nyanti. He's still just a kid that wants to have fun. He doesn't want to think about his destiny or powers, or too much of anything besides cavorting with Erany. He hasn't figured out who he is or what he truly wants. He's pretty averse to big-picture thought, and easily distracted by smaller-picture novelty and fantasticality. Because of that, he misses details and he can be somewhat oblivious. He started out as a grumpy old man (in spirit), discovered there's a lot more to life that he wants to explore, but hasn't yet committed to it.

And that's where the story resumes...

Weapons Of Old

We've been gone for two days. Due to the time-twisting quirks of interdimensional travel, over a year has passed on Evermoor.

Thanks to Gyrax's aviad-borne message, we know Lyderea declared war against the Freecast Territories (whatever those are). They deadlocked her Knights at Algulis Devari (wherever that is), giving rise to a sweeping no-man's land. Now, Gyrax wants to meet us at Glimmersend City (a major trading hub).

Before his message, I was thoroughly enjoying my time with Erany—basking in the glow of our side-quest success, eating tasty food by a hot fire, and engaging in multiple helpings of wink-wink sexy time.

Not anymore. Everything's changed.

I can't stop thinking about my supposed destiny. *I'm* the Traveler? *Me?* The guy who beats Lyderea, reaches the Unbound Realm, and goes on to save the *ENTIRE FREAKING WORLD???*

Part of me wants to head back to Earth. The white-picket life doesn't seem that bad, not compared to my existential burden.

Predictably, my anxiety affects my relationship with Erany. Aside from a handful of travel-related exchanges, we haven't spoken in the last three days. We're not sleeping together, either. (We're still sleeping next to each other, just no more sexy time.) On the fourth day of gloom and doom, she steps in front of me and blocks my way forward.

"What?" I ask.

"Quell your worry. You have plenty of time before—"

"I'm fine." I say it roughly; I don't want to talk about this.

"Jon." She lays a hand on my shoulder.

I close my eyes, struggling with everything that's come to pass. A gateway into another dimension. Losing a year on Evermoor during our two-day trip. The guilt of living free and happy, while the others were doing God knows what.

I take a shaky breath. "Thanks. I just…"

She pulls me into a solid hug, filling my brain with her sweet-summer scent.

"You smell so good," I murmur. "How do you always smell so good?"

"My Elven heritage." I can't see her grin, but I can definitely hear it in her voice. "You're not so bad yourself. Somewhat musky…though I have learned to enjoy it, oddly enough."

"Mmm. Sorry for being grumpy." I nestle deeper into her hair.

"It's understandable." She squeezes me tight, then holds me out at arm's length. "Nevertheless, I would have you remember: our childhood isn't long behind, but that doesn't excuse us from our duties."

"Adulting," I grumble. "That's a cuss word back on Earth."

"Jon—"

I blow a sigh. "Yeah, you're right. I've been spiraling out. Over my future, yeah, but over the others as well." I stick my hands in my pockets and stare at the ground. "They're probably fine."

"Better than us, mayhap."

"Doubt it." I reach for her waist, intent on stealing a sloppy kiss. *"Grabbies grabbies grabbies!"*

She yelps with delight and twitches into a shrug, slapping my tricep with her forearm and sending me rocketing past her. While I'm off-balance, she clinches my waist, curves her calf behind me, and drags me over her bent leg.

I flop on my back like a complete noob. *"WHOOF!"* As she hurdles my belly and sits on my chest, I gasp, "Who taught you MMA?"

She pins my wrists to the dewy ground. " 'Em-em-ae?' "

"Mixed Martial Arts. What you did just now. And come to think of it, what you did to that cop back on Earth."

"It's called 'fighting,' Jon." An amused grin.

"Yeah, I *know* it's called 'fighting,' " I retort. "It's just that it took us a while to integrate grappling and striking. They were kind of piecemeal until the UFC—" I suddenly remember she has no idea what that is. "—sorry, I mean open-rules tournaments—started becoming popular. Is that what happened here on Evermoor?"

"Ah." She nods knowingly. "Before the Bright Age, we too, were limited to disparate techniques. But as peace spread and folk mingled, different masters exchanged their knowledge. I can't wrestle like an Aksu Hillsman, or kick with the finesse of the Senlaedyn Fair Folk, but..." She straightens up and lets go of my wrists. (Kinda wish she hadn't.)

"Huh." I prop myself up onto both my elbows. "Interesting. On my world, Bruce Lee was the first to combine styles in a public forum. He made people mad, but he eventually became known as a uniter of knowledge."

"Well Lyderea is a divider of it." Erany sighs. "Countless folk have gone into hiding, or banded together into isolated tribes. Consequently, our grasp of fighting might splinter and fragment, and eventually resettle into limited styles." She gets to her feet and pulls me up.

"Seems like things are heading in that direction." I dust off my thighs.

She grunts in acknowledgment. "I hope it is simply a bump on the road."

"Me too." My eyes drift across the horizon. "No worries. It'll all work out."

That's what I say. But it's not what I feel.

The slope before us drops away, revealing a span of peaks and vales. Glimmersend is built on a lattice of hills, kind of like Rohan in *The Lord of the Rings,* only way bigger and a lot busier. This isn't a stretch of horse-soldier territory, it's a metropolis ringed with gorges and ridges. Merchant hills, blacksmith hills, farmer's hills...there's dozens (maybe hundreds) of highland mini communities, stretching long and wide across the green. Off in the distance, glaciers score the sunny horizon, providing a gorgeous backdrop for the city below.

"Wow," I breathe. "This is *incredible.*"

"As much as any other city, yes," Erany replies distractedly. "Telnoc is known for its dewshine trees, whose leaves store and refract the sun. And before Delán fell to the Queen, it boasted several districts made from crystal."

I roll my eyes. "Silly me. How could I forget those dewshine trees?" Doubt flares up, prompting me to give her a suspicious once-over. "Hey...back on Earth, when Alijyar took us to his redwood grove...were you actually impressed, or were you just pretending?"

She tilts her head, puzzled. "Why would I pretend? Your home is just as beautiful as anything on Evermoor."

"Are you *insane?*" My eyes bug out. "There isn't a city on Earth that could even come *close!* Glimmersend is a *kajillion* times better than—"

"Jon, your Earthling house was partly machine. And you rode around in a lightning-powered cart."

"It was gas, actually. The battery recharges off the—"

She cuts me off with a raised finger. "Stop comparing Earth to Evermoor. They both play a part, no? Shun that premise, and you shun the True's inherent harmony."

"That's a religious worldview," I argue. "Might as well throw in some gibbering snake handlers, along with an undead savior that wants you to eat him."

"I disagree, for such a worldview entails constant comparison and perpetual judgment. You are forced to weigh virtue on a continual basis, so you can justify your place among the blessed or the damned." She mutters, "Though it would be more accurate to call it transactional and hierarchical. Religious folk aren't necessarily bound by—"

"What does that have to do with—"

"You said certain locales are better than others. That sentiment is based on worth, which is the very foundation of what you are criticizing: a view that determines who is worthy and who is not."

"Wait a second." My face reddens. "We're not evaluating *my* worldview, which is anything *but* religious—"

"You were evaluating mine. Which, quite justly, reflects your evaluation back onto you."

"—this is about *yours*. You're wrong, Erany. Admit it. *Admit it.*"

She smirks without malice: a blend of amusement and weary compassion. "Here you stand, judging me for my belief that everything has a part and a place. And now you want me to change that belief, simply because you find it distasteful? Which of us embodies what you claim to oppose?"

I open my mouth. Nothing comes out. Finally, I manage, "Well if you're not religious, then—"

She touches my cheek with a gentle palm. "I seek to maintain a transcendent perspective."

"What does that even *mean?*" I sputter.

"That we don't have to pay a price for our happiness. That it can transcend the conditions arising around us."

I try and retort, but she interrupts with a kiss. Quick and abrupt, but also heartfelt.

I study her face, then grudgingly chuckle. "Did we just have a fight? I guess you won."

"So did you. You cried off long before you caused yourself harm."

"That sounds like praise for letting you win," I grumble.

"You could see it as such," she allows. "Or you could see it as wise and astute. You chose to abandon a fruitless battle. In so doing, you skirted a bout of strife and regret."

She isn't messing with me. I can tell by her expression and clear tone, free of judgment and *I-told-you-so* righteousness.

"Well..." I rub the back of my neck . "You could put it that way, I suppose..."

"You can put it any way you want. But if you try and impose your thought upon mine, the ensuing frustration will be your own reap." She starts walking down the hill.

"Ever get tired of being right?" My irritation dims and fades.

She turns and beams, filling my chest with smiley butterflies. As far as I'm concerned, that's answer enough.

Because sometimes, words just can't cut it.

————

Halfway down, she asks if Ailura is in her pouch. After a cursory pat-check, I respond with, "Yep."

"Good. I would rather avoid unwanted attention."

I can't put Ailura inside my carry. She's way too strong; she'll cut right through the storage-boosting charms. Her triangular pouch, unlike my holster, will actively conceal her blast-furnace aura (it took me a while to realize the pouch was enchanted, but gimme a break—I just learned how to Shift my perception).

Speaking of realizations that are long overdue, I find myself mulling the issue that every fantasy geek encounters when they run into firearms. "If there's guns on Evermoor, why use a bow and arrow? For that matter, why does anyone wield a sword?"

"Clapfires are averse to arcane energy," she explains. "Simple charms can explode their bullets, and they are easy to repel with minor shields."

"Interesting." Then: "Does anyone else carry a gun? It can't just be me."

"The majority of sailors are partial to clapfires, as they fight in odd quarters and varied range. But they prefer flintlocks and muskets because they're easier to ward. Revolvers, however, are almost impossible."

"Huh? Why?"

"Magic springs from connotation, from the underlying feel of ideas and notions. As a general rule, mechanical items are harder to enchant."

"I still don't get it."

"Magic and machines are conceptual opposites. That dynamic becomes especially pronounced when it comes to clapfires, specifically revolvers and quick-chamber guns. If a sorcerer tries to enchant such a weapon, a high rate of failure will plague their attempt. In almost every case, the spell is hindered by a sense of dysfunctional conflict."

"So flintlocks, maybe. Revolvers, no."

"Aye. Excepting Ailura, six-guns are laughably vulnerable to spells, and are widely seen as a pauper's weapon. Flintlocks and muskets enjoy a bit more esteem. Nevertheless, they are mostly found among sailors and peasants."

She intuits my next *Why* and preemptively explains: "By and large, they are still hard to ward—a half-decent mage can foul their shot." Erany pauses at the edge of Glimmersend. There isn't any gate. It's just grass and bushes, then a wide dirt road that leads into the hillscape.

She turns and raises an inquisitive eyebrow. *Ready?*

I sweep the air with an open hand. "After you, Princess."

———

Our first stop is Yonfir Baily, a busy jumble of trinket-hawking kiosks. *(Baily* is short for bailiwick, which is what they call their hilltop mini communities). Yonfir connects to some agricultural bailys, then a blacksmith baily on its northern slope.

From higher up, the city looked neat and orderly. It's the exact opposite down below. Everything here is fast and ragged, awash in a sea of hustle-hustle-hustle.

"Kinda disorganized," I mutter as we pass by an amulet-laden stall.

"Wot you say?" A hag with one bulging eye steps out from her booth. "Wot you say?" She pokes my chest with a gnarled finger.

My mouth goes dry. Partly because I meant no offense, and partly because she's a dead ringer for a fairytale witch. "I...I..."

Erany dips her chin in respectful deference. "We plead your grace, Sha..."

"Alsiníce. Pirily Alsiníce." Her buggy left eye examines me angrily. Her right eye (squinty instead of buggy) does the same, only with hostile suspicion instead of vein-powered rage.

"A pretty name," Erany offers. "Pardon my friend—his tongue runs ahead of his diminutive brain. When he was a tot, he was spared the rod and spoiled with glut."

"And no serprise!" Witch-Lady (sorry, Pirily Alsiníce) screeches. "Yer lips are smart, young Kai! A little too smart fer yer own scabbin' good!" She reaches in her cloak and draws a ratty piece of wood.

"What the—" I cover my face as she batters my cheeks. "Ow! *Ow!*" Her stick snaps on the fourth hit, but she replaces it with a spare from the depths of her cloak.

"Ow!" I peek at Pirily through raised forearms. "You just—*ow!* You just keep those on you? *OW!*"

"Aye!' she crows gleefully. "Always carry an extra walloper! They're a damned necessity fer ill-mannered whelps!" She is *clearly* enjoying this.

And so is Erany, what a surprise. She's covered her mouth in a pathetic attempt to conceal her smile. (Glad to see she's willing to stand up for me. Ride or die, my ass.)

"Right in the yib-yobs!" Pirily fakes a chop, flourishes twice, then buries the stick in my unguarded nuts.

"OOF!" I drop to the ground, cupping my sack with both hands. She must've been saving her strength for that final hit—it felt like a punt from an NFL kicker.

Pirily wags a finger in my face. "Don't go fergettin'!"

"No...ma'am," I gasp. She gives me a puzzled look and I correct it to, "I mean no, Sha. I won't forget, Sha Alsiníce." *God* this hurts!

"Serpose you've learned yer lesson," she grouses. "Hope I wasn't too hard on yer wrinkly little babymakers."

"Babymakers are fine," I wheeze. Erany reaches down and gives me a hand. "They're up in my throat, but give it time—they'll come back down when they're good and ready."

"Which won't be long, I hope," Erany teases. "There's plenty of taverns with virgin beds. We should do our best to break them in."

"Ha!" Pirily slaps her knee. "I like you, Elf lady! You remind me of me, when I was young and sassy!"

"Still pretty sassy," I mutter.

"Unfortunately, we aren't seeking leisure." Erany releases my elbow. "Do you know of a Wolven named Gyrax Aclasian?"

Pirily shrugs. "Plenty of Fenrics come and go. O'er half the folk here are just passing through." She contemplates the sky for a couple of seconds. "Might want to try the Isle of Plen. Biggest pub in all of Glimmersend." She hawks a loogie into the dirt. "Go five blocks east through Farrier's Baily, a quarter turn left at Falconer's Circle, then two blocks north on Kyslinger's Straight."

Erany repeats the directions in a quick mutter. Pirily confirms them with a solid nod. "Ayep. That'll do ya."

"Our thanks, Sha Alsiníce." Erany touches her brow with her index and middle finger, then brings her palm a few inches out, turned in toward her face (the Evermoor version of a casual wave, only way cooler and a bit more formal). "May light find you in dark places."

"Aye, Elf lady. May it ease your eyes and guide your feet." Pirily gives me a contemptuous once-over. "Mebbe hold off on icing them yibyobs. They're small enough without the cold."

"What?" I bluster. "Hold on, that's not—"

Erany gives my arm an affectionate squeeze. "His yib-yobs are plump, good Sha. I can attest to that myself." (My girlfriend is sporting an ear-to-ear grin, which I *so* do not approve of.)

"If you say so," Pirily grunts.

"Come, Jon." Erany giggles. "Let us tend to your overly small—"

"Yeah, yeah—*I got it!*"

She giggles again, buoying my spirits and soothing my pain. I'm not sure if I lost or won. My balls got busted (literally and figuratively), but Erany's laugh is beauty incarnate. After a minute, I decide to count it as a win. I could care less about my aching yib-yobs; they're like the ugliest part of a human body.

(They're not small, though. I'd say they're at least average, maybe a little on the larger side. Pirily needs to check her damn judgment. What does she know, anyway? Does she have a degree in yib-yob statistics? Can she chart modes and deviations on a testicular bell curve? I'm betting NO. Stupid old crone.)

———

As we make our way through Farrier's Baily, I can't help but gawk at our fantastic surroundings. The streets are lined with Wildlyre blacksmiths, straight out of a D&D Monstrous Compendium. Most of them are Minotaurs (head of a bull, hooved feet, super-yoked torsos) or extra-large Wolven. They're pounding steel, quenching it in water, or stirring beds of red-hot coals. The rise in temperature is undeniable—it's like walking in front of an open oven.

Scattered throughout are clusters of mages, blessing the metal with various charms. The majority are imbuing it with runes or designs, while a few are performing the arcane version of a blacksmith's quench: they're guiding weapons and armor into light-woven constructs. Instead of inducing a heated boil, the magic triggers a chromatic blaze. Each time it happens, a strong body-high rolls up my spine.

"Ooh. Ah. That feels...*yeah.*" I close my eyes and crick my neck, trying but failing to keep from jerking and fidgeting.

Erany throws me an exasperated look. "These are minor enchantments, Jon. You're acting like they're chrisms from a Brightsworn Paladin."

"I can't help it!" I exclaim. "I'm super sensitive! Everything has gone into tenth-gear Shift!"

"I can see it in your aura," she says apprehensively. "Perhaps you should dim it."

"Dim it?" The hammers are starting to build and intensify—now they're accompanied by mind-bending warbles. It's the same with the magic. The script-laden flares burn extra bright, roping me in with hypnotic glitter.

"Jon? *Jon?*" Erany grips my arm.

"Have to get out of here," I mumble.

"This way." She pulls me along by the crook of my elbow.

The peal of metal on metal is raking my brain, making it hard to think or speak. The magic is similar—it's slamming me with waves of need and relief. Like making it to the bathroom in the bare nick of time, but over and over and over and *over.*

As the strength and frequency ratchet up, my chest tightens and my legs jelly. "Whoa." I almost collapse, but Erany pulls me straight. "*Whoa.* I think I'm gonna..."

And then it stops.

"What...what..." I open my eyes and look around. We're standing in front of a ratty apothecary, marked with paintings of potions and vials.

"Jon? Did you hear what I said?"

"I'm sorry—what?" I wipe away tears and meet her gaze.

"I was telling you to relax and dim your aura. You were glowing like starfire."

"Okay, but how do I..." I trail off and study my hands, which are now surrounded by translucent armor. (That's how my aura visually manifests). "Did I...did I make a scene?" Passersby shoot me uncertain glances.

"Quell your worry," she assures. "These are well-traveled traders and wanderers. They observe eccentrics on a regular basis."

"Good to know." A sheepish grin. "Ironic—back on Earth, I spent my life craving novelty and meaning. Now that I've got it, I kinda miss being a fly on the wall."

"As Deláni royalty, I can relate."

"How'd you deal?"

A nonchalant shrug. "Sometimes you're key, sometimes you aren't. It was a gradual insight, realized through my time on the road."

I blow out a sigh. "Too much adulting. I wish I could rewind time and relive our vacation."

"Vacation?"

"The four weeks before Gyrax's message."

"There will be other opportunities." She cracks a smile. "Be—"

"—dust upon your breath." I sigh again. "Yeah, yeah."

"In the meantime, you need to learn some auric control. Unless, that is, you wish to shine like a moonglimmer pond."

"Definitely not." I pat the air with both hands: *Take it easy on me.* "Okay, so as you know, I have zero experience in casting spells. What exactly does magic entail?"

"Typically, it requires several years of visualization, along with countless hours of poetic harmonics. However, you are markedly different than conventional students, so we'll skip ahead to Primal enchantments."

"Wait," I say guardedly. "You started with the basics, right?"

"I did."

"So why am I skipping 'em?"

She puts her hands on her hips. "Would you rather I glut you with study and drill? I thought that was why you wished to leave Earth: you were sick and tired of your rote existence, which you have described as a perpetuation of perpetuity itself."

Damn. Check and mate.

"Okay," I cede. "I'll opt out of the arcane grind. But are you qualified to teach me Primal Magic? Ren said that only masters can shape it."

"He was referring to middle and high-level charms, woven entirely from emotional force. Technically, Primal Magic is accessible to all. No one could cast if that wasn't the case, as it lies at the base of every enchantment."

"So this is a Primal version of 'Hello World?' " She opens her mouth to ask what that is, but I interrupt with, "Sorry. I meant to ask if we're starting with something easy."

"Of course," she assures. "Dimming your aura is literally child's play."

"Okay, then." I clap my hands and rub them together. "Let's get to some aura-dimming."

Over the next few minutes, she teaches me how to contract my aura. Traditionally, mages focus on visuals and vocals, but Erany wants me to focus on *feeling*. "Shift your gaze and soften your mind," she instructs. "Let thought arise without conscious judgment."

Her words trigger déjà vu—Gyrax said something similar when I healed Nyanti. "Okay," I mutter. "Let it all go, let it all go..."

"No," she interrupts. "Let it all *in*."

I open my eyes. "What's the difference?"

"When you let things go, you fixate on whatever you're trying to release. When you let things in, you allow your desire to bloom and take shape."

"Right." I respond with a nod. "Let it all in."

Let it all in, let it all in...at first, I wrestle with nagging frustration (this isn't working and if it is, it isn't happening as fast as I want) but that gives way to resignation. Resignation shifts into mild optimism, then gradually congeals into ease and surety.

"Think I got it," I murmur. "I can feel...pulsing."

"Good." She nods. "Move into that cadence. Merge with it. Your thought will recede of its own accord."

I resist the urge to make a dirt-munching hippie joke. *Be the ball.* But as cliché as it is, Erany's right—there's a palpable rhythm to my arcane vibration, and it'll allow me to blend with it if that's what I want. All I have to do is give it some space, and...

My sight goes into full-on Shift.

I'm surrounded by networks of see-through plates, drifting in time with my movement and breath. They're lashed together with lines of energy, dotted with blips of fast-moving color. If my aura was a hologram of citywide traffic, the lines would be the roads and the dots would be the cars. (These are meridians. I've seen them before, but only in passing.)

At certain points along my body—palms, belly, feet, and several points up the length of my spine—the meridians coalesce into blazing reservoirs: pure white cores limned by multicolored light. Their glowing edges are smoky and frayed, as if they were threatening to spill over their designated boundaries. (These are loci. *Very* cool.)

"Interesting," she says.

"What?"

"Your aura...it has fully adopted an Evermoor aesthetic." She leans in and peers at my contours.

I crinkle my brow. "You're right. It doesn't look sci-fi anymore. Why, though?"

"Strange...I didn't notice until I held it in focus, and I have been traveling by your side for a decent stretch. It might be Laiddinic, or perhaps it is something roundabout causal..."

"Roundabout causal?"

"According to my tutors, the past and future transcend linearity. Theoretically, you can change the past in the present moment, though speculation abounds as to how it is done."

"You're saying I reached back in time and altered my aura?" Queasiness rises and prickles my gorge.

She shrugs in response. "That would explain why it was easy to overlook, as our collective perception would adjust to your act. Even now, when I mull the prospect, my psyche feels…I believe *dissonance* would be the right descriptor." She clears her throat. "Unless it induces dysfunction and strife, I am not concerned. As the Prophesied Traveler, you are a walking invitation to strangeness and oddity."

"Uh…" I *really* don't want to think about this. Laiddinic powers are crazy enough, and now she's saying…honestly, I don't know *what* she's saying. So I change the subject with, "What's next?"

"Focus on the sensation of narrowing and shrinking," Erany advises, "but don't fixate on either of those words. *Feel* your way into it."

It's a delicate balance—I'm holding a concept in my attention, but not with any intensity or fervor. Soon, my meridians dim and so do my loci.

"Wow." I spread my arms and study my aura. "You can barely see it. Primal Magic, huh?"

Erany shakes her head. "That's like calling a ripple a river. Primal Magic is so far beyond this it's almost a different thing altogether."

"Hold on." I put my hands on my hips. "What about your non-hierarchical worldview? Primal Magic is Primal Magic, no matter what the scale or level of difficulty, right?"

Erany rolls her eyes and groans in frustration. "I knew you would twist my—" She spreads her fingers, a gesture that says: *Listen close, I don't want to have to explain this again.* "A transcendent perspective is not a certificate—it either is or it isn't moment by moment. Also, in order to advance in a given context, you must compare and contrast within that context. So in order to indulge in the model of progress, you must occasionally break from an inclusive view."

I slice a hand back over my scalp. "Jon no follow."

"When we enjoy a tumble, you do not think of the world at large, do you?"

(*Enjoy a tumble.* Way more innocent than making love, smashing, or…yeah.) "Definitely not," I chuckle. "All I think about is—"

"Don't be crude. My point is that comparison and contrast, when properly framed, serve to enhance your personal fulfillment. They only become problems if they cause you misery—when you believe whatever you're doing is anything more than a game."

"Our 'tumbles' aren't a game," I intone gravely. "Each one is a matter of life-and-death. I couldn't go a day without—"

"Jon." She covers her eyes with a thumb and a forefinger. "I'm trying to explain how—"

"I got it, I got it. I'm just messing with you."

She lurches forward in mock anger, causing me to squeal and jump a couple feet back. "Come on, now—my Earthling body is weak and puny compared to your half-Elf lusciousness! Don't—ow!" As her knuckles dig into my upper arm, I spin with the punch and cup her butt. Before I can sweep her off her feet, she clinches my waist, roots her weight, and dips me low like a swooning damsel.

"Don't forget: warrior-princess," she teases.

"I'm the Prophesied Traveler!" I huff. "That's gotta count for something!"

"Allow me to extol your virtue and grace." She stops my breath with a heady kiss.

After that brief burst of heaven, she hauls me up. "Wow." I smile dazedly. "I so do not care that you're the sailor. I'm totally fine with being the nurse."

"Sailor? Nurse?" She tilts her head, puzzled.

"Back on Earth, this sailor goes viral for kissing a nurse. He dips her down while he does it."

"Only one of us is going to be dipped." She crosses her arms. "And it won't be me."

"Just you wait," I warn. "Once I'm good with these Laiddinic powers, I'm giving you the dip."

Amusement and skepticism. "If you say so. Until that day, I shall do the dipping."

"No complaints here, but..." I trail off and stare into the distance."

"What?" Her expression turns curious.

"Do you think I should train in weapons and magic?" I meet her gaze. "I feel like I should learn some basic spells. Chain lightning, ray of frost..."

"What are you talking abo—never mind." (She can easily recognize when I slip into Nerd Speak). "You wish to learn swordplay? And how to manipulate arcane energy?"

"Not all the time, but you know...a few days a week?" I tense with uncertainty. "I'd like to be able to hold my own, and...well, it'd be nice to be the sailor, every now and then."

She throws her head back and roars with laughter. "Jon, you will never, *ever* be the sailor!"

I flap a hand in annoyance. "Yeah, yeah. Thus far, I've been completely underpowered, or when it's time to whip out the Laiddinic mojo, a last-ditch option. I'd like to have some in-between choices, you know? At the same time, I don't want to be end up like Elier or Nyanti. They're nice and all, but there's more to life than swords and sorcery. Do you get what I'm saying? I'm not sure if—"

"Jon." She lays a hand on my shoulder. "I was raised as royalty; I am all too familiar with onus and duty. If you wish to learn swordplay and magic, I am happy to proceed at your chosen pace."

"Good." I blow a sigh of relief. "So far, I've felt like a giant liability. Remember Elerica, when I healed Nyanti? That was the first time Ren gave me an actual compliment. It may seem trivial, but after months of his judgy face—"

Erany groans in exasperation. "Deliac's Gleam, would you cease your puling?"

My mouth opens and closes, trying to form words. "I...uh...I'm sorry, I—"

"I jest, Jon, I jest." She flashes a smile. "As I said, we shall train at your leisure."

"Oh. Okay," I reply hesitantly. "I knew you were joking, by the way. It was just a test." My voice picks up confidence. "It was just a test, yeah."

She repeats my words in an oafish tone: " 'It was just a test, yeah.' " Her smile returns. "Did I pass?"

"Come find out." I pull her close and dip her low. This time, she lets me.

"Jon." She palms my cheek, searching my face with her lavender gaze. "Just remember…"

"Yeah?"

"Ren is an idiot."

"Couldn't agree more."

As we kiss, an emphatic declaration rings through my mind:

Best. Girlfriend. *Ever.*

2

On the way back to Farrier's Baily, arcane feedback tickles my brain. This time, it doesn't wreak havoc on my perception.

"Nice," I mutter. "Dimming your aura's the way to go."

"Indeed," Erany agrees. "You were starting to unravel."

"What does that mean?"

"Auras are like bodies. With infection and damage, they shrink and wither. In milder cases, your magical strength will dwindle and fade."

"And in not-so-mild cases?"

"Your capacity for hope is stripped away, leaving you bereft of solace and joy."

Gulp. "Okay then. Guess it pays to take care of your aura."

"Aye," she affirms. "In a similar vein, they are also capable of self-repair."

"There are some injuries, I'm guessing, that are too severe to heal on their own."

"Wrong. Every injury, both physical and auric, has the potential to mend itself. Aid, however, can still be of use—it can shift your vantage away from disease, allowing your innate wellness to re-entrench. Remember Terrelly? He's an adverse example of what I'm invoking. He clung to ire with all his might, and it prevented his health from coming to the fore."

Terrelly Jindow, Explorer Captain of the Wayfarer Advance, led a wanderer army in service of Evermoor. After he was crippled at Sidehelm Pass, he retreated into the equivalent of palliative care.

"Man, it feels like a lifetime since I last saw him." I scratch my temple. "How do you think he's doing?"

Her face goes blank. "I cannot say. Even with a quality remedy, the outcome would depend upon his perspective."

"Huh? Why? A remedy's a remedy, isn't it?"

She shakes her head. "Perhaps I wasn't clear. The strongest cure will fail to heal, if the injured refuse their own well-being. They may enjoy a bit of reprieve, but…"

"What about Nyanti? I was able to heal her with Laiddinic powers. And afterwards, she was able to heal Lucky and Elier."

She shakes her head again. "It is not my area of expertise. The best I can explain it is that at a soul-deep level, you and Nyanti agreed on her wholeness. Afterward, she did the same with Lucky and Elier. If that hadn't been the case, it wouldn't have worked."

"I get it…I think." (Not really, though.)

"I spent a year under Terrelly's wing." She stares at the ground. "He taught me much and gave me hope. When I learned of his illness…"

I reach out and rub her back. "Ren said he would find an elixir. Take it easy and hope for the best."

A rueful grin. "How the tables have turned. I said that to you, only in regard to Gyrax and the others."

I imitate her voice in a party-girl whine: " 'My worldview is *soooo* transcendental. Yours isn't—you're a judgy drama queen, always comparing Earth to Evermoor!' "

Her eyes widen in shock. "That is *not* what I sound like!"

I prance away, tilting back so I can look down my nose. " 'My name is Erany—I'm a half-Elf princess, but I am *soooo* down to earth!' "

"Why you—*come here!*" She snatches my arms and twists them together.

"All right, all right." I open my hands in capitulation. "You win."

She lets me go with a teasing smirk. " 'Ware my revenge. It will come without mercy in the dead of the night."

"Promises, promises." I sigh in defeat. "I wish we could just keep goofing around. Adulting rears its ugly head."

"Try and enjoy it." She threads her hand into the crook of my elbow.

(*Love* it when she does that.) "It'll be easier later, when we get around to 'enjoying a tumble.' " I make quote marks with my fingers.

She rolls her eyes in exasperation. "Deliac's Gleam, do you ever think about anything else?"

"I'm the Prophesied Traveler!" I retort. "Prophesying and traveling require a boatload of tumble-time!"

Her grin returns. "Doubtful, but I yield for the sake of my own enjoyment."

Halfway into the next baily, I'm struck by a flash of cognitive dissonance. Due to my arcane seizure, I had no idea we went this far. I thought it was only a couple of blocks, but we're already coming up on our seventh.

"What's with all these pharmacies?" I look around at the glut of apothecaries.

Erany gives them a passing glance. "Sickness is rampant among the poor, and it begets a demand for these shoddy cures. Also, many of these shops are criminal facades. To mislead taxmen, felons must—"

"Wait, what?" I'm surprised into laughter. "You guys have money launderers?"

Her expression turns quizzical. "Why would anyone wash their coin? No, I meant they conceal or distort their actual revenue."

"Yeah, that's what I meant." I cycle my hand in an impatient gesture. "Money laundering is slang for...for what you just said."

"Glimmersend is part of Lyjeia Asir. As that is the case, the outlaws are probably Ash Tip Cudgels." She shrugs in defeat. "Lucky would know more."

Lucky. Our charming friend (I think?) who took great pride in his ability to steal. "I haven't thought of him since we got back. Kind of ironic, because I've been practicing what he taught me."

"I know. I've seen you training in sleight of hand."

I straighten in surprise. "Why didn't you say anything?"

"To avoid undue pressure. You voiced a desire for ease and repose. I feared my attention would be seen as meddlesome."

My cheeks flush red. "Sorry, I didn't mean to—"

She cuts me off with a dismissive wave. "You are tasked with saving all of Evermoor. Take it moment by moment, step by step, or your peace will shrink and wither away."

"Uh, yeah..." Dubious head tilt. "That doesn't really help."

"Your problem, not mine."

"I'm still practicing deception and thievery. Doesn't that make you—"

She sighs in exasperation. "Would you cease your dithers? You aren't Lucky—I have yet to see you lighten a carry."

"Right. Sorry." An embarrassed chuckle. "I think it's just a mental reflex. Back on Earth, I never felt like I had anything to contribute. Like I didn't have worth or practical value."

"Given a scenario, certain folk are of greater use, but that isn't a reflection of their personal worth. You would do well to remember that, or your joy will be tied to others' regard."

"Interesting. I've always tied worth to an outside measure." I take a moment to digest her words. Then: "Just to be sure, you approve of my—" I catch myself being needy and reword the question. "You think training in theft is a good idea?"

"Without a doubt. It might come in handy, as I do not wish to learn the specifics. I know enough to fend off urchins, but..." She gives a shrug. "It seems you have achieved a measure of skill, one I cannot match without dedicated study."

"Um...okay." My brow furrows in thought. "Yeah. I'll keep it up."

As we step back onto Farrier's Bailey, I can't help but dwell on her words: *It might come in handy.* For some reason, my gut agrees.

It's going to play a part. I'm all but sure of it.

———

During our trip to Earth, Erany used up all her arrows. Fortunately, there's pockets of fletchers on the edge of the baily, which gives us a chance to reload her quiver.

Over the course of her barter and purchase, I try to hide my growing excitement. The blacksmiths have triggered my inner geek, bringing to mind D&D swords and their badass powers. Frostbrand, Dawnbringer, Wyrmsheart ...the list keeps growing and so does my glee. Two blocks in, I'm almost giddy with it.

"Erany?" I resist the urge to twiddle my fingers.

"Mmm?"

"Do you think that...could I get a..." My cheeks flush with nerdish enthusiasm. "I would really like a *magic sword.*"

"Of course." She cocks her head, amused. "Why wouldn't you—ah, I forget they are rare, back on your world."

(Rare? Try nonexistent.) "Really? You'll get me a sword? A *magic* sword?" My voice trembles with held-back excitement.

"Most prefer a plain-steel blade, but—"

"What?" I blurt. *"Why?"*

"Unless they are weak or exceedingly strong, magic weapons require specialized care. However..." She shrugs. "It is up to you."

I can't believe this. *I cannot believe this.* Every hero in every fantasy gets to wield a *magic sword.* (Every fantasy worth its salt, anyway). And now, *I* get to do it. This is like every Christmas rolled into one.

I shove my hands in my pockets to keep them from shaking. "Can we get one here, or..."

She looks around. "Let's hold off. These smithies live off haste and volume. Good for arrows, but swords are best left to accomplished artisans."

"Oh. Right." I force a smile, trying to hide my disappointment.

"Boys and their blades." She shakes her head, grinning. "Another trait our worlds have in common."

"Oh you *know it!*" I stack my fists and swing an imaginary lightsaber, accenting my slashes with buzzy sound effects. *"VVmm. VVmm.* Man, I can't *wait!* Ailura's cool and all, but—"

She covers her eyes with a thumb and a forefinger. "Jon, please. Whatever you're doing...it isn't swordwork."

"Says you!" I swing a couple more times and bow my head, deactivating my saber with an intricate flourish. "Gotta think of a badass name. Something like Blastravage, Megaslay…Dawncracker, maybe?" I scratch my temple. "No, that sounds like an evangelist hillbilly…"

"Oddly enough, I find you adorable." She chuckles. "Worry not. We shall find you a blade."

"Awesome. Hey, she said a quarter-turn left at Falconer's Circle. Is this it?" I point ahead at a circular street. There's a sign by its lip, but it's too archaic for me to read.

"It is," she affirms. "Good eye."

We take a left onto Kyslinger's Straight, which leads us onto another baily. This one is brimming with pubs and taverns.

"Stay alert for the Isle of Plen," Erany cautions.

"Can't read signs, remember?"

"Of course. My mistake." She picks up the pace and scans the exteriors. "I'll just—ah, there it is." She gestures at a building, roughly three times as large as its squat-bodied neighbors. Due to its waist-high, half-walled front, I'm able to see into its depths. The Isle of Plen is raucous and lively, filled with an assortment of humans and Wildlyre.

Erany puts her hands on her hips. "Neither calm nor quiet, but that's to be expected. I'll search left, you search right."

"What? Like split up?" Vague alarm ripples through my gut.

"We shall cover more ground," she replies. "Unless you'd rather—"

"No, I'm good," I say hurriedly. "We'll meet outside, yeah?"

"Agreed. I'll question the folk and see what arises."

"Cool. I'll do the same."

"No. Your accent will draw unwanted attention. Also, I wish to be sure: you're hale by yourself?"

I wave a dismissive hand. "Prophesied Traveler, remember?"

She gives me a skeptical, *why-are-you-being-weird* look. "There is no reproach in asking for help."

"Let's go." I head for the tavern, simultaneously ashamed and embarrassed. Part of me wants to stick with Erany, but I'm sick of being an incompetent kid.

As I approach the Isle, I make note of my daggers, mentally rehearsing my draw and parry. Deep breath, Jon.

Remember:

You asked for this.

3

As a nascent Dungeon Master, I've started plenty of campaigns with a stereotypical open—where the heroes walk into a rough-and-tumble bar. Now, instead of playing the cliché, I'm actually living it.

Trippy and meta, to say the least.

The patrons inside are motley and varied, a mishmash of humans and exotic Wildlyre. Some are familiar—Wolven, Saura, Minotaurs, Goblins—but there's a bunch of species (sorry, designates) I haven't yet seen.

Off to my right, I spot a cluster of humanoids that seem demonic. Not in a scary or dramatic sense (they don't have fangs, and there isn't any fire leaking from their mouths) but their eyes glow red, they have stubby little horns, and their skin ranges from purple to crimson.

Off to my left, a group of changelings are playing a card game where the players morph in accordance with the draws. Their expressions stay fixed, but their features continually shift and mutate. *(Awesome.)*

Directly behind them, there's a dozen folk that are partially comprised of the natural elements. One of them has a liquid head, another has a torso made of swirling wind, and a third has an arm that is *literally fire.* The flames aren't spreading or causing any damage, even though she's leaning against a wood beam.

Adjacent to the element people, I spot some humans with holstered revolvers, staring at the ground and avoiding eye contact. Erany was right (only peasants carry six-shooters) but it's weird to see it in the flesh.

Lastly, there's handfuls of Elves scattered throughout. Like Gyrax said when I first arrived, the Fair Folk come in a variety of colors. There's Whites, Blacks, and everything in between.

And they. Are. *Gorgeous.*

Think stunning celebrity with impeccable makeup, perfect lighting, and a balanced helping of Crossfit muscle. Michael B Jordan, BTS, Ryan Gosling...they'd all look sloppy next to the Fair Folk. It's the kind of beauty that makes you question your own, replacing your desire with worry and doubt. If I ever dated one, I would low-key suspect they were pulling a scam, because there's no way in hell they would stoop to my level on the humanoid dating scale. On that note, I can't understand why Erany chose me, when she could have snagged one of these ultra-model specimens.

I shake my head, forcibly dispelling my insecurities. Come on, Jon—if Erany wanted a fighter/mage hottie, she'd be spoiled for choice. She picked you over Elier, Ren, and Lucky, all of whom are handsome and decidedly accomplished.

All right, that's it for my half. I should go back now, unless...hold on, there's a set of stairs in the far right corner. Still gotta check the second floor.

As I push through a mob of descending bodies, sullen grumbling fills my ears. It alternates between "beg pardon," rough utterances of "make way," and rougher utterances of *"ONE SIDE!"*

Halfway up, vague alarm nettles my brain. My sleight of hand radar just went off.

I easily spot the hand on my chest, checking for items as it heads for my carry. I snatch it by the wrist, intending to...well, I don't know what, but one thing's for sure: I won't fall prey to some random thief. I've been trained by Lucky at his sociopathic best.

Imagine my surprise when I see that it's him.

———

"Beg pardon, good Kai, I was jostled a bit hard, and—" His eyes widen in shock. *"Jon?"*

Folks nudge past, snapping angrily at us. I couldn't care less; their voices fade into a background drone.

"Lucky! What are you—" At the same time, he exclaims, "I thought you were dead!"

"Dead? Why would you…" I struggle for words, but nothing comes out. Finally, I manage, "Where are the others?"

He glances past me and jerks his chin. "I would rather palaver in calmer airs."

"Yep. Sure." My defensive awareness comes to the fore, highlighting the shift of cloth and drift of hands. I know it's silly, but it's an instinctive reaction to his larcenous presence.

Once we're clear, I keep walking and wave him onward. "Let's talk outside."

He agrees with an "Aye," and follows me through the saloon-swing doors. A second later, we're standing in front of the Isle of Plen, regarding each other with disbelieving grins.

"You've been gone for a year! I can't believe…" He trails off, incredulous.

"I know," I chuckle. "You thought I was *dead?* Why? I told you where I was going!"

"Aye, but…" A dismissive wave. "Other planes? That's a little far-fetched, don't you think?"

I respond with an *are-you-crazy* stare. "Lucky, you live in a world with magic and beast-people!"

"But other *planes?*" His voice rises with ridicule. "That's like saying dragons are real."

"What are you *talking* about?" I sputter. "Of course they're real! The Queen made wyverns from their eggs!"

"That's a *conspiracy,* Jon." Exaggerated patience. "Concocted by nobles to keep us in rein."

Wow. *Wow.* I knew our worlds were somewhat alike, but this is…man, he's the Evermoor equivalent of a conspiracy-theory nutjob. How am I just now realizing this?

"I…okay." I rub the back of my neck. "But…you don't believe in other dimensions? How do you explain my year-long absence?"

The thief shrugs. "A magical coma, if I had to guess."

"I had to cross planes to complete Ailura. How do you explain that? I can show her to you now, if you want to see proof."

Another shrug. "The Sygress could have completed the revolver, planted it somewhere on your person, then woken you from your arcane sleep."

My expression goes from quizzical to bewildered. "Why would she do that?"

"Lyné Anir is a woman of power." Exasperation creeps into his tone. "Her actions are based on wolfish calculations."

"So anyone with power...they prey on folk beneath their station?"

"Aye. 'Tis an endless cycle between predator and prey, with everyone vying for dominant rule." He pats the air, as if to say, *Take it down a notch*. "If you dwell on our sorry, hard-bitten lot, your peace will dwindle and fritter away. There's a saying among thieves: 'Keep the world small.' Stay focused on your task, whether it's something as small as picking a pocket, or as complex and knotted as a seduction-based con."

I can't believe this. Lucky's dispensing sound advice, but in a way that rationalizes social predation.

He takes my silence as tacit agreement. "I am glad we share vantage. And I am also glad you have continued your training. It takes considerable skill to stymie my hand."

His compliment produces mixed emotions: accomplishment and pride, followed by a rush of indignant anger. He really thinks I share his perspective?

Before I can speak, Erany emerges from the Isle of Plen. "Jon, I couldn't find Gy—" She stops in her tracks and grabs the hilt of her rapier.

"My thanks, Princess." Lucky responds with an easy smile. "The blade comes out, more often than not."

"Lucky?" She releases her weapon.

"The one and only." He offers a bow. "It does me glad to see you hale. As I was just telling Jon, I thought you had perished."

"Why would you—" She shakes her head. *Forget I asked.* "We need to find Gyrax. Do you know where he is?"

"I do, milady. I am still in his service."

"Wow." I raise an eyebrow. "Never saw you as a long-term hire."

Lucky chuckles. "Typically, you would be right to think so. But Gyrax surprised me—he gave me every penny of what I was owed, along with an overlarge bonus for Elerica City. Afterward, he offered me employ. I almost declined, but I have never met a soul as capable and good as our Wolven friend."

Erany crosses her arms. "Do you now believe in the kindness of others?"

He stiffens in shock, then barks out a laugh. "Aha! *Ha!* You think..." He bends at the waist and slaps his thigh. *"AAAAH-HAHAHA-HAHA!"* Tears stream down his reddened cheeks.

She sighs in disgust. "As I suspected."

The thief straightens, wiping moisture off his cheeks. "You...you thought..." He blows out slowly, controlling his mirth. "Priceless, Erany, priceless."

"Not my intent," she snaps.

"As you say, as you say," he replies. "Just to be clear: when I refer to the qualities of grace and competence, I do not speak of the world at large. 'Tis Gyrax Aclasian and no one else."

"Good to know you haven't changed," she says coldly.

The thief shrugs. "I am a reflection of Evermoor. When the world changes, so will I."

I glance back and forth between Lucky and Erany, praying she won't punch him or choke him out. She is *pissed.* Although I'm not sure why...up until now, she's never had a problem with his selfish behavior.

Doesn't matter—gotta get us back on track. "You said Gyrax is close, right?"

"Aye. He is residing within the Wanderer's Idyll."

"Take us there," Erany hisses, "before I crack your nose and stop your breath."

"Very well." He gives her a puzzled look. *What did I do?* "On my heels."

Two bailys over, my gut tightens with dread. He's led us onto a hill full of Knights. The cobbles are lined with barracks and armories, all plastered with Lyderea's sigil.

"Guys?" I continue looking straight ahead. "Is it just me, or are we right in the middle of Stormtrooper Central?"

Erany leans toward Lucky and whispers, "If this is a trap, your head will roll across this street."

"Soft, Princess, soft." The thief gives a lighthearted chuckle. "These Knights are guards for Protectorate convoys. Wanderers fall outside their purview."

Her anger is replaced by curiosity. "Convoys?"

"Provisions and stock for their dominant front. They're fighting rebels at—"

"Algulis Devari," she finishes. "Thanks to Gyrax's aviad, I know bits and pieces. The bare strokes and nothing more."

Lucky straightens in mild surprise. "He launched it a year ago, yet it still managed to find its way to you..." He clears his throat. "In any case, it is best to avoid the Deadlocked Strait."

Her brow furrows. "The Deadlocked Strait?"

"How most refer to Algulis Devari. Deadlocked due to the current standoff, and Strait because—"

"It used to channel free-running water. But it has been a day and an age since that soil ran wet. Why would anyone call it a strait, when it has lain dry since the early Bright Age?"

Our surroundings give way to a jumble of merchants, hawking all manner of charms and wares. "See?" Lucky teases. "The Knights are focused on other matters."

Erany's expression doesn't change. "Answer my question."

The thief responds with an amicable shrug. "While you were gone, a horde of Knights poured through Algulis. Folk began saying it was brimming with rain: a flood of blades and sheer white mail."

"And the deadlock?" she presses. "How did it form?"

"Desperate souls flocked to the Strait, and held off the Knights with pitchforks and clapfires. At first they were comprised of peasants and felons, driven to rage by privation and lack." He flips his palms in a gesture of bafflement. "Tools and gadgets against armor and magic? I would rather fight wolves with my hands and my feet."

"They must have had help, right?" I ask. "I mean, if they were that outmatched…"

"Aye. News of the rebellion swept the lands. In the span of a week, the peasants were bolstered by Fair Folk and Wildlyre. Lyderea's armies are vast and strong, but they cannot push through into her northern cities. The resistance at the Strait is too severe."

"And the first wave of Knights?" Erany asks. "A fair amount cleared the gap. What became of them?"

"They settled in a muddle of strongpointed towns. If Algulis is the central blaze, the Knights beyond it are smoldering flames."

I interject with, "We're in the North, right?"

"Of course," Lucky chuckles. "If we were to venture south of Algulis, there would be twice the Knights and thrice the malice. They would concoct an excuse to throw us in gaol, and that's only if they were feeling bonny and charitable. If they happened to be feeling the least bit sour, they would free our heads from our low-shadow necks."

"Oh, okay." *Whew.* "What's so special about Algulis Devari? Why is everyone trying to claim it?"

Erany explains, "Between its vales, the pass-through terrain is wide and firm, a perfect channel for large-scale supply. Without control of Algulis Devari, Lyderea's north-south goods are slowed to a trickle."

"There's nothing comparable?" I ask. "No other routes she could use for transport?"

"They are rugged, tangled, or both. And they are also riddled with feral Wildlyre."

"What about ships?"

Lucky says, "The water is rife with giant serpents, drawn by the presence of three or more craft. In order to replace Algulis Devari, the Queen would need chains of freighters, guarded by armadas to ensure their cargo. As rich as she is, that much outlay would cripple her efforts. Make no mistake, she uses every route we have just discussed—the smaller trails and the north-south currents—but unless she clears the Deadlocked Strait, her strategic tempo will remain at a crawl." He thinks for a moment, then adds, "Sidehelm Pass could serve as an alternate, but it remains impractical due to the peril."

"The Watchers of Erendor, right? What's their deal, anyway?"

"They erode their prey into restless ghosts." He averts his gaze, clearly uncomfortable. "The Pass is filled with lesser haunts—those who fell to the Watchers' blight."

"Lesser haunts?" I ask. "Why not just kill them?"

"They provide the Watchers with ongoing sustenance. Living folk provide a feast, the fallen serve as sips and crumbs."

"Christ." I wince in dismay. "Glad we're not heading there."

"We are, actually," Erany corrects.

"*What?*" I shoot her a panicked look. "No! *Hell* no! Why would you even—"

" 'Tis the only way to Yom Dagur."

I close my eyes and sigh in resignation. "Which is where we find the Rosecraft Blade."

Erany nods. "The Pass feeds into a winding trail, one that traverses the Skytooth Ridge. Yom Dagur is the third peak west of Sidehelm Fortress. We shall walk by its flank en route to the Blade."

"Oh come *on!*" I throw my arms up in frustration. "We're walking *right by it?* The doom-scarred castle with the *phantom vampires?*"

"I share your mien," Lucky mutters. "I shan't set foot upon the Pass. No amount of coin will convince me otherwise."

"See?" I thrust an upturned hand in Lucky's direction. "No amount of coin, Erany—*no amount of coin!*"

Erany glares at him. "There is more to this life than glimmering metal. Your view of the world is stunted and choked."

The thief replies with a knowing smirk. "Isn't the Blade an arrangement of metal? Does it not glimmer like ordinary coin?"

"You grasp at the shade and swear off the shine. True riches elude your eye."

Lucky belts out a laugh. "If I am not mistaken, it is I—not you—who is focused on riches."

Erany's jaw tightens with anger. "Stow your prattle, lest I cut your tongue from its low-shadow perch."

"Are we almost there?" I ask nervously. If these two fight, Erany wins ninety-nine-point-nine percent of the time, but what would be the point?

"Aye. Around this corner, and...here." Lucky points at a two-story tavern. It's boxy like the others, but the upkeep is better. Fresh paint, clean windows, and a solid roof without any holes. "The Wanderer's Idyll. You'll find him inside."

I take a steadying breath. I've only been gone for a couple of days, but Gyrax hasn't seen me in over a year. Be cool, Jon. Be dust upon your breath.

Erany nudges me. "Ready?"

I respond with a nod. "Yep. Let's do this."

4

The walls and the floor are worn and polished, aglow with the sheen of soft-tuned lamps. Clusters of folk are chatting and smoking, resting in the shadow of their hooded cloaks. It feels like I'm surrounded by a bunch of Aragorns (right before he meets the Hobbits) only they don't give off any brooding menace.

"This way." Lucky veers right, toward a screen of bauble-threaded strings.

As we step into the hallway beyond, Erany whispers, "Be on guard. This may be a trap."

A couple turns later, we end up in a homey dining room. Our friends are clustered around a knee-high table, piled with exotic Evermoor dishes.

Everyone freezes...then breaks into a round of warm-hearted greetings. Even Ren manages a faint grin (I think anything more would hurt his face).

"Come! Sit!" Gyrax beckons. "Eat!"

I hunker down and assess the spread. There's roasted poultry, mashed tubers, and heaps of colorful fantasy-world veggies. "What are those?" I point at a platter of sky-blue stems, marked by stark white stripes that define their middle.

Erany chomps on a glistening bird leg, twisting her head to rip off the meat. (My girlfriend eats like a Viking powerlifter—*love* it.) "Those?" Due to her chewing, it sounds like *thothe.* "Sydiferan winter root. Here." She holds a stalk up to my lips. "Try it." (I have to stifle a giggle—her insistence reminds me of a Korean *halmoni.)*

As I crunch down, it dissolves into a scatter of tingly crumbles. The flavor pendulums between sweet and sour, fading in time with the shrinking granules.

"Jon?" She stops chewing and examines my face. "Are you well?"

"Huh? Yeah." I meet her gaze. "Why?"

"You've been staring into space."

"Oh." A self-conscious chuckle. "Sorry, it's just..." I examine the root with mild wonder. "Nuckin' futz."

"Is that good?" She's genuinely concerned. It's kind of adorable.

"Yes," I assure her. "Absolutely, yes."

Her concern gives way to a relieved smile. "Then try the other dishes. They too, are 'nuckin' futz.' "

A minute later, Elier asks about our Earth-side adventures. I kick things off with a recap and intro, then Erany steps in and refines the details. We both take turns with the dinner-chat baton, leading me to realize we're a genuine couple—we're acknowledging and exchanging nonverbal cues, fleshing out each other's incomplete points, and occasionally taking over if the other is struggling.

This. Is. *Awesome*. I never thought I would enjoy a Korean-style dinner (by that I mean the table and arrangement, not the food) with a half-Elf hottie, my Wolven BFF, and a motley assortment of badass wanderers.

As the convo progresses, I find myself mulling our recent adventures, and how for the past few months, I've been living the life of a D&D character. Man, I should write a campaign when I get back to Earth. I'm thinking Forgotten Realms, maybe Greyhawk. (Definitely not Ravenloft. Hard pass on the liches and zombies). Hmm...maybe I'll try an exotic setting...something like Spelljammer, or—*ooh!*—Dark Sun! I love that post-apocalyptic fantasy vibe they put togeth—

Erany pierces my reverie with, "Lucky took us through a Knight-infested baily, and not a single one questioned our presence. I find that credible in the Aureate Pastures, but it is almost unthinkable in a city this large."

"They both know of the Deadlocked Strait." Lucky elaborates. "Other than that…"

Gyrax interjects with an open paw. *I'll take it from here.* "Before you left, the Queen was content with physical taxes. Now she wishes for an auric equivalent. The Knights responded by adjusting their spread, re-settling according to logistical value. They have no interest in—"

"An auric equivalent?" Erany demands. "Bad enough she would beggar the world, now she would cull it of mystical force?"

Lucky glances from person to person. "I fail to see the problem."

Her expression flares with white-hot rage. "Because your aura is *weak,* Lucky! Much like your excuse for a *low-shadow soul!*"

He ducks his head and mutters, "As you say, Princess. All I meant was—"

Erany closes her eyes and raises a finger. "Do not speak. I would keep my sword inside its sheath." She scowls at Ren, who seems indifferent to Lucky's selfishness. "Typically, you are the one who keeps him in line."

The Wayfarer shrugs. "I do not care for his predatory view, but he has served us well as a capable jack-broker."

" 'Jack-broker?' " I ask.

"Someone who does a bit of everything," he explains. (Ah—okay. Same thing as a jack-of-all-trades.) "His contacts are many. That proved useful when dealing with Ardos."

"Oh yeah!" I snap my fingers. "How'd that go?" Before my trip to San Francisco, Gyrax was going to convene with Ardos Rygar: the ruthless leader of the Birthright Alliance.

"Better than expected," Gyrax answers. "His agents are headed for the Deadlocked Strait, ready to engage in disruption and sabotage." He gives Lucky a nod. "If not for our rogue, it would have been harder to strike a pact, as I have no rapport with the Bandit Czar. Lucky, on the other hand, knew several of his aides from days of yore."

Erany stares at Lucky, dumbfounded. "You did this? *You?*"

His brow wrinkles in confusion. "Does this mean I can—"

"Yes." Erany sighs and cycles a hand. "Speak."

The thief responds with a dazzling smile. "Spare me your praise. I was well paid."

"Everyone knows of your mercenary spirit. This, however—"

He dips his chin, as if she had just paid him a solid compliment.

"—seems overly generous."

"Not at all," he replies breezily. "For when I say well paid, I mean *well paid.*"

"Incredible." Her lip curls in disgust. "Nevertheless, you have shown your worth. From what I have heard, Ardos isn't interested in anything but himself."

"Probably helped Lucky strike a deal," I remark, "since they both have a similar mentality."

Lucky's face wrinkles in agreement (a bit like De Niro) and he gives a series of thoughtful nods (a lot like De Niro).

I catch Gyrax's eye with a lift of my hand. "I wanted to ask: you wrote your message way back when. Yet somehow, you knew you'd be at Glimmersend a full year later. How?"

"Sygress Anir foresaw our reunion. If not for her guidance, I wouldn't have known when you'd return, or where to direct you after you did."

"Nice." I nod approvingly. "So what's next for Gyrax and company?"

"We seek advice from the Volant Oracle," Nyanti says.

Elier, who's been characteristically quiet, murmurs his assent. "Her wisdom is always highly invaluable."

"Why, though?" I tilt my head, curious. "Aside from Lucky, everyone here is an awesome fighter. Why not lend a hand to the rebels?"

"They're firmly entrenched in the Deadlocked Strait," Elier says. "Bladeshadows, Duelists...even some Brightsworn have joined their ranks."

"Gotcha. So they have plenty of ammo and sufficient artillery."

"Aye," Gyrax affirms. "We could bolster their efforts, but we are of greater use in other capacities."

"I get it." A knowing nod. "You want a gamechanger. A weapon or an ally that'll help turn the tide."

Gyrax nods back. "Or knowledge of a weakness we must protect."

I sigh in disappointment. "Damn. I was hoping we could squad up and travel together. But you guys are seeking some all-knowing Oracle, while we have to get the Rosecraft Blade."

"What do you speak of?" Erany gives me a quizzical look. "The Oracle resides in the Silvered Caves, which are on the way to Yom Dagur. There isn't any reason to part with our friends."

"Sweet!" My eyes light with excitement. "In D&D, it's a lot more fun when the group sticks together. Sometimes, you gotta split people up, but it's really annoying if you have to play in separate roo—"

Erany interrupts with, "Cool story, bro!" Then follows up with a crooked brow. "That's how you use it, is it not?"

Gyrax, who's spent several years as my Earthling dog, gets the humor and roars with laughter.

My mouth opens and closes as I fish for a comeback. It ain't gonna happen; her timing was perfect. "Uh...yes. That's how you use it."

"Thank you, thank you." She bows and grins, milking the pwnage. "I am ever at your service."

I can't help but chuckle. The others express amusement in varying degrees. They might not get the detail or nuance, but they understand the overarching gist.

Gyrax says, "I share your sentiment, nerdish as it is. It is better to—"

" 'Nerdish?' " I mutter.

"—stick together and travel as a group. Competent folk are hard to come by. Competent and trustworthy, however, are as rare as Lyderea's long-term favor." (When Gyrax says *trustworthy*, Erany shoots Lucky some glaring side-eye.)

"It seems that fate has set our course," Elier states. Nyanti reaches up and rests a hand on his back. (Nice to see they're still together. They had just started flirting before I left.) "We shall break trail for the Volant Oracle. Afterward, we shall continue on to Yom Dagur, then summit its peak and claim the Blade."

I turn to my girlfriend. "What's its backstory? You mentioned bits and pieces..."

" 'Tis a winding yarn, better suited for our time on the road," Erany answers. "I'll spin the tale as we thin our soles."

Lucky raises a finger. *Hold your horses.* "The edge of the Pass is as far as I'll go. Yom Dagur is out of the question."

Gyrax says, "If it's a matter of coin—"

He shakes his head with firm insistence. "I refuse to negotiate haunts and specters."

"It is good to know the limits of your troth," Erany says coolly.

"Maybe we could teleport?" I look at Nyanti. "Skip the Pass altogether?"

" 'Twouldn't be wise," she says hesitantly. "As you saw in Elerica, the strain is enormous and potentially lethal. To do it safely, I would need several days to refine the ontology, and the distance would still be incredibly limited." She chews her lip. "Even if I could use the Velic Tessellate, its original network of slipworld passages—" She registers my uncomprehending stare and explains: "A pre-established weave of teleport byways."

"Ah." I nod sagely. "I knew what you meant. I was just testing you to see if—anyway, go on."

My attempt at humor goes unnoticed. "The byways are all in disrepair. If I used them to fold a relevant span, there's a good chance it wouldn't work."

"It's worth a shot, isn't it? What's the worst that could happen?"

"I could open a portal into the Stillfae, or maybe one of the thirteen Banes. That could invite the Temporal Fell, or perhaps a clutch of Dyrack Fiends. And should it open into Skaynewrith or Krai, we would face an army of Rotsink Hags. Personally, I prefer the Fiends, as the Hags would transform us into vectors for—"

"I got it." I pat the air with both hands. "If we tried to teleport, we'd roll out the carpet for Cthulu and company. Sheesh. What about horses?"

The Witch shrugs. "If you wish to part with a kingly sum, then by all means go and buy one."

"They're that expensive?"

"Lyderea has claimed them as part of her taxes," Elier explains. "Justicers enjoy their pick of steeds, while the folk are left with dregs and scraps. Even donkeys are considered a luxury."

"What about Wildlyre?"

"They are not for transport," the Duelist says. "If you are lucky enough to gain their trust, they may offer to bear you through imminent peril. Easing your travel, however, would insult and demean them."

"So more like a partner, instead of a pet."

"Exactly."

"Okay," I sigh. "Guess we're hoofing it."

Gyrax chuckles. "This isn't *Fallout,* where you can fix up a car and skip the slog."

"Don't I know it." I sigh again. *"Lord of the Rings* looked cool on screen, but damn—they must have gotten tired of all that hiking."

"If you wish for a horse, I can put up the coin," Gyrax says. "But keep in mind that their care is a chore. If the terrain is rough or they're rendered lame..."

"Nah." I wave him off. "I can barely remember to change the oil. Caring for a horse seems way more complicated."

Erany scans the table with a faint smile. "I must say: I did not expect to journey with friends. Your presence will serve as a welcome diversion."

"Aye Princess. I feel the same." Gyrax pauses, throws me a grin, then solemnly proclaims, "You have my axe."

Wait—what? *What?*

"Are we doing this? *Are we really doing this?*" I slap the table with my hands and look excitedly around.

Gyrax dips his chin and lifts an upturned palm at me. *Go ahead. Get it out of your system.*

I put on my best Serious Face, clear my throat, and gravely intone, "You have my gun." I stare ahead for a couple of seconds, then glance at the others without turning my head.

Absolute silence.

"A-a-*hem. You have my gun.*"

Nothing.

"Are we...should we say something?" Elier asks hesitantly.

"Oh come *on!*" I throw my hands in the air. "You guys are the *last* people that—" I point at Elier. "You're supposed to say, 'And my sabers,' " at Lucky, " 'And my bow,' " at Ren, " 'You have my sword,' " at Erany, "Same with you, (well maybe say rapier, just to mix it up.) And..." I falter at Nyanti. "I'm not really sure when it comes to you." I sweep the table with an accusing glare. *"God!* I'm surrounded by heathens!"

Everyone exchanges a mystified look, then acquiesces with murmurs and shrugs. "You have my sword," Ren says indifferently. The others follow suit, delivering their lines with zero panache.

"No!" I clench my jaw and grip my hair. "That's even worse! You guys are just—*AGGHH!*"

"Are you referencing a play?" Erany asks. "One of your lightning-powered 'movies?' "

"Yes. I thought you would...never mind."

"Mm." Nyanti gives me a guarded look, that one you reserve for your extra weird friend. "Are we done with the theater, or—"

"Yes, *yes!*" I cover my eyes with a thumb and forefinger. "We're done with the...yeah, we're done."

"Ah...right." The Witch responds with a blank but polite, you-do-you judgy face. "To each their own. Would any of you care for an enchanted smoke?" She reaches in her carry and produces a leaf-rolled cigarette. "I have plenty of loken."

Lucky claps his hands and rubs them together. "My favorite way to end the night!"

Nice—a change of subject and a chance to flirt. I lean close to Erany and whisper, "Not mine, though." And throw her a sly, knowing grin.

"Jon." She tries to stifle a smile, fails *(yes!)*, and curls a lock of hair behind her ear.

The others light up with arcane snaps, summoning blue-fire sparks from their enchanted fingers. I fit mine to my lips and turn to my girl-friend.

"Can a guy get a light?"

In her overly deep, Jon-is-a-moron voice, she booms, "You have my sorcery," and ignites my loken.

I shoot her a glare as she cackles and snickers. "That doesn't even flow! It's why I skipped Nyanti!"

"Sorry, sorry. Couldn't resist." She subsides into giggles.

"Can't believe you guys." I take a drag and exhale smoke. "New side-quest: I'm gonna make you appreciate *The Lord of the Rings.*" My voice drops to a mutter. "Just the movies, though, not the books. I mean, how many times do I have to read about a mountain, or some random guy's entire family tree?"

"Jon." Erany nudges me.

"Mm?"

"You're...what is the phrase? 'Nerding out?' I find it charming, but it lacks context." She glances at our puzzled friends. "An explanation, if you please."

"Um...sure." I tap some ash into an empty cup. "So on my world, there was this guy named Tolkien, and he wrote a story called *The Lord of the Rings...*"

For the next two hours, I regale my companions with Middle Earth lore. Lucky, conspiracy-theory cynic that he is, occasionally scoffs as if to say, *Yeah, RIGHT.* Elier listens with polite interest. It changes to disgust when I describe how Tolkien wrote more about armies and forma-tions, instead of boots-on-the-ground, blood-n-guts action (the Duelist throws up his hands and yells, "Then what's the *point?*"). Nyanti nods at the magical bits with an air of, *Check, check. Yep, seen it.* Every so often, she clicks her tongue and hisses in displeasure. *Nope, nope. All wrong.* Ren seems interested in Strider/Aragorn, but as I wax on about Frodo's journey, he becomes straight-up pissed. (If our grumpy Wayfarer had his way, Frodo would've whooped Gollum's ass on a thrice-daily basis.) Gyrax, who's seen all the movies, smiles or chuckles at the others' reactions.

Erany, meanwhile, intersperses my tale with disgruntled murmurs. When I ask her what's wrong, she angrily states that there aren't any women. I spread my fingers and start ticking off names: Galadriel, Eowyn, Arwen...she interrupts with a snort, retorting that a sprinkling of side characters don't make up for a giant sausage-fest. (My words, not hers.)

"This tale is *renowned?*" she demands. "Why would anyone—"

"Easy." I raise my palms and hold back laughter. "Like I said, the movies are better. Arwen gets to kick some ass, and Eowyn—"

"*Fah!*" She flaps a hand. "As a half-Elf child, I suffered countless bullies, but at least I was exposed to capable women!" She glares at Nyanti. "You share my vantage—why aren't you riled? This tale is farcical, through and through!"

The Witch shrugs, unperturbed. "Build and body are trifling matters. I fail to see why you are vexed."

Erany takes a breath and exhales slowly. "I plead thy grace. I have let my ire best my carriage." She stares at the table. "I believe the answer lies in our upbringing. You have enjoyed an inclusive childhood. I have not. I may be royalty, but I never felt like it, as I was mocked and taunted for my human father. So when Jon mentions these insidious devices, these sly omissions that embolden one and discount the other...well, it fuels my temper, as you can see. Children have a right to believe in their worth, along with their potential and inherent promise. To hem their minds with exclusionary drivel is—" She takes another breath. "Apologies. I harry your ears with my long-running tongue."

"I understand," Nyanti says. "But do not let it eat at your peace."

I may be new to this supportive boyfriend stuff, but I'm pretty sure this isn't the right time to zing her about her transcendental worldview. So instead I say, "Just to be fair, Tolkien was raised on a different world. Back then, societal norms were—"

"Spare me!" Erany snarls. (Crap. Wait to miss the mark.) "He could have just as easily—" She cuts herself short and forces a sigh. "Yes...I suppose you are right. Our varied pasts have shaped our perspectives, and sifting malice from ignorance is how we progress. Otherwise, we might as well live as Reft-stricken folk, and act purely out of reactive fury." A rueful grin. "Transcendental worldview, correct? I needn't obsess over outward conditions, nor use them as an excuse to wallow in rage."

"Uh, yeah." I hiss through my teeth. "I wasn't going to mention it, but..."

"Wise." Erany smiles.

"I definitely think Nyanti's right. You do what you can and try to downplay the negative. I'm not endorsing willful ignorance, just a focus on solutions instead of the problem. If Ren can do it—"

He raises his glass and dips his chin in acknowledgment.

"—anyone can. And just so you know: Earth has way more prejudice than anything on Evermoor. We're still trying to sort it all out."

Lucky raises an eyebrow. "Evermoor teems with social disparity."

I shrug in defeat. "You got me there. It's the same back home."

" 'Tis a fact of life," the thief asserts. "An enduring tenet of existence itself."

"Your vantage is flawed," Gyrax counters, "due to your incomplete view of our greater reality."

"I have merely discarded any pointless context."

Gyrax takes a drag and examines the wall. "On that point, you and I must disagree, though I do not seek to change your view. Your right to its fruit, be it sour or sweet, is entirely your own and no one else's."

Lucky chuckles. " 'Tis plain to see why you are king. You care for others, yet allow them to retain their own perspective. For the time being, you have even made a follower out of me."

"I haven't been king in quite some time," Gyrax admonishes. "I have appointed a Steward to—"

"You stay connected through your trio of aviads. Also, whenever we encounter a courier exchange, you ensure that a letter is sent to your folk."

"Aye, but—"

"Whether you are journeying abroad or residing at home, you set an example nonetheless. And it is an august one, Gyrax. I do not believe that anyone at this table—or anyone with the least bit of sense—would seek to dispute me on this issue."

Lucky's compliment is met with *Ayes.* Gyrax waves them off with good-natured humor. "Pretty words, Lucky. Yet a test of my faith looms before me: I believe you will bow to the greater good."

"Ha!" The thief responds with a raucous guffaw. "Do not wait with bated breath."

"We shall see."

"Lucky won't change," Erany mutters. "Let him rot. Along with your tale of rings and Hobbits."

"Easy now," I warn. "Tolkien fans are a dedicated bunch. If we go back to Earth, then—"

"They would do well to keep their cursed distance," she growls, "lest I blacken their eyes and redden their rumps."

"Some might like it," I joke. "Not me, though. I prefer my rump pristine and unreddened."

Erany responds with a wry grin. "Then mind your tongue and keep me merry."

As laughter and mirth sweep our table, I reflect on the state of present-day fantasy, and how much it's changed since Tolkien's epic. Props to the guy for breaking new ground, but there's no way in hell I'd trade my fellowship for his. Sexy time with Erany versus nine smelly dudes? Their collective funk must've been *out of control.* Still, credit's due where credit's due; without Tolkien, we wouldn't have *Dungeons and Drag-*

ons, Assassin's Apprentice, The Dark Tower...you can't deny his creative influence.

Erany's laugh draws my gaze. For a timeless moment, I'm lost in her beauty. Her graceful neck, her perfect lips...

Yeah, I'm grateful for all that came before, but what I've got now is so much better.

5

Midway into our evening chat, Gyrax pays for lodging and breakfast. Before we adjourn, everyone agrees to meet outside before dawn.

Erany grabs me and hauls me upstairs. Doors and hallways blur through my vision, then we barge into our room and get straight-up hormonal. I catch a glimpse of our cushy surroundings (lamp, desk, linen-coated bed) but all that's just a fleeting impression, because hotel sex is as awesome as they say.

————

I wake up to Erany's hand on my chest, slowly creeping down to my belly (morning smashes? Yes, *please!*). At the same time, she nibbles my ear. "*Jo*-ooonnn...time to *go*-ooo..."

"Mmm." I nuzzle into my pillow. "Five more minutes. But keep doing whatever you're doing—it feels amazing."

She clamps my nipple with viselike force. "Get *up*, you layabout! Time runs thin!"

"*AHGODNO!*" I desperately try to pry her off, but she's way too strong for my weak little gamer hands.

"Up, Jon, *UP!*" She releases my nerp and starts tickling my ribs.

"No!" I gasp. "*DON'T!*" I writhe and squirm like a fish out of water, but she keeps me pinned with her Elven jiu-jitsu. After what seems like a manic eternity, she lets me go and I squirt out of bed.

"Not. *Funny.*" I pant.

She's tangled in the rumpled sheets, deep in the throes of sidesplitting mirth. Our neighbor bangs on the adjacent wall, yelling something-something-something about shutting our gams.

"Aaah…" She wipes off a tear and gets to her feet. "Priceless."

"Gotta start training," I mutter. "Gonna make you the nurse, just you wait."

"Never, Jon, except in dreams and passing fancy." She slips on her pants and throws me a grin. "Don't lie—you *love* it!"

I shrug into a shirt and chuckle agreeably. "I kinda do, actually."

She nods at the door as she fastens her belt. "I saw a wash-byre three rooms down. If you wish to bathe…"

I sniff-check my pits and flinch in disgust. *Whoof.* "Definitely."

"I as well. I shall meet you outside."

Once she's gone, I join my hands in a palm-to-palm prayer, stare up at the heavens, and mouth, *Thank you, God.* My half-Elf girlfriend is the best thing ever.

Even with the purple-nurples.

———

What do you know…they have showers on Evermoor.

Instead of a nozzle, they're each fitted with a wooden half-pipe, canting down at a diagonal angle. Their curtains are made from a glaucous membrane, webbed throughout with pinkish-red veins (I think they're cut from a giant plant.) In place of a knob, a metal-beaded cord hangs from the ceiling. Our room came stocked with soap and towels, so everything else is smooth sailing.

As I lather up my arms, Lucky enters the stall to my right (his cheerful humming gives him away). I'm glad there's a wall. Showering naked with a master thief…for some reason, it gives me a case of the heebie-jeebies.

Once I'm done, I step out and lock eyes with Elier and Ren. They've just dried off and they're starting to get dressed. (Jesus Christ, they are *ripped.* Swear to God, if they hit on Erany, I am gonna…no, Jon, *no!* Do *not* become a jealous boyfriend!)

Elier dips his head in casual greeting. Ren grumbles, "Sun on your brow." (Points for consistency—he's still a black belt in dickhead energy.)

"Hey guys." I clear my throat. "I've given it some thought, and I'd like to start training in swordplay and magic. If you're willing, maybe you could—"

"Maybe you could act with a semblance of haste," Ren snaps. "While you stand there and gibber, Freecast rebels hold fast at the Strait." As he throws on a shirt and slips out the door, I stifle the urge to give him the finger.

Elier chuckles and shakes his head. *That's Ren.* "I shall gladly instruct you. Teaching another will sharpen my skill."

"Thanks!" Then I hiss through my teeth, suddenly nervous. "But could we keep it to like, every other day, maybe less?"

"What? Why?" He stops mid-button.

"I've got other stuff to learn, and...well, I'd like to have some time to myself. For personal enjoyment, you know?"

"Swordplay *is* enjoyment." His voice is slow and careful, as if he's talking me back from the brink of insanity.

"Maybe for you, not for me. You like duels, I like other stuff."

"I...*suppose...*" His brow wrinkles in confusion, then he shrugs. "To each his own."

Lucky grabs his towel and steps out from his stall. "Canny, Jon, canny!" He throws a backhanded flick at Elier's shoulder. "He cannot match us skill for skill, so he has decided to learn a bit from each! If swordplay fails, he will turn to magic. If magic fails, he will turn to grift. He is preparing for our wrath or potential betrayal." He wags a finger at me. "I fully approve!"

"No, that's not what—" I sigh in frustration. "I'd like to contribute, but I still want time to chill and relax. Does that make sense?"

They both say, "No."

"Forget it." I wave my hand in defeat. "Just...yeah."

I finish getting dressed and hustle out the door, keenly aware of their perplexed expressions.

———

Seconds later, I run into Nyanti at the top of the stairs. With great reluctance, I ask her to teach me how to cast magic, with the same stipulation I asked of Elier and Lucky. Much to my surprise, she responds with easy agreement.

"Whew," I chuckle. "I thought you'd make me—"

"Slave day and night over charms and glyphs? If you were a tot, that is exactly what I would do. But you are well past that age, and you are also the Traveler. As that is the case, you are better off with Primal Magic, and that entails abidance in ease and grace. Forcing a spell will only slow your progress."

"Nice," I reply. "Erany said something similar, when she was showing me how to dim my aura."

"So you've learned that already. Good." An approving nod. "If you wish to train, let me know and we shall train."

"Will do." I smile. "Funny—out of all the stuff I want to learn, I thought magic would be hardest."

"We'll see." She returns my smile. "Come." She glances at the bar. "Breakfast awaits."

As we approach, the attendant holds up some burlap bags. "Sack meals, per Gyrax Aclasian." (He must have given her our physical and/or auric description. How else would she know we were traveling with Gyrax?)

Once we're outside, I pull a wax-paper bundle from the depths of my bag. Its folds shine with melty-cheese bread, stuffed with chunks of garlicky sausage.

I take a moment to ogle my noms, then crane forward and take a bite.

"Oh my God," I exclaim. "Oh my *God.*"

The cheese is spicy, but the herby bread is a perfect offset. It's golden crusty brown on the sides and the top, just enough to add some yum-malicious texture. A second later, in a happy-dance-worthy nombastic explosion, the sausage floods my palate with greasy meaties.

Erany walks out with Elier and Ren, mocking me in her Jon-Is-Stupid Voice: " 'MMMM! Oh my *GO-oooddd!*' If ever we need a catch-penny laugh, throw my lover a Gomptown biscuit, so all can revel in his bovine pleasure."

I tighten my lips in mock reproach. "Really don't approve."

She flashes a grin, making my heart beat noticeably faster. "Because I have captured your dullard spirit, if not the tone and off-world pitch."

"Pretty much," I chuckle. "Gomptown biscuit, huh?" I examine its steamy fragrant edges. "These would sell like hotcakes back on Earth."

"The Wanderer's Idyll is known for its fare. Supposedly, their dishes hark back to the Faldarrin Age." She takes a bite of her food and closes her eyes. *"MMMmmm..."* Two seconds in, her expression tautens with self-aware horror.

Too late. My turn, lady.

"MMMmmm..." I roll my eyes and flutter my lids. *"MmrrRRAGHH..."* I sound like Jabba on weed, trying to beatbox through a mouthful of yogurt.

Erany knows I've won this round—she breaks into loud, unchecked guffaws. *(Yes!)*

Ren samples his Gomptown biscuit. "It's good, but...food is food." His expression crinkles in puzzlement.

Elier takes a bite and agrees with Ren, cueing Erany and Nyanti to exchange exasperated looks. Before they can ridicule our tough-guy swordsmen, Lucky and Gyrax step outside. The Wolven is holding a leathery waterskin, paired with a sheaf of conical cups. They look like a stack of oversized cones, made from sanded-down bark with yellow-green stripes.

"Kheva." He lifts the waterskin. "We'll drink it on the road."

"Shall we?" Lucky prompts. "My legs and feet are a tad bit chill."

Ren breaks west. "On my heels."

Aside from a smatter of early bird merchants, there aren't any people out and about. Three blocks in, the sun crests the glaciered horizon, dappling the ground with slanted gold light. We may be crossing a rag-tag city, but the brisk-aired shine makes it seem fresh and new.

Two bailys over, the merchants give way to vertical farms (between three and five stories, with a couple that are taller) lined with sills of plants and herbs. Their windows are built with fanciful curves, their walls are fitted with gears and rods. It's clear they were made with a purpose in mind.

I gulp the last of my biscuit and peer at the buildings. "Why do they look like that?"

"Under Glimmersend statutes, lots and structures are hard to acquire," Nyanti explains, "even harder to share or divide. These botanicals maximize space and choice. Each one moves with the sun and the moons, to allow for a wide variety of crops."

My brow furrows in confusion. "You need moving buildings to grow a range of produce?"

She answers with a nod. "Their mobility controls the incoming light, which allows them to meet conflicting demands. A plant may require the dawning sun, while its companion might need the lunar quadrivium. Alaewyn sepaia, for example, will blossom in the early dusk, then wilt in the rays of morning and noon."

I throw her a puzzled look. "How could it ever live on its own? Unless people controlled its exposure to light, then—"

"Not people," Erany interjects. "Trees. Sepaia grows under yenlif boughs. Their leaves and branches move and adjust."

"What?" My brow wrinkles in confusion. "So the boughs provide shade during the day, then move to the side as the sun starts to set?"

"That is correct."

Elier adds, "Khairach is known for its alypsy vines. They trip the unwary and move your belongings."

"Um...okay." I give him a dubious look. Then a months-old memory comes to the fore, prompting me to ask, "Can any of them speak? On the way to Elerica, some of the vines grumbled and coughed."

"Those were pengrips," Elier says. "They are somewhat grumpy, like cranky old dodders. Alypsy are closer to mischievous tots. And yes, certain flora are capable of speech, though most are halting and spare in rhythm."

"Wow." I shake my head in quiet amazement.

"Pengrips and alypsy are lower caste," Nyanti adds. "Nothing compared to the stately Eka." She moderates the E, pronouncing it *EH-kah.*

I shift back to the Witch. "Eka?"

"Enormous fungi. Roughly as tall as these vertical farms."

"No *way!*" I breathe. "Magic mushrooms! Like, *literal* magic mushrooms!"

"Aye." A faint smile. "Many are wizards, though in a different manner than humans and Wildlyre."

"What do you mean?"

"Their spells are bound to the soil and sea."

"How is that different from regular sorcery?"

"In traditional magic, a mage will rely on preestablished patterns of thought. The Eka, however, draw their power from the heart of Evermoor—the arcane marrow of the planet itself."

"Huh." I scratch my temple. "I'm guessing they're strong?"

"Ridiculously so," Nyanti confirms. "As the Tessellate expanded in breadth and clout, they withdrew from sight and lapsed into slumber."

Lucky interjects with a cynical scoff. "Eka are simply a half-witted lie."

The Witch regards him with tired amusement. "Wonder and marvel have fallen out of fashion. Now we are plagued by doubt and mistrust."

The thief shrugs, clearly disinterested. *Whatever.*

The Witch turns back to me. "In days of yore, Eka ruled kingdoms across this world—palatial forests that beggar description."

Man, that sounds cool...kind of like dinosaurs, only with sentient vegetables instead of bird-lizard giants. "You said they're asleep? Where?"

"No one knows."

The buildings around us creak to life, surprising me into halting and drawing my dagger.

Erany beckons me on with an irritable wave. "Would you cease your dithers? We just told you they shift and move."

I sheathe my blade and clear my throat. "Sorry. It's one thing to hear it, another thing to…"

The structure in front of us—a three-deck stack of circular floors—cants in place, striking a forty-five degree angle against the sky. As each floor begins spinning on its axis, its windows and doors fold and split, its walls retract and its corners flatten. The surrounding architecture follows suit, rumbling and sliding in a brick-and-mortar symphony.

This. Is. *Amazing.*

Erany places a finger under my chin, gently closing my slack-jawed mouth. "Mind the slobber." She wipes her hand off on my cloak.

"Oh! Sorry." I swipe my lips with the back of my wrist.

"Quell your worry." She gives me a fond once-over. "I find you endearing. Even with the smelly drool."

Her compliment evokes a sheepish laugh. "I'll work on the saliva."

"Grace and thanks."

As the buildings around us grumble and settle, Glimmersend's border comes into sight. Beyond its edge, a low-curving trail stretches into the distance, cutting through a swath of cloud-wreathed bluffs. Half are hidden by swirling mist, the rest are coated in rich blue trees.

The rolling terrain, the sun-dappled vapor, the arresting hue of the cobalt leaves…it's absolutely stunning.

"A beautiful way to resume our journey," Gyrax states.

I couldn't agree more.

6 |

Fog spills across the path, refracting the sun into slow-moving spears. A few of them condense into rainbow globs, bounce-roll along for a couple of seconds, then break apart into muted flickers.

"What the…" I trail off, overcome by awe.

"Fair Folk call them *lyaedim sinaeri,*" Nyanti explains, "which loosely translates to 'skyfire kiss.' Others use a plainer name: flare-pours."

"Huh." I watch as a flare-pour trundles along, ablaze with hues of silky luminescence, before wisping apart into ringlets and tendrils. "Do they just happen on their own, or…"

"More or less. This arcane topography is somewhat unusual. It facilitates the expression of prismatic phenomena."

Gyrax beckons us over to the side of the road. "Partake of this kheva while it is hot." He begins to fill our bark-formed cups. Each one gets passed to the right.

I lift mine up to take a sip, but Ren stops me with a half-gloved hand. "Wait. It's pulling flavor off the greenspaeth bark."

"Oh, okay." (The bark adds flavor? Wait to outdo yourself, Evermoor.) "So it doesn't taste good in a mug or a glass?"

Gyrax shrugs. "Like plain coffee."

"Interes—wait, when have you had coffee? Does it grow here on Evermoor?"

He ducks his head in a bashful smile. "Two years back, you were pulling an all-nighter for AP English. You left a cup out on your desk, then fell asleep on your midterm study guide."

"Did I? I don't remem—" The memory crystallizes, surprising me into a raucous guffaw. "You drank the *entire cup!* I freaked out and called the emergency vet—I thought your heart was gonna explode! How'd you get up there, anyway?"

"Your easy chair. It presses against the side of your desk." He chuckles ruefully. "Never again. I couldn't sleep for a day and a half."

"You woke me up with full-on zoomies," I laugh.

"Never again," he repeats. "I was damnably sore for the rest of the week. My current body is strong and hale, but my Earthling form is old and weak." He nods at my cup. "It should be ready."

Kheva tastes like sweetened cocoa, mixed with creamy-delicious, peanut-buttery undertones. "Man." I shake my head, thoroughly impressed. "Kheva is *life*. I want this every morning when I get back to Earth."

"All in the bark," Gyrax says. "Unless there's a greenspaeth somewhere on Earth, I regret to inform you you're out of luck."

"The bark, huh?" I take another sip. "Maybe there's a substitute."

"Maybe you could make one," Erany says.

"Maybe. I dunno..." I gaze into the distance. "When it's all said and done, I think I'd rather stay here. I kinda miss pizza, but..."

Ren grunts in approval. "Wise. You have much to do in the foreseeable future."

"Right." I rub the back of my neck, struck by a flash of sudden panic. It's easy to forget I'm the Prophesied Traveler.

It's easy to forget I have to *save the world.*

Erany nudges me. "You have plenty of time to grow into your role."

"Of course." I muster a grin. "Plenty of time."

"Onward." Ren gulps his kheva and resumes walking. As we fall in behind him, dread takes root in the pit of my stomach.

Why does everything have to change?

Why can't things just stay the same?

———

Over the next few days, I make an effort to be cheerful and talkative. Every so often, I laugh a little too hard and draw puzzled glances. That puts me on edge, but my social anxiety feels a hell of a lot better than contemplating my Frodo-esque destiny. (Just to be clear, I am *not* Frodo Baggins. I'm dating the hottest half-Elf in the history of half-Elves, while Frodo was stuck with Samwise Gamgee. Unless Sam was played by a young Brad Pitt, he wouldn't stand a chance against my girl.)

The doom-vibe gradually lessens and fades, allowing me to relax and enjoy our D&D road trip. For the others' sake, me and Erany keep the PDA to a minimum. But whenever we stop to eat and sleep, off we go into the woods, where we can enjoy our sexy time in relative privacy. It's kind of exciting: a fun, giggly game that alternates between forcibly composed and shamelessly intimate.

On our second week of travel, I ask Erany about the Rosecraft Blade. She gives a mild start (she forgot she didn't tell us about it) then proceeds to bring us up to speed.

The Blade arose from a magic teardrop, left by an entity named Saedra ValFae. Saedra was born as one of the Elder Folk: half-dream, half-smoke creatures that were the first race of beings to appear on Evermoor. One day, while contemplating impermanence, her tear fell on the peak known as Yom Dagur. There it sat for countless millennia, blessing the wilds with peace and serenity. Meanwhile, Saedra became pregnant. The father was a deadbeat named Quare Althaelis.

Saedra gave birth to fraternal twins: a girl named Telse (rhymes with "else") and a boy named Vyde (rhymes with "slide"). Telse favored wind, Vyde favored water. (Elder Folk can manipulate any element, but they each have a personal preference). During the Second Age of the Continuance Reverie, the twins fought over a network of rivers. Their clash manifested as a raging storm, rife with enchanted supercharged lightning. One of the bolts hit Saedra's tear, shocking it with a burst of eldritch power.

The tear went nuts. It sucked the life from its mountainous home, turning everything around it dusty and gray. After the storm faded away, a single rose was all that stood, growing from the spot where the tear had fallen. The rose was locked in a transitory state (its aura was blinking through multiple possibilities) as it hadn't yet chosen its final form.

Eons after the Elder Folk vanished, a trio of dryads (nature-bound spirits who protect the wild) happened upon the lone rose. They sat and watched it for over a decade, waiting to see what form it would take. Eventually, it settled into an orphic stasis: a state of uncertainty between rose and sword. If someone channels their will into the rose, it'll solidify into a rune-scriven blade.

To this day, the three dryads guard the weapon, ensuring it won't be plucked by a careless soul. It's also guarded by a stone golem: a semi-sentient, enchanted automaton. (The dryads summoned it in the early Bright Age).

"Dryads and golems are fine and dandy," I remark. "It's Sidehelm Pass that creeps me out. Why do we need the Blade, anyway? I get that it's important, but..."

"It's one of the Seven Great Weapons," Erany replies.

" 'Great Weapon.' What does that mean, exactly?"

"Due to its power, it has strategic value." I give her a puzzled look, prompting her to elaborate: "It can sway the course of kingdoms and nations." She begins ticking names off on her outstretched fingers. "Ailura Qartesi. The Elderean Staff. The trident Sendaefir. The Shadefire Bow. The Redmordent Scourge. Ijeltir the Axe. And, of course, the Rosecraft Blade. While it cannot match the Velic Tessellate, it can stymie or bulwark armies and fleets."

"Why did you pick the Rosecraft Blade? Were the rest of them taken, or...oh yeah—" I conk my forehead. "You have a magical homing brace."

"The Blade also favors Elder Folk blood. I am a prime candidate, as the Ailahdi line is descended from Saedra."

"What?" I blurt. "You're related to a *demigod?*"

"Mm," Erany replies distractedly. "All Fair Folk are."

While I'm struggling to process this, Nyanti prompts her with, "Your locator brace—you said you received it from a sage named Yondi…"

Erany nods. "After I saved his crustacean familiar, I told him I wished to acquire the Blade. He gave me this brace as a gesture of thanks." Erany raises her left wrist, displaying a shiny gold weave with a ruby in its center. "It was fashioned by a Witch named Dybera Tyjaric. She too, desired the Blade, and spent over a decade enchanting this armlet. Sadly, she vanished in the depths of Sidehelm Pass. Most assume she encountered the Watchers. They likely mazed her and drained her aura."

"Awesome," I grumble. "Can't wait to meet 'em."

"Not for a while," she chides. "Remember: we aren't going into the castle itself. We are simply walking by the Pass."

"Tomato, toh-mah-toe."

Silence descends. And not the good kind either; it's heavy with the weight of doom and gloom. Thankfully, Lucky starts humming. I throw in some nightclub-esque percussion—*MM-tsst MM-tsst MM-tsst*—and he launches into a raunchy ditty, one where he sleazes his way through seven sisters, then seduces their mom while they're all at the fair. Predictably, things go south: he ends up fleeing naked into the woods, chased by the sisters and their pissed-off mom.

Elier's up next. The Duelist's offering is similar to Lucky's: a fight-song laden with tons of innuendo about stabbing and thrusting. Everyone claps along to the beat, and upon his signal, lets loose with a "HA!" or "WO!" (like "woe" but shorter). Once he's done, most of us break into hearty applause (Ren doesn't clap, but to his credit, he manages to look a little less sullen.)

"Gyrax?" I throw him a pointed look.

He raises his hands in polite refusal. "Wolven howls would test your grace."

"Makes sense," I chuckle. "When I left you at home, you would bawl your eyes out. It sounded like someone was literally beating you."

"That was only when you first adopted me," he grumbles. "Within the bounds of my Earthling form, my psyche struggles with complexity and nuance."

"Ren?" I turn to the Wayfarer. "Care to entertain us with—"

"No."

Shocker. I sidle up to Erany. "You gotta have something—you're a dead ringer for Taylor Swift."

"Like for like," she replies coquettishly. "Sing me a song and I'll match your bid."

"Deal. You first, though."

She chews her lip, then gives a nod. "Very well."

As the trail steepens, Eralindíany begins to hum. My legs tire and my breath roughens, but I barely notice because her voice is *beautiful*. There aren't any lyrics, it's a continuous flow of pitch-perfect sound. Through exclusive use of lilt and tone, she's conveying a story without any words.

Here's how I read it: at first there's a rush of mutual attraction, which gradually deepens into rock-solid love. That gives way to distrust and unease, opening the way for heartbreak and grief. Insidious epiphanies arise and bloom, crystallizing into betrayal and resentment. It now resembles the score from *Requiem for a Dream*—grim determination, burning drive, and a hate-fueled desire for justice and revenge.

Her voice flares, intensifies, then slowly fades into a haunting whisper.

After a respectful silence, I start to clap. "Wow." I shake my head. "That was...wow." The others don't applaud, but I can tell by their expressions that they feel the same way.

Erany shrugs. "When I was a tot, I loved to sing. A foolish dream, given my duties—"

"Not at all," Ren says quietly. "Those were honeyed tones."

Erany blushes and averts her gaze. "Grace and thanks."

I stifle the urge to shoot him a glare, then mentally kick myself for being an ass. He isn't hitting on her, Jon. Calm the hell down.

Lucky exclaims, "If I had known of your skill, we could have been rich as Lyderea's nobles!"

Erany responds with a puzzled grin. "Minstrels aren't rich, Lucky."

"No, that's not what I—" He throws his hands up in exasperation. "Do you know how many folk we could have swindled if—" He registers her darkening expression and amends it to, "Ah…never mind. I was merely hypothesizing."

"Your conjecture is fell," she says icily.

The thief recedes with a sullen glare, muttering something nasty under his breath. Erany catches it and looks angrily back at him. At the same time, she flares her cloak and grips her rapier.

"If you would have it out with me, then—"

I grab her arms and turn her around. "Whoa! Same side, remember?"

"Right," she grumbles. "Transcendental worldview, Erany, transcendental worldview."

I lean in and whisper, "Why are you pissed? Ever since we got back from Earth—"

"I don't know," she whispers back. "For some reason, the very sight of him triggers my rage."

"Well for the foreseeable future, he's gonna be with us, so you should probably—"

"I know, Jon, I know," she says irritably. "Cry off, will you? I'll keep my peace with the Nok-damned rogue." She looks at Nyanti. "Care to go next?"

The Witch chuckles. "Thank you, but no. Compared to you, I would sound like a passel of cats in heat."

Her compliment restores Erany's cheer. "Another day, then."

I clear my throat. "Does that song have words?"

She shakes her head. "Fair Folk music never has lyrics. The narrative is told through rhythm and pitch."

"Wow," I say appreciatively. "You'd make tons of money writing cinematic scores."

"Your turn." Her eyes twinkle with mischief. "Did you think I forgot?"

"Okay, let me think." I study the sky and rack my brain. No lyrics... maybe I could do the same... "Ooh!" I perk and straighten. "Okay, this one's famous. It goes something like..."

I take a breath, then belt out the *Star Wars* opening theme.

The others burst into raucous laughter. Clearly, they think it's ridiculous. Nevertheless, they form a motley chorus and shore up my warble. For the next few minutes, the air rings with X-wings and Jedi, epic duels and majestic space opera. They all seem to like it, so I segue into "The Starfighter Attack Theme" then "The Imperial March." Much to my delight, both are met with cheers and applause.

"More!" Erany yells. "Give us more!" The others respond with hearty approval, shouting, *"More!"* and *"Again!"*

"All right. One more." I walk out in front and face the party. This way, I can pretend-conduct while I sing.

Elier cups his mouth and yells, "Give us adventure! Give us thrills in the unknown wild!"

I point at him and affect a radio DJ voice: *"Coming at you with a blast of wanderlust, requested by the Duelist off to my right!"* My announcement is met with hoots of encouragement.

I might have spoken a bit too soon. Adventure...wanderlust...what do I know that—

Ooh! Got it.

I take a breath, then ease into the fanfare for *Indiana Jones*. The others exchange thoughtful looks—*okay, okay, I see you*—then commit to the melody, booming out the promise of far-flung lands, paired with the thrill of daring escapades.

My offering concludes with a round of applause. I respond with a bow and an Elvis-esque *Thangyew, thangyew very much*. I almost fall back in when it suddenly hits me: I have one more tune up my Earth-music sleeve.

I clear my throat with theatric gravity: "A-heh-*hem. A-heh-HEM!*"

They all quiet down, eager to hear my next number.

Which just so happens to be the *Lord of the Rings*. "DAAA DAAA deh deh DAAA! Deh deh *daah,* deh deh *daah,* deh deh daah, dah da—"

A chorus of groans arise from the party.

"Jon! *Jon!*"

"Save our ears and still your breath!"

"No! *Please,* Jon, *NO!*"

"Deliac's Gleam, where is your *taste?*"

I spread my arms in a WTF gesture, glaring them down like the haters they are. "Come on guys, this was *made* for you!"

Lucky hisses like a pissed-off cat, cuing the others to do the same (apparently, that's how you boo people here on Evermoor). Pretty soon, I'm surrounded by a pack of disgruntled wanderers, expressing their wrath with a sibilant buzz.

"Just *try* it, okay?" I plead my case with an exasperated look. "Let's end on a high note, huh?" (My voice almost cracked. Thank God it didn't).

Mutters of *Fine* and *As you wish* ripple through the party.

As I launch into a repeat performance, the others hum along with zero emotion. I raise my eyebrows, give them my best *do-not-test-me* face, and turn it up a couple of notches. They match my volume but not my spirit—it's like someone's holding a gun to their head.

Then, much to my relief, Elier begins singing with lively exuberance. I smile and point, acknowledging his support, then spread my arms again. *What about the rest of you? Come on!* One by one, they reluctantly shift from resentment to enthusiasm.

As our voices mingle, the incline begins to level out, revealing blue-forest ridges hemmed by towering waterfalls. Right before we crest the trail, I fall back in so we can recreate that iconic scene from the *Fellowship of the Ring,* the one where they summit the pass in epic slow motion.

"DAAA DAAA deh deh DAAA! Deh deh daah, deh deh daah, deh deh daah, dah dah..."

Say what you want about the books or the movies, but you gotta love that dope-ass theme music.

————

Down below, the trail narrows into a stone bridge. The rightmost waterfall gushes toward it, feeding into a turbulent lake. The lefthand waterfall does the same, only it gushes in from the opposite direction. Due to the pressure, the lake splits into fast-moving rapids—one goes north, the other goes south. Thanks to the elevation and majestic backdrop, the bridge below looks super tiny.

"With treacherous footing, it helps to walk sideways." Ren turns his body and starts down the hill. "I mention this tidbit solely for Jon, as he is generally lacking in practical know-how."

"Thanks, Ren," I say loudly and dryly. "Really enjoy the subtle dig."

"It is not without merit. If we set you against a hapless child, there is a good chance that—"

"Yeah, I *got it!*"

The scenery's stunning, but it takes a backseat to my razzum-frazzum saltiness. Stupid Ren and his dickhead zingers. I swear to God, I'm gonna pee in his next biscuit. Think that's a hunk of nommalicious cheese? Think again, asshole—it's an extra-strong dose of Eau de Jon.

"Jon?" Erany nudges me, startling me out of my juvenile reverie. "Why are you smiling?"

"Uh...didn't know I was."

Nice—I was low-key mad, then I let it flow and let it go. Now I'm thinking about funny pranks to pull on Ren. I look to my right and lock eyes with Nyanti. Judging by her stare, she's been assessing my response.

A moment later, she confirms it with a nod. "Remember: emotions are like streams of long-running water. If the current is strong, 'tis counterproductive to force their heading. At that point, it is much easier to redirect them."

Gyrax claps me on the shoulder. "We'll make a wizard of you yet!"

Damn. Thanks to Ren's jerk-faced jerkiness, I just leveled up in Primal Magic. Who would have thought?

The stone bridge stretches before us, glazed in swirls of particulate mist. From higher up, the waterfalls resembled picturesque columns. Up close, it's a different story. Roaring torrents bound our flanks, rattling my bones with deafening sound.

Ren shouts, *"Short steps, slow stride!"*

We follow behind one by one. The wind picks up and lashes my face, forcing me to close my eyes, dip to a knee, and palm the rock to steady my balance. A second later, the wind changes course and blows away the fog to our front.

Hold on...is that...

Shit.

Shit.

Arganti Knifelock, Lyderea Fairdyle's Nightkeeper Captain, is standing at the end of this goddamn bridge.

Everyone freezes.

Back in Elerica, we encountered his simulacra: a magic double that could interact with matter. This time, it's *actually him*. His snow-white hair is fluttering in the wind, his pitch-black armor is shining with moisture. The tails on his blindfold whip and twist, the runes on its surface pulse and glimmer.

Ren breaks the silence with: *"KILL HIM!"*

Glyph-laden auras spin and accelerate, concentrating into eyes and foreheads, hands and chests. Lucky rolls sideways off the bridge, clutching a pair of silver spikes.

I scream, *"Lucky, what are you DOING?"* Too late. He's already gone.

Nyanti throws a sweeping backhand, launching a fifty-foot slash of crimson energy. It whips through the air like a giant boomerang, sizzling as it flows into Knifelock's breastplate. The dusky metal glows cherry red, then diffuses her attack into multicolored ripples.

The others unleash a destructive barrage—violet rays, green spears of light, and shrill white flares that arc and twist. Knifelock swats a bunch of it away, the rest is absorbed by his impenetrable armor. Gradients surge across his plates, imbuing them with fluxing iridescence.

The Nightkeeper Captain shouts and waves, but I can't make head or tails of what he's saying. Everything around us is rumbling and quaking, jarred by the roil of arcane power.

He shakes his head in seeming frustration, then claps his hands and raises them high. Ebony fog pours from his fingers, forming an oversized blade made of shadow and night.

The others cast harder, hurling wave after wave of violent magic. It doesn't faze him. He cuts downward, left shoulder to right hip, releasing the buildup of rune-limned black. It boils forward in twitchy spurts, enveloping us all in lightless gloom.

"Gyrax!" I scream. *"Erany!"*

I can hear my own voice, but that's about it. Same goes for sight. Everywhere I look, it's blacker than black. If it weren't for the wind and the spray-laden mist, I would have no idea I was standing outside.

So I get on my knees and start crawling forward. I know how to swim, but the water below is super turbulent. Gotta be careful, or I could—

An unfamiliar voice catches my attention: "Jon."

"Huh?" I crane my head up.

Knifelock—he's *right there.* Five yards away, maybe less.

I scoot frantically back on my hands and my butt. "Shit—*NO!*"

He dives toward me, clinches my waist, and rolls us off the side of the bridge. Mid-tumble, we break free of his magical veil. I catch a glimpse of Lucky, hanging off the side with his silver climbing spikes, then we plunge into the liquid churn.

———

Time decelerates, flooding my mind with deep-rooted calm. I can't move my eyes (or anything else, for that matter), but I'm able to process the bubbles and ripples, the bleary distortions and water-bent sun. Remember that scene in Tobey's first *Spider Man,* when Flash threw a punch and Peter observed it in super slow-mo? It's not quite the same 'cause I'm frozen in place—

[Jon.]

That was Knifelock. Speaking telepathically into my mind.

[Yeah?]

[I don't want to hurt you.]

(Got a funny way of showing it—you threw me off a goddamn bridge.) But I don't want to irk him, so I project, *[Um...that's great. I don't want to hurt me either.]*

[I'm sorry I had to cast at your friends.]

[Are they okay?] Mild fear creeps through my psyche.

[Yes. That was a smokescreen, nothing more. If they hadn't attacked, I would have refrained from throwing shadow.]

[Thanks...I guess? Not to be rude, but why are we talking? You aren't on my side, so—]

[I am, actually. Arganti Knifelock is dead and gone. I am someone else altogether.]

What the hell? *[All right...who are you, then?]*

[I used to be known as Dake Harkness. In another life, I trained a man named Kishchan Atriya.]

My eyes try to widen. *[You mean Chris Atriya? The Marine recruiter who sent me to Evermoor?]*

[Interesting he'd become that, but yes, they are one and the same.]

[What did you train him in?]

[That's a story for another day.]

[Uh...okay. So is Knifelock real? Or was it you all along?]

[He was real.] he assures. *[During the Bright Age, he contacted entities throughout the multiverse. I was one of them.]*

[What did he want with you?]

[He jailed me in his putrid mind, then tried to lock me into a weapon. As you can imagine, that wasn't to my liking. I spent decades in his mantic gaol, privy to every torture he could inflict or imagine.]

[I'm...I'm sorry. That sounds horrible. How did it end?]

[Battle of wits. I won.]

This guy is giving off *serious* Batman vibes. *[So now you're chilling in Knifelock's body? And you're some kind of...double agent spy?]*

[That is correct.]

[What do I call you? Dake or Knifelock?]

[For the sake of clarity, call me Knifelock.] He projects the psychic equivalent of clearing his throat. *[I am hampered by my duties as the Nightkeeper Captain. I have saved a few here and there, but they were paltry wins in the grander scheme.]*

[Not so paltry to the ones you saved.] I argue.

[I am better suited to large-scale efforts. So are you.]

[Not sure what you mean by—]

[You are the Traveler. I am Deepened.]

['Deepened?' What does that—]

[You have experienced it yourself. You already know.]

[I really don't.]

[You only think you don't, because you purposefully forgot so you could revel in the joy of expanding into a new iteration of your inherent omnipot—] He senses my confusion and projects a sigh. *[Never mind. Focus on your upcoming task.]*

[What are you talking about?]

[You need to retrieve the Veric Glass. I would get it myself, but I am busy with—]

[Hold on.] I project the mental equivalent of lifting a hand. *[What the hell is a 'Veric Glass?']*

[Conceptually, it's…] I get the psychic impression he's chewing his lip. *[It's hard to put into—]* He takes a pause and gathers his thoughts. *[Think of it as a magic mirror. That's how it appears on the physical plane.]*

[Okay…what does it do?]

[Once it awakens, it will reflect the metaphysical—what you call 'truth'—back from its surface. Keep it covered. Do not look into it.]

[Why?]

[It can expand your perception in unexpected ways. That might lead to anything from insanity to godhood to interdimensional collapse.] He pauses again, and—this is hard to describe—*quests outward* with his spirit. *[I…yes, that makes sense.]* He directs his attention back onto me. *[Look into the Glass after Lyderea has done so.]*

[Is that how I beat her? Wake the Glass and make her look into it?]

[Yes.]

[Good to know.] (It really is—I haven't given any thought as to how I'm supposed to beat an evil queen sorceress.) *[How do I wake it?]*

[That possibility wave has not yet collapsed.]
[Come again?]
[The information will reveal itself in time.]
[Helpful.] I quip. *[Can you tell me where it is, at least?]*
[Gracelyn Keep.]
[How do you know?]
[It has what you call a Laiddinic signature, perceptible to you and I and a handful of others.]
[Wait...you can use Laiddinic powers?]
[Everyone can. But that too, is another story for another day. Focus on your particular tale. It would be an existential shame if you spurned your own genesis.]
[Uh...okay. Anything else?]
[I will try and contact you in the future, but I have much to do and time runs thin.] He stares at my mind. *[Tell your friends I'm on their side.]*

I radiate doubt and skepticism. *[They all think you're a god-mode doom-wizard.]*

[Do your best. Now brace yourself. I'm going to re-instantiate your perception of time.]

———

I'm thrown by a froth of violent cold, tumbled and slammed by raging swells. The burn in my chest throttles my brain, triggering a flash of redline panic. My gulping throat gives way to the pressure, and a stream of bubbles rip from my mouth.

If I don't get some air, I'm gonna—

I'm sucked to the bottom, then launched to the surface just as quick. I catch a muddled glimpse of trees and sky, then break into a series of water-threaded coughs. Before I can take another breath, I'm pulled back under and spun around. The walls of my sight begin closing in...

Then someone grabs me and pulls me out.

I push to my knees and try to speak. I can't form words—just guttural wails and watery vomit.

"Jon!" Erany crouches beside me.

"Yeah." (due to my stupor, it sounds like *yuh*). I burp, blink, and clear away tears. We're on a strip of land near the lefthand waterfall. "Where is he?" I gather my legs under my torso, then slowly rise with Erany's help. Everything is shaking, even the soles of my goddamn feet.

"Floating north," Gyrax says. "For the moment, we are safe from his daggers."

"Safe?" Lucky blurts. "He knows where we are, Gyrax! His assassins are en route, preparing to—"

"No," I gasp. "He's on our side. Knifelock imprisoned a foreign consciousness. It broke free and hijacked his body."

Ren regards me with overt suspicion. "Who is this 'consciousness?' "

"A man named Dake."

Nyanti's brow furrows in thought. "Dake? As in Dake Harkness?"

"Wait..." I run a hand through my sodden hair. "You know him?"

"Only from grimoires. He is said to live on a different plane."

"A different *plane?*" Lucky throws up his arms in disbelief. *"Ridiculous.* He is obviously toying with us." He gestures angrily at me. "At the very least, he's filled your aura with traps and snares!"

Nyanti peers at me. "I do not detect any magical tampering."

"You don't detect any—" Lucky covers his face and groans in frustration. "Because Knifelock's power is beyond your *KEN!"* He grabs my wrist, pulls me close, and rakes me with an unhinged glare. "Will you serve us up as spoils and riches, to be divvied and consumed at the White Queen's leisure? Or are you simply a bundle of arcane shot, ready to detonate at her say?"

"Neither!" Erany shoves him away. *"Cry off, Lucky!"*

Veins bulge from his forehead and neck. "Just because you two are rutting—"

She flares her cloak and grips her sword.

"ENOUGH!" Gyrax steps between them and levels a finger at Erany. *"Keep your weapon in its sheath!"*

Her rapier stops a quarter-way out. Her eyes blaze with hate and bloodlust.

"Do it," Lucky hisses, "Before Jon becomes a clockwork weapon. Kill me now, and save us the pain of—"

Gyrax interrupts with a single word: *"Lucky."* He swings back to Erany. *"Don't."*

Something inside me cracks and breaks. These are my *friends,* dammit. We've traveled together, fought together...and now they're ready to cut each other down?

"Erany." My voice trembles as I tug on her arm, trying to pry it off her sword.

She slowly pushes it into its scabbard. "I...I..." Her features are still ugly with rage.

"Do not speak," Gyrax cautions, then stares at the thief. "You are free to leave at any time. Our world is still healing from the Reft. We needn't see it rise anew, fueled by mistrust and baseless allegations."

"This is nothing like the Reft!" Lucky spits. "This is—" He closes his eyes. Opens them. "I will stay, but only if you agree to certain conditions."

"Name them."

"I will flee at the first sign—*the very first sign*—he becomes a threat." Lucky jerks his chin at me. "Lastly, double—no, triple—our agreed-upon fee."

"Done."

Lucky glowers at me. "Keep your distance."

"Got it." I force a nod. "If you ever want to talk—"

"I won't."

"What if Jon's right?" Elier hedges. "Siding with Knifelock might—"

"And what if he's wrong?" Lucky roars. "Sparing Jon is a perilous gamble; it could mean the difference between life and death! Not for hordes of nameless folk, but for the *seven souls beneath these falls!* Will you damn us to the Clear for a trifling hope, made slack and weak by its faithless herald? A man who wears a Nok-damned *blindfold?"* The

thief barks a disbelieving laugh. "He cannot distinguish the light from the dark!"

"His cloth is enchanted," Erany hisses. "It does not mean he is truly blind."

Lucky responds with a flap of his hand. "He is using Jon as a weapon or a pawn."

"Then why did he save us in Elerica City?"

"Was that his aim?" Lucky counters, "or was he there to murder the competition? Remember: powerful mages were in our midst."

Nyanti scoffs. "Two Sytíshí against the Nightkeeper Captain? He would tear them apart in the blink of an eye. And that's exactly what he did, if memory serves."

"Ah." He favors the Witch with a deranged grin. "But what about three? Four? A dozen, mayhap? If they banded together and attacked en masse..."

She crosses her arms, clearly skeptical. "I do not see it."

"We need to keep moving," Gyrax states. "Bury your spat or take your leave."

The thief looks around, mouth open like he's about to speak. As he registers the lack of receptivity, the fervor in his eyes dims and fades. "I...very well."

Gyrax looks at Ren. "If you are ready to lead..."

"Always." Ren steps off and pulls his hood over his head.

Gyrax draws abreast of Lucky. "Triple your fee, this I promise. And despite our contention, I would rather you stay."

"I would rather you didn't," Erany mutters. "Vest us a favor and show us your heels."

Lucky glances at me, then at Gyrax. "For now...for now I will stay."

The Wolven smiles and claps his shoulder. "Good man."

I'm struck by a wave of heart-wrenching sorrow. Gyrax is the only one of us who could have said that and meant it.

8 |

Lucky stays near the front of our line, deliberately avoiding me and Erany. I'm not gonna lie, I'm hurt by the freeze-out. It's not my fault, I know, but I still feel like I somehow failed.

The next day, I ask Nyanti and Elier if I can start my training. They readily agree, which paves the way for my new routine: weapons and combatives before I eat breakfast (Erany lends me her rapier so I can drill and spar, then jiu-jitsus me into a pretzel after Elier's lessons), magic in the afternoon, and thievery when I've got nothing else to do. I have to wake up early for classes in melee (it's hard to practice while I'm on the road) but magic isn't nearly as restrictive—Nyanti teaches me while we're walking.

Aside from learning some online dances, I was never big on physical exercise, so the fight stuff and swordplay tire me out (to his credit, Elier keeps his word—he doesn't give me crap if I don't want to train). The exertion, however, comes with unexpected benefits. It loosens me up (which is good for Primal Magic), and it also relieves me of my Lucky-induced stress.

A couple weeks in, I add some basic conditioning: pushups, burpees, and squats. It'll help me fight, but I'd also like to pack on some muscle. Elier and Ren are ridiculously cut, while I'm stuck with a sloppy four-pack, and that's only if I'm tensing under perfect lighting. Most of the time, it's flat and plai—Jesus, Jon, stop obsessing over your goddamn body! Erany likes you for you! *Idiot!*

As promised, Nyanti's instruction is easy and gentle. In order to channel Primal Magic, I need to remain open and light, in touch with possibility and the present-moment flow (usually, that means some form of positive expectation). From there, I narrow my focus onto a result, but I gotta *feel* my way into it—concentrate on what it feels like to throw fire and night, or change running water into glittering ice.

There's similarities from mage to mage, but the connotation is ultimately subjective. Nyanti likens it to three different people staring at a tree. The first might see it from a good ways off, in which case it would appear as a blip of color. The second might see it in heavy fog, dappled with patches of shifting sun. The third might see it in the dead of night, as a menacing snarl of shadows and branches. With each perspective, the same tree would evoke a different connotation.

That's Primal Magic in a nutshell. I need to focus on how it feels to *me.*

Eventually, Primal energy will carve grooves in my aura, making it easier to channel previously casted spells. However, if my emotions aren't aligned, the enchantment won't "pop." So if I throw a fireball over and over, I'll be able to do it through the equivalent of muscle memory, but it'll be weak and faint compared to a Primal spell. It's of utmost importance, Nyanti stresses, that I pay attention to my emotional state, or I'll cut myself off from my true potential.

————

The vales and peaks flatten and level, slowly transforming into grassy plains. Spherical bushes begin dotting the ground, complemented every so often by a scraggly tree. During the day, it's the American Midwest. Come nightfall, the bushes light up and turn the prairie into a sorcerous wonderland.

Ren says they're called "driftglimmer friends." Most are warm, which means we don't have to worry about starting a fire; we just set up camp around a glowing bush. Their branches are edible (although it's considered bad luck to eat them), and their leaves can be made into a cooling salve. According to legend, they lived as explorers in a previous life, then chose to reincarnate as a luminescent bush. Supposedly, it's their way of helping out fellow travelers.

The downside is that it never gets dark. When I mosey off with Er-any, we have to walk twice as far to ensure we're a good ways away. (She always conjures a root/branch igloo, but it'd be weird to summon it in view of the others. *Doo-bee-doo-bee-doo...don't mind our nasty-deeds igloo—just go on about your fantasy-world business.* Yeah, I'd rather not.)

Other than that, I can't complain. I could wander these fields for the rest of my life, relishing the cloud-swept sky during the day, and chilling with the Evermoor Lite Brites throughout the night. I'd probably take up landscape painting—it's that beautiful.

As the weeks roll by, I start making progress in basic swordplay. Most of the time, my limbs erupt with the urge to just *GO* and I end up bungling whatever I'm doing. But every so often, I have the presence of mind to parse through my options. It's not like I think through A, B, and C, it's more like a deep-seated knowing with a physical cue. The feel of each option twitches through me, alerting the appropriate muscles with increased sensitivity (like a feather-light touch or an electrical tin-gle). Elier says that's where the "art" begins. As my body gets smarter, it'll ditch the need for conscious direction, and I'll be able to express nu-anced combos. Right now I'm speaking in monosyllabic grunts. Even-tually, I'll be able to converse in clauses and sentences, with varying pitch and dramatic pauses.

Primal Magic is similar to fighting, but the emphasis is backward. Through drills and reps, Elier is training my feelings and instincts. Nyanti, however, wants me to work on my inward state, then allow ac-tion to flow from my calibrated psyche. The results vary—sometimes I cast, sometimes I don't—but her message is clear: emotions first, ac-tion second. Occasionally, she refuses to train me if I'm emotionally off. I have to get my shit together (my words, not hers) and try again later. Back on Earth, it was all hustle-hustle-hustle, earn your sleep, bil-lionaires wake up at 3am, blah-blibbity-blah-blah-blah. Primal Magic doesn't work like that. You turn the wheel, give it some gas, then let the engine do most of the work.

Initially, all I can summon are cluster of sparks. Midway into my third week of training, I manage to throw a green spear of light. It's not that impressive (Nyanti says it would feel like a tickle if it actually hit) but I'm still pretty jazzed. I never, *ever* in my life thought I would cast anything resembling a Jedi lightning bolt.

During the gap between magic and dinner, I usually get in some sleight of hand. After a close call with one of my knives, I decide to switch to my warded medallion, the one Ren got me when I first arrived. I don't need it anymore (since I can generate wards with my own aura) but it's my first magic item, so I'm kind of reluctant to throw it away. I like the boots embossed on the front. Something about 'em kindles my sense of adventure—*grab your boots, because we're about to step off.*

A month into our prairie-crossing journey, Erany points at a lake to our right (she's the first to see it, thanks to her hawkeye vision). "Ren. Are you certain of our heading?"

He throws an irritable glance at her. "Terrelly drowned me in maps and charts. He also trained me as a Wayfaring dowser, which means—"

"You are able to read the arcane topography." Erany finishes. "He imparted that knowledge onto me as well. Tell me: do you remember a lake on the Driftglimmer Plains?"

Ren cranes forward and stares at the lake. "I..." Confusion plays across his face. "No, but..."

Gyrax squints and mutters, "I'll be a Dagonite's tail-spike..."

Ren summons a holographic dashboard, filling the air with rune-bordered layouts. "We are still en route to the Silvered Caves." His brow furrows as he swipes and taps. "Either we have all been mazed, or the world around us is shifting and changing."

"Allow me." Nyanti closes her eyes and becomes utterly still.

Seconds become minutes. The breeze whispers and the grass swishes. I reach for my medallion (might as well get in some sleight of hand) then she opens her eyes and regards us apprehensively.

"This is hard to believe, but..."

"But what?" Gyrax prods.

"We are not ensorcelled."

Lucky bursts into laughter. "Do you...do you mean to say that..."

"Yes," she affirms. "The physical world is reconfiguring."

"Impossible!" he scoffs.

"The Reft arose from our bickering and quibbling; 'twas a manifestation of our collective intolerance. I suspect this is simply a follow-on effect. Pervasive mistrust has split us apart, to the point where the earth is gapping and breaking."

"Not according to my arcane guidance," Ren argues. "We are going the right way. I am sure of it."

Nyanti gives him a speculative look. "Your auric navigation...'tis a thrice-removed cousin of Primal Magic, correct? It does not reveal the greater relation—it divulges specifics through doubt or conviction."

"That is correct."

"So you cannot determine if the earth has been shifting. You can only determine if we are on the right path."

"I...that is to say..." His mouth opens and closes. Then: "You are right. If the soil was in motion, I would not know it."

"This is..." Lucky groans and rolls his eyes. "Take a moment to ponder your claim: *Evermoor is moving beneath our feet.* How can you humor such rot-brained tripe?"

"It isn't nonsense," I insist. "On my world, every continent was once connected. Eventually, they broke apart into—"

" 'On my world.' " He covers his eyes with a thumb and a forefinger. "Please—I am not in the mood for delusional fancy."

I react with a shrug, quietly pleased with Lucky's reply. This is our first exchange in over a month. Maybe it isn't all hugs and rainbows, but it's a hell of a lot better than ice-cold silence.

Erany crosses her arms and chews her lip. "I wonder if it will affect the Deadlocked Strait. If Knights can detour around the impasse..."

"Doubtful," Nyanti opines. "Algulis is home to a long-running nexus—an interwoven flow of sorcerous conduits. Those channels manifest as a physical passage, conducive to transport and large-scale movement. A comparable byway would not arise unless the primary ley lines tied to Algulis—"

Ren mutters, "Elwin's Surge, Nyadia's Run, Tavarack's Cut..."

The Witch nods. "Correct. If they were redirected into another crux, they would instantiate into an equivalent route. However, the outrush would echo across the Protectorate, and the weakest apprentice would instantly sense it."

"What about the lake?" I challenge. "Why didn't you sense it?"

"It resulted from a shift in minor ley lines. As the turmoil was small, it escaped my notice."

"Onward," Lucky grumbles. "My ears tire of this imbecilic drivel."

"Very well." Ren starts walking. "On my heels."

As I fall in line, I'm nettled by unease. Pangaea took millions of years to break apart. The fact that Evermoor is changing with noticeable speed...

I don't like it. It creeps me out.

———

Slowly but surely, Lucky warms back up to me. I wait for a week, then ask about his change of heart. He says we've been on the road for over a month. If killing us was high on Knifelock's list of priorities, he would have already taken us out.

"Keep the world small," he reminds me. "It does no good to fret or worry, as it is clear I am not his intended target. When he finally decides to lay you low, I trust in my ability to cut and run." He goes on to say that he's fine with training me, if I'm still interested in his tutelage. I eagerly accept, and we dive back into sleight of hand.

Three days into our larcenous studies, he praises my technique on a twisty flourish. The mood is chill, the journey's copacetic. If I wanna know more about his past, now's the time to bring it up.

"So...if you don't mind me asking, what's the deal with you and the Queen? When Ren compared you to Lyderea Fairdyle, it sent you into a violent rage."

The thief regards me with narrowed eyes. In the span of a second, he's gone from happy and cheerful to straight-up hostile. "Why?"

"Uh..." I gulp nervously. "Never mind." An awkward laugh bursts from my lips. "Stupid question. Forget I—"

"You asked. I shall answer." He stares at the ground with a deadened expression. "After Lyderea declared herself Queen, she visited her nobles to gauge their devotion. In reality, she was culling the dovish from their ranks, ensuring that all with a title were unthinkingly loyal. It took several years, but she got her wish—they slaughter and torture without question or qualm."

"If you don't want to talk about it, I totally understand." (Honestly, I hope he doesn't—Dark Lucky is scary as hell.)

His expression doesn't change. "My kinfolk, Clade Yetshaw, held sweeping reign over the Kysidian Rush. 'Tis a river that cuts through heavy briar, making it valuable to traders and merchants. That piqued Lyderea's interest. While others hosted her every quarter, we entertained her on a weekly basis."

"Sounds awful."

He gives a nod. "Aye. She left our clade with boons and devices. At the time, I simply thought she was being gracious. It was only later, after my parents died of poison, that I realized she had been pitting my family against each other. Shortly after my tenth birthday, my brother Syjé killed his twin. I barely escaped his bloody knife."

What? When he first brought it up, he didn't mention any patri-matri-fratricide. I get it, though—it's not something you'd mention in a casual conversation.

"I'm sorry." I mean it too. Lucky's story is a Darwinian nightmare, a hellish example of survival of the fittest. It didn't play out in tooth and claw, but it was savage and bloody nonetheless.

The thief shrugs, nonchalant. "I understand why she did it. If I were king of this low-shadow realm, I would likely do the same."

"What are you—" I sputter for a second. "Lucky, that is *ridiculous!* You're not Lyderea, goddammit!"

His smile is haunted, so unlike him it gives me chills. "In a sense you are right. I am nothing like her—she rose, I fell. But make no mistake: both she and I are reflections of this world. So are you, and so is everyone else. And while I fervently wish that wasn't the case, it does me not an ounce of good, for wishes are merely foolish dreams."

"That's not true. Once I harness my Laiddinic power, I'll—"

"Jon." He stops walking and stares straight ahead. "The Prophesied Traveler is naught but a lie. You might have a knack for Primal Magic, but don't confuse it with sham and deception."

"The others say—"

"The others are fools, through and through. The sooner you accept that, the better." He contemplates the horizon for a couple seconds. Then he nods to himself, as if he's made an important decision. "You seem committed to learning my craft. As that is the case, you deserve a measure of professional candor. So listen close and listen well: the world does not bow to our heart's desire. If it did, I would be the first to know. For several years, I prayed every day for Lyderea's death. Yet she continued on without a care, flush with riches and extravagant luxury. That is but a single example—if I recounted the horrors I have witnessed since, your hair would turn gray before I was done. Life has taught me there is no justice, save that which you claim through guile and force. And even that is a fool's errand—justice pales before dominion and rule."

"That's...wow." I shake my head, at a loss for words. "I don't know what to say."

"Say you agree, for it will ease my heart if your perception is clear, and you can better protect your heart and your mind."

We start moving forward. "I'm sorry, Lucky. I just don't see it that way."

"How do you see it?"

I drop my gaze. "I'm...I'm not sure. But it can't be as bad as what you've described."

"Spurn my view, and you will never reach your true potential. You will be at the mercy of men like me."

"That's a risk I'm willing to take."

The others trudge on, ignorant of the tension growing between us.

After a minute, he sighs in regret. "So be it. Your tale will be dark and full of woe, but it is yours to write and no one else's. I cannot quell your self-deceit."

Typically, I would lighten the mood with a dorky joke, but this goes way beyond disappointment or sorrow. From his tone and his bearing, you'd think I was dying and he was saying goodbye.

It's like he's completely given up on me.

9

In less than a minute, Lucky's back to his old self. It's super unnerving—he went from morose to baseline in no time flat. When I ask him about it, he replies that we've chosen our respective paths, and that I should enjoy my life before it unravels.

Not what I was hoping for, but I guess I shouldn't be surprised.

As the prairie morphs into rolling slopes, the bushes give way to sporadic mini forests. They're large enough to obstruct your view, small enough to detour around (between ten and twenty yards across). They're also filled with spooky-ass trees—the bark bulges with disturbing faces, ranging from mischief to sorrow to straight-up anguish.

Gyrax says they're called trapwood husks. "The faces belong to folk who passed on, then became entangled in the surrounding wood. That, however, is merely an oft-told rumor. No one has verified the reason or process."

"Hold on." I give him a guarded look. "It might be true, right? They could actually be —"

"GAH!" Someone grabs me from behind and pulls me off-balance.

I jump and shriek and take off running. As blurred scenery flashes by, panicked gibbers burst from my mouth: *"Yerdibberribb McGOOBIEoobies!"* After twenty seconds of breakneck cowardice, I realize it was just my half-Elf girlfriend.

I coast to a stop and bend at the waist, panting and gasping as I struggle for breath. "Very...*funny.*"

Everyone's howling, clutching their bellies or slapping their knees. I rake 'em all with a Glare of Doom, then cede my defeat with a grin and a chuckle. "You guys suck."

As their laughter subsides into muted giggles, we form back up and continue walking. Erany leans in and smooches my cheek, softening my desire for prank-driven vengeance. She's still gonna get it, but I can hold off for now.

Because half-Elf kisses are the absolute best.

————

Three days later, a cylindrical tower comes into view. The top floor is dotted with circular windows, capped by a parapet with gap-toothed battlements. It's like something out of an old-school fairytale—a lofty pillar made of smooth gray stone, disrupting the countryside with its looming presence.

Ren stops and appraises the tower. "We should look inside. Just to make sure that all is well."

"If any folk are residing within, they are in possession of adequate shelter," Lucky argues. "And they can't be short on food and water—this land is rife with plants and streams."

"What if they're injured?" Nyanti challenges. "Perhaps they require an arcane remedy."

"Perhaps they wish to injure others," Lucky retorts. "And by 'others,' I mean us."

"I welcome the malice," Elier grumbles. "Knifelock served as a refreshing break, but..."

Gyrax interjects with, "If peril lurks in yonder spire, best to vanquish it here and now."

"Untrue," Lucky counters. "Best to avoid it altogether. Leave it for the next fellow."

"The welfare of others is a practical matter," Gyrax replies. "With time and perspective, their pain and ours are one and the same. Also—we seek the Oracle to gain an advantage, and one might lie inside that tower."

Lucky shrugs. "If you wish to dawdle and lengthen our journey, I do not object. I am bound by coin if little else."

"So be it." Ren steps off the path and heads for the tower.

———

The base is marked by a double-door entry. Fresh varnish shines from the wood, complementing a sprawl of intricate filigree. A stone platform juts from the doors, serving as a median between tower and grass. The platform is topped by a hide-fashioned mat, emblazoned with a pair of dark bold words:

GO AWAY.

Unlike most of Evermoor's signage, the words are legible to my Earthling brain. "Maybe Lucky's right." I chuckle nervously. "I've seen plenty of welcome mats, but who's ever heard of an *un*welcome mat, amirite?"

Everyone ignores me. Jerks.

Nyanti cranes forward and studies the doors. "This wood is infused with complex wards. I believe they were cast by the Perific Society. Yes..." she nods with growing certainty. "The panache and flamboyance are unmistakable."

"You will have to enlighten us," Gyrax says, "as none of us are steeped in arcane history. What exactly is the Perific Society?"

"Mages who favored labyrinthine glyphs. They once gathered in Fairliff and Wence, when those cities were known for adventure and romance."

"Hard to imagine," Lucky mutters. "Fairliff and Wence are both cut-throat slums."

"That's not all..." Nyanti stares at the upper floors. "There's a faint hint of Avalonian magic. I could be mistaken, but..."

"Avalonian magic..." I chew my lip. "You've referred to my gun as the 'Avalon Clapfire.' Is there a matching revolver inside this tower?"

"Doubtful. Ailura Qartesi is one of a kind."

"Well on the off chance she isn't..." I grin at Erany. "Dual-wielding gunslinger. Bad. *Ass.*"

She rolls her eyes. "Nerd."

Nyanti glances at us. "The wards have frayed with the passage of time, but they are still sharp and lethally charged. To add snarl upon snag, there is another set of wards beyond the first. 'Tis a fair bit strange...they are woven in the opposite direction."

Elier's forehead wrinkles in puzzlement. "The only reason for that would be—"

"—to keep someone in," Erany finishes.

"Correct," Nyanti affirms. "The master of this tower has cordoned a prisoner. No way in, no way out."

"Well there you have it," Lucky declares. "Whoever's inside is clearly dangerous."

"Can you undo the wards?" Ren asks.

"Aye," Nyanti answers. "It will take an hour, maybe two. You should make yourself comfortable whilst I work."

"Joy," Lucky grumbles. "Boredom and torpor before we are slaughtered."

"We haven't determined if danger is nigh," Gyrax admonishes.

"Fah." Lucky responds with a flap of his hand. "At the first sign of shades or haunts, I will bid you all a hasty farewell."

Erany scowls. "You made that clear when Knifelock attacked."

"It wasn't an attack," I protest. "He wanted to—"

"Ah." The thief wags a finger. "Thank you for the reminder. If we happen upon that cursed vampire, I shall take to my heels with zest and aplomb."

"Come." Erany grabs my elbow and pulls me along. "Let us away before I carve him apart."

"Whoop!" I stumble for balance, then fall in beside her. "What—okay."

As we depart, I glance over my shoulder. Ren and Gyrax are extending their arms and projecting blue-green energy, enlivening the wards and their runic designs. Meanwhile, Nyanti is twisting her black-nailed hands, summoning a clutch of glowing crescents. They seem like the equivalent of supportive lockpicks, designed to keep tumbler pins out of the way. She's wedged them into some pulsating glyphs; they're pushing aside spells or infusing them with color.

Man...I kinda wish I could stay and watch. The wards are beautiful (longish calligraphy spinning in concentric circles) and whatever Nyanti's doing looks pretty cool. Oh well. I've already seen my fair share of magic. Plus, this is a good opportunity to earn some boyfriend points. Hmm...maybe I can talk Erany into a wham-bam quickie. Been almost a day since—no Jon, *no!* Respect her space, goddammit!

(Still...I won't turn her down if she wants to get frisky. Just throwing that out there, Universe. Hint hint, wink wink.)

———

Erany slows down. "I am sorry, Jon. I did not mean to—"

I interrupt with a quick kiss. "Save it. Not a big deal."

"Thank you." Her lavender gaze brightens and warms.

"Don't mention it." I clasp her hand. "Alone-time's important, you know?"

She probes my eyes with a faint grin. "Just to be clear, this isn't the place to enjoy a tumble. We should turn around soon, as Nyanti might finish earlier than expected."

(Dammit! There goes my secret evil plan!) "What? No, that's not what I meant," I bluster. "Matter of fact, I was just about to say we should start heading back."

"I'm sure," she replies dryly. "Nevertheless, I appreciate your company." She leans in and kisses my cheek. "Before we return, I need to make waste. Wait here, will you?"

"Yeah, of course."

Then it hits me: she has never, *ever* excused herself to go use the restroom.

"Wait a sec." I clear my throat. "Uh...do you hold it in when I'm up and about? Don't worry about me—everyone's gotta go, you know?"

"What?" Her face goes blank with surprise. Then she throws her head back and erupts with laughter. *"No!* Do you take me for a dainty consort?"

"Not at all." (Crap. I can feel myself blushing.) "But then why—"

"I am a half-Elf, Jon." Her features crinkle with amusement. "I only pass waste every other month."

"Every other *month?*" My jaw drops. "Are you *kidding me?*"

"There is room for variance, but once a month at the most. On the rare occasion I have had to excrete, you were busy training or fast asleep."

"Um...okay, then. That's..." I close my eyes and chuckle. "Yet another reason I want Elven genetics."

"There are drawbacks," she adds. "Although overall, I do feel blessed."

"Drawbacks? Like what?" I raise my hands in a *no pressure* gesture. "If it makes you uncomfortable..."

Erany scoffs. "Not in the least. I am referring to the relief that comes with the act. You experience it on a daily basis. I do not."

"Um..." (Tread lightly, Jon. This could easily get weird and super gross). "I see your point. On the other hand...man." I rub the back of my neck. "You must see me as a poop-crazed heathen."

"Please," she retorts. "My bullies saw my needs as barbaric, and took every opportunity to assert their view. Why would I mock you about the exact same thing?"

"Wait...full-blooded Elves don't have to poop?"

"They do, but not nearly as much. Every other year, at the most."

"What?" I'm shocked into laughter. "Every other *year?* Yeaaah..." I hiss through my teeth. "I can see why they're cranky."

She flashes a smile. "Wait here. I won't be long." She puts some distance between us, then summons a pond covered by a root-branch igloo. I turn my back so as not to be creepy, and contemplate the top of the soaring tower.

Man, every other *month*. Maybe that's why Elves are uptight—because they don't drop logs on a regular basis. Not that I know any full-blooded Elves, but from everything I've heard, they seem like a bunch of crotchety pricks. Whenever Erany mentions her childhood bullies, I wanna kick Legolas in his non-wrinkled nuts. (The lack of wrinkles is just a guess. Obviously, I've never seen a Wood Elf ball-bag.) I'm just glad she's okay with my humanity. Specifically, the funk that comes with being a dude. Her bullies pushed her towards compassion, but it could have easily gone the other way; she could have passed on her trauma in the way she was traumatized.

Back when we visited Alijyar SyCajister, he implied that existence was infinite, which means that every iteration of cause and effect would have to be playing out somewhere, some when. So if *Lord of the Rings* is occurring in another dimension, I can't help but wonder for the umpteenth time: how in the hell did the Fellowship stand each other? Nine smelly dudes who spent most of their time hiking? I'm just glad that everyone in our party can summon a nature-woven bathroom (me included, thanks to Nyanti's Primal training), because that sounds like a recipe for olfactory disaster. Take *that,* Tolkien! You should've mentioned their face-melting hygiene! On the other hand, I can see why he didn't. I mean, how many stories address number one and number two? I doubt it would be a topic at your local book club, or pique the interest of a high-browed literature profess—

"Ready?" Erany asks, interrupting my scatterbrained reverie.

"Yep. Let's do this."

We start heading back, in a much better mood than when we first headed out. After a minute, I snap my fingers. "Oh! I wanted to ask: why did Lucky call Knifelock a vampire?"

She gives me a sideways look. "He's extended his life through unnatural means. Records of Knifelock predate the Bright Age, when he still fought to keep the night at bay."

Keep the night at bay. The phrase triggers a memory: Ren telling me the Nightkeeper motto—*We keep the night at bay*—but how people now joke that it's *We keep the night in place.*

I do a quick calculation. "Predate the Bright Age...so that would make him what—three hundred years old?"

Erany nods. "Older, mayhap. In order to maintain his aberrant longevity, many believe he drains shortfall peasants."

" 'Shortfall?' "

"Those who can't pay their taxes or debt."

"Gotcha."

During my Earth-side visions of Evermoor, on-the-spot torture wasn't a big deal. But if the Justicers decided to drag off a peasant, the entire community screamed and begged. I'm guessing it was because they were scared of Knifelock.

This rebellion is beginning to make a lot more sense. A crippled aura...that sounds so much worse than an empty wallet.

Erany continues, "In many regions, he inspires more fear than Queen Lyderea, as auras are tied to your dreams and potential—the invisible clockwork that drives your existence. Even so, the aurically sick can vanquish their lack, if they consistently align their emotions with the True."

"Ah," I nod knowingly. "But they couldn't do that without Primal training."

"Wrong. Formal training is not a prerequisite. The determinant factor would be easing the flow of feelings and thoughts. From what I understand, 'tis a gateway into Laiddinic energy. Keep in mind, however, that I am not an expert—I am merely parroting what I heard as a tot." She points at our friends. "They seem to be ready."

Nyanti and Elier are sitting on the grass, chatting and smiling and low-key flirting. Ren and Gyrax are exploring transitions and entries, miming slow-motion attacks and appropriate counters. Lucky's observing with crossed arms, regarding them both with mild disbelief. *Why bother, when you can just cut and run?*

Nyanti spots us and gets to her feet. "Ho! Jon and Erany have come back around."

"Impressive," Erany remarks. "I though you would take a good while longer."

The Wise Woman throws her a cocky smile. "You forget who I am, Princess."

"My mistake," Erany chuckles.

"Who shall go first?" Lucky puts his hands on his hips. "Due to the wards, Nyanti might be the prudent—"

"No." Ren draws his sword. "I am a Wayfarer. I am designed to navigate peril and risk."

"As you wish," Lucky snickers. "But if I were a horse, would I be destined to suffer a saddle and mount?"

Ren glares at him, bringing a smile to Erany's lips. I open my mouth (not sure what I'm gonna say), but Gyrax intervenes with, "Go, Wayfarer." He gives Ren a nod. "Guide our steps and keep us hale."

Ren grunts in acknowledgment. "Eyes open, weapons close."

Then he opens the door and steps inside.

10

The far wall is lined with books, packed into rows of built-in shelves. A stately fireplace interrupts their length, carving out a sitting area off to our right (furnished with sofas and a rectangular coffee table) and an imposing desk off to our left (ringed by a trio of attendant chairs). Marble flooring runs throughout, coating the deck in expansive shine.

This place reeks of culture and intellect. If I were alone, I'd be tempted to whip out some fancy reading glasses, sit with my legs crossed at the knees, and pore over the works of Dostoyevsky and Kierkegaard.

"Stay keen," Ren warns. "Pleasant decor says nothing about character."

"I dunno..." I survey the room, drinking in the Victorian vibe. "Ever heard the phrase 'Manners make the man?' "

The Wayfarer scoffs. "Manners have little to no bearing on moral fiber."

Politicians and businessfolk flash through my mind. "Yeah, you're right," I concede.

Suddenly, a guttural howl sounds from above. While it's distant and echoey, the anguish in that voice is undeniable.

"The hell was *that?*" My voice quivers. Just a little, but I still wanna facepalm. Come on, Jon, you're the Prophesied Traveler. Time to start acting like it.

Ren points at a curving stairwell, nestled into the corner across from the desk. "There's our way up."

The second floor is lined with torches (bulbous glass spheres, lit by a core of magic blue light) that burnish the walls in aquamarine glow. Unlike the study, there's no marble and no furniture. It's just gray stone and wooden bins, arranged in a grid of parallel rows. Don't know what's in 'em, don't think I want to. I might stumble onto a mithril vest, but what if I awaken a sleeping Necronomicon? I doubt I could fight off an evil grimoire (or the accompanying horde of Deadite spawn), even if I had a shotgun and chainsaw.

On the far wall, another set of stairs feeds into the corner. We cross over and make our way up.

The third floor is more of the same—tons of bins in parallel rows—and so is the fourth. Five through seven are also storage, but they're an absolute mess. The bins and chests have been thrown and smashed. Tattered paper spills from their edges. Most of it's stained and yellow with age.

There's something weird about this tower...an eerie surrealism, if I had to describe it.

The eighth floor is bare and dusty. Dangly cobwebs hang and twist, sagging down in feathery wisps.

Halfway across, another roar sounds from directly above us.

"ARRRRAAAAAAUUUUUUHHH!"

Everyone freezes. That was a hell of a lot louder. And a hell of a lot *closer.*

I whisper, "Guys?"

For a long moment, no one moves. Then Ren starts walking, slow and careful.

My senses are magnified. I can hear our boots rubbing against stone, along with the shift of our cloaks and our weapons. When I reach the stairs, my heart jumps into red-line overdrive: *THUHthump THUHthump THUHthump.* If whatever's up there is as big as it sounds—

"ARRRRAAAAAAUUUUUUHHH!"

My foot pauses mid-step. I blow out hard...then force myself to keep ascending.

Natural light gilds the walls, glazing the stone in a soft white sheen. That means the next floor up has some windows. I'm hit by a surge of demented relief, followed by the urge to break into giggles. At least I get to see the sky, before whatever's up there rips me apart.

Gyrax halts, cuing me and Erany to do the same. Ren has stopped but I can't see why; he's hidden behind the curve of the stairs. After a minute, our line starts moving, and we come face to face with the tower's inhabitant.

Whoa.

It's a bare-chested giant—eight feet tall, built like a scary-strong, rotund hillbilly—lying fast asleep on a dilapidated mattress. If he wasn't breathing, I'd swear he was dead, because there's a *goddamn sword sticking out of his skull.* Half the blade is buried in his dome, the rest is protruding from his thick-browed noggin.

A ratty loincloth hangs from his waist, but that's it as far as clothing (unless you count his coarse body hair, which, at a distance, might be able to pass as a patchy fur coat). In between his trunk-like thighs, there's a moldy loaf of half-eaten bread.

The rest of the room is ringed with windows: eight portholes with intricate gold molding. There's deflated waterskins in the far-right corner, and rusted debris (gears, rods, miscellaneous parts) scattered around the last set of stairs.

Before anyone can speak, the giant sits up and rubs his eyes. He isn't human (fangs poke up from his bottom lip) but his facial features are distinctly Asian. If I had to guess, I'd say he's Korean. (I'm okay at guessing nationalities; I get it wrong about half the time).

I'm hit by a synchronistic sense of camaraderie, as if the giant and I shared a deep-seated bond. I'm fully aware it's hella weird—I'm only half-Korean, and I'm also not an eight-foot behemoth.

"Roffy have nightmare." He squints at Ren. "Roffy still dreaming?"

Ren sheathes his sword and raises his hands. *Easy, buddy.* "Wind at your back and sun on your brow. Are you well, Kai Roffy?"

"Roffy fine." He scratches his temple. "Why?"

"There is a tolerably long sword embedded in your cranium."

Roffy clambers to his feet and yawns loudly. "Sword in head for many years. Hurt at first. Now just tickle."

Ren turns and nods, cuing us to sheathe our assortment of weapons, then addresses the giant with deliberate calm. "Why not remove it?"

"If sword come out, Roffy will smarten."

"And that's...bad?" The Wayfarer's voice lilts in confusion.

"Too much brain, too much fight. This much better."

Nyanti's eyes widen in astonishment. "Hold, are you Raefingh—"

Gyrax gives her a pointed look. "I understand, Kai Roffy. A surfeit of thought can lead to dismay."

"Too much think in old life," Roffy agrees. "Much better now." He picks up the loaf of half-eaten bread—blue and gray and crawling with maggots—and maows down a larvae-flecked bite. "Mmm!" He rubs his belly and holds it out. "Hungo?"

We respond with a scatter of polite refusals.

Roffy shrugs and gulps the bread. A couple maggots make it onto his lips, but he slurps them down with greedy fervor. I try to hide a reflexive wince.

Elier clears his throat. "Whence comes the bread, Kai Roffy? If the wards sealed you in and kept others out..."

"Just Roffy. No Kai." He rubs his temple, coming dangerously close to the protruding sword. "Bread come from mechabug."

" 'Mechabug?' " Erany prods.

"Mechabug." He gestures at the mechanical debris. "Try and hurt Roffy, but Roffy beat and Roffy smash. Pick off shell and take out noms."

"May we inspect the fragments?" Gyrax asks.

Roffy squints through a window. "Bug-men come at any minute. If dog-man want, he can see real live mechabug." He begins plodding toward the stairs.

"Forward, then." Ren falls in behind the giant.

The steps lead onto an open-air parapet, ringed with a quartet of stone gargoyles. Unlike traditionally built grotesques, these are all facing inward. A couple feet below their perches, busted metal shines from the deck, just like in Roffy's decrepit bedroom. But the stuff up here is helter skelter, as opposed to just clustered around the stairs.

Nyanti glances at the statues. "They're casting a beacon. I can deactivate it if—"

"No!" Roffy shakes his head. "How will mechabug know where to go? Bring Roffy food and water!"

"As you wish." She dips her chin in respectful deference.

Roffy grunts, then goes back to studying the sunny horizon.

I Shift my sight (it's only a partial Shift, which means I'm holding on to some internal resistance) and examine the gargoyles. Two are flaring their bat-like wings, the others are clawing the air with their talons. All of them, however, are coursing with magic. Smoky blue runes spill from their maws, forming a locus in the middle of the deck. The glyphs extend into an enchanted X. At the end of the X's three-foot tines, it splits into a series of smaller Xs. Those fractalize into yet smaller Xs, and so on and so forth.

"There!" Roffy points into the distance. Four black specks are approaching the tower, growing from dots into humanoid figures. "Mechabugs!"

Ren draws steel. "We are fighting automata. Do not hold back."

"No!" Roffy snarls. *"Leave them to me!"*

The Wayfarer opens his mouth to argue, but Nyanti silences him with an open palm. "If he is who I think he is, he is more than capable. And even if he isn't, he is still an Ogre."

"I...very well." Ren sheathes his longsword.

As the mechabugs approach, their features resolve into visible detail. They're fitted with a set of canvas wings, veined with gears and thin brass rods. Faceted eyes bulge from their skulls, kind of like a fly's, but nowhere near as complex or intricate. Their humanoid bodies are made from red-brown metal, plated together with rivets and hasps. Puffs of fog spurt from their joints, adding a cartoonish touch to their mechanical anatomy. Last but not least, they're all imbued with janky enchantments; the assembly-line magic is creaky and primitive, designed to keep them in motion and nothing more.

"Stay low!" the Ogre yells.

The bugs fold their wings and dive at Roffy, dogpiling his torso in rapid succession. Ren and Erany both lurch forward, but Gyrax stops them with a curt, *"Wait."*

The Ogre stumbles and weaves, then grabs two by the legs and slams them together. Both explode into a million pieces—washers and sprockets fly every which way. Roffy flails for a couple of seconds, seizes the one on his back, then snatches up its buddy down by his thigh. He pins them beneath his massive foot, yells, "Bash and *BEAT!*" and pitches backward, smashing them to bits with a People's Elbow.

The Ogre scrambles up and pries them open, revealing bread and waterskins in their rusted chests. As he maows down the blighted food, larvae erupt between his teeth. It's simultaneously gross and endearing, because Roffy's galumphing is unabashedly childlike: *"Mmf ompf nompf! YUM!"*

"Oh!" He conks his brow with a meaty palm. "Forgot to share." He holds out a waterskin. "Runts want drink?"

We decline his offer, to which he responds with a determined nod. He lifts the skin to his bearded lips, pauses...then looks down and pats his hairy potbelly. "Have to go bloop." His stomach issues an ominous rumble. It culminates into an iffy squeak.

"Flee, little runts. Otherwise, Roffy's gas will kill your face."

Seven bodies turn and run, intent on escaping his maggot-tinged ass. We sprint through his bedroom, pile up in the stairwell's curve—get *off,* no *you* get off—then tumble onto the seventh-floor deck.

"You..." I look uncertainly at the others. "You think we're safe?"

Gyrax says, "One more floor, just to be sure."

Once again, we dart down the stairs. As soon as we're clear, Roffy cuts loose with an omega-level beefer. Remember that scene in the *Two Towers,* when Gimli blew into the ginormous horn? Roffy's fart is just as loud—I can feel the vibration inside my *brain.*

Elier claps Gyrax's arm. "A wise decision," he pants. "Your leadership saves us once again."

The Wolven responds with a vigorous nod. "I'll take the credit. In this case, at least." He straightens up and shakes his head. "I cannot believe it. We happened upon the Detective Savant."

Elier gives him a skeptical look. "Do you truly think he is—"

"Who and what is a Detective Savant?" I ask.

"Raefingham Bask," Nyanti explains. "One of the most brilliant minds to grace this plane. During the Bright Age, he lent his wit to different constabularies, assisting with crimes that exceeded their savvy. On two occasions he foiled powerful cabals, villains that would have gutted our world."

"His efforts were in vain," Lucky grumbles, "as Lyderea did exactly that."

"It would have been worse if not for Bask," Ren counters.

"As you say." The thief shrugs. "Though I remain unconvinced. He could simply be a nameless Ogre, confined to this tower by a spiteful wizard."

Elier's brow wrinkles in puzzlement. "Why would a mage go to the trouble?"

Lucky shrugs again. "With power and time, their primary foes would be languor and boredom. They would naturally be drawn to cruelty and torture."

Erany scoffs. "Only you, Lucky. No one else would reach that conclusion."

"Then you haven't mingled with other thieves. Or royals, for that matter."

"I was raised by nobles," she retorts. "They might have seen me as brutish and low, but they were fair and brave and cared for Delán. I do not condone their elitist ways, but I cannot deny their selfless ethic."

Lucky responds with a checkmate grin. "Pretenders, all. If they were truly royals, they would have disabused you of your ridiculous altruism."

Erany flaps a disgusted hand. "Neither logic nor wisdom will shift your vantage. Cling to your peace for as long as you can—the world will steal it soon enough."

"You plucked the words straight from my brain," Lucky counters. "I was about to say the same to you."

"Enough," Gyrax admonishes. "Do we tell him who he is, or do we leave him in this tower?"

"Maybe he knows," Elier ventures. "He calls himself Roffy. 'Tis remarkably similar to his given name."

"The sword in his skull," Nyanti states. "We need to remove it."

"He said he wanted to leave it in," I reply.

The Witch throw me a disbelieving look. "He cannot make an informed decision. We must pull out the blade in order to—"

"What if he put it there?"

Everyone stares at me.

Finally, Ren asks, "Why would he do that?"

"He might have burnt out." I look around expectantly. "He said, 'Too much brain. Too much fight.' This might be his way of keeping things simple."

Lucky surprises me by nodding agreeably. "At certain points along our journey, most of us wish to shuck our burden."

"All I have heard is conjecture and guess. What to do next?" Erany prods.

Surety blooms inside my gut. He'll take out the sword, but it has to be of his own volition.

"I think I can get him to do it by himself."

Gyrax studies me. "Are you sure?"

"Yeah." My voice firms with resolution. "I can't explain why, but…" I give Nyanti a lopsided grin. "It's a Primal thing, you know?"

"Very well." Gyrax looks at the others. "Ready?"

His question is met with scattered assent.

"Lead the way, Jon. We have your flanks."

"Right." I head for the stairs, awash in a mix of excitement and nerves.

I just hope to God he doesn't fart.

11

"Hey man, how's it going? I was wondering if—"

Roffy plunks onto his dirty mattress. "Don't go up for next hour. Magic is cleaning poop and pee."

"No, that's not..." I rifle through my brain, trying to think of the right approach. "I want to talk to you."

"Why?" the Ogre asks irritably. "No talk good."

I look at Gyrax, who assures me with a nod—*you got this*—and turn back to Roffy. "How long have you been living in this tower?"

He studies the ceiling. "Umm...many years. Roffy lose count."

"What did you do before you were..." I almost say *imprisoned,* but I don't know the circumstances. "What did you do before you arrived?"

The Ogre perks up. "Wear nice clothes. Travel far. But then..." Sorrow washes across his face.

"That's why you left the sword in your head," I say gently. "So you could try and forget."

"It take away memory. Some, not all." A tear trickles down his cheek. "Folk argue and fight and argue and fight."

"The Crimson Reft. You saw it happen."

"Yes." He stares at the floor like a brokenhearted kid.

A lump of emotion grows in my throat. He wanted everyone to live in peace, but he was up against impossible odds. And it hurt so bad he left a sword in his brain, just so he could dull the pain.

"Roffy."

"Hm?" His face gleams with fresh tears.

"The Reft has long since come and gone. You can take out the sword and live your life."

He shakes his head. *Nuh-uh.* "Might come back."

"You can't just rot in a stone tower, fighting for water and maggoty bread."

"Why not?" he demands. "Roffy only hurt mechabug!"

Gyrax steps forward. "The world has moved on. It would be a shame to ignore its potential and promise."

"Roffy no want hurt," he mutters.

"There is more to life than pain and despair."

He stares out the window. "Roffy once have friends." His eyes tick back and forth. "Laugh and make merry. Bring Roffy joy. Then Reft come along and tear us apart."

It has to be of his own volition.

I sink to a knee, taking his massive hand in both of mine. "Roffy..."

"Hmm?"

"You can leave the sword in, if that's what you want. I..." I swallow hard. "I understand why you would."

The Ogre studies me for a long moment. Then he says, "Roffy *feel* your belief." His expression intensifies, as if it's super important that I get what he's saying. "Roffy thought no one understand. But you..." He falls silent. Then: "You think now is time?"

"I..." I look at the others, but they don't have an answer. "Yes." I turn back to Roffy. "I think it's time."

He dips his head. His brow tenses into a maze of wrinkles. A couple minutes pass—his contemplation radiates a palpable gravity—then he gives a somber nod.

"I think as well."

The Ogre lumbers to his feet, seemingly doubling his size and presence, then curls his fingers around the hilt. Slowly, solemnly, he pulls out the sword. It rasps and grinds as it leaves his skull, a grisly scrape of metal on bone.

The brutishness vanishes from his posture. His face tightens with savvy and wit. The Ogre tosses the sword off to the side, and a sharp *CLANG* sounds from the deck.

"Raefingham Bask." He scans our party with a penetrating gaze. "At your service."

————

Erany dips into a respectful curtsy. " 'Tis an honor to meet you, Detective Savant." The rest of us offer greetings and bows.

Raefingham Bask holds up a hand. *Please don't.* "Call me Raef or Raefingham. I am divided on whether to thank you or curse you, though I believe that is born from my loutish fragility. In deepest truth I owe you credit and grace, as the Wolven was right through and through—this plodding tedium is less than I warrant."

Wow. Loinclothed Raef could pass as a backcountry mutant, but his comportment is that of a master statesman.

"I am curious," Gyrax ventures. "Who locked you inside this tower?"

Raef sighs. "I did, in spirit if not action. 'Tis a long tale, better told over smoke and tea." He raises an eyebrow. "The floor below us still lies bare?"

"It does."

"Splendid. With a touch of arcanix, it should be easy to make into a suitable wash-byre."

We follow Raef into the chamber below. He strides to the center and extends his arms, summoning red-orange haloes around his hands. Rune-laden chains fill their cores, streaming clockwise with fluid velocity.

"Hmm..." He moves his hands (and consequently, the haloes), studying the designs with a thoughtful expression. "I see." He twists his wrist, causing a halo to rotate, then spreads his fingers and imbues it with a gleam. He does this several more times, muttering, "There, there, and...*there.*"

Raef drops his arms and looks expectantly around.

A second later, the walls begin quaking. Stone blocks protrude and retract, folding and stacking with Tetris-like precision. They quickly congeal into familiar structures. Sink, shower, toilet...pretty soon, we're standing in the middle of a posh bathroom, comprised of polished stone and shiny metal. Every fixture is abnormally large, a nod to Raef's hulking physique.

"I shall meet you in the study," the Ogre says, "though it may be a while. As you can see, there is much of me to wash." He runs an upturned hand down his enormous torso.

"Of course," Gyrax replies. "We look forward to your presence."

————

We spend the next hour in his study, lounging on elegant Victorian furniture. Lucky, predictably, thinks we're all being stupid. Raef could be a malicious impostor, trying to fool us into dropping our guard. His recycled paranoia is met with eyerolls and sighs. Gyrax remains the one exception; he listens politely and engages with the thief.

Lucky warns that you never know with Lyderea Fairdyle—she has access to magic beyond our ken. Gyrax replies that you never know anything a hundred percent, and that you occasionally have to take an educated risk. Lucky counters with, "You are employing hyperbole to evade the problem." Gyrax rebuts that given the evidence (signatories embedded in the Ogre's aura, corresponding with bits of the Detective's history) it's almost certain that he's Raefingham Bask. And since Bask was never a skilled sorcerer (he relied instead on his intellect and strength), we've got him outgunned if it comes to a fight.

"I don't like it," Lucky grumbles. "We are still inviting unnecessary peril."

"Perhaps," Gyrax cedes. "But we are also courting substantial reward. He would make a formidable ally or partisan."

"Of whom do you speak?"

We all turn as the Ogre enters. He's balancing a tray with eight saucered cups, arranged around a floral-patterned teapot. His hair is slicked back, his beard is groomed, and he's wearing a rich blue vest over a solid white shirt. His neck is adorned with a red cravat, complemented by a burgundy pocket square in his left breast pocket. A gold-link chain runs from his right lapel into his right breast pocket, adding a touch of attractive shine. High-waisted trousers (the same blue as his dashing vest) streamline his frame, flowing down to his black leather shoes.

While all of that's cool, it doesn't hold a candle to his low-key grace. As he crosses the study, the tea on his tray remains perfectly still.

"Yseniel tea." He lowers the tray onto the coffee table. "Please—help yourselves."

As we each take a cup, he walks to the fireplace, reaches into a bag atop the mantel, and produces a handful of dried kindling. He piles it in the hearth, positions his hand above its center, and snaps his fingers several times. Sparks fly onto the bunched-up twigs, evoking a lash of roaring fire.

Whoa. Those twigs are the equivalent of full-size logs—the resultant blaze is lively and thick.

Raef nods in satisfaction and walks back over, sinking onto a chair and crossing his legs at the knees.

This. Is. *Nuts.* A couple hours back, he was eating maggoty bread and pooping on the roof. Now he's a cross between a Kingsman and Sherlock, oozing old-school swag and suave debonair.

"No cream, no sugar." He gestures at the tea. "I plead thy grace. My perishable stock has gone to rot."

" 'Tis not a concern," Gyrax assures. "If you fancy a smoke, we have delectable lokens, courtesy of our Wise Woman Nyanti Eldara." He looks at Nyanti, who acknowledges the compliment with a dip of her head.

"Thank you, but no. I prefer the feel of a calabash pipe." Raef sips his tea and appraises Gyrax. (If he was pinpointing me with those super-thorough eyes, I'd stutter and stammer and derp it all up.) "You have many questions and so do I. I propose an in-depth palaver."

"Very well. Who shall begin?"

"As I am your host, I shall go first. Also: my tale is smaller and fits into yours. Or so I believe, mayhap."

"I believe so as well," Gyrax replies. "Before I forget, I shall bless my lips with Elerican smoke."

"I shall do likewise."

Raef crosses the study and stops at his desk, where he produces a wallet from one of its drawers. Its pockets contain a tied-off sack, a long-stemmed pipe, and a couple of other tools and gadgets (for maintenance and cleaning, I think).

Raef turns the sack on to its side, shaking tobacco onto his desk. He carefully separates the earthen clumps, then packs the top of his burnished pipe. After a test-draw, he summons a flame from the tip of his thumb. He chars the tobacco with careful swipes, tamps it down with his non-flame fingers, then lights the bowl with slow circles. As he does so, he coaxes out smoke with shallow puffs. Once it's flowing to his satisfaction, he concludes the ritual with a reverent drag.

"Ah," he sighs. "Perfect." A funnel of gray spills from his nose.

Man, this guy has *style.* If I had access to online shopping, I would be scouring the interwebs for Victorian menswear, along with pipes and high-end tobacco.

Erany holds out a cigarette. "Loken?" While the others were busy passing them around, I was full-on admiring our sophisticated host.

I clear my throat, embarrassed by my man-crush moment. "Uh, yeah. Thanks." I fit the smoke to my lips and light the end.

Raef sits down, takes a couple puffs, and commences with his tale.

———

Before the Reft, Raefingham Bask was a freelance detective. When he wasn't busy solving a case, he would putter away in his lab or his study, exploring everything from electrodynamics to psychedelic medicine. He knew some magic, but it wasn't his thing. He studied it from an academic standpoint: as a philosophical expression of self, and how that expression interacted with others.

Over the course of his storied career, he amassed a fortune and won countless accolades. That, however, was simply a footnote—he was never interested in money or fame. Raefingham Bask loved what he did.

Slowly but surely, that began to change. As the Ogre harried Evermoor's underworld, a new breed of criminal emerged from its midst—

skilled, dedicated, and utterly ruthless. Eventually, one proved a match for Raef: a genius assassin named Morteri VySade.

VySade was born as a Wildfae Kinetic. When I whisper-ask Erany what that is, she replies they're partially human, partially made from a natural element. I respond that I saw 'em at the Isle of Plen: the folks who were made of fire/water/wind. Erany confirms that yes, those were Wildfae. She goes on to explain the suffix *Kinetic,* which means they're comprised of a dynamic substance (air, light, or something insubstantial), as opposed to Wildfae Quiescent, who are fused with something solid and inert (like sand or glass or a spider-silk weave). Morteri's kinesis manifested as shadow—his arms were made of pitch-black night.

Vysade and Bask grew networks of spies, then engaged in an epic Great Game that spanned dozens of kingdoms. Their conflict was fraught with venom and malice, but it held relatively even until the Reft. While the Ogre fought to contain the curse, VySade targeted Raefingham's agents.

After a year of loss and defeat, Bask was ambushed inside his home. He managed to escape and live on the run. Six months later, Morteri cornered him at Rakebyre Falls. The assassin beat him within an inch of his life, then held him above the rushing water.

Raef was certain he was about to die. Morteri, however, had thought of something better: he would pierce Raef's brain and damage his wit (Morteri had tortured many an Ogre, and knew that a sword in the brain needn't be lethal) then seal Raef inside his last remaining satellite outpost. Vysade would build it into a tower, a soaring tribute to his criminal skill.

Meanwhile, Raef would live in filth and ignorance. Every day he would fight to exist, a reactive animal incapable of betterment. The catch was, he could regain his intelligence at any time—he simply had to remove the sword. But they both knew he wouldn't, didn't they? Bask was a shell of what he'd been.

Raef falls quiet and stares at the wall. Then he takes a puff, exhales smoke, and continues with his story.

"I didn't feel a need to restore my wit. Morteri was right—I was drained of hope. I had wrestled with the gears of a heartless world, only to be smashed between their teeth."

"Well it didn't last," I say. "You changed your mind."

"Because of you." His hyper-smart eyes lock onto mine. "I can't say why, but I sense that we share a similar quandary."

I hiss through my teeth. "Uh...yeah, maybe. What happened next?"

"I subsisted here for over a decade, dining on rot and stale water. Even now, part of me yearns to pick up the sword and..." He closes his eyes and shakes his head.

Gyrax clears his throat. "If I may assume the narrative..."

"Please." Raef yields with an upturned hand.

Gyrax gives him a brief overview—Lyderea's rise, Sidehelm Pass, the rebellion at Algulis—before drilling down into specifics. When he mentions Terrelly, Raef perks up.

"I aided his Wayfarers many a-time. Does he still rove the land with his army of rangers?"

The Wolven glances over at Ren. "You are better suited to speak on such matters."

Guilt roils through me—I forgot to ask about Terrelly Jindow. I was busy making out with my half-Elf girlfriend, or losing myself in sword-play and magic.

Ren describes Terrelly's wounds (auric infections cast by Lyderea's sorcerers), then elaborates with a new tidbit of info: after we freed the Witchcraft City, Ren obtained a salve from one of their Wise Women. (It was made of stuff that sounds extra magic-y: a fistful of shade from a Khel-touched Wraith, a trio of scales from a Basilisk king, and an enchanted kiss from the Sygress herself.) Salve in hand, Ren traveled to Naversé and gave it to Terrelly. Unfortunately, it didn't take. At the deepest levels of Terrelly's being, he wasn't ready to accept a cure.

Bask gives a reluctant nod, then tells us we should give it more time. That much trauma doesn't heal overnight.

During the exchange, I lean over to Erany and whisper, "Did you know about Terrelly?"

"Of course," she whispers back.

I'm shocked. Hurt, too. "Why didn't you tell me?"

"Your quibble with Lucky, then your ongoing training. Due to your role and future duties, you are ill-served by distraction and bother."

"Terrelly isn't 'distraction and bother,' " I hiss. "He needs my help like everyone else! The fact you don't think so is absolutely—"

"—correct." She pins me down with her lavender stare. "It's absolutely correct, and you know it to your core. You are meant to serve all of Evermoor, while the rest of us deal with specifics like Terrelly."

"But—"

"Specifics that aren't lesser, simply different, and just as relevant in their own right." She tilts her head, issuing a challenge. "Or does your intuition disagree? Tell me it does and I shall cede you this quarrel."

"I...I..." I shake my head, frustrated. My gut tells me she's in the right. "No, that's correct. It's just..."

She lays a hand atop my leg. "Be true to your heart, and you will help us in ways you cannot imagine. Do not give in to false perception, even if it appears to be noble and just."

Damn. I was about to do exactly that. I was gonna use Terrelly as an excuse to get angry, then indulge in a bout of recreational outrage. Before I can lapse into self-flagellation, I remember my training and manage my guilt: everyone slips, everyone falls. Trust in the process, take it step by step.

Once Ren's finished, Gyrax reassumes the verbal reins. When he mentions Knifelock and the Veric Glass, Raef interjects with a raised finger.

"I believe I can shed some light on this subject. If you would be so kind as to give me a moment..."

"Of course."

The Ogre strides to the book-lined wall, third section down from the rightmost end. He rifles through some dusty tomes, then extracts a green book with a button-snap hasp. Tome in hand, he sits at his desk and tugs on his collar-chain, fishing its monocled end from his right breast pocket. (Is there such a thing as monocle envy? Because if there is, I think I have it.) He affixes the glass to his right eye, licks his finger, and begins perusing the archaic manuscript.

"Where did...ah!" He runs his finger along the page, murmuring softly under his breath. "This text, the *Existentia Nobilis,* bears mention of the Veric Glass. I wished to confirm what I already suspected: the Glass must be woken by its one true love."

"And who would that be?" I stifle the urge to pump my fist. Sweet! Knifelock told me I had to wake the Glass, but he didn't say how. At least now I can—

He shakes his head, dousing my hopes. "That is it. There is nothing more."

" 'One true love,' " I mutter dejectedly. "Feels so retro. Like we're in the *Princess Bride* or something." Before anyone can ask, I add, "It's a fairy-tale adventure."

Gyrax divulges our next destination—the Volant Oracle—explaining how we hope to gain some critical knowledge. Afterward, we'll set a course for Yom Dagur, where Erany will claim the Rosecraft Blade. Somewhere along our winding journey, we'll visit Gracelyn Keep and find the Glass.

"And that is where we currently stand," he finishes.

The Ogre draws a mouthful of smoke, his prothagonous brow wrinkled in thought. "Would you care to share travels? Our crossing seems fated."

Gyrax ashes his loken into an empty cup. "If I had endured your trials and troubles, my nerves would be taut with fear and rage. Why travel with a passel of strangers?"

Raefingham gives him a knowing smile. "You are no stranger, and neither are your friends." He points at Gyrax, "Royalty. Your phrasing is tinged with High Fenric Speech—" then at Erany, "and yours with a trace of fine court Deláni." Ren's up next. "Wayfarer. There is a talic decagram in your cardiac aura, known in the Advance as the Lydiliant Glimmer." Then it's Lucky. "Criminal, though not by birth—your carriage hails from Yetshaw nobility." He homes in on Elier. "Duelist. High Taire, would by my guess. Your twitches express combative maneuvers, a form of subconscious practice developed in the Taires." On to Nyanti. "You have already disclosed you are a Witch and a Wise Woman. However, I would hazard you were trained by the Nightclaw Coven, as your aura bears vouchers from Tsetsimon the Shade, as well as the Elemental Arinia D'Sae." I'm last. "The Prophesied Traveler, though I am least certain when it comes to you. I would never declare it in court of law, but you reek of fate and far-reaching destiny."

Everyone stares.

He puffs casually on his pipe, as if he didn't just drop an old-school Sherlock. "You offered plenty of clues throughout your tale. Combine that data with physical cues—eyes, lips, tics of the limbs...'tis an imperfect art, but I have honed my deduction on countless felons."

Gyrax chuckles. "Impressive. I believe I speak for us all when I say I welcome your presence."

"Truly?" Raefingham raises an eyebrow and smiles at Lucky.

The thief responds with an easy grin; pleasant enough to redirect scrutiny, mild enough to avoid engagement. (It's easy to see the reason behind it: thieves and detectives are probably like oil and water.)

"Well." The Ogre slaps his thighs and pushes to his feet. "Allow me to retrieve my cane and my carry, then we can—"

Nyanti says, "Hold."

He stops mid-sentence. "Milady?"

"Before we entered, I sensed Avalonian magic within these walls. I wish to investigate, if you do not object."

He cocks his head, puzzled. "Avalonian magic? I'm not sure what you...ah!" He snaps his fingers.

"The holster!"

12

Raef tromps up the stairs. Minutes later, he tromps back down with a sheathed rapier, a rotund sack, and something hidden in his right fist.

He uncurls his fingers, revealing a sleek black holster. Its leather is marked with a cobalt flourish—distinctly serpentine and a little celestial—while its conjoined belt is flush with bullets-loops.

"Ailura Qartesi's original holster, along with roughly a thousand cartridges. I won them from a lich named Alistair Vekhmire." (A *thousand?* Back on Earth, Alijyar said they were hard to come by. How the hell did that lich get a *thousand?)* He hefts the ammo-sack and gives me a once-over. "As you are the Traveler, I assume you have claimed the Avalon Clapfire." He tilts his head in a low-key challenge: *You* do *have her, don't you?*

"Yep. Right here." I pat my gun-pouch and stare at the holster. "Man...that looks way better than mine."

"Perfect. As now it is yours." He extends his arms, offering both holster and ammo.

"What?" My eyes widen in shock. "Are you *serious?"* I almost reach up and clutch my hair. (I know, I know: what else would he do with 'em? Nevertheless, it strikes a chord.) I glance at the others—*can you believe this?*—then turn back to Raef with a bashful grin. "I...I don't know what to say. Wow. Thank you." I tuck the ammo into my carry (it weighs less than a pound, which I'm guessing is significantly lighter than non-magic bullets), remove my old holster, and buckle the new one around my waist.

"Shift your perception," Nyanti urges. "It's designed to conceal Ailura's strength."

"Really?" I slide Ailura into the holster, then assess the weapon with Shifted sight. "Whoa!" Magically speaking, there's no way to tell that I'm packing a Great Weapon. I pull her out and drop her in, checking to see if her mojo is still there. Then I do it a dozen more times, so I can be absolutely sure and erase all doubt.

"What are you doing?" Elier asks, startling me out of my OCD fiddling.

My face reddens. "I wanted to see if...you know..."

"If she was still Ailura?" He raises an amused eyebrow.

"Yeah. Something like that." Then I sigh. "Unfortunately, I'll have to keep her in my pouch so I can protect her from—"

"Why?" Erany interjects. "The holster conceals her orphic presence, and you have made leaps and bounds as a swordsman and wizard. Swindlers and brigands are a trifling concern."

"You think so?" I straighten in surprise. "I mean, yeah...maybe you're right." I adopt a thinking man's posture—left arm crossed over my stomach, left hand cupping my right elbow, right hand cupping my chin—and gaze thoughtfully at the wall. "I'm kind of a badass, aren't I? I know some moves, I'm decent with magic, and I can see my bottom two abs if I flex really hard. Throw in some Laiddinic powers, and—"

Erany scoffs. "Spare me. My lover has become a brainless oaf."

"Get ready to play nurse," I declare. "Sailor-time's a-coming!"

"As I said before, you will never, *ever* be the—"

Raef interrupts with an a-a-*hem.* "Does anyone desire an enchanted blade? If not, I can sell it at the next—"

"You're gonna sell *a magic sword?*" I swing around and grab its scabbard and hilt. "Oh *hell* no!" I try and yank it away from his gigantimous hands, but to no one's surprise, it doesn't budge.

The Ogre gives me a weighted look.

"Um...I mean..." I let go and twiddle my fingers. "If you don't mind, I'd really appreciate it if..."

"Here." He hands it over, lips twitching in a held-back smile.

I sheepishly accept, embarrassed and humbled by my Gollum-like flareup. That lasts for all of a second, because I just acquired a *MAGIC SWORD*. "What does it do?" I pull it out and give it an excited once-over. Nice! It's a medium-size rapier that looks like Erany's, but a little heavier and with a plainer guard. I wonder if it ignites like a Jedi lightsaber, or maybe it shoots icy death-rays. Ooh! Maybe it—

"It glows," Raef says.

"Excuse me?" I lower the blade and stare at the Ogre.

"It glows," he repeats. "If you are in the vicinity of a disembodied haunt, its flat will gleam with rich blue light."

"It *glows?*" I stammer and sputter for a couple of seconds. "Like *Sting?* Why the hell would...this sword is *bullshit!*"

Raefingham shrugs. "I have never heard of a sword named Sting, but it doesn't sound like anything special. A glowing sword is rather unim-pressive."

"Exactly!" I yell, shaking my good-for-nothing, *Lord of the Rings* knockoff. "Why would anyone make such a *stupid-ass weapon?*"

"It was probably crafted by a first-year apprentice," Nyanti offers. "As part of their training, arcane smiths create throwaway trinkets. They're often traded for goods and chores."

"Great," I mutter. "My sword is worth a meal and a backrub. At least it's not racist against Orcs and Goblins."

"You said you wanted a magic sword," Erany chides. "Why are you being so—"

I throw my head back and scream, *"I'M NOT A HOBBIT!"*

Blank stares all around.

"I'm not a Hobbit," I mutter. "Why couldn't I pick from the *Player's Handbook?* Something cool like Flametongue or Frostbrand."

"You have Ailura," Erany reminds me.

"Yeah, yeah," I grumble. "It's just all my characters had magic swords, and I was hoping for—" I wave dismissively. "Never mind." I give the weapon a dubious look. "Hmm...it'd be a little on the nose if

I called you Sting. When you stop and think, that's a lousy name, isn't it? Swords don't *sting,* they rend, cleave, slash, decapitate…Sting is the most weak-sauce name you could pick for a…" My eyes widen in sudden epiphany. "That's it! That's the name!"

I hold up the sword and dramatically intone, "From this day forth, I shall call you…*Weak Sauce!*"

Once again, pin-drop silence.

Elier clears his throat. "Ah…whatever suits you. Blades are named in accordance with their spirit, so…"

"No, it's perfect," I insist. "Just gimme a minute to…" I strap Weak Sauce onto my left hip, opposite Ailura on my right. My weapons are now set for a cross-body draw. I'm not worried about shooting with my left; the last time I fired Ailura Qartesi, she guided my sights and steadied my aim. Also, as I've gotten better at Primal Magic, her presence has strengthened along with my aura, which—thanks to Nyanti's arcane instruction—I know will translate to an increase in accuracy. At this point in my training, I'd go so far as to say that missing a shot is almost unthinkable.

Raef gives me a quick once-over. "You look quite formidable. Dashing, as well." (I can't tell if he's being sarcastic.) His gaze drifts across the party. "Shall we?"

Ren grunts and heads for the door. As Erany and I trail behind, I give her a nudge and point at my hip.

"Weak Sauce. Pretty good, huh?"

She rolls her eyes and sighs loudly. *Good God, you are a NERD.*

Whatever. She's just jealous that I thought of it first.

13

Shortly after we hit the road, Raef busts out a bowler hat and cane. Instead of a hook, it has a detachable telescope that snaps onto its end. *(Very* cool.) His snazzy accoutrements also double as weapons; he can use the hat to conceal and distract, and he can throw his pocket square into an assailant's face. If he needs some more oomph, his cane is imbued with four explosive spells (he doesn't want to show me 'cause it's a pain to re-enchant).

Between Erany, Elier, and Raefingham Bask, I'm getting a solid bachelor's in brawling and dueling. Elier's the most technical, Raef's the most stylish, and Erany's the most knowledgeable in hand-to-hand combat. I'm starting to experience body/mind epiphanies, like why I should entangle same-side posts (arm and a leg) before sweeping in that direction, or the concept of weakening your opponent's limbs (by lengthening them), so you can peel off their hooks and move where you want. Once I download the bird's eye view, the setups make a lot more sense. I wouldn't have understood when I first started training; I had to experience the techniques before I could get it. Don't get me wrong, Erany still kicks my ass on a regular basis, but I'm absorbing new levels of the why and the how.

Fight training requires sensitivity and openness, but it doesn't directly train those qualities. You do it over and over and over and *over,* until it sinks into the fibers of your brain and muscles. Primal Magic is the exact opposite. Everything is based on emotional intelligence, which often requires faith and surrender. For auric fluidity, yeah, but also because it's hard to match a result to a specific emotion. I have to let go of details so the spell can take shape. It's not predictable (if I'm trying to burn something, I might summon fire, a heat ray, or a blast of lava) but it's way more potent.

Over the next few weeks, I pick up the muscle-memory equivalent of traditional spellcraft (it goes by different names depending on region—hedge magic, arcanix, faeweave, and a bunch of other labels that everyone seems to know. Kinda like the arcane version of soda/pop/soft drink.). It's pretty messy (since I was never taught oodles of chants and diagrams) but I now have a grasp of basic charms: lighting my own cigarette, checking food for rot and spoil, or summoning a pond for personal hygiene. I even start helping with arcane security. (I didn't realize we were setting alarms, but I should've guessed; during our travels, no one stood watch). Nyanti warned me about traditional magic—while it's more predictable, it will tire me out a hell of a lot faster—and now I've got some firsthand experience. Unless I'm casting a throwaway spell, Primal Magic is the way to go.

I'm also starting to refine my perception. I used to Shift without regard for depth, but now I can home in on mild (things seem brighter, with a little haze around contours and outlines) medium (symbols and auras clarify and sharpen, until they're evenly balanced with physical input. This is what I go for most of the time.) And deep (I become immersed in the flow of magic, to the point where it's hard to navigate the material world. Nyanti says this is rarely useful, unless you're weaving complex spells for extended durations).

There's subtle gradients between mild/medium/deep, which I'll become more familiar with through practice and drill. Apparently, different spells match different Shifts. The wrong Shift isn't a dealbreaker, but the right one will save you energy, streamline your magic, and also demonstrate professional competence.

I think it's safe to say that I've hit a groove. Back in Elerica, the Sygress said my ability to Shift would depend on whether or not I'm embracing my destiny. Apparently, I'm doing alright, because Shifting my perception is easy as hell.

Lucky, meanwhile, has become more withdrawn. He still instructs me in tricks and deceit, but as more of a professor than an easygoing friend. I'm pretty sure it's because of Raefingham Bask. Lucky's a criminal, and he wants to be careful around the Detective Savant. I'm good with it. At least he's not being outright hostile.

On a whim, I combine sleight of hand with illusionist spells, imposing shadows and mirages onto Ren's medallion. For some reason, I keep this to myself. Whenever I think about bringing it up, a surge of revulsion grips my brain. (As I've gotten better at Primal Magic, my intuition has gotten a hell of a lot stronger).

The medallion protects me from ward-checking barriers, but that no longer matters because I can fashion my own declarative wards. Whenever I Shift, a ring of holographic runes appears by my right shoulder. Within their perimeter, my wards rotate in a dreamy gyre: a pair of boots, crossed swords, and a snarling monster face (it looks like a super-angry Shrek). The boots identify me as a visiting wanderer, the swords are an admittance I'm carrying weapons, and the monster is an assurance that I have a basic understanding of civility and etiquette (contradictory, I know—why use a monster to denote those qualities?). Those three pronouncements will get me into ninety-nine percent of Evermoor cities.

I know what you're thinking: barriers that rely on self-declaration? Is that what they call "arcane security?" But it makes sense if you factor in Evermoor's history. The majority of Reft-stricken couldn't cast magic, so ward-checking barriers were an effective deterrent. Nowadays, the barriers serve as arcane pest repellent. They're not a hundred percent effective, but they definitely make a noticeable difference: whenever I'm in a warded community, there's an observable decrease in bugs and rodents.

Last but not least, my relationship with Erany remains as awesome as ever. After dinner, we wander off into the summery night. One of us will summon a small enclosure, then we'll make out and smash to our heart's content.

Five weeks into our bucolic trek, we're interrupted by a rude surprise.

We're hanging out in a conjured hut (I'm entertaining her with a ridiculous striptease, humming a hip hop version of the *Lord of the Rings* theme), when she abruptly stops laughing and draws her sword.

I bow my knees in and cover my junk. "Uh...what are you—"

She screams, *"Nightkeepers!"* and charges past me. I spin in place and spot a pair of silhouettes.

"Crap!" I yank up my jeans and fall to my side, flailing around for Weak Sauce the rapier (can't remember where I threw Ailura). I stumble to my feet, draw steel, and assume low-middle guard.

Before I can rush to Erany's aid, my Primal training comes to the fore: someone behind me wants me dead.

So I flip-circle Weak Sauce and thrust him backward, sinking into a crouch like a badass samurai. As a hostile blade whooshes overhead, my sword pierces cloth and flesh. The accompanying scream is angry and female—that's all I register before my spidey-sense demands that I tuck and roll.

I let go of Weak Sauce and tumble right. Just in time—she misses my leg with a downward slice. I grab some dirt, rise to a knee, and aim for her eyes with a backhand fling. (Crap, that was stupid—she's wearing a goddamn magic blindfold.) Lucky for me, some of it flies into her mouth, causing her to break into coughs and sputters.

As I snatch up Weak Sauce, she matches my *Bloodsport* cheap shot by flicking her hand and releasing peppery dust. I see it coming and spin to the left, gaining momentum as I slip clear of the irritant. A bit of it gets inside my nose, but that doesn't stop me as I whirl into a slash—

—and cut through a swath of empty air.

Damn. She just pulled a Ninja Vanish.

I dash out of the hut and glance quickly around. Erany's attackers are running away.

"You see that?" I beam at my girl as she swivels in place. "I just fought off a bona fide Nightkeeper! That's gotta be worth at least two hundred experience poi—"

"Back to the others!" She sprints past me, sword at the ready.

I follow behind, mentally kicking myself. This isn't a game, Jon. Help friends now, crack jokes later.

"Stay keen!" Erany shouts. "Flanks and rear!"

"Yep! Got it!"

As we crest the hill between us and the party, I glimpse Lucky ducking behind Gyrax's torso. The Wolven parries a thrust, sweeps his opponent with the haft of his axe, then cuts her in two while she's still in the air. A moment later, Lucky spins past Gyrax, stabbing a second Nightkeeper high on the arm. The thief keeps spinning, snapping his wrist and releasing another dagger into his palm. It slices neatly across the Nightkeeper's throat and unleashes a jet of arterial blood.

A dozen yards left, Elier and Nyanti are fighting two apiece. The Duelist is grinning, toying with both of his blindfolded opponents. He throws a series of languid slashes, driving his foes into a compromised scramble, then dispatches them both with a flurry of cuts.

Meanwhile, Nyanti's assailants blitz her with runes. She dissipates their spells with red-infused hands, then conjures a trio of hovering green dials. The runes around the dials blossom into new sets of dials, then the new dials flare and give birth to more dials.

Her opponents cast with desperate speed, trying to repulse the swarm of hexes. Not gonna happen—the Witch's dials pour into their loci, morphing into jags of crackling light. Turbulent energy floods their auras, dropping them both like they were hit by a sniper.

A dozen yards right, Raef trips a Nightkeeper, throws his pocket square into the other's face, then smacks them both with the end of his cane. He follows up with a thrust and a feint, then straightens on his toes in a whirling pirouette, dodging their knives with balletic grace. The Ogre finishes in a rightward lean, opening his posture and throwing a sweeping backhand. As his cane smashes a Nightkeeper's skull, the second one turns and—

—slumps onto his knees, revealing Arganti Knifelock standing behind him. He pulls his dagger from the assassin's neck.

"I am not here to—"

Ren snarls, *"VAMPIRE!"* and slashes twice with his blue-steel sword. Knifelock ducks and tries to speak, but Raef jumps in with a busy combo, striking sparks off Knifelock's daggers. Elier, never one to miss out on a fight, whirls his sabers and leaps into the fray.

Gyrax and Erany are both shouting—something along the lines of *calm the hell down*—but they're overtaken by Lucky's screams: *"Kill him! Kill him now, before he summons more blades!"*

Knifelock spits a harsh-toned phrase—dozens of white orbs materialize across the nighttime field. Nyanti blows out a plume of serpentine dark, snuffing them all with pitch-black shadow. Raef disengages, ratchets his cane with a decisive twist, and sights down its length at the Nightkeeper Captain.

BLAM!

A ball of rainbow light flies out from its end, crashing into Knifelock and knocking him backward. He lands, rolls, and continues dueling with Ren and Elier. Raef strides forward, gives his cane another twist, then kneels and aims at Arganti's torso.

"Stop!" he yells. *"I'm—"*

BLAM!

The Nightkeeper Captain clutches the air, halting the blast with his clawed fingers. The rainbow discharge begins shaking and churning, intensifying as it crumbles into supercharged wisps. It erupts with spears of dancing red light, then peaks in a massive, spectacular explosion.

————

All I can see is a blotchy smear. All I can hear is a high-pitched keen.

"What...where..." I try and rise, then plop back onto my butt and palms. As my senses resolve, Erany hooks my elbow and helps me up.

"Whoa." I lean into her side to keep myself stable. "Just gimme a...just..."

"Easy." She shifts her weight and gives me a stronger brace. "Don't—"

"I'm good. That was...wow."

Gyrax spreads his arms in a WTF gesture. "What were you *thinking?*" he shouts. "Why did you—"

"He's a *Nightkeeper Captain!*" Ren shouts back. "Would you rather I gift him with smoke and a meal?"

"Where is he?" I whisper to Erany.

"Gone," she whispers back. "Escaped in the chaos."

Gyrax thrusts a finger at the livid Wayfarer. "We have already settled this! I *specifically told Lucky—*"

"Lucky is *right!*" Ren yells. "You truly believe that Knifelock is with us? His personal testimony is all we have! His *personal testimony,* Gyrax! If Lucky said that he wasn't a thief, would you trust him around your coffers and carry?"

"You have lost all sense," Gyrax growls. "Once again, Knifelock refrained from hurting our party, yet still you cling to a verdict of malice. You." He turns to Raef. "I expected better of the Detective Savant. You as well." He eyes Nyanti. "A Wise Woman should act with tact and prudence, with a firm grasp of context and evidence. And *you,*" he homes in on Elier, "You know damn well you should have stayed your sabers."

Elier scoffs. "Spare me your judgment. I was simply—"

"You are no mere Duelist!" Gyrax snaps. "Why have you traveled so long by our side, when you could have been amassing rank and prestige? Could it be that you care for the folk of this world?"

Elier's mouth opens and closes. "I..."

Raef looks sideways. "My hate for Knifelock exceeded my wit. He worked hand in hand with Morteri VySade, and I—" He clears his throat. "I am making excuses. I plead thy grace."

"I as well," Nyanti mumbles.

Gyrax closes his eyes, takes a calming breath, then regards us all with a steely glare. "Listen close and listen well: if we happen upon Arganti Knifelock, keep your weapon in its sheath. He doesn't mean us harm. And if there is any truth to Jon's claim, then—"

" 'Doesn't mean us harm?' " Lucky bristles. "He ambushed us, Gyrax! *Twice!*"

"And fled our wrath on both occasions," Gyrax counters. "Why would he let us still draw breath?"

Lucky throws his arms up in exasperation. "Who knows? Who *cares?* But let me assure you that Arganti Knifelock—*Lyderea Fairdyle's Nightkeeper Captain*—does not wish to laugh and make merry!"

"I never said as much," Gyrax says evenly. "But your view of his aims fall short of his deeds."

"Gyrax is right," Raefingham states. "His motives break with murder and spite."

Lucky hisses, *"Idiots,"* and flaps a hand in angry dismissal.

"Then it's settled," Gyrax asserts. "When next we see him, give him a chance to make his case."

"Why do you think he showed up now?" I ask.

The Wolven adopts a reflective expression. "To foil the assassins? What do you think?" He turns to Raef.

The Detective's brow furrows in thought. "From everything I've heard...yes, that would be my guess."

"We need to move," Ren urges. "Our wards cannot dampen this much bustle. Feral Wildlyre will be drawn by the battle."

"Feral?" I mutter.

"Quell your fear," Erany teases. "You are safe by my side." She reaches up and rubs my back (which is embarrassing and awesome all at once).

Elier turns his sabers back and forth, giving them both a cursory inspection, then slides them into their respective sheaths. "Shall we?"

"On my heels," Ren orders.

"Jon and I will join you soon," Erany replies. "We fled our den in yonder field, and we need to retrieve a couple of items." She gives my bare-chested torso a playful once-over. "As you can see by the state of his dress."

Nyanti stares at my hip, then recoils in shock. *"You left Ailura behind?"*

Erany covers her mouth in sudden dismay.

"Um...I..." I glance at the others. "I wasn't...uh..."

"Hurry!" Gyrax breaks into a four-limbed gallop.

A minute later, we catch up to the Wolven. He strides out of our conjured root-hut, gun and holster in his paw.

"Oh *man,*" I bend over and clutch my knees. "Thank. *God.*" I accept Ailura from his outstretched hand. "I'm sorry. I wasn't—"

"Do not let it happen again," he warns. A grin plays across his face, leavening the severity in his rebuke. "Great Weapons are hard to come by."

"Absolutely." I buckle the revolver around my waist.

Ren clears his throat. "Once you are ready, I shall resume breaking trail."

"We'll catch up," I protest.

He crosses his arms and stares me down. "No. That was a shade too close for my personal comfort."

Erany puts a hand on my shoulder. "Do as he says."

"I...all right." I blow out a sigh. "I...yeah."

We walk into the hut and grab our stuff. As far as managing emotions, it's an epic fail.

Jon, you are an *idiot.*

14

Due to the noisy wind and low visibility, I feel cut off from the rest of the party. Combine lack of sleep with my post-fight crash, and you get a super tired, zombified Jon. Outlines and contours bleed together, taunting my brain with phantasmagoric shapes. My hands keep twitching down to my weapons, an instinctive reaction to imaginary threats.

When we finally stop, I feel drunk and high. Nonsense plays at the edges of my mind, forcing me to concentrate on logical follow-on.

Shortly after I crawl into bed, I fall into a deep, dreamless slumber.

———

I desperately want to catch up on sleep. My brain, however, is wired to get up right before dawn.

Murggh...I want a dryer-warm snuggie, an extra-large pizza, and something mindless to watch on TV. No one else seems to care. (Stupid adventurers, forcing me to adventure when I'm feeling all lazy.)

Slowly but surely, my irritability dims and fades. As the sun climbs higher on its arc, it vanquishes the last of my morning oogies.

Ren, much to my surprise, apologizes to Gyrax. The Wolven responds with measured thanks—he's grateful Ren has come around. At the same time, he warns against indulging in self-flagellation. If Ren doesn't forgive himself, he'll subconsciously find ways to become less forgivable.

"Something I'm working on," Ren admits. "Not my forte, I'm sad to say."

"You're in good company, for much of Evermoor shares your predicament." Gyrax throws me a pointed look, the meaning behind which is crystal clear. I can't stress out about misplacing Ailura. I have to let things flow and integrate the lesson, or I'll set myself up for another mishap.

When I first arrived, I thought I'd have to prioritize classic hero stuff (facing my fears, pushing through adversity, embracing my darkness to outthink my dark-minded foes), all the tropes I explored as a writer. I had no idea I would have to learn self-forgiveness, or anything to do with emotional intelligence. For most of my life, I've locked up my feelings and denied their existence. But it's pretty clear that if I'm not staying positive and solution-oriented—if I'm not concentrating on making things work—I'll bungle my timing and make all the wrong moves. At a certain point, it's not about technique or practice. It's about focusing on where I want to go, or at least how to improve my current position.

Emotions. Who knew?

———

The next morning, I feel loose and energized. Yeah, I messed up, but I held my own against a bona fide Nightkeeper. I wish I'd recorded it, especially that part where I stabbed her without looking. At this point, I'm probably like a seventh level fighter/mage/thief. (Eighth level, maybe? I'm allowed to dream.)

After lunch, I'm struck by a surge of irrational shame—I feel like I've been dunking on Tolkien since I got back from Earth. So I try and make up for it by singing my ass off, because Middle-Earthers liked to burst into song. Ironic. It used to irk me when the Fellowship acted like they were in a Broadway musical. Now here I am, leading the charge with my cringey acapella.

Much to my delight, the others join in. On a whim, I bust out some Earthling pop music. Just for the record, it is straight-up *hilarious* when fantasy-world adventurers try to rap, beatbox, or pop lock and moonwalk.

Everyone's chill, which is a welcome change from our past discord. Even Erany seems okay with Lucky—they're both maintaining a cautious civility. You know that discomfort after a fight with a friend, when you've just made up and things are still awkward? It feels like that, only less uncomfortable, because they've both accepted they'll never be friends. I'll take it, though, if it means that he muzzles his darker half. There's a lot of vinegar under that honey.

As the hills flatten into a rocky expanse, craggy stone towers begin to appear, anywhere from three feet tall to two stories high. Some are clustered in tight little groups, while others stand as singular monuments. A foot above their crystal-jagged peaks, cores of energy burn like stars. Each one is ringed by light-woven slashes, differing in brightness, color, and rotational speed.

I can't help but gawk. "What are *those?*"

"Orphic cauda," Nyanti replies. "The arcane tides have formed a long-running eddy. Its excess is funneling into these towers, filling them with stores of concentrated magic."

"Whoa." My brow wrinkles. "So they're like arcane trees? And their cores of light are like enchanted fruit?"

"An apt comparison," Nyanti affirms. "The lights are called starfae. With skill and training, it's possible to store them in a telestic canister."

Raef adds, "During the Bright Age, starfae were harvested for various reasons. Research and invention, mostly, but also the upkeep of Tessellate byways."

"Those are teleport conduits, right?"

The Ogre nods. "Aye. Before my confinement, I made frequent use of them."

"Why doesn't Lyderea harvest the starfae?"

"More complication than she's willing to bear," Ren grumbles. "Harvesters require an abundance of training, telestic containment an abundance of care."

"A shame," Raefingham sighs. "They led to the advent of wondrous discoveries."

"Too much trouble," Lucky mutters. "The complexity and nuance leave no room for theft."

"Observe." Erany extends her hand toward a red-orange cauda. A second later, it erupts into flares.

"Whoa!" I shield my eyes in reflexive fear. "What the *hell*, Erany?"

"All is well," Gyrax assures. " 'Tis little more than a spectacular flicker."

"Really?" I give him a doubtful look.

"Try it." He nods at a blue-green orb, causing it to erupt into voltage and runes.

"Okay, let's see..." I mentally reach for a black-violet ball, and—

KABOOM!

—it detonates into an expanding blue ring. The energy surges a hundred feet out, then gradually fades into sparkles and glimmers.

"Jon!" Nyanti admonishes. "A brush of intent is all you need!"

"Sorry." My voice cracks, adding to my embarrassment. "They can't hurt us, can they?"

"Not unless you touch the actual starfae. The discharge might tickle, but it won't cause any lasting damage."

"Right," I squeak. "I'll back off then, just to be safe."

"Don't be ridiculous." Erany points at an emerald core. "Touch it with your mind."

"I really don't—"

"Disgruntlement comes in many forms, one of them being protracted abstinence."

"What the hell?" I grouse. "Abstinence? Really? That's outdated, crude, and just plain mean."

A devilish smile. "It would hurt me more. You need to hone your sensitivity, and these starfae present an excellent opportunity."

"Erany is right," Nyanti agrees. "You haven't yet explored how to cast with delicacy, but it is something you will eventually have to learn."

"Fine," I grumble. "But if I crack a hole in the fabric of space-time, my 'I-told-you-so' is gonna be the most epic 'I-told-you-so' in the history of 'I-told-you-so's.' "

For the next three hours, Nyanti instructs me in nuanced focus. It's a new level of emotional IQ. I'm working with snippets of feelings and notions, well before they've gained any mass or momentum. Willpower's useful (unlike with fully formed thoughts) because the emotional pull is still pretty weak.

Every so often, the floating cores will explode on their own, which does nothing to calm my frazzled nerves. Fortunately, that comes with a silver lining: from a distance, no one will suspect that anything's amiss, since detonating starfae are a natural phenomenon.

Soon enough, it starts to click. Instead of unleashing a chaotic torrent, I conjure dazzling fluxes and exquisite contortions. Cerulean peals of butterflied light? You got it. Kaleidoscopic twists of bladed pink rays? No problem. I never thought emotion could be this subtle. Back on Earth, it seemed like passion and zeal were proof of substance. Now I realize it's all about rhythm—there's a time for volume and a time for quiet.

Speaking of rhythm, I know the perfect accompaniment to these arcane fireworks: Tchaikovsky's *1812 Overture,* specifically that part with those beast-ass cannons.

I begin to hum and wave my hands, mock-conducting along with the music. Whenever I get to one of the cannons, I lunge forward, point at a cauda, and make it erupt with brilliant flares. The others roll their eyes—*just Jon being Jon, what a doof*—but soon enough, they give in to my adorkableness and start humming along. Ren, predictably, refrains from singing, though I'm proud to say that I catch him smiling. He even jumps in on a couple of fireworks, triggering starfae in time with the melody.

Ha! Who says training can't be fun?

15

Ten days into our cauda-filled trek, muggy warmth rolls in from the east. Accordingly, Ren alters our routine so we sleep through the heat. On night four of our modified schedule, the Wayfarer stops and points to the south.

"Erany. Do you see them?"

After a bit of intensive squinting, I spot a handful of dots atop a hill, rising and falling in rapid sequence. (I have twenty-twenty vision, but I'm legally blind compared to Erany and Ren.)

Erany draws abreast. "Nightkeepers."

Lucky startles. *"Nightkeepers?* We need to—"

"Hush," Gyrax chides. He turns to Nyanti. "Can you fell them at range?"

"The spell would run wild." The Witch chews her lip. "Best to wait until they are closer."

"They're clustered together...a perfect chance to thin their ranks." Ren clicks his tongue in a frustrated hiss. " 'Tis a Nok-damned shame."

Elier extends an arm, stretches left, then extends the other and stretches right. "All for the best. I could use the practice."

"What about Ailura?" I ask.

Gyrax shakes his head. "Save your bullets for hardier foes."

"Perhaps we can lengthen your arcane reach," Raef gives Nyanti a speculative look. "Instead of throwing a bolt of energy, could we store it inside an envoy receptacle?"

"An arrow, mayhap?" Elier asks.

"Don't look to me," Lucky states. "I shan't waste an arrow unless it is dire."

Raef turns to Erany. "Could you make such a shot?"

Her face crinkles in thought. "Not if I try for a limb or a head…"

"The arrow would not be aimed at a person," Nyanti clarifies. "You would enchant its shaft with catalyst energy, then launch it into a designate cloud." She points at a clump of moonlit puffs, drifting west above the hills. "I see five vortices of magical force, in varying degrees of torpor and stir. If I rile a vortex and you hit it square, I can harness the resulting destruction and ruin."

"Time runs thin," Lucky snaps. "Hasten your draw and lay them low."

Erany produces her collapsible bow, priming it with a decisive, spell-powered shake. It flares with runes and a sequence of gleams, then its string whips out and snags the top. She nocks an arrow, pulls it back, and aims high into the moonlit sky. A second later, her naval loci spins and glares, directing power up her arm and into the arrow.

"At your say." The missile blazes with emerald shine, surrounded by glyphs and slow-winking sparks.

Ren prompts Raef with an open hand. "Your scope. May I?"

He detaches his cane's telescope handle, then expands it with a nimble twist. "I assume you are trained in longshot report."

Ren accepts the optic with a dip of his chin. "My lessons were sporadic and informal in nature, but I remember enough to assist in the strike." He lifts the scope up to his eye. "I have the field. Erany?"

"My arrow is charged. Nyanti?"

The Witch's eyes glow and pulse. "Hold. Center cloud, second from the right…" She trails off and falls silent.

Then: "Now."

As Erany releases the spell-charged arrow, Nyanti projects a laser-like line into the designated cloud. When the arrow hits, it triggers a boil of crackling radiance. Sapphire lances shoot down from the churn, forming glowing blue domes wherever they land. The domes glimmer with brazen light, then erupt with lashes of cerulean fire.

Half the Nightkeepers die in a flash, striking fleeting silhouettes before they're consumed.

"Six on the field, shifting left," Ren says. The scope remains glued to his eye. "Await your span...fifteen metnic."

Erany nocks an arrow and charges its shaft. "Nyanti?"

"Aim one cloud left of your previous mark." She projects a thin violet line into the target.

This time, the sky erupts with scarlet lightning. It rakes the assassins with dancing red bolts.

"Oh yes." Ren surveys the carnage and beams with pleasure. "Well done. You as well, Nyanti."

"Any survivors?" Lucky asks anxiously.

"Two are alive, though now in withdrawal." Ren lowers the scope and looks at Gyrax. "I can track their prints and finish them off."

"No need. If they return, we shall reacquaint them with Nyanti's ire."

"A shame." Elier sighs. "I was hoping the survivors would mount an assault."

Nyanti's lips curl in amusement. "If they had any skill, they would have deflected my enchanted barrage."

"True." The Duelist shrugs.

Gyrax glances at Ren. "If that is all..."

"Aye." He collapses the scope, hands it to Raef, and takes his place at the head of our column.

————

The cauda give way to lively waterfalls, ranging from three feet tall to four stories high. Our path is now flanked by low-high spills. At first glance, they seem pretty old—they've cut parallel moats into the rock below—but when magic is involved, you can never be sure.

"Be ready," Ren cautions. "We are fast approaching the Oracle's lair."

"Ready for what?" I ask. "Is he dangerous?" (Crap. Between training and Erany-time, I completely forgot to ask about the Oracle.)

"She," Nyanti corrects.

"The Oracle emerged in the Elder Folk Dawn," Gyrax explains. "She appears throughout our recorded history, but her origin and persona remain shrouded in mystery, and her presence is never a guarantee. However, Sygress Anir foretold our meeting, so I trust she will grace us with requisite knowledge."

"Any advice?" I ask.

"Cleanse your mind of any deceit. She is a candid reflector of greater truths."

"What does that mean?" I give him a skeptical look.

"She expresses what you know in your heart of hearts."

"Then why even see her? If we already know the answer..."

"Over the course of an outward journey, events can highlight an inner truth. It's dependent on vantage, though more so upon your soul-deep intent."

I slice a hand across my scalp. "Jon no follow."

Gyrax smiles. "Let intuition mesh with logic, then draw a conclusion and venture forth."

"Take it moment by moment, step by step."

"Exactly."

"I've heard that before, but you always make it seem new and fresh."

"If it didn't resonate in days of yore, you weren't yet ready to grasp its meaning, or it was said in a manner devoid of life. In the end, you only receive what you're ready to accept."

"How do you do it?" I give him a faint grin. "You're always dropping these feel-good wisdom-bombs. Kind of practical, but also uplifting."

"I do my best to articulate truth. That is it and that is all."

"I'm glad." I glance at Lucky, trailing a dozen yards behind us.

"Too many people have bought into lies."

————

Statues of monks begin appearing beneath the falls. I instantly recognize their cross-legged posture.

"These used to be flesh." Raef examines the spaced-out figures.

"Wait..." Panic rises in my chest. "Something turned them into stone?" My inner nerd leaps to the fore, calculating saving throws and modifiers versus petrifying gaze.

"No, you dundernonce," Erany chuckles. "When the Reft spread wide, the journey here became increasingly dangerous. These statues were left as a proxy memorial.

"Oh, okay." I sigh in relief.

Two faires later, silver veins begin streaking the cliffs. They all look buffed and highly polished. You'd think they'd be rough (since they're natural deposits and not jewelry-store metal) but I'm not complaining, because they're straight-up gorgeous.

"Wow," I breathe. "The Silvered Caves are *literally* silver."

"We have yet to reach them, but yes," Elier says. "The Caves are known for their natural beauty."

"When do we get to the actual ca—oh." Right on cue, a gaping cavern shows up beneath a waterfall.

I clear my throat. "The Volant Oracle. How do we find her?"

"She found us." Ren gives a nod, directing my attention back to the front.

Twenty yards ahead, the Oracle flaps her wings and settles on a mossy overhang. I thought she would be a cranky old hermit, like Yoda or Obi Wan.

The last thing I expected was a six-foot tall, two-headed raven.

———

"She's a *bird!*" I blurt.

The head on the right screeches, "I'm a bird! You're a bird!" Her other head is fast asleep, turned sideways and nestled in her body.

"It's in the name." Elier says, mildly puzzled at my not-so-mild puzzlement. "Volant Oracle."

"Uh..." I give him an uncertain look. "What does 'Volant' mean?"

"Relating to flight."

"Right. I knew that." I mentally kick myself. You're a writer, Jon—words are supposed to be your Nok-damned forte.

"What next?" I glance at the others.

Nyanti shrugs. *No idea.*

All righty then. Time to step up. "Hi." I face the Oracle and wring my hands. "I'm Jon. I used to live in a parallel dimension, then I stumbled across a portal leading into Evermoor, and—"

"Evermoor!" it screeches. "Ever! *More!*" A brief pause, then: "EVERMOOR! Ever more of the same! Ever more to sustain!"

"Um...right." I look around at the others. "Is it supposed to parrot everything I say?"

"Parrot merit tenet!" it screams. "Inherit tear it declare it!"

"I'm not certain..." Nyanti studies the raven. "Perhaps the Reft drove her insane."

"She has another head," Raef points out. "Let us see what it has to say." He cups his mouth and yells, "We seek palaver with your articulate half!"

"Half an art!" she barks. "The artful half!"

The other head emerges and turns to its partner. "Sleep." Head number one promptly obeys, ducking into her feathers and disappearing from view.

Wow. I heard at least three different tones, accompanied by faint chimes and a harmonic crinkle. She sounds like an interdimensional, auto-tuned angel.

The Oracle shifts, giving head number two a better angle. "I haven't had visitors in quite some time."

Gyrax responds with an Evermoor salute: he touches his brow with his index and middle finger, then brings his hand a few inches out. "Wind at your back and sun on your brow. We have journeyed far in search of your counsel."

"Why seek what you already know? We are all pieces of a greater whole. If you quested inward—"

He cuts her off with an open hand. "Your premise holds an implicit flaw: that consequence hinges on the inner versus outer, when it is actually a matter of a personal focus—how attention settles onto lack or bounty."

"Then why ask me?" she challenges. "When you could ask anything and everything, and interact with a similar veracity?"

"As fragments of the True, we are designed to weave stories through personal constraints. In our case, these constraints have left us with a series of clues—clues that end at your taloned feet. So from one fragment to another, I ask that you yield the knowledge that is our True-born right."

The Oracle smiles. "Well said. I apologize for the stint of tail-chasing discourse, but I wished to ensure your perception was aligned. In the past, folk have made a religion of my words, and forgotten the spirit that brought us together." She looks me in the eye. "Throughout my life upon your plane, I told my students to refrain from depicting me, to discourage them from clinging to my transient semblance. I wanted their minds to remain free and expansive, so they could revitalize existence through novelty and joy." A regretful sigh. "They chose to do otherwise. I will never understand that particular tendency—your willingness to renounce your True-born power." She clears her throat. "When I say 'you,' I am referring to the whole of folk, not you in the singular."

"Of course," Gyrax replies. "I am quite familiar with intention and context."

"I have no doubt." The Oracle smiles. (Never realized a bird could smile. It's weird and cute at the same time). "Or you wouldn't have answered as you did. Now. What is your query?"

"War burns hot at the Deadlocked Strait. We seek to quench the growing blaze, before ruin follows war and leaves nothing but ash."

"Lyderea Fairdyle." She closes her eyes in quiet pain.

"Aye."

The raven opens her eyes. "Despite all she has hoarded, she has failed to slake the craving within. It seems much of the world has joined her in lack."

"We did not *join* her!" Lucky tromps forward, suddenly livid. "She pushed us down into the mud, so she could step on our necks and boost her own vantage!"

"You would do well to leaven your wrath, for you share the same vantage as the White Veiled Queen. In her last incarnation, she was known as Enthimy Nilena. Even though she claimed to serve the True—"

Lucky slashes the air with a furious backhand. "How dare you compare *me to her!*" His face twists into an ugly sneer. "Look at you! You are little more than a talking beast—an eloquent fool with a penchant for drama! But your folly is there for all to see, as we have this life *and that is it!* The world does not care for our pain or joy—we are conjured from a haze of disparate chance, doomed to compete for the dregs and the scraps! All we can hope for is to hoard a bit more than our fellow wretches!"

"Is that what you are?" the Oracle asks coolly. "A faithless wretch?"

Lucky's face goes red with fury. "My blade has remained within its sheath. If you wish me to free it—"

"I would speak with you in private."

Lucky freezes, taken aback. His expression flickers with conflicting emotions. Suspicion, mostly, but also doubt and a bit of fear. "I..." A second later, he straightens and gives a caustic laugh. "Ply your con on someone else."

"You needn't suffer, but if you insist..." The raven sighs. "I hope you choose an easier path."

"The path I have chosen is shored by facts," Lucky snaps. "Spare me your sermon along with your lies."

"As you wish." The Oracle shifts back to Gyrax. "You came for advice and here it is: chart a course for Lanctom Downs."

" 'Tis a modest settlement," Ren says quizzically, "inhabited by farmers and humble artisans. Why in Khel should we break for Lanctom?"

"Are you aware of the shifting earth?"

Nyanti nods. "Due to the tumult in the arcane tides."

The Oracle nods back. "The magical fallout surpasses terrain."

"What do you speak of?"

"The Downs will give birth to a space-time vortex. This is no mere crease or rimple—once it is gels, it will be able to transport millions of souls."

"When?"

"Four months at the soonest. No more than a full year."

"A slipworld passage," Nyanti murmurs, "on a scale unseen since the Elder Folk Dawn. And since Lanctom is north of the Deadlocked Strait..."

"It would be of incalculable value to Lyderea Fairdyle," Elier finishes. "If she conjured an ingress south of Algulis, she could bypass the Strait altogether." His jaw clenches in determination. "That cannot happen. We must stop her."

I'm baffled by his concern. In the past, all he's cared about is whooping ass with his sabers. The others feel the same—they're regarding the Duelist with confused expressions.

He drops his gaze. "After my orphaning, the villagers in Lanctom took me in. Under their care, I displayed a knack for the blade, rightly believing it would pave my way. And so I sneered at my gracious keepers, deriding their poverty and lowborn caste. On my twelfth birthday, I stole away in the dead of night, without so much as a thanks or farewell." He lifts his chin and meets our eyes. "They deserve more than ruin and woe."

Nyanti squeezes his shoulder. "We shall ensure their safety."

Ren mutters, "Six months to reach the Downs..." He swears in frustration. "If I had known in Glimmersend, we could have gone north and halved the faires."

"As I have said, the earth has been shifting," the Oracle says. "And this time, it is to your advantage: the Bysajic now flows straight to Lanctom."

"Truly?" Erany asks excitedly. "If we sail its breadth, it will cut our journey down to a month!"

"Aye," she agrees. "Kessreach lies beyond these caves. Upon its docks, there are myriad crews that can ferry your party."

"Kessreach." Elier searches our faces for objection or doubt. "We break for Kessreach."

Lucky rolls his eyes, but everyone else is fully on board. I'm no exception. Now that I've got a bit of experience (still patting my own back for jacking up that Nightkeeper), I'm eager to help in any way I can. We can thwart Lyderea, assist the townfolk, and give Elier closure in one fell swoo—

The Volant Oracle interrupts my thoughts. "You cannot go with them."

"Who, me?" I point at my chest.

She jerks her beak at Raefingham Bask. "You have much to do, and it does not play out at this particular scale. You know this, don't you?"

He dips his head, shading his eyes with the brim of his hat. "I know it well." He clears his throat and addresses the party. "During my time as the Detective Savant, I trained covert agents known as Clandestine Inspectors. When the Reft took hold, I ordered them all to go into hiding." He raises his chin, lifting the shadow off his eyes. "I have yet to determine if any are alive, and if they are, to what extent they are able to help. Additionally, I must verify the stock in my emergency caches. Those stores of wealth will serve us well, if they haven't been plundered by enterprising thieves."

"You're *leaving?*" I blurt. "But—"

He gives me a smile. "Jon. You, more than anyone else, know I must go. Search your unfettered self, if you have any doubt."

I drop my gaze and study the ground. "I...I don't need to." I can feel the truth of it deep in my bones.

"Good." He reaches up and pats my arm. "Follow your path, Jon. And if you ever fear you have gone astray, remember this: in the infinity of time, we cannot finish and we cannot err."

"A surprising view," Gyrax remarks. "Given your focus on logic and reason, I thought you would be reluctant to invoke the True."

The Ogre waves a dismissive hand. "I have pored through science along with philosophy, and the conundrum that arises is always the same: are we random organisms, at the mercy of chance and unknowable forces? Or is it somehow possible to determine our fate? The first view implies we must stay on guard, unceasingly vigilant against arbitrary malice, while the second implies there is another way. I am a proponent of the latter vantage, which I believe is dependent on person and viewpoint—on whether or not they meld with a nameless unity. This unity, I maintain, escapes definitions and shuns labels, due to its constant expansion and unconditional benevolence. And because it draws breath through novel occurrence, everyone's path to it differs in nature. Otherwise, what would be the point of contrasting perspectives? If the same journey applied to us all, there wouldn't be a use for disparate beginnings." The Ogre turns to me. "I knew it before through books and texts, but you, Jon...you helped me live it."

His words trigger a respectful silence.

For some reason I can't articulate, I desperately want him to stay with the party. "Are you leaving right now?"

"No." He shakes his head. "I will travel to Kessreach, then find a ship that will take me east." He offers a tip of his stylish hat. "Once I am done, I shall make my way to Lanctom Downs."

The others acknowledge with *Ayes* and nods. I murmur assent, but without any feeling.

My gut says he's only the first. And that change is coming and it won't be pleasant.

16

As we progress, the falls inch closer to our sides. Two faires later, they end in a spill directly to our front. Beneath the curtain of free-flowing water, a silver-veined cave looms before us.

Ren stops and addresses the party. "These caves have been known to bewilder the weak. Continually scan your flanks and your rear, and ensure that everyone around you is present and hale."

The caves turn out to be a visual treat. In addition to the veins of shiny ore, they're lit by clusters of soft-glowing crystals. Each one serves as a lucent conduit, channeling long-running flashes that culminate in sparkles. They also emit low mellow tones, as if they were connected to a muffled xylophone. I've poked around in Earthling caves, but they were all shadows and nooks and jump-scare tension. This is more like the Fortress of Solitude. There seems to be zero chance of encountering any weird-ass bugs, pale and creepy with freaky little eyestalks. (Cave bugs—*gross.*)

Nyanti elaborates on Ren's warning: folk have entered and never come out (the singing crystal can be hypnotic) but since we're fairly decent at magic, that shouldn't be a problem. Lucky's the exception—he's limited to things like starting a fire, summoning a bathroom, and basic illumination. Accordingly, Nyanti shields his mind with an enchanted filter, weaving extra runes into the pyramid-shaped loci between his temples. (If I remember correctly, it's called the greater cognat.)

While she's casting the spell, I ask, "Could we stumble across a decaying corpse?"

Nyanti shakes her head. "Not unless their passing was recent. The ambient energy decomposes matter. Eventually, it would incorporate their flesh into the surrounding rock."

"Okay, cool." I breathe a sigh of relief. "That's beautiful and spooky at the same—"

My spidey-sense buzzes, prompting me to swing toward my girlfriend. She's raised her hands in downward claws, ready to oogie-boogie the absolute crap out of me.

"*Nope.*" I level a finger at her glee-charged face. "Nope, nope, and *nope.*"

"Fah." She lowers her arms, disappointed. "To Khel with you and your Primal training."

"The day is coming," I warn. "Get ready to play nurse, 'cause I'mma go full-on sailor." My teasing elicits a good-natured scoff.

We spend the rest of the day traversing the caves, marveling at their gorgeous interiors. An hour before dusk, we emerge onto the soil and rolling green. Part of me wants to keep on spelunking, but that's the life of the Prophesied Traveler—gotta get busy with the Prophesied Traveling. It's all good. The old routine is still pretty cool: fight training, magic, and Erany using me like a cheap piece of meat on sale at Costco.

After a week, the slope drops away, revealing Kessreach off in the distance. Its bigger structures are closer to the water, its smaller buildings are further inland. They visually form a subtle hierarchy, kind of like an architectural tide. Right by the shore, it's jampacked city. As you withdraw, it gradually recedes into spaced-out shacks.

"Nice." I put my hands on my hips and survey the docks. (Man, the river is *huge.* Even though we're standing on top of a hill, I still can't see the opposite shore.) "Kessreach, huh? What's a 'Kess,' anyway?"

"A mythical plane that folded and split," Raefingham explains. " 'Twas rife with portals to faraway lands." He points at the coast. "From here on the river, a mariner can access much of the North. That's the meaning behind its name. While it may fall short of its legendary title, Kessreach connects to hundreds of ports."

"Isn't the water infested with serpents?" I glance at Lucky. "Back at Glimmersend, you said—"

"They are," he replies. " 'Tis why a skilled crew is—"

A deafening horn sounds from the city, accompanied by a flurry of movement and shouts. Violent swells whip back and forth, then—

Holy. *Shit.*

A reptilian head breaches the water, followed by a length of soaring torso. The yellow-green titan unleashes a roar, flooding me with fear and awe and a sense of utter insignificance.

Two dozen ships launch from the docks, paired with a scatter of angular hang-gliders. The vessels begin flaring with rune-laden globes. They only last a couple of seconds, but it's enough to establish a consistent rhythm, ensuring that two of them are always casting a spell. The swooping gliders are doing the same, only their arcane globes are smaller and weaker.

The serpent squints as if it smelled something foul, then turns and plunges into the waves. When it's a quarter mile away, the ships start heading back to the docks. At the same time, a glowing red dome materializes around Kessreach, extending hundreds of yards out from the city's edge. A trio of serpents burst from the river, test the dome with a couple of bites—their fangs elicit sparks and flashes—but they fail to break through the defensive shield.

This. Is. *Nuts.* I just saw a real-life Kaiju attack. What's even nuttier is that it's obviously a part of the day-to-day grind, because the folk below are just going about their business.

"Wow," I breathe. "I guess serpents hate magic."

"A particular type, yes," Nyanti clarifies. "Those ships were casting revelatory spells, typically used for uncovering traps. Strange that a serpent would respond to such charms, but I cannot deny their protective effect."

"I never heard tell of aquatic ophidians," Raefingham muses. "Fascinating."

"They appeared in tandem with Lyderea Fairdyle," Ren grumbles. "A fell coincidence, as both served as portents of woe."

"What about those?" I point at the hang-gliders, diving low in alternating swoops. Before pulling up, they flash with bursts of rune-charged energy, driving the serpents further out to sea.

"Follow-on deterrents." Ren tracks the gliders with his scout-ranger stare. "Wealthier vessels employ them as well."

"If ships were caught outside the barrier, they would risk getting mauled by angry serpents. How do they—"

"A lone ship needn't worry. Typically, it takes three or more to attract a beast. Even so, most are equipped with an emergency measure, similar to the magic you just beheld."

"Gnarly." I fall quiet, struck by respect for the monster-braving sailors. Then I give him a puzzled look. "Lyderea can't use the water due to the serpents, right?"

"Correct."

"Why, though? Her ships have wizards, right? And if the city has hang-gliders, then—"

"Skyfoils," Ren corrects. "And she can't use her fleet because there aren't enough mages. Those deterrent spells might have been simple, but they were high in volume and auric charge. You saw that, correct?" He raises an eyebrow, as if to say, *You* did *see that, didn't you? Your Primal training wasn't a waste of time, was it?* When I respond with a nod, he grunts in approval. "Each ship is staffed by a coterie: a trained team of nautical wizards."

"And they were going off in a specific rhythm, which means the coteries have to work together..." I nod slowly. "Okay, I get what you're saying—a lot more mages, a lot more training. Is that why she wants to tax peoples' auras?" I glance uncertainly at Nyanti. "To beef up her wizards and guard her fleet?"

"That's possible," Elier allows. "Though I believe she prefers the Deadlocked Strait. Breaking the impasse might be expensive, but it would still be cheaper than fleet-borne cargo. Unless the war carries on for decades, the Strait remains the obvious choice." He cups his chin. "If I had to guess, I'd say her auric tax is for personal use."

"I'll go with your answer," I cede. "I'm not really savvy on wartime strategy."

"I agree with Elier," Erany says. "And even if the serpents weren't in play, seafaring elements make everything trickier."

"The water, right?" I venture. "It adds a layer of complication."

"Not just the water. The wind, the weather, the crew...there is less room for error in all that you do."

Ren adds, "Good mariners are steady and sharp. It takes a keen mind, steely gut, and the ability to maintain a flexible routine. Otherwise, they will fail to navigate the inevitable chaos."

"Man," I mutter. "Not sure I could hack it."

In a rare display of non-dickishness, Ren shakes his head. "You would do fine. I have described the ideal, not the average."

"Gotcha."

I'm fairly creative (I think?) so I might be okay with the unexpected risk, though not so much with the shipboard monotony. Still, I've been pretty consistent with swordplay and magic...I don't know. I guess it depends on whether or not you're enjoying what you're doing. Or at the very least, if you find it engaging.

Emotions. Can't get away from 'em.

"Come," Ren starts walking. "Let's go find our captain."

———

The space between buildings gradually lessens, until they're bunched together on well-worn roads. By the time we reach the piers and the docks, we're surrounded by merchants and zoomy street urchins.

"Do not engage with random folk," Ren cautions. "Ports are rife with predatory scum." He grimaces and mutters, "I much prefer the untouched wilds."

"What do you speak of?" Lucky exclaims. "This place is full of life and zest!"

Raef clears his throat. "It has been decades since I roamed these streets, but I will happily take lead on finding a captain."

Ren's features crinkle in protest. "Thank you, but no. I am perfectly capable of—"

"Nonsense!" Lucky interrupts. "If we follow in the steps of Wretched Ren, death and ruin will trail in our wake!"

Ren shoots him an irritable glance. "You're being overdrama—"

Lucky slams his fist into his palm. "I have spoken!"

I try not to laugh, but a giggle slips out. The others feel the same; everyone smiles or stifles a chuckle.

Not Ren, though. "Lucky, I can lead us through a Nok-damned city. You're being—"

"*I have spoken!*" Lucky declares. He sweeps the party with his gaze. "Only one of us can navigate these lively docks! I submit my vote for Lucknar Hap, Master Thief and Handsome Bastard!"

While the rest of us break into outright laughter, Ren tries to hide a grin. "Very well. If the party is willing."

His offer is met with nods and assent.

Lucky pulls his lapels and cracks his neck. "Right. As you have seen, gobs of thieves are prowling these streets. Keep your eye on hands and carries. If something happens to draw your gaze, mind your flanks as well as your rear. A good thief will combine deceptions, and subdue your guard through instinctive reaction." He looks at Erany. "Much like grappling, no? You pull before you push and push before you pull, to coerce your opponent into aiding your efforts."

Erany straightens, taken aback by his incisive comment. "That...is correct."

"That is what happens during a con, only with belief and perception instead of balance and poise." The rogue turns businesslike. "On my heels. And don't forget: hands and carries, hands and carries. As my colleagues like to say, 'A mind adrift is an invite to grift.' "

———

Over the next ten minutes, I thwart five attempts to steal from my carry. Four from children (probably no older than five or six) and one from a tween. The others seem annoyed (Lucky's the exception; he doesn't even look as he swats away hands). Gyrax is the chillest, Ren's the most irritable, and the rest fall somewhere in between.

"How much longer?" Ren slaps a hand off his dagger bandolier. Its owner, an apple-cheeked klepto around eight years old, gives him a raspberry and takes off running. "This is ridiculous."

"It's damn good practice!" Lucky chides, employing a Neo-like defense where he smacks, blocks, and stymies three different pickpockets. Then he cedes, "Although it is a little much." He allows a Goblin to lift his carry, then reels it back in with a twist of its strap.

Man, that was *smooth.* So damn smooth the robber doesn't notice—he just keeps on running past storefronts and alleys. After a second, he registers the lack of tension and weight, and gestures rudely at Lucky before sprinting onto a cross-street.

"This rampant crime...my guess is it springs from kingdom-wide levies," Raefingham ventures. "Lyderea's front hungers for coin."

"More than likely," Gyrax agrees. "The price of goods has risen considerably. Collectors and merchants are squeezing the commoners."

"Those who evade audit are probably rich or criminal," Ren grouses.

"Same thing," Lucky remarks.

"Our reputation precedes us," Elier observes. "The imps are hunting easier prey." Sure enough, the urchins are avoiding us. Some give us a cursory glance—*should I try my luck, nope not worth the trouble*—and move right on past.

"Lucky." Erany points at the signage. "Could we find a captain in one of these taverns?"

"Mayhap. But I would rather try at the Watery Crux, as it serves as a hub for visiting sailors." He jostles past a swordsman, snatching three daggers, a ring, and a big hunk of bread from his unguarded carry.

I'm struck by a mix of conflicting thoughts. *Why does he need that much crap?* And: *those lifts were smooth as all get out.*

He looks over his shoulder at us, grabbing a bracelet, an armband, and an embroidered scarf off another passerby. "Unless any of you object?" His hands flit to his side, depositing the bounty into his carry.

We respond in the negative. *Nope. No problem.*

"Good." He picks up the pace, brushing past a mixed-race woman. "I am sure we will—"

She grabs his collar and slams him against a brick wall. "My pendant," she snarls. "Or I open your neck and bleed you dry."

Lucky raises his hands (her pendant's in his right), and laughs nervously. "Soft, milady. My fingers caught on your looping cachet. I did not intend any—"

"I am sure," she hisses. "Somehow, it bypassed my coat and fell into your grip." She slaps his cheek, earning a yelp, then produces a dagger with a snap of her wrist. "Give it." A line of blood creases his skin, marking the press of steel against flesh. Before we can react, she says, "I hear one of you move, I hear one of you *breathe,* and I will end his life in a fair-weather jiff." She lasers in on the guilty thief. "My pendant."

Lucky gulps. "Ah...I..."

"Give it. Now."

"I am going to move," he announces. "Slowly." His pendant-draped hand drifts toward her. "There." Its gold-link chain is adorned with a stone, emerald green and stunningly bright.

Raefingham startles. "Is that—"

"Do not speak. Or I make good on my vow and open his throat." She snatches the pendant and holds it up to the thief. "This was my father's. He fought and strove for a better world, free from wretches such as yourself." She fixes Lucky with a resolute gaze. "You are not fit to touch my keepsake. Speak your accord, or I'll send you into the Eventide Clear."

"Yes," Lucky whispers. "I understand."

"Good." The knife vanishes into her sleeve. "Show me your heels."

Lucky takes off, hand pressing his bleeding throat. "Come now, you heard her!"

"Wait," Raefingham calls. The thief turns around, indignant, but the Ogre ignores him and studies the woman.

Her face is a blend of exotic features—milky brown skin, sharp high cheeks, and a stunning bright pair of blue-green eyes. Her dark blue tailcoat is somewhat military; two rows of buttons mark its center, deep red piping accentuates its cut. Below its hem, fitted white breeches run down her legs, disappearing into a pair of knee-high boots. Last but not least, two weapons adorn her waist: a cutlass on her left, and a flintlock pistol on her right.

She grips her pistol and squares up with Raef. "I do not care for your overlong stare."

Raef bows and doffs his hat. "Apologies, milady. Your greenstone pendant caught my eye."

"Has it, now?" she asks sarcastically. "Well direct your eye onto something else, or I'll direct it onto my barrel and blade."

"It is just..." He holds a fist to his mouth and clears his throat. " 'For every shadow, shroud, and shade...' "

She stiffens in shock. " 'There is a wealth of light that will never fade.' Who *are* you?"

He stacks his hands atop his cane. "Raefingham Bask. 'Tis a pleasure to meet you, Clandestine Inspector."

———

She shakes her head in firm denial. "Impossible. The Detective perished during the Reft."

"I am happy to report he is very much alive. I do not recall you, Inspector..."

"I am not an Inspector," she snaps. "My name is Syfaedi Kysaire, and I serve as the captain of the *Offset Knife*. If you are who you say, then you know my father, who went by the name of..." She falls silent, challenging him to finish.

"Estelic Kysaire," Raef answers. "Out of all my agents, he possessed the sharpest wit and quickest blade."

She studies him for a hanging moment, then turns on her heel and starts walking. "Follow me."

We fall in behind her. I thought the urchins were avoiding us before, but now it's blatantly obvious. Apparently, Syfaedi enjoys a good deal of street cred.

Lucky draws abreast. "We are on our way to the Watery Crux, in search of a crew of able sailors. As I have imparted personal offense, I understand passage on your ship is out of the question. However, if you could—"

"The *Crux?*" she snorts. "Were you looking to hire bilge rats and swabs?"

" 'Tis a respectable tavern!" Lucky protests. "I know plenty of thieves who would vouch for its folk!"

Syfaedi scoffs. "I have never, in all my years of wind and sail, *ever* suggested the Crux as a place to seek a vessel."

"I am a man of broad horizons," Lucky insists. "Where you see shroud, I see shine. If I may offer a bit of advice—"

"You may not," she says curtly. "I do not care for incompetent thieves."

"*Incompetent?*" he sputters. "I am the very definition of a quality criminal! Allow me to prove it: I will lift your pendant a second time, only you shan't detect me in the slightest de—"

She draws her flintlock and jams it into his temple. Her body is sideways, much like a fencer's, funneling her entire being into the muzzle. In a remarkable display of fine-motor skill, she cocks the hammer without disturbing the gun.

"Sully me again with your Nok-damned hands, and I'll paint the deck with your rotted-out brain."

Raefingham pushes the thief behind him. "Grant him reprieve. Lucky was raised with unusual values."

She points her gun skyward and decocks the hammer. The weapon spins in a neat little whirl, then slips in its holster with practiced ease. "If he touches me, his life is forfeit." She nods at a weather-faded sign. "The Calmer Swell. Let us palaver beyond its doors."

As we follow her into the dockside tavern, a rush of excitement surges through me. We just met up with a fantasy-world pirate.

Bad. *Ass.*

17

The Calmer Swell is homey and warm. Slivers of wind blow in through the cracks, but that only adds to the homey warm snugness—it's like nestling in bed when it's pouring outside.

Syfaedi grabs a table and orders some tea. After a round of introductions (just our names and nothing more) she gets down to business.

"Listen close and listen well: I am not a pirate."

(What? Dammit...pirates are one of my nerdy obsessions.)

"There is nothing wrong with buccaneers," Lucky argues. "I know plenty of—"

Syfaedi doesn't glance in his direction. "They are low-shadow swabs, by and large. I should know—I used to be one." (Nice! She doesn't check the box of "Real Live Pirate," but "Former Pirate" isn't far off.) "I did it out of need. After my father succumbed to wrack, I tried to live as a dockside urchin. The pickings were slim and the peril was great."

Our server returns with tea and condiments. Syfaedi hands him a coin and says, "The leavings are yours." (Cool way of saying keep the change.) He accepts with a thanks and bustles away.

She reaches in her coat and pulls out a flask. "Splash of rum, if anyone fancies."

Nyanti and I both decline, the others accept with outstretched cups. As she pours out dollops, Raef says, "I am sorry to hear that Estelic is dead. I trusted him with a range of difficult tasks, and he failed in not a single one."

Syfaedi caps her flask and slips it into her coat. "Ironic. He shone in your service, but he failed as a father. When I was a tot, he led a crusade against corruption and malice, at the expense of our bellies and steady coin. On the day he transitioned into the Clear, he left me naught but his knife and his khydonite pendant." The captain sighs. "But as with everything, it is a mixed bag. If he hadn't taught me to fight or deduce, I wouldn't have lasted a day at sea. When I served as a deckhand aboard the *Steady,* I fought off debauchers thrice my age."

(Jesus. I was into pirates because of *Pirates of the Caribbean.* But if she's saying what I think she's saying, it sounds more like *Hunger Games* with perverts.)

She lifts her cup and takes a sip. "Our ship was stacked to the Nok-damned rafters, o'er five hundred souls who knew nothing but lack. I fought every day for a solid month, and pared their count by a solid dozen. Our captain, a low-shadow jack named Faithless Bran, wanted to keelhaul the skin off my famished bones, but his first mate convinced him to spare my life. My supposed reprieve was thankless and bru-tal—our seavokers were unable to emplace any basic toiletry, so I was tasked with scrubbing countless chamber pots. Five weeks in, my deck-hand partner leapt off the prow, driven to madness by stench and dis-ease." Her eyes go distant. "I can't remember the name of that deckhand..."

After a brief pause, I ask, "What's a seavoker?"

"A mage who controls the wind and the waves, along with any magic entwined in the ship." She gives me a once-over. It's similar to being studied by Raefingham Bask, only a lot less friendly and way more in-trusive. "Jon, correct? From whence do you hail?"

Raef begins, "Inspector Kysaire—"

"Now we get to the heart of the matter." She lasers in on the Detec-tive Savant. "As I have said, I am not an Inspector. I am simply the cap-tain of a merchant carrack."

"Then why keep the pendant, when you could have sold it in your time of need?" Raef challenges. "That token binds your father to my kith."

"Tell me who he is." She jerks her chin at me. "I can map an accent in a fair-weather jiff, but I have never heard brogue adjacent to his."

"Why do you care?" Gyrax prods.

"My reasons are my own. You seek passage, correct? I can provide it. A party of eight will not be—"

"Seven," Raefingham amends. "My friends are bound for Lanctom Downs, while I have business in the port of Fairliff."

Syfaedi gives nothing away—her poker face is masterful—but there's still that sense of razor-sharp wit. She's poring through data with dizzying speed, winnowing it down into conclusions and options.

"Fairliff. Your former base of operations, stocked with coin and materiel."

The Ogre remains silent. A hint of a smile plays on his lips.

"You..." Her expression falters. "You're truly him. The Detective Savant." Next comes rage. "Where *were* you?" she hisses. "Where did you hide when the world fell apart? When my father and I fled from Reft-stricken mobs?"

The cheer disappears from Raefingham's face. He opens his mouth, closes it, then stares at the table. "VySade. He hunted me down and locked me in gaol. The fault is mine, as I could have escaped at any time. I was jailed by my sorrow and rampant despair."

"I despised you," she says evenly, "with every ounce of my low-shadow spirit." A single tear wells in her eye. She palms it away before it spills. "But if I flame that toxic malice, I will follow in your steps and rot in a gaol. Mine would be hate instead of despair."

"I am sorry," he whispers. "If I could take it all back—"

"I would be a different woman than I am today," Kysaire finishes. "Two choices lie before me: to harry my peace with if, perhaps, and maybe, or to see that a measure of good has come from my pain."

Damn. As far as emotional intelligence goes, she's got me beat by a country mile. Typically, it takes lengthy introspection to restore my perspective. She just did it in a matter of seconds.

"I am a relic of a bygone era," Raefingham states, "worn and frayed by the gears of this world. I trifled away in a stone-tower cell, due to my lack of spirit and mettle. You, however...you have sidestepped your hate with remarkable skill." He looks her in the eye. " 'Tis a shame you are a captain, for I believe you would shine as the Detective Savant."

"No. A thousand times, no." She sips her tea, grimaces, and pours another splash of rum into her cup. "I live a life of incomparable wealth. And though my coffers are brimming with coin, I do not speak of gold or treasure. I love what I do, and I am damn good at it."

Raef raises his cup. "Then we might be denied a Detective Savant, but we are blessed with a mariner of the highest caliber."

She accepts his praise with a curt nod. "Grace and thanks. I shall grant you passage and waive your fare. On this matter, I will not be challenged."

"Captain!" Gyrax protests, "I have plenty of coin!"

She waves him off. " 'Tis a tribute to my father. He would see friends of the Detective as friends of his own. Also—we have much to offload, and the folk in the Downs pay sumptuous rates."

Elier looks puzzled. "Lanctom is peopled with croppers and serfs."

"It used to be." She sips from her cup, regarding him over its porcelain edge. "The Downs have expanded into a healthy river-town. In the next few years, its folk will grow lavish."

"Unless the Queen floods it with Knights," Lucky mutters.

Erany hisses, "Lucky!"

The thief spreads his arms in irritation. "She's a master sleuth! She figured it out the instant we—"

Syfaedi stares at him. "Why would Lyderea care for the Downs?"

Ren covers his face with his hands—*Lucky, you IDIOT*—while everyone else sighs and/or groans. Raef and Gyrax exchange a quick look—*should we tell her?*—to which Gyrax cedes with a short nod. *Be my guest.*

The Ogre clears his throat. "What do you know of the arcane tides?"

Syfaedi shrugs. "I know of the shifting topography. Other than that..."

"Lanctom will give birth to a slip-world passage."

Her expression sharpens. "On what scale?"

"It will be capable of transporting millions of souls."

"When?"

"Perhaps a year, likely sooner."

Syfaedi studies the table. "Lyderea...if she anchored its end in the southern reach, she could easily bypass the Deadlocked Strait."

"And if that happens, she will win the war and reap countless auras," Gyrax concludes.

"I..." The captain reluctantly shakes her head. " 'Tis not my concern."

Elier's expression turns impassive. The others seem disappointed. Not me, though, I totally get it—Syfaedi's been through hell and come out strong. Throwing it away to fight Lyderea...well, it's a big ask, to say the least. Even Luke took a while to come around, and he didn't really have any long-term prospects (aside from becoming a yawn-worthy vapor farmer, or a uselessly armored Imperial Stormtrooper). Syfaedi's the opposite. She's found her purpose and she's good at her job.

"No matter," Raef says, breaking the silence. "Does Fairliff still lie east of Kessreach?" He arches an eyebrow, inserting a second question beneath the first: *Has the shift of the earth changed my heading?*

"It does," Syfaedi confirms. "Seek the *Blue Follow Breeze,* and ask for its captain: Elfidi Barsaech. Tell him I sent you, and that he owes me a brandy for that time he was marooned."

"Grace and thanks." Raef offers the Evermoor salute: his index and middle finger touch his brow, palm facing in, then his hand moves out six or seven inches. "May light find you in dark places."

"And may it ease your eyes and guide your feet."

Raef exchanges goodbyes with our party, then collects his belongings and heads for the door. Syfaedi watches him as he departs. She doesn't have his physicality or charisma, but I suspect she's a match in raw intellect.

"Well." She stands up and adjusts her tailcoat. "If there are no objections..."

Gyrax rises. "Lead the way, Captain Kysaire."

18

As we walk along the docks, I give Erany a slight nudge. "Most of these people aren't wearing cloaks. What's their deal?"

"Port town culture is unique and varied," she explains. "They aren't as encumbered by tradition or custom."

"I'm guessing that bleeds into shipboard life."

"Aye. By and large, sailors are tetchy—they take great pride in their savvy and skill. So bottle your nerdery and save it for later. They may interpret it as meddling or criticism."

Maybe it's a leap, but I think I can relate. When I shared my writing with various groups, there would always be haters who nitpicked my stuff. Not in the interest of helping me out, but out of a dickhead urge to gatekeep my stories. I got the impression they were super insecure, looking to dump it on an easy target, and high school Jon was as easy a target as anyone could ask for. Eventually, I stopped with the groups altogether, due to their overwhelming crab-in-the-bucket vibe.

Syfaedi turns right onto a quay, where the *Offset Knife* is moored to the posts.

Majesty and *breadth* are the first words that come to mind. Its wooden hull runs long and sleek, promising speed and thrills and high-seas adventure. Its triple-mast rig stands tall and proud, dotted with sailors that are climbing, descending, or performing some form of nautical maintenance. Its sides are graced with stone pillars, all tipped with a sculpted dragon's head. Upon closer inspection, I spot a pair on the front and the back.

My voice drops to an awestruck murmur. "Your ship has cannons?"

"Nothing so crude," Syfaedi says briskly. "Those are bombardier obelisks. Magic artillery designed for the sea."

"Whoa," I whisper.

"They won't repel a Protectorate cruiser, but everything else is fair game. The *Offset Knife*, I'm proud to say, can broadside as hard as a Khelfire drake." She crosses her arms and scans her ship, exuding a sense of bone-deep pride. A few seconds later, she asks, "Shall we?" and invites us aboard with a sweep of her arm.

My excitement grows as I walk up the gangplank. A fantasy-world pirate (sorry, *former* pirate) is about to lead us on a riverine adventure.

This. Is. *Awesome.*

———

"First Mate Blythe, these seven folk are now our guests. Brief them on the lay of the *Knife,* then settle them inside the travelers' cabins."

First Mate Blythe is a big bald tough guy. His sleeves are rolled halfway up, exposing a pair of knotted forearms. Stained breeches run into his boots, which—while ugly and worn—look ridiculously comfortable. As a super piratical cherry on top, a scar cuts through his right eye, interrupted by a colorless pupil. Despite the damage, it still seems to work, because it tracks along with its unfaded twin.

"Still on course for Merfolk Stay?" he growls.

"Still on course, with a minor detour. Prior to the Stay, our guests will debark at Lanctom Downs. That should help us maximize yield. Our holds are filled with helshy and vekkel, and demand for those spices have doubled in Lanctom."

"Smart," he grunts. "But the rates in the Downs are in constant flux. If their prices drop and we don't make coin, our cargo will lose flavor before the Stay. We'll be lucky to get half from a Merfolk broker."

"Double or half." Syfaedi replies. "When it comes to profit, I have never known you to curb your zest."

Blythe grins. " 'Cept when we were pirates aboard the *Steady*. We must have dodged o'er a hundred frigates."

Syfaedi nods and shifts into Captain Mode. "Haul anchor."

"Aye, Captain." Blythe jerks his chin at us. "On my heels." As we follow him across the deck, he bellows, "HAUL ANCHOR!"

The command echoes throughout the ship, evoking a surge of busy movement. Blythe follows up with rapid-fire orders, directing painters and swabbers and anyone hanging off the side of the ship (I think they're checking for leaks and tarring up holes) to climb aboard and get ready to make sail.

Once he's done, he guides us frontward toward the bow, halting at a large green circle drawn onto the planks. It's centered around a half-oval stone—roughly waist-high—that protrudes from its pulsing, magic-charged breadth. Six mages are standing on the perimeter, passing arcane voltage back and forth.

Out of curiosity, I Shift my perception and examine the spellwork.

Holy. *Magoobers.*

Radiance soars from the circle's designs, reaching hundreds of feet up before splitting into tendrils. Each curl snakes and winds, imbuing the *Knife* with glowing runes. It's like there's a completely different ship—one that's comprised of runes and magic—superimposed over its physical counterpart.

Blythe's already intense expression becomes way more intense. "This right here is our seavoker coil. *Don't go messing with these Nok-damned spells.* I don't care if you're Circle SyCajister, you are not to alter these charms and markings. Now speak your accord or I'll leave you in Kessreach."

Everyone gives their verbal assent, evoking a grunt of Bald Guy approval. "Your cabins aren't much, but they're a damn sight better than what you'd find on a—"

"Aegelton Blythe, why do you insist on being so gruff?"

Blythe locks eyes with a mage on the coil, a woman who's a few shades darker than Syfaedi Kysaire. She's got bright yellow pupils (not demonic or zombified, more of a stop-you-in-your-tracks, striking shade of gold), and she's dressed in a gray-sheened robe with cut-off sleeves.

Both her arms have sinuous tattoos. They start at her shoulders, flow onto her hands, and taper onto her longish fingers.

"Beg pardon, Mister Eledy. I was telling them all to mind the coil." Blythe's manner abruptly shifts, going from take-no-crap to civil and courteous.

Mister Eledy sighs in disappointment. "I told you—call me Arisse. There isn't any need to be so damned formal."

"You're a seavoker," Blythe argues. " 'Twouldn't do to short you respect."

I lean over to Erany and whisper, "What's with the 'Mister?' Isn't she a woman?"

Erany whispers back, "A derivative of 'Master.' 'Tis a seafaring term." Her expression turns quizzical. "What does gender have to do with it?"

"Oh...nothing, I guess. On Earth, it's usually a word reserved for men, which is kind of silly, now that I think about it." (Come on, Jon—you're a writer, aren't you? How are you getting schooled on verbal etymology?)

Arisse rolls her eyes. "One of these days, I'll get you to call me by my Nok-damned name."

"Already do," Blythe says mischievously. " 'Mister Eledy.' If ever you beat me at a game of knuckles, I'll doff all custom and call you the other." He follows up with a doubtful squint. "Mebbe."

Another sigh. "We both know that will never happen. You've been playing that game since you were a tot." She gives us a once-over. "If all is well, I wish to palaver with our guests."

"Aye, Seavoker." His gruffness returns as he surveys our party. "Once you're done, seek me out and I'll show you to your quarters."

"Leave it to me," Arisse says distractedly.

"Mister Eledy!" Blythe protests. "You have more important things to do than—"

"Away with you." She flaps a hand at him.

Blythe bows deeper than necessary, drawing an exasperated groan from Seavoker Eledy. As he turns and walks away, Arisse folds her hands in front of her waist. "I am the *Knife's* lead voker. If you value your life and my fraying sanity, refrain from calling me seavoker, mister, or anything that resembles or ends with Eledy."

Nyanti examines the seavokers' coil. "I have studied your magic, though not up close. Nautical spells are a specialized niche."

"Ah." Arisse nods knowingly. "You wear the robes of a veteran Witch. Elerican, if I am not mistaken."

"Nyanti Eldara, Third Wise Woman of the Nightclaw Coven." She chuckles self-consciously. "Although it has been a day and an age since I have acted as such." Her tone softens with professional curiosity. "I have secondhand knowledge of your vocation, but I would thoroughly enjoy a firsthand primer. If you would be so kind as to expound on your craft…"

" 'Twould be my pleasure."

Lucky clears his throat. "These matters are beyond me. I am off to find lodging and settle in."

"I as well," Elier says. He glances at Nyanti. "Unless…"

"Fine, fine." She shoos him away.

As Lucky and Elier wander off, the sails bulge taut, timber creaks, and the deck begins rolling with weighty insistence.

Arisse cants her head, addressing a seavoker from over her shoulder. "Heffin—wind and currents?"

A human male looks up from the coil. "Clear on storms, clear on Dwellers. We can set a watch and let her coast."

"Draw up shifts. Make sure I'm scheduled."

"Wish be done."

" 'Wish be done?' " Ren's face crinkles in puzzlement. A moment later, his expression relaxes. "Ah. Short for 'your wish be done.' "

"Aye," Arisse affirms. "You'll hear a good deal of slang aboard the *Knife.* Pardon the bother."

"Quell your worry," Nyanti says impatiently. "As you were saying…"

"Right." Arisse's knees bend and straighten, instinctively absorbing the roll and the pitch. "Seavokers shape the drafts and the currents, tend to a range of magical amenities, and maintain the battery of bombardier obelisks. Lastly, we operate the ship's aegis umbrella." She nods at the half-oval stone within the coil, roughly two feet in diameter and three feet in height. "If a voker rouses its dormant spell, a butterfly shield will envelop the *Knife,* forming translucent barriers that join at the stern and the prow. They're hard to detect in peace and lull, but they brighten and sharpen under incoming fire. The destructive energy is diffused and re-fracted, spread into a ripple that highlights the aegis."

"Fascinating." Ren puts his hands on his hips. "Seavoker Eledy—"

"Call me Arisse, or I will change you all into frogs and newts." Her mock-threat elicits a round of chuckles.

"My mistake. Arisse. Manipulating weather is a tricky endeavor. Did you study at an academy, or..."

Arisse shakes her head. "Vokers learn through informal means. Un-less, of course, they serve aboard a Protectorate ship. In that case, they would receive their training at a Protectorate school."

"Do all of you handle the wind and the sea?" Gyrax asks.

"Aye. Most of the time, the surface swells align with the breeze. But every so often, a Greater Dweller will roil the water."

Erany raises a loose-fingered hand. " 'Greater Dweller?' "

"Titanic beasts that frequent the trenches." Arisse gives her a quizzi-cal look. *Where have you been living—under a rock?*

"Ah." Erany nods. "In Delán, we referred to their kind as Lightless Gargans."

"Wolven call them Deep Crawl Bulks," Gyrax says. "I was unaware they affected the currents."

"Historically, they haven't." The seavoker shrugs. "But in the last four years, they have started to clash. The New Isle Pair, for example. Have any of you heard of them?"

We shake our heads. *Nope.*

"Two years back, a pair of Dwellers mortally wounded each other. Now their corpses drift on the surface, six faires west of Lesinger

Province. They have both been deemed singular islands, as flora and fauna have taken root on their bodies."

"Islands?" I whisper. "They're *that* big?"

"Some can grow as large as Texas," Gyrax informs me distractedly. Then he turns back to Arisse. "I hope they do not pose a threat."

"Dwellers have been known to wreck seagoing vessels, but it is a rare occurrence. In every case, it stemmed from inept sailing, not from a Dweller's hunger or malice."

The others nod, expressing varying degrees of thoughtful interest. I don't understand how they're all so calm. There's Texas-sized monsters beneath the water? And they're strong enough to change the currents? *What?*

"Not to worry—that would never happen under Syfaedi Kydaire. She is a captain amongst captains." Arisse stares into the distance. "Though she seems distracted as of late. It could be the Dwellers, or perhaps it is Lyderea's endorsement of thralls..."

"What?" Erany sputters. *"Slaves?"*

Arisse focuses on Eralindíany. " 'Tis a recent development. The Queen has drawn up letters of yoke."

"Explain." Erany's brow wrinkles in fury.

"They're charters signed by Lyderea's ministers, authorizing nobles to enslave debt-ridden folk. From what I have heard, they primarily target shortfall peasants. I have yet to see a slaver vessel, but if one of them sailed across our prow..." Her expression tightens with disgust. "I know what it is to live without joy, bereft of dreams and hope for the future."

I'm hit by a flash of intuition. "You used to be a pirate."

"Not just I—all of us. Half know Syf from days of yore, when she served as a rake aboard the *Steady.*" The seavoker chuckles. "Swordplay, sailing, mutiny...Captain Syf has many talents."

"Mutiny?" Ren raises an eyebrow.

"Mutiny," Arisse replies, issuing a challenge through her unruffled tone. *You have a problem with that?* "She led a rebellion against Faithless Bran. Does that tie you in knots?"

"Not at all," Ren says coolly. "This world cries out for good-hearted rebels."

Arisse guffaws. "More grandiose than I would have put it. Nevertheless, I'll take your poetry."

"I didn't mean to speak posh or fair," Ren says quickly. "I was simply—"

"As you say, wanderer, as you say." Arisse gives him an amused once-over.

Am I imagining things, or are these two flirting? (I should clarify: is Arisse flirting with Ren? Because I'm pretty sure he would explode if he ever let up on his resting bitch face.)

Nyanti clears her throat. "The bombardier obelisks. If you wouldn't mind..."

"You wish to inspect them?"

The Witch responds with an eager nod. "I would greatly enjoy that, Seavoker Ele—Arisse, I mean."

"Very well." Arisse heads for a starboard hatch, beckoning us on with a wave of her arm. "Follow me."

19

The bombardier deck is two floors down. Within its dingy confines, thirty-six pillars (all lashed to wheeled platforms) protrude from the flanks of the *Offset Knife*.

I Shift my perception and scan their enchantments. They're visible as sheaths of slow-pulsing glyphs, accented by gleams that flash up the obelisks' engravings. This may sound weird, but these weapons give off a quiet majesty. I'd probably feel the same if I was staring at dormant fighter jets—their presence and craftsmanship are undeniable.

Arisse guides us toward the centermost pillar. "They're typically referred to as lisks or bombards." She rests a hand atop its butt. "Each one is run by a three-sailor team: an actuate, mark, and a temper. The actuate fires, the mark aims, and the temper diffuses the arcane feedback. Actuates require minimal skill, they simply channel their aura into the trigger. Accordingly, they serve as the obelisk's informal leader—they are responsible for communicating and maintaining awareness. The very least of that is working with the temper, so the weapon doesn't fire before it is ready. If a lisk overheats, it will shut down for several hours."

"Incredible." Nyanti circles the bombard, studying its engravings with an awed expression. "They spoke of these in Elerica, but..." She extends a glowing hand toward the obelisk, querying Arisse with her eyes. "May I?"

The mage replies with an upturned hand. *Be my guest.*

Nyanti lifts her arm, raising and tilting the obelisk's runes. With a snap of her fingers, she expands them into a magical layout: a web of glyph-circled clusters and holographic lattice. A foot above the enchanted weapon, a glowing circle floats and sizzles. Ten orange nodes shine on its edge, set equidistant on a circumference of light.

"Each of these nodes..." Her gaze drifts across the pulsing sparks. "These are the charges."

"They are."

Ren ventures, "In a nautical duel, you would match your aura against hostile vokers."

"Aye," Arisse says. "The initial struggle is between seavoker coteries. We seek to becalm the enemy's craft, then maneuver behind them and broadside their stern."

"Why is that better than hitting their width?" I ask.

"If a discharge travels down their length, it could potentially rake the entire ship, doing far more damage than punching through their flank. Also, there is a better chance of smashing their rudder."

"A high-flying shot would tear their sails," Ren crosses his arms and nods along, "denying them use of the local winds. Still—they could shape the water below their keel."

Arisse laughs. "At that point, with raggedy sails and a broken rudder, there's not a voker on Evermoor that could handle their ship. And re-member: our first priority is to becalm their vessel. If we've done our job, we've wrestled away their currents and drafts."

"Ah," Ren acknowledges. "My mistake."

"It is all too clear you are steeped in knowledge," Gyrax says. "You have the bearing of a consummate expert."

She accepts the compliment with a dip of her chin. "Thank you."

Nyanti keeps fiddling with the obelisk's layout. "This arcane engi-neering...incredible."

"Why don't people use them on land?" I ask. "Or do they?"

"Sometimes they're placed in castles or bulwarks," Nyanti says dis-tractedly. "But catapults are easier to move and entrench. They can be disassembled and transported piecemeal."

"Could we see a demonstration?" Erany asks. "If it isn't any trou-ble..."

"No trouble," the seavoker assures, "although Gafflock might complain and grumble." In response to our puzzled expressions, she explains, "Our junior seavoker, in charge of reloading the bombardier ordnance."

"No need," Erany says quickly. "I do not wish to impose on the crew."

"Quell your worry. He spends much of his time reading or napping." Arisse strides to the ladder and cups her mouth. "REQUEST FIRE, LARBOARD SIDE!"

Sailors yell, "REQUEST FIRE, LARBOARD SIDE!" in rapid succession. There's a momentary pause, then Syfaedi's response comes echoing back: "FIRE APPROVED! THROW YOUR SPELL!"

Arisse spreads her fingers in front of the arcane layout. Runes swirl and lock into place, brightening and thrumming with insistent vibrance. On the bombard's right, a light-formed display begins to materialize, marking the air with bright violet lines. They congeal into a circle with a crossways axis: a magical version of an Earthling gunsight.

She gives me a nod. "You can be actuate." She points at Nyanti. "You shall be mark. The rest of you can serve as the obelisk's tempers."

I raise a bent-armed hand. "What uh...what do I do, exactly?"

She points at a filigreed vortex above the weapon, floating a few inches back from the ten-spark ring. "Affix that trigger in your mind, and shove your willpower into its center. Don't be shy—it won't respond to anything light." She eyes Nyanti. "Lock your perception onto the guidesight," her pointer-finger shifts to the magical crosshairs, "and direct the blast wherever you wish. In your case, less is more. The rest of you..." She glances at Erany, Ren, and Gyrax. "A crew only needs a single temper. But since we have the extras auras, we might as well put them to use."

Ren says, "Aside from diffracting the obelisk's feedback, there doesn't seem much else for us to do."

" 'Tis the long and the short of it," Arisse confirms. She catches my attention with a jerk of her chin. "The lisk is primed. Fire when ready."

As I settle my focus onto the trigger, it fills my senses with brimming force. My inner nerd leaps to the fore, inspiring to me to mime a pistol with my fingers, intone, "Engage," and push into the trigger as hard as I can.

A spark from the ten-charge circle feeds into the pillar, imbuing its grooves with a scintillant flash. Light flows up the smooth-grained stone, then roars from the mouth of its dragon-headed tip. For a brief instant, blue-bordered purple eclipses my sight. Then it resolves into a haloed comet, lining the river with brilliance as it rockets away.

Nyanti curls her fingers, controlling the guidesight with auric pressure. She twists her hand and the discharge responds, zagging left and furrowing the water. A second later it touches down, triggering an explosion and a sky-high plume.

"Tempers!" Arisse calls. "Cool your bombard!" The obelisk is flush with lambent energy, akin to a coal or a smoldering ember.

Gyrax has the head, Ren's got middle, and Erany has the butt. Shimmering feedback pours off the weapon, flooding their auras with heightened shine. After filtering through their spinal loci, it diffuses into clouds of multicolored sparkles.

Five minutes later, the obelisk is back to its original state.

Arisse grins wryly. "If you wish to pull your weight as a temper, you'll have to cool it thrice as fast. Even then, you would still be slow—our best teams fire every ninety seconds."

"And those would be your next seavokers," Nyanti ventures. "Your finest bombardiers."

"Aye," Arisse confirms. "It's an easy way to scout for talent. I have my—"

Before she can finish, salt-crusted boots appear on the ladder, followed by a torso and a meaty pair of arms. A human seavoker touches down, puts his hands on his hips, and favors Arisse with a sour glare.

"I was dozing in my quarters. Why?"

"It's good for you," she replies. "When I was a pirate, I had to recharge twice the bombards and we had—"

"Half the vokers." Gafflock waves a dismissive hand. "You climbed the rigging night and day, and your aegis was constantly leaking magic. I have it easy, right?"

"I'm glad you understand." Arisse grins. "It shouldn't be hard to load the ring. We only used a single charge."

"That isn't the issue," he grumbles. "If one of the deckhands shouted you awake, you'd be as cross as a Khelfire drake."

"This isn't so bad, is it?" Arisse teases. "Charging the lisks and working the coil, instead of scrambling across the ropes and the masts?"

Gafflock links his aura with the obelisk. "You're enjoying my pain," he mutters. "A voker needs their Nok-damned sleep."

"I concur," she agrees. "So I'll make good on your word and relish a nap." She looks at our party. "Shall I show you to your quarters?"

Gyrax dips into a slight bow. "If you would be so kind."

"Very well. Follow me."

We climb back onto the main deck. She leads us astern, then down a ladder and into a cabin-lined hallway.

"If a door isn't locked, you are free to claim it. Speak with Blythe if you have any issues." Arisse unlocks her room and slips inside.

We spread out and start turning knobs. Seconds later, Erany beckons me into a starboard room. Glass windows line the hull, offering a scenic view of the sea and sky. On the non-windowed side, a neatly made bunkbed abuts the wall. A pair of keys are dangling from its lefthand post, hung by twine from a protruding nail.

I grab a key and toss the other to Erany. "We're officially settled in. What do you want to do?"

She crosses her arms and chews her lip. "Speak with the vokers, mayhap? It would be interesting to see how they fashion their spells."

I wrinkle my face in speculative thought. "I *guess*...but we're going to be sailing for at least a month. We'll have plenty of time to pick their brains."

Erany cocks her head. "What do you have in mind?"

A nonchalant shrug. "I dunno. Maybe we could...you know..."

"No, I don't know. What do you speak of?"

I study the ceiling and whistle an innocent little tune.

She rolls her eyes. "You fancy a tumble. What a surprise. Lock the door and draw the curtains."

"Good call. I've seen deckhands hanging off the sides. Wouldn't wanna give 'em an eyeful of booty." I slide the curtains across the glass, then click the latch on our cabin door. "Hey, why am I the one who always locks up? Whenever we get frisky—"

"I told you, Jon." She drapes her arms around my neck, rivets me with her lavender eyes, and melts my brain with a gorgeous smile.

"I'm the sailor, you're the nurse."

20

Life on a ship is pretty damn cool. It might be different if I worked as a deckhand, or if my half-Elf girlfriend wasn't on board. Lucky for me, that isn't the case—this is like a D&D version of an Age of Sail cruise.

The *Knife* was built as a ship of the line (which means it was designed for nautical combat) so it's got plenty of room for extra bodies (some of these spaces were made for prisoners). Syfaedi, however, has traded quantity for quality. There's more room for crew, more room for cargo, and half as many obelisks. Each deck has several bathrooms (operated through enchanted bilge pumps and pipes), there's a hot-food galley, and we even have showers.

Our party of seven dines in a stateroom, temporarily designated as a traveler's mess. The food isn't fancy, but it's a lot better than what you'd expect (thanks to my interest in all things pirate, I'm well aware that Earthling sailors endured terrible food, stuff like salted pork and hardtack biscuits). Aside from a couple of time-honored staples—a cup of soup and ration of rum—there's decent variety from meal to meal. The kudos belong to our high-level vokers. Due to their magical expertise, open flames are safe to cook with, and the ingredients are immune to spoil or rot. If we had second-rate mages, they would be fully preoccupied with the wind and the sea, and they wouldn't have the juice for bathrooms and food.

Surprisingly, the deckhands have their own cabins. Their quarters are small, but they seem pretty happy with the spare accommodations. On most ships, they'd be forced to sleep in open-air bays. These guys, however, enjoy a modicum of privacy.

While they're on duty, they reserve their chitchat for fellow deck-hands. It's always salty and always sharp, a competitive banter that keeps them engaged. Off duty, it's a different story—they're uniformly chill and relaxed. When I'm not with Erany, I hang out in their staterooms, watching them gamble and tell bawdy stories. Their diversion of choice is a card game called knuckles, and every so often a board game called cradle.

Unsurprisingly, the *Knife* enjoys high retention—every hand has served for at least three years. Occasionally, they'll take on a newbie, but they're super picky about who they hire. Thanks to the *Knife's* pay and amenities, Syfaedi and Blythe get their pick of the litter.

"Still vote on it, though." Sheffid, an older human deckhand, slaps a card on the table and raps twice with his knuckles. "Syf upholds some pirating customs, e'en though we couldn't care less. All the newjoins are as solid as a rock. No one's called for a real vote in..." His brow crinkles. "I can't recall. 'Twas before I came aboard."

One of the three players, a surprisingly Elvish-looking Goblin named Lafa, adds, "I am with you—I care not a whit. She offers a good deal more'n any other captain. This stateroom, for example." She glances around at the varnished walls, dotted with a line of onyx-ringed port-holes. " 'Twas meant to be a mates' lounge, but Syf gave it to us junior deckhands. Between our quarters and jangling carries, there's never been a reason to fuss over ballots." She studies her cards with her lime-green eyes, then favors Sheffid with a knowing smirk.

"Aye." This from a sailor named Jaeka Fedlock, a Wildfae Quiescent (he's got an arm made of quartz) in his early twenties. "Honestly, I wish she would just do away with 'em." He throws a handful of metal into the pot.

"Whoa!" I uncross my arms and push off the wall. "Are those *pieces of eight?*"

Jaeka gives me a puzzled look. "What else would they be?"

"Uh...I just..." I clear my throat, trying to hide my enthusiasm. "I've never seen them before. They look nice, that's all."

Fedlock chuckles, looking briefly at the others while jiggling a thumb at me. *This guy.* "It's not like they're rare. Here." He grabs a piece off the table and flicks it toward me. I pluck it from the air with a reflexive snatch.

The others watch as I turn it back and forth, amused by my fascination with a simple piece of metal. I couldn't care less, because this right here? This right here is *pirate booty.* For the last two weeks, I kept my nerd flag hidden (didn't want to annoy the crew) but now that I've established a bit of rapport, it's time to let that bad boy fly.

Visually, it's not a big deal (a glimmering little slice, engraved with some tentacles and a cut-off squid-head) but that isn't the point. I'm holding a piece of corsair culture. Brisk ocean breeze, bulging sails, hefty chests laden with treasure....if you've seen your passion take physical form, you know what I'm talking about—it's like a fresh injection of excitement and potential.

I can vividly remember the first time it happened. Shortly after my sixth birthday, my mom took me on a trip to the Smithsonian. As soon as we got to the dinosaur exhibit, my imagination sent me into a different world. I was gaping at bugs as big as a dog, large enough to look you in the eye. I was basking in the presence of reptilian giants, made all the more regal by their seeming indifference. My lungs were full of Cambrian air, weighted with heat and carbon dioxide. Thanks to that exhibit, I went on a jaunt into another realm, triggered by some glass-encased factoids and reconstructed bones. The outward portrayals were static and fixed, but they ignited my mind and quickened my soul.

That epiphany inspired me to write. In a similar vein, I realized the symbols on a page can serve as a portal, if we only allow them to work their magic. I just have to place them in the right order, evoke the right cadence through words and sentences. If I do it correctly, my story will trigger an electric synergy, where my descriptions are given life through a reader's perception. Their boosted imagination, in turn, will feed the world with more innovations, which will serve as inspiration for ever more stories...

"Keep it," Fedlock says, interrupting my reverie.

"I'm sorry?" I blink dazedly.

He slaps down a card and raps the table. "Judging by the hang of your slack-jawed gam, it's worth more to you than it is to me."

"Um…thanks." I stuff the piece into my carry. "I—"

Before I can finish, a cry echoes throughout the ship: *"ON THE WEATHER DECKS!"*

Lafa, Sheffid, and Fedlock yell *"ON THE WEATHER DECKS"* while shooting to their feet and leaving the pot on the table. (It isn't much—a modest scatter of trinkets and coins—but their snap-to professionalism is still impressive.)

I trail behind Lafa, unsure of what to do. "Am I invited to this meeting, or—"

"You are not of this crew. Go where you please."

"Um…" I stare at her boots as she clops up the rungs. *Screw it.* "I'll come with."

Most of the hands are already topside. They're standing in a circle, divided between the middle two decks (I think the one further to the rear is called the quarterdeck, while the one closer to the front is called the waist.) Blythe and his mates are huddled together, conversing in a series of businesslike murmurs. I'm pretty sure they're taking roll…yep. Syfaedi walks up to 'em and confirms my suspicion.

"All hands present?"

"Aye, Captain. Even the guests." He points briefly at me, then at the rest of the party.

The captain gives us a cursory glance. "You are free to leave. This doesn't concern you."

"One affects all," Gyrax replies.

The others nod in agreement. Lucky's the exception—he crosses his arms and rolls his eyes.

"Very well." Syfaedi regards the assembled crew. "Your promptness, as always, is greatly appreciated." She begins walking in a circle, drawing their attention with her lingering gaze. "All of you have sailed as pirate raiders. Do you still recall those days of yore?"

The crew responds with a hearty, *"Aye!"*

She folds her hands behind her back. "I know you grumble about our votes, but I believe it is important to uphold some pirating customs, as I will not always be your captain. Come that day, I hope every one of you has the power to be heard, in a manner devoid of fury or gall. That is why I switch out your duties. While many of you think it is Blythe's ill will, made all the more crass by his unsightly features—"

A round of chuckles sweeps the crew. Blythe gives them a wry grin. *Ha ha, laugh it up.*

"—know that it has been my personal design, a deliberate attempt to broaden your view. I cannot eliminate factions and cliques, but I strongly believe we should soften their temper. In so doing, I hope that when you cast a vote, it will remain untouched by tribal passions. Down that road lies ruin and woe. If we vie against neighbor in winner take all, we'll spurn our ethics for pyrrhic triumph, and focus on foes instead of our cause. Over time, nuance would vanish in favor of hate, and become hijacked by rancor and toxic dichotomy. Eventually, we would risk domination by two brutish parties, utterly consumed with ruling the other. And then what? One of the parties would emerge victorious, leaving tyranny in its ruthless wake. Or the two factions would collude and conspire, and make a lie of the choice they pretend to uphold."

Murmured agreement bubbles through the crowd.

Syfaedi continues circling the deck, riveting the crew with her blue-green eyes. "This ship is run by allied folk. Folk who share their pain and bounty, who honor difference without venom or malice. In my early days as a madbrain pirate, I dreamt of a crew that would make me proud. The crew on this ship, I am happy to say, have exceeded my dreams in spectacular fashion."

A mate cups his mouth and yells, "Let's hear it for the Captai—"

She interrupts with an open palm. "For the first time in a long while, we must hold a vote of true consequence. Whatever the result, I will gladly accept, as each of you are sound in mind and heart." She dips her chin and stares at the deck.

Silence blooms. My ears are drawn to the creak of timber, the billowing sails and the waves on the hull.

She clears her throat. "Cast your gaze toward the bow. You will see a vessel on the horizon."

Sailors turn and study the water. Syfaedi reaches in her coat, produces a spyglass, and gives it to Blythe. He expands it with a practiced twist, peers through its lens, then hands it off to the nearest sailor.

"Pass it around and take a look," Syfaedi orders. "That ship, the *Spiral,* is chock-full of captured slaves. Note the design upon its flag." She turns to the sailor holding the glass, a Wildfae Quiescent with an arm made of vines. "What do you see, Tylefi?"

"A starred cross," she replies.

"That sigul denotes a vessel of thrall. When last we docked, I heard of such pennants from drunken rakes." The captain sweeps the crew with her gaze. "Have the rest of you heard of any such emblem?"

Her speech is interrupted by an astonished cry: "They're throwing corpses in the water!"

Bustling chatter envelops the deck. Syfaedi waits for nearly a minute, then cuts it off with a lift of her hand. "Now we come to the heart of the matter: those Nok-damned slavers deserve to be punished, but are we to be the instrument of wrath? If we attack, our way of life will come to an end. As all of you know, slavers are chartered by Lyderea's ministers. She would interpret a raid as a personal affront, and hunt us into the distant yonder."

The crew stands rapt, transfixed by the decision looming before them.

She reaches in her jacket and produces a silken coil. "It will take several hours to close the gap. Accordingly, I will allot one hour to cast a vote. If you wish to refrain from attacking the *Spiral,* tie a knot into this line. 'Tis an abbreviate bind, common among the Elsíny Isles." She hefts the cord. "You've seen its like, aye?"

The crew responds with a collective *Aye.*

"So you know it serves as a temporary clasp, and that for a designated time, its knots will refuse to come undone. This one will hold for the next three hours. Mister Blythe?" She holds out the bind.

"Aye, Captain." Blythe takes the coil from her grasp.

"If I see a knot in an hour's time, we shall pull forthwith into a port, and rewrite our articles as the crew sees fit. In this matter, I will brook no dissent. No one here will sail as a pirate, should it runs afoul of their personal wishes. If there is any doubt about this order, you can vote on my captainship here and now. Anyone?"

The crew remains silent.

"Very well." She nods at Blythe. "The ship is yours."

"Back to your stations!" Blythe yells. "Make sure that we're fair, then come see me topside!"

Syfaedi beckons to our seven-person party, prompting us all to bring it in. "If the *Knife* chooses to engage those slavers, I shall pen you letters of noninterference. I apologize—as guests on my ship, you should not have to endure any peril or risk."

Gyrax replies, "Quell your worry. We support any and all action against the Queen."

Lucky says, "Count me out of your foolish sentiment."

"You're not concerned?" I ask him. "If everyone votes to attack the *Spiral,* you're going to end up in harm's way."

"Jon," he says with exaggerated patience. "Did you not hear the captain's terms? There are hundreds of souls aboard this ship. You think *every one of them* will fight for those thralls?"

Erany scoffs. *Typical.*

"I'm not sure." I look uncertainly at Syfaedi. "There's always a chance, right?"

The captain smiles, but that's the extent of her answer.

Lucky regards us with disbelief. "Hold. Am I to believe—" A bark of laughter flies from his mouth. "Ha! *Ha!* I'm sorry," he giggles. "It's just...you are of the mind that..." He takes a calming breath. "The crew has endured piratical life. Now they live on a well-stocked ship, with gold in their carries and food in their bellies. A unanimous vote defies reason and sanity—you must see that."

"There is more to this life than comfort and coin," Erany says evenly.

"Yes, yes." Lucky cycles a hand in exasperation. "I've heard this before: the damn-fool notion that each of you serve a greater cause. Understand, however, that ideals will fall before hatred and greed. The Reft and Lyderea are living proof of it."

"Expand your view beyond pain and hardship," Gyrax urges. "You will see benevolence in this world."

"Fah." Lucky flaps a hand. "I should charge you double for your high-minded nonsense."

"Nonsense?" The Wolven lifts an eyebrow. "So we are meant to live in perpetual lack, constantly watching our flanks and our rear?"

Much to my surprise, the thief becomes livid. "We aren't meant to live *any sort of way!*" he shouts. "We were born into strife and random misfortune, encouraged to become the very thing we hate! If there is any order to this Nok-damned life, it comes from a force that guts our dreams, then lets us writhe before the Clear!"

"And I?" Gyrax prods. "Why have I not become the very thing I hate?"

Lucky's grin is downright mean. "You are a piece of glorified bait: a fraudulent example to any with faith, as you show it is possible to sidestep woe. 'Tis the perfect evil, when you stop and reflect. Those you inspire will preach to the masses, conning a lucky few into becoming like you, while most will fall to misfortune and cruelty. In the end, you are nothing more than a tragic shill, luring the sheep into grief and regret." The thief shrugs, nonchalant. "I do not fault you, Gyrax. You are naught but a pawn in a malicious existence. But the actions you take, the example you set...'tis insidious villainy at its absolute finest."

Ren takes an angry step forward. "Listen, you—"

"No, it's all right." Gyrax stops him with a hand on his chest, then lasers in on the cynical thief. "So if all is random, I am a fluke. And if there exists a hand behind our lives, it has made me into bait for the sheep."

"That is correct," Lucky affirms. "I am sorry, but..." He turns up his hands and shrugs again.

Gyrax's eyes slide over to Blythe, who's standing before a line of sailors. He's writing their names in a tattered ledger, making sure everyone gets a chance to be heard.

"We shall see, Lucky. We shall see."

21

For the next hour, I pace back and forth across the deck. I absolutely want to free those slaves, but I don't want the crew to die or get hurt. At this point, I'd go so far as to call some of them friends.

Lucky's acting like he couldn't care less. He's leaning against the mast, hands in his pockets, and—judging by the expression on his face—seemingly over all of it, but I'm pretty sure he's secretly worried. If he wasn't, he'd be relaxing in his cabin (that's where he's spent most of the journey).

Any minute now, Syfaedi's gonna—yep, there she is. The captain strolls up to Blythe and asks, "Mister Blythe. Has everyone cast their personal ballot?"

He closes his tally book. "Aye, Captain. Shall I cry out the verdict, or…"

"No. Assemble all hands. This vote is momentous. I wish to vanquish all doubt, in full view of all who are affected."

"Very well." Blythe cups his mouth and yells, *"ON THE WEATHER DECKS!"* His order echoes throughout the ship. In a couple of minutes, everyone's topside.

"Mister Blythe. Walk to my cabin and hold the coil by your chest. I shall take the end and walk to the bow."

"Aye, Captain." Blythe and Syfaedi head for the rear. Once they're set, he offers the coil with odd solemnity. Thus far, everything on the *Knife* has been loose and fluid. Now it feels like a formal ceremony.

Syfaedi takes the end and heads for the bow. Lucky is still leaning against the mast, openly smirking at the proceedings. *Idiots, all of you.*

But as the line keeps flowing, off the quarterdeck and onto the waist, a glimmer of doubt takes root in his eyes.

It's halfway straight. And there aren't any knots.

Lucky pushes off the mast, craning forward and inspecting the cord. When it hits the three-quarters mark, he clenches his fists and mutters something livid. I didn't want to admit it, but deep down I thought he was right—there's no way in hell that *every single sailor* would voluntarily risk their life and livelihood. I should have given them more credit, because…

Syfaedi halts at the forecastle. "Mister Blythe?"

"Captain?"

"Confirm the length."

"That's the last of it."

"I see no knots. You?"

"Not so much as a twist or a curl."

Her gaze drifts across the crew, all of whom have fallen pin-drop silent.

"We are pirates once more."

———

A lusty roar erupts from the ship. Lucky gestures and shouts with manic fury, but I can't make head or tails of what he's saying—everyone's cheering at the top of their lungs.

Syfaedi points at a nearby deckhand. "Aikaba."

The smallest Wolven I've ever seen (six feet tall with a face like a pug), stops and turns. "Captain?"

She offers the line. "Nail this onto the primary mast. Straight and proud so all can see."

"Aye, Captain." She grabs the cord and scampers off.

"Travelers." Syfaedi glances at our party and starts walking aft. "I wish to palaver in my quarters."

As we match her steps, Lucky draws abreast. "Captain, you are on the verge of a grievous error. If we attack that ship—"

"It is not my choice." She keeps striding across the deck. "I am an extension of this crew and I serve at their will. If it were my decision and mine alone, I would have prepped the attack an hour prior."

"But—"

"Folk are not meant to live under yoke," she continues. "We are meant to explore life and all it can offer, painting time and space with our inner truths. Denying a person their reason for being and confining them to a lightless hole—"

"Listen to me!" He grabs her shoulder and swings her around.

She snatches his wrist and circles behind him, locking his arm and forcing him down to a knee. At the same time, she draws her pistol with her right hand.

Dozens of sailors stop in their tracks.

Gyrax steps forward. "Captain—"

"Stay where you are." She cocks the hammer and zeroes in on Lucky's skull.

Gyrax meets our eyes and pats the air. *Be cool. Let her speak.*

"You now exist at my whim." Her voice remains calm and steady. "This is but a taste—a taste of what those slavers inflict." She releases the thief and kicks his butt, flattening him onto his face and his belly. "Get up."

Lucky rises and offers a smile. "Ah...you see, I..."

Syfaedi glances to either side, at nearby crew who are watching the drama. "Back to your posts."

They answer with a hearty, *"Aye, Captain!"* and hastily scatter.

She fixes the thief with a dead-eyed stare. "I told you before: *do not touch me.* Speak your accord or I will fill you with shot."

"I understand." He gulps hard; his Adam's apple bobs up and down.

"Good," she says evenly. "Now. This dynamic we have, where you live and breathe at my say, this is what those slaves endure. How do you like it? Tell me—do you feel worthy of your chosen name?"

"I—"

"That was rhetorical. Keep your mouth shut."

Lucky's mouth opens and closes.

"Yes," she nods. "Exactly. You speak at my bidding, just like those slaves. Believe it or not, I regret this impasse. No one should learn ethics at the end of a gun." She de-cocks her pistol, points it skyward, and slips it into its holster. "As you were, highwayman."

He lowers his arms and averts his gaze. I seriously doubt she changed his mind, but it's nice to see her put him in his place. Maybe he'll come around and see the reason for it. (Probably not, but one can hope.)

Syfaedi resumes walking. "We have business in my quarters. Let us attend to it."

As we file inside, the bustle of her crew is replaced by overhead tromping (her ceiling is the poop deck). Her stateroom is...well, stately. The walls are adorned with weapons, curios, and a handful of beautiful musical instruments. Near the stern, there's a weighty desk covered in maps, ledgers, and an old-school globe. Unlike an Earthling globe, it isn't mounted on a metal crescent. Instead, it's hovering above a filigreed base (a thick stone ring that could be mistaken for a paperweight) as if it was supported by magnetic levitation. It's also ringed with light-woven haloes, comprised of runes and magic designs.

Syfaedi notes my fascinated stare. "A celestial diaglobe. You may access it, if you so wish."

"Oh, uh...maybe later." I chuckle nervously. "Thanks, though."

She takes a seat, pulls a sheaf of paper out from a drawer, and plucks an old-school pen (a lavish green feather, graduating from striking bright jade into deep shiny black) from its desk-affixed mount. "I require your names, parentage, and a physical print of your cardiac loci."

"No need," Gyrax assures. "We are ready to stand with you and your crew."

"*What?*" Lucky sputters. "You would make us into criminals?"

"You *are* a criminal," Elier says dryly.

"Carries are one thing, but—"

"If you fight, they will judge you guilty without review." Syfaedi focuses on the Wolven. "This is not a trifling matter."

"Perhaps it is time to reveal our cards." Gyrax surveys the party, all of whom respond with affirmative murmurs (all except Lucky).

"Of what do you speak?" Syfaedi asks.

"Before you stands the Prophesied Traveler." Gyrax nods at me.

Lucky throws up his hands. *Here we go.*

Syfaedi regards me with unblinking scrutiny. The silence in the cabin stretches and thickens.

Finally, she says, "The gun on your hip. I would see it uncovered."

Gyrax encourages me with a dip of his chin. *Go ahead.*

"Sure." As soon as Ailura clears her holster, shocked cries sound from outside the cabin—they're an instinctive response to her unfettered power.

[Jon.] Ailura floods my mind with a telepathic smile.

[Yep.] I return her smile (mine is bashful because I'm low-key intimidated). *[Good to see you again.]*

[As it always is, as it ever was.]

I begin to lower her onto the desk, but Syfaedi interrupts with a brief wave. "Put it away. I have seen enough."

Someone pounds on the cabin door. "Captain! Are you—"

"Hale as ever!" she yells. "Back to your duties!"

I holster my gun, struck by a pang of vivid regret. Holding Ailura is like a Christmas wakeup. Even before you unwrap your presents, your cells are buzzing with elation and glee.

[Later, Jon. We'll have our time, you and I.] Her star-bright aura fades and vanishes.

"The Prophesied Traveler...you seek to depose Lyderea Fairdyle," the captain states, "not just thwart her or contain her designs, but fully topple her from her reign."

"Aye," Erany affirms.

Syfaedi's in Detective Mode, calculating options at a million MPH. After a bit, she says, "I foresee us together on a long-term basis."

"Joy," Lucky grumbles. "Cheers and mirth for all and sundry."

Syfaedi gives him an impassive stare. "You and I must curb our temper—resist the temptation to bicker and fight."

Lucky blows a frustrated sigh. "Agreed."

She scoots back and gets to her feet. "During the raid, you seven will stay on the *Knife.*"

"Captain!" Elier protests. "I am a High Taire Duelist! I can lessen the chance of trauma and death!"

She considers his words. Then: "Can you spearhead the push? Can you serve as a bulwark and distract them from raiders?"

He dips into a bow and flourishes an arm. "I am well acquainted with both my sabers. They will guard my flanks with zest and aplomb."

"And who shall watch your van and your rear?" Erany demands. "You can't assail them all by yourself!"

"*Why not?*" he snarls. "Do you question my skill? I would have you know that—"

"No, you dundernonce!" She flings up her hands. *What are you TALKING about?* "Are you *trying* to—"

"Enough." Syfaedi's rebuke is clear and cold. "Eralindíany has a point. Your blades will be shored by mast-high snipers, but..." Her gaze settles on our resident Wayfarer. "There is anger within you. Enough to eclipse a Reft-stricken mob."

Ren tilts his head, mildly offended. "Perhaps, but I have been working to quell it. Frankly, I don't see why it is any of your—"

"It will serve you well as an advance boarder."

"Oh," he replies, thrown by her backhanded compliment. "In that case..."

Syfaedi looks alternately between the Wayfarer and Duelist. "Upon the call 'first boarders,' cross onto the *Spiral* as fast as you can. Expect the opposition to be savage and fierce."

Elier shrugs. "The more, the merrier." Ren nods grimly. "So be it."

"I can provide you with firearms, if you so wish."

Elier looks affronted. "And waste the opportunity to hone my swordplay? Out of the question."

Ren dismisses the captain with a curt wave. "I am well-versed in combat magic."

"Very well." She looks at Ailura. "Keep your clapfire in its holster. Slavers don't warrant a Great Weapon round."

Huh? "I don't unders—"

"If any survive and slip our grasp, they will catch someone's ear with mention of your gun."

"Yeah, but—"

" 'Tis wise and astute," Gyrax interjects, "as we have plenty of spells at our disposal. Unless the clash turns surprisingly dire, there shan't be a need for Ailura Qartesi."

"Aye," Syfaedi agrees. "The rest of you will follow upon the call, 'second boarders.' I assume none of you have engaged in shipboard combat, so allow me to brief you on the order of battle. Our first objective is to becalm their ship. That falls under the purview of our seavoker coterie. Once we control the wind and the waves, we shall harry them with our bombardier obelisks. Optimally, the *Knife* will lie perpendicular to the *Spiral,* ready to broadside her from the rear. However, our nautical spells might lag or slip. In that case, our ships could end up broadside to broadside, exchanging bombardier fire shot for shot. We may or may not have to board, depending on what happens during the exchange. Don't assume that—"

"Captain." Lucky clears his throat.

"Yes?"

"I would appreciate a letter of noninterference."

"Allow me to finish the order of battle. I shall pen it for you afterward. Fair?"

"Aye."

"Very well." She eyes the rest of us. "The air will be rife with shouted commands, but the one that concerns you is..." She trails off, prompting us for a reply.

Ren and Elier: "First boarders."

"And?"

"Second boarders," I answer.

"Correct. Try and face inward, toward the center of their ship. Ensure you are constantly looking about, accounting for the folk on your flanks and your rear. If all goes well, your friends will be trailing and your foes will be facing, but that can change in a fair-weather jiff. Now repeat my instructions—I would hear you speak them of your own accord."

"Try and face inward," everyone murmurs. "Look around to your flanks and your rear."

"Good," she affirms. "When they drift into range of our bow-mounted lisks, that's when things will begin to pick up. Stay out of the way and stay alert for your calls. Lucky." She locks onto the thief. "I shall draw up a letter and allow you an audit. The rest of you may leave."

As I exit her cabin, I'm hit by a wave of giddy nerves. In less than an hour, I went from an easygoing passenger to a high-seas raider.

My mind flashes back to Atriya's contract. It seems like a lifetime since I signed it.

SOMETHING DIFFERENT.

For better or worse, I'm getting what I wanted.

22

The post-vote excitement quickly dwindles, giving way to an uneasy calm. (Uneasy for me, anyway. The crew are all seasoned pirates, so this is old hat for 'em). As we coast along, the *Spiral* grows from a far-off dot into a slightly bigger dot, then eventually into a triangular outline.

Syfaedi remains glued to the forecastle, peering through her spyglass and conferring with Blythe. The First Mate replies with grunts of acknowledgment, paired with an infrequent one-word answer. Occasionally, he'll turn around and yell at a deckhand, telling them to tighten this or adjust that.

Lucky is somewhere down in the holds. The rest of us are topside, careful to steer clear of the hands and their mates. I'm part of the team, but it sure doesn't feel like it, because all I'm doing is—

Arisse strides up to me. "Antsy?"

"What? No." I uncross my arms, push off the mast I was leaning against, then shove my hands into my pockets. Then I re-cross my arms, but that isn't as comfy, so I stick my hands back in my pockets. That's weird too, so I take them out and rub the back of my neck. "Why, uh...why do you ask?"

The seavoker chuckles, refusing to dignify my BS question. "Quell your worry. We're steady on their rear, but the winds and the tides are a fickle mix. If they luck into gusts or surging water, they can leverage the flux and slip our pursuit."

"Oh. Right." I laugh nervously, try to conceal it with a forced cough, then mentally kick myself for being a derp. "Shouldn't you be with the other vokers?" I glance at the coterie, standing equidistant on the seavoker coil. I'm not very Shifted (way too anxious) but I can still see energy rising from the circle. The vokers are shaping it with fluid gestures, passing constructs and layouts back and forth.

She follows my gaze and responds with a shrug. "They know what to do. Right now, it's a matter of filling our sails and smoothing the currents. Once we're close—a couple of faires, give or take—that's when our vokers will wrestle with theirs."

"Like I said, I'm willing to help. I'm all right with Primal Magic."

Eledy studies me. Then she offers her bent-elbowed hands. "Palms on mine."

I peek at Nyanti, who's standing near the hull and observing our chat. She dispels my reservations with an approving nod.

"Right." I take a breath and lay my hands on hers.

"Try and relax." She closes her eyes.

"Relax. Sure." I do my best to expand my aura. My anxiety keeps everything tight and constrained.

[Didn't I just tell you to try and relax?] Her telepathy is tinged with playful reproach.

[Sorry.] I project sheepishly. *[Still kinda new to this.]*

[I shall link your aura to our coil. Don't worry about fouling our spells—I will cordon you off from anything vital.]

[Let's do it.]

She starts pushing and squeezing my auric loci. This is...well, it's kind of pleasant, actually. There's a soothing gentleness to her presence, similar to that of a top-notch waiter. She's not overbearing, she's just *there,* imparting an easy pressure that puts me at ease.

A second later, information floods my psyche, cohering into visceral awareness of the ship's arcane infrastructure. Man...it is *intricate.* The *Knife's* enchantments—which range from small and discreet to straight-up titanic—flow seamlessly between the sails and the rudder, along the hull and throughout the obelisks.

[Wow.] I zero in on the deep-current spells. *[You guys built those?]* There's enchantments for earthquakes, volcanoes, and clashes between trench-walking Dwellers.

Arisse laughs. *[I'm flattered you would think so, but no. They were woven during the* Knife's *construction, refined and sealed by orphic masons. My coterie simply tweaks the magic.]*

[Ah.] I project a nod. *[Gotcha.]*

She directs me onto the defensive aegis. *[Can you sense how it's designed to repel the enemy?]*

I feel along the mesh-like spell, noting the balance of tension and give. *[It suffers damage from outgoing fire.]* I realize.

[Very good. Our shots will degrade it, though not nearly as much as hostile bombards. We have to sustain the uneven polarity, or it will settle into a neutral state.]

[A neutral state? So that would mean—]

[It wouldn't repel any incoming fire. It would simply be a marker of arcane potential.]

[A blank field laid over the ship, waiting to receive any old enchantment.]

[Correct.] she affirms. *[That is the nature of magical energy. Without intent, it will revert to a state of fresh possibility.]*

[So it favors inertia?]

[In a sense. If we fail to maintain its layered arcanix, it will gradually weaken and become increasingly responsive. Ironic, isn't it? Given time, its external influence will dwindle and wane, but it will become easier to influence through external forces.] She nods at the aegis. *[In terms of spellcraft, 'tis a relatively complex design. With training and experience, it ceases to vex.]*

[Can't you re-weave it by ditching resistance, and allowing your desire to rise and take shape?]

She roars with laughter. *[Unless you believe in the Prophesied Traveler, what you have just described is outright impossible.]*

I chuckle nervously. *[Yeah, that would be ridiculous. Prophesied Traveler—what a load.]*

[Your speech is odd.] she remarks. *[I have visited scads of far-off shores, but I have yet to hear anything close to your accent. No matter.]* A dismissive wave. *[My eyes have beheld stranger than you.]*

[Um...thanks.] I reply apprehensively. *[I get that a lot. So all this requires a lot of know-how. The obelisks alone...they're like the arcane equivalent of a fine piece of art.]*

[Aye. The Knife *requires precision upkeep.]*

[Could have fooled me. You're way more relaxed than Blythe and his sailors.]

[Partly from skill, partly from need.] she responds. *[We must harmonize with the ship and the sea, which means emotional calm is of the utmost importance. When I crewed with Syf as a pirate voker, I—]*

Blythe shouts, *"They're coming within range! Beat to quarters!"*

Arisse breaks our telepathic link. "I have to—"

"Go." I settle into my body and rub my temples.

She nods and turns inward toward her vokers. Their magic is now on full display, intensified into a glaring column. A dozen yards aft, Elier and Ren are shouting up at the snipers, making last-minute arrangements with the overwatch marksmen.

Gyrax walks up and nudges my side. "How goes it?"

"Um...I think I'm still processing. I never thought I'd participate in a high-seas raid." A flag ripples upward, replacing the *Knife's* pennant with a black standard.

Gyrax pulls his signature move: he lays a paw on my shoulder and gives it a squeeze. "When the battle picks up, you will be tempted to ignore the greater picture. Find rhythm in the moment. Let it steady your mind and guide your hand."

"Be dust upon your breath?" I smile wryly.

"Always." He gives my shoulder another squeeze.

Captain Kysaire cups her mouth. (Whoa, she's wearing a Blackbeard-style harness with six flintlock pistols—two near her hips, and four around her chest and belly.) Her fingers glimmer with eldritch power, then she booms, **"SURRENDER YOUR SHIP AND PRE-PARE TO BE BOARDED!"** in a magically charged voice.

The *Spiral* fires its rear obelisks, releasing two streaks of hissing energy. One of the discharges grazes our flank, the other curves into our aegis. It startles me into taking an involuntary step back. Much to my relief, the blast diffuses into lava-red flashes. They weaken into a mess of yellow-orange licks, then sweep our shields with fading blaze.

Our bow-mounted obelisks respond with blue-purple comets. Sizzling tails burn in their wake, scorching the air before hitting the slavers. Their butterfly shield isn't nearly as strong; it bulges ponderously inward as it diffuses our shots.

Syfaedi glances over her shoulder at the seavoker coil. *"Arisse! When are you going to calm that ship?"*

"Ten, maybe fifteen minutes. Their vokers are fair, nothing special."

"Then why aren't we—"

"They're making up for it with sheer desperation." Irritation creeps into her voice. "Keep your peace. You needn't yell."

The captain takes a steadying breath. "Apologies. Those damn slavers..." She shakes her head in muted frustration.

"Captain! Broadside ahoy!" Blythe points at the *Spiral,* now veering left. Its flank kindles with obelisk blaze.

Syfaedi lasers in on the helmsman. "Safen! Hard a-larboard!"

Safen spins the wheel, matching their turn with our own. As the *Knife* and the *Spiral* get ready to brawl, my gut tightens in anticipation. Sharp hisses sound from below, accompanied by fractalized light from our dragon-headed bombards.

Syfaedi turns to the coil. "Arisse?"

The seavoker's eyes flick between runes. "We have two of their sails. We'll seize their currents soon enough. In the meantime, we shall have to trade salvos."

"Very well." Syfaedi's words are tinged with excitement. "Let us see whose mettle is greater."

A moment later our ships line up, and all hell breaks loose on the water.

23

I've already experienced bombardier fire, but those were shots off the bow and the stern. These are full-on broadsides involving dozens of obelisks. Unlike the movies, where the visual is restricted to discharge and impact, I can *see* the ammunition coming our way. Swarms of energy drench the air, arcing and curving before striking the *Knife.*

Our aegis turns from a barely-there sheen into a gorgeous aurora. As storms of color explode and flatten, enveloping us in ripples of fractalized vibrance, I'm hit by a roil of conflicting emotions—half of me wants to pee my pants, the other half revels in the untrammeled beauty.

The *Spiral* doesn't fare nearly as well. A pair of our shots pierce their aegis, dinging their bow and clipping their foremast. It galvanizes our scrappy bombardiers—they all start shouting with fresh enthusiasm, exhorting their tempers to cool their obelisks. Faster, Nok dammit, *faster!*

"Mister Arisse," Syfaedi calls. "Status?"

"Five minutes, maybe less. We've got their sails and most of their current."

A mast-perched sailor yells, *"Incoming!"* as the *Spiral* hurls another broadside.

Furious hues rocket toward us, blanketing the *Knife* in destructive iridescence. Our bombards respond with eighteen blasts, piercing their aegis with two more rounds. Both of them split into fiery showers, carving char-lined divots into their hull.

"Syf!" Arisse calls. "Their ship is becalmed!"

"Fill our sails!" Syfaedi roars.

Our sails bulge taut as we pick up speed, drawing creaks and groans from the straining masts. As we swing around to the *Spiral's* rear, I notice the water around her is flat and dead.

Syfaedi looks at First Mate Blythe. "If they blitz us again, rake their decks from stern to bow."

Blythe points at the *Spiral*. "Doesn't seem likely—they're all taking refuge." Sure enough, they're scrambling down rigging and disappearing from view.

"Arisse, how is our aegis?"

"Still holding strong," the voker replies. "Theirs, on the other hand, is about to collapse."

Syfaedi glances at Safen. "Once we're astern, await my command."

"Aye, Captain." The helmsman coaxes the wheel and softens our turn.

Arisse orders, "Easy on the wind. Cross up the water." Her vokers acknowledge with low-toned mutters.

As our canvas slackens, the waves around us flatten and smooth. The *Knife* settles into a lazy drift, crawling slowly along the rear of the *Spiral*.

Syfaedi chews her bottom lip. "They've gone below or hidden behind cover. Why not just yield?"

Blythe's eyes narrow in suspicion. "They likely think we're after their slaves. Mayhap they'll kill 'em if we don't cry off. A hostage situation, if you ken my meaning."

"If they're hoping we won't fire because of their thralls, they've judged us correctly." She pulls her tailcoat straight. "No way around it—we'll have to board her. All teams off their bombards. Four fifths as second boarders, the remaining fifth as topside defense."

Blythe cracks a lopsided grin. "Like old times, eh? Becalming ships, storming decks..."

Syfaedi responds with a slight smile. "There are similarities. Back then, however, we were fighting to survive. Now we fight for the survival of others."

Blythe tips an imaginary hat. "True." Then he turns and starts hollering at the crew.

Syfaedi cups her mouth, imbues her hands with auric energy, and turns them into a spell-boosted megaphone. **"I WOULD SPEAK WITH YOUR CAPTAIN!"**

No response.

"Close on their larboard," she orders.

As the wheel spins, Blythe shuffles across the deck in a hunched crouch. "Get low," he hisses. "Behind the hull." His order is repeated in muted echoes.

I hunker down beside my girlfriend. "What about our shields?" I whisper. "Won't they protect us?"

Nyanti crouches next to me. "Not from snipers or smaller missiles. The aegis is made for burly projectiles: obelisks and cannons and heavier siege engines. If it blocked every form of kinetic power, the wind and the currents wouldn't pass through."

"Hush," Gyrax chides. "Keen your eyes and clear your senses."

After a seeming eternity, we halt parallel to the *Spiral*.

Blythe calls, "First boarders!"

Elier and Ren leap across, boosted by a surge of propellant magic. I peek over the *Knife's* hull, watching as they flow into easy rolls.

"Grapnels!"

Hooks fly out, catching on netting and wooden edges. Our planks stand tall, ready to yaw forward onto their ship.

Ren yells, "I think they're—" then bodies pour out from hatches and corners.

The Duelist and Wayfarer get to work, slashing, stabbing, and entangling a mess of hostile weapons. In between chains of strikes and parries, Ren throws spells with his half-gloved free hand. Meanwhile, Elier channels energy into his sabers, casting short-range arcs of debilitating violet. Whenever they hit, his unfortunate targets collapse and vomit. (Nice—the slavers aren't trained in combat magic. If they had any skill, they would diffuse his spells with relative ease.)

Blythe roars, *"Snipers! Clear us some deck!"*

Scores of guns crack and snap, limning muzzles and hammers in puffy white smoke. Down on the *Spiral,* handfuls of slavers twist and drop, giving Ren and Elier room to press forward.

Syfaedi stands tall and levels her cutlass. *"Second boarders—FOR-WARD!"*

Sailors rush across the planks, gripping an assortment of pistols and swords. As my feet thump onto the *Spiral's* waist, our snipers fire another volley. I lurch forward, ready to join the embattled perimeter, but Erany halts me by grabbing my shoulder.

"Stay one layer back and null their shot!" She parries a thrust, kicks a man in the chest, and casts a spell at some flintlock-wielding slavers. Her magic takes form as rune-coated mist. It spills and swirls across their guns, imbuing them with flashes of blue-purple-green.

A moment later, their pistols click in rapid succession, surprising me into a reflexive flinch. Thankfully, none of them fire. Iron shot rolls out from their barrels, clacking loudly on the wooden deck.

"Got it!" I spot four on our left. Nyanti's got middle, Erany's on the right, so these guys are mine.

I blow out quickly, releasing tension as fast as I can, then reach toward them with my non-sword hand. As they sight in, I pivot to futility, a reliable go-to in my emotional toolbox. *In the long run, none of this matters. You die, they die, everyone dies. Relax into grace and focus on the task.*

My worry vanishes, replaced by surety and mild optimism. Loci open, meridians connect, and magic streams out from the tips of my fingers. It materializes as a mess of red-orange curls, surrounded by haze and fanciful symbols. Since it's Primal in nature, it honors my intent with a novel iteration—their guns wither into sooty dust, then blow away in a crosswise breeze. (I thought warded firearms would be hard to disrupt, but that was easy as hell. Probably because these are low-ranking troops who don't have access to quality magic).

Nyanti confirms it with, *"Their guns are cheap and easy to repel! Keep them at bay while I shield our crew!"* In a flare of robes and black-nailed fingers, she paints the air with stylized glyphs. Bright gold spheres blaze into existence, coating friendly sailors in protective glitter.

At first I'm confused. Why didn't she do that before we attacked? Then I realize: while the slavers' guns are poorly warded, they still vary in protection and strength. Multiple shields could needlessly drain her auric loci—or worse, be ineffective—without precision sorcery. She couldn't have known her magic would work until she was closer and had eyes-on.

"Join the fray!" she yells. *"I will keep us hale!"*

I stop hunting pistols and rush into battle, paying attention to my weight and posture. I suddenly get why Elier loves this. I can viscerally feel what's going to happen, and capitalize on my array of openings and positions. This is his reward—this continuous bloom of ease and flow.

As I take out a slaver with a high-low combo, I catch a glimpse of the *Spiral's* vokers. They're all sprawled across a darkened coil, probably unconscious, possibly dead.

"We surrender!" A gravelly voice rings out from the mob, hitting me with a blast of cognitive dissonance. *That was quick.* "We surrender!" Slavers drop their weapons and raise their hands.

"Strip them of arms!" Syfaedi orders. "Put them in lines!" She stares at the man who called for surrender: a bull-necked human with a handlebar mustache. "First Mate, I presume? Lower your hands."

He lets them drop. "First Mate Tallix. You are their captain?"

She nods in response. "Syfaedi Kysaire."

Tallix glowers at her. "Our ship has been granted a letter of yoke. As a vessel chartered for live-cargo bondage—"

Her expression turns cold. " 'Live-cargo bondage?' 'A letter of yoke?' Garish words, Mister Tallix, for a transgression against existence itself."

"We live by the law and the law lets us live," he growls. "You and your crew are marked for the Clear."

"As are we all." He tries to retort, but she holds up a hand. "Your captain, Mister Tallix."

"Lower hold," he grumbles. "Defending the cargo."

"Call them slaves or thralls. At least acknowledge their beating hearts."

Tallix doesn't reply. He just keeps on glowering.

"Mister Aclasian." She turns to Gyrax.

The Wolven strides over. "Captain?"

"Can you and your fellows guard my person?"

"Of course."

"Blythe," she calls. "You and three mates will remain by my side."

"Aye, Captain."

"Very well. Lead the way, Mister Tallix."

Tallix guides us two floors down, then walks toward the fore of the ship. After a series of cage-bordered hallways, we halt inside a windowless room. Centered on the floor is a vault-like hatch: a gritty metal slab with a large keyhole, topped by a hefty four-spoke wheel.

"Their quarters?" Syfaedi asks.

"Aye."

"Open it."

Tallix lifts a key-loop off his neck, kneels down, and unlocks the hatch. As he spins the wheel, gears and tumblers clunk into place.

The noise triggers a fearful query: "Who goes there?"

"First Mate Tallix, Captain Deybau. Along with a clutch of enemy boarders."

"Stay where you are!" Deybau shouts. "Or I'll send you into the Eventide Clear!"

Tallix pulls up the hatch, revealing a ladder, and queries our party with a surly glance. "Well?"

Ren says, "I shall go first," to which Syfaedi answers, "No. It has to be me."

"I am a Wayfarer," Ren argues. "Breaking trail is my reason for being."

"I am the de facto captain of this entire ship," Syfaedi counters. "The folk in this hold are under my care."

"But..." Ren sighs. "Very well."

Syfaedi catches Nyanti's attention with a lift of her chin. "In all likelihood, Deybau's weapons are highly enchanted. If you would be so kind as to bolster my shield..."

"Of course." Nyanti raises her hands, causing her aura to quicken and pulse. "Hold still." Her voice drops to a low-octave hum, causing scintillant energies to pour off her loci. After an elegant series of revolutions, they fully lock into the captain's aura, reinforcing her contours with extra runes.

"There," Nyanti says. "For the next half hour, you will enjoy a significant boost in arcane protection." She clicks her tongue and examines the shield. "It won't repel lichfrost, but for anything equal to Serion's Fusillade..."

"I am sure it will suffice," Syfaedi interrupts, startling the Witch out of her musing. "My thanks, Wise Woman."

"Ah..." Nyanti clears her throat, trying to hide her embarrassment. "Of course." (Ha! I'm not the only nerd!)

As Syfaedi descends, Deybau shouts, "Back! Back, Nok damn you!"

She touches down, casts a brief glance around, then looks up at us through the hatchway. "Blythe. You and your mates. Gyrax. You and two others."

"Wish be done." Gyrax points at me and Ren. "Jon. Ren."

I almost question him—*Me? Why?*—but the protest dies inside my throat. I'm a decent fighter and a trained sorcerer. Time to start acting like it.

Gyrax jumps in the hole, absorbing the impact with a flex of his knees. Blythe and his mates clop down the rungs, then me and Ren follow suit.

My first impression is the hellish smell: a blend of unwashed bodies and old waste. Wall-mounted sconces give off sullen red light, contributing to the oppressive vibe. Unfortunately, the oppression goes a hell of a lot further than smell and vibes. Dozens of folk are sitting on the deck, arranged in a grid of networked shackles. They're staring straight ahead and refusing to make eye contact.

My breath catches in my throat. A second later, I'm trembling with rage. I've studied this before in textbooks and lectures…I never thought I would see it in person. There's marked differences (the main one being this isn't about race) but now that it's right here in front of me, I can't ignore their hollow gazes.

"These are *debtors!*" Deybau shouts. "They're short on their due and they're paying the price!" He's retreated all the way to the back of the hold.

"You exceed your bounds," Syfaedi says tightly. "This doesn't serve anyone."

"I am doing them a favor!" As Deybau creeps forward, crimson-tinged shadows prance across his face.

I can't believe this…he's the same age as me.

"They would never amount to a Nok-damned thing, unless someone detained them and forced them to work! I am not their captor—*I am their savior!*" He jabs his pistol at her.

Syfaedi folds her hands behind her back. "Choose to fight, and you will depart this life with stunning speed. Lay down your arms and declare your surrender, and I shall guarantee safety and release you in port. Lastly, you may opt to serve as a crewmember deckhand."

"A crewmember?" His brow wrinkles in confusion. "Under Tallix?"

"No." Syfaedi nods at the slaves. "Them."

"*What?*" he sputters. "How could you even—"

"Mister Tallix." Syfaedi cants her head and catches his eye.

The First Mate straightens. "Captain?"

Deybau thrusts his flintlock at him. "She is not your captain! Know your place, Mister Tallix! *Know your place!*"

Syfaedi remains unfazed by his outburst. "Unshackle the crew."

Tallix hesitates. Deybau continues to shout and gibber, gesticulating with the end of his ornate pistol.

"Now."

Her order startles Tallix out of his pause. "Aye, Captain." He moves toward the nearest slave.

Syfaedi squares up with Captain Deybau. "Kindly stop waving that Nok-damned gun, or I will turn it on you and fill you with shot."

"You cannot do this!" he screams. *"I have a letter of yoke from QUEEN LYDEREA!"*

Syfaedi ignores him and examines the slaves. "Are there any among you who speak for the whole?"

A tall wiry guy with stubby little horns, purple skin, and glowing red pupils (one of those half-demon types I saw back in Glimmersend) rises to his feet and rubs his wrists. "Aye."

"Your name?"

"Keybra Elahqua."

Syfaedi's gaze drifts across the prisoners. "This Daemos is your leader?" She's met by a series of murmurs and nods. "And none take issue?"

No one speaks.

"Very well." She homes in on Keybra. "Distribute aid, quarters, clothing, and food. Refer to First Mate Blythe for specifics and contacts." She indicates Blythe, then addresses Tallix. "Mister Tallix?"

He stops unlocking a woman's shackles. "Captain?"

"Once you are finished, assist Mister Elahqua."

"Aye, Captain."

Deybau continues spewing out threats. No one's listening. The nexus of command has settled around Syfaedi, Keybra, and Tallix.

As the first slave climbs through the hatch, Syfaedi looks again at Deybau. "Captain, if you would please calm down—"

"—just you wait! My father will rack you and hang your crew! You have no damned clue what you've gotten yourself into—"

"—if you would please calm down—"

"—rue the day you took this ship! I am the nephew of Castigan Syric; he flies a dozen armies beneath his banner! Savor this moment when your limbs are attached, when your organs still lie beneath your skin! It is only a matter of time before—"

"Captain. *Deybau.*" She grips a pistol holstered near her sternum. "If you insist on running your low-shadow mouth, I will lay out my terms at the end of a gun."

Deybau stiffens. After a moment, he says, "I plead thy grace. It's just...I was entrusted with cargo and a royal charter, and now it is all..."

I'm hit by a wave of cognitive dissonance. This guy is a friggin' *slaver captain*. I thought he would look villainous and evil. The last thing I expected was this apple-cheeked frat boy, teetering on the verge of openly crying.

Syfaedi lets go of her black-and-gold flintlock. "Very well," she says curtly. "Remember: you are still a captain until your relief. As that is the case, I advise you to act with a measure of poise."

Her words have a sobering effect. Deybau straightens and clears his throat, attempting to project a bit of authority. He falls woefully short, but that's to be expected. Any leader (which Deybau clearly isn't) would be hard-pressed to match Syfaedi's presence. *Captain Kysaire* isn't just a title; it's woven into the core of her being.

"Captain Deybau," Syfaedi prods, "I have stated your options."

He takes a steadying breath. "I agree to your offer of safe passage, contingent upon a single request."

"Name it."

"I wish to transfer command in a formal ceremony."

"Very well."

"Grace and thanks." His lip quivers and his voice trembles. "Captain Kysaire...I..."

"Yes?"

He picks up a pair of unlocked cuffs. "I need a moment alone." He stares morosely at the rusted iron. "To quell my turmoil."

"Of course," Syfaedi replies. "Ren? Lead us out."

The Wayfarer glances at Deybau with blatant disgust, then follows the last of the prisoners up the ladder. Blythe and his mates trail behind him.

Gyrax nudges me. "Time to go."

"What? Oh. Sorry." I was distracted by Deybau. He's nothing more than a spoiled kid, which somehow makes him way more scary—he's proof you can be weak and indulgent and still inflict ruin.

Halfway up, I chance a look back. The slaver captain is standing all by himself, staring down at the shackles like they're all he's got left.

24

Tallix and Blythe report to Syfaedi, who paraphrases everything for Keybra Elahqua. It's kind of awkward—a four-person relay with tons of redundancy—but it's an interim necessity. The crews need to co-ordinate their efforts, and Keybra needs to settle into his captaincy.

Half the slaves are still in good health. While the remainder need care, only a few are in dire straits. Accordingly, Nyanti and the vokers set up an aid station. Erany, Gyrax, and Ren do their best to help out. They're not as versed in magical healing, but they know enough to make a difference.

Over the course of their care, we find out some of the slaves have ex-perience as sailors. Keybra, however, is still their pick for captain-elect. His ability to communicate, delegate, and supervise (all the stuff that corporate leadership nerds are super keen on) is top notch.

Keybra's guys have two decent mages, but that isn't enough for a sea-voker circle. While some of his crew have arcane potential, it's gonna take a while to bring 'em up to speed. In the meantime, Deybau's vokers will continue in their roles. If worst comes to worst, the *Spiral* can sail without any magic. It's the nautical equivalent of going from a car to a bicycle, but it worked on Earth and it can work on Evermoor.

Once everyone's fed and bandaged, we start preparing for the change of command. Deybau, annoyingly and predictably, is all about the pomp and circumstance. It's probably because he never earned respect, except as a knee-jerk response to his designated rank. Syfaedi, however, is the polar opposite—she could exude authority in any scenario. Hell, you could chain her up in the *Spiral's* dungeon, and she would still come off as a three-mast captain.

An hour before dusk, most of us gather on the *Spiral's* deck (I say *most* because the *Knife* has been assigned a stay-behind crew in case of emergencies.) Syfaedi's humored Deybau with a fresh outfit. There's a couple of changes (bicorne hat, white gloves, and she's replaced her triple brace of pistols with a single flintlock) but she looks pretty much the same. Her sailors follow suit—they're wearing clean garments and tricorne hats.

In sharp contrast, Deybau and his mates are wearing garish costumes. It's easy to spot the nautical influence—coats, hats, neckerchiefs—but the reams of accessories are downright cartoonish. Gold ropes, epaulets, countless rows of medals on their chests...it's funny and sad, but mostly gross.

We assemble on the *Spiral's* deck, leaving room in the center for the formal changeover. Captain Kysaire halts before Deybau, cuing him to flourish an arm and bow deeply at the waist.

Syfaedi responds with the Evermoor greeting: she touches her forehead, then moves her hand a few inches out. "Wind at your back and sun on your brow."

"May your sails run full, may your hull run slick," Deybau declares. "May the tides bring fortune to you and your crew."

His fancy greeting is a little much—sailors clear their throats and hold back chuckles. Syfaedi, however, doesn't break character. "Are you ready to surrender command of the *Spiral?*"

"I am." Deybau presents his sheathed cutlass, balanced atop his open palms.

Syfaedi bows as she receives the weapon. "Any last words before we conclude?"

Deybau pauses...then his face spasms with vicious rage.

Uh-oh.

"What is my crime?" He thrusts a finger at her. "I have merely followed Protectorate law! These debtors are not *sailors!*" As he says the word *sailors,* his voice rises with toxic ridicule. "Once tainted, forever rotten—they're bound to their past and so are you! Just you wait: I shall see you twist at the end of a rope!"

Syfaedi holds the cutlass out to the side. "Captain Elahqua?"

Keybra strides up and accepts the weapon. "Grace and thanks."

"Do not enslave them." Syfaedi turns and searches his eyes. "Open their throats if they force your hand, but don't break faith unless you must. Promise me this and you owe me nothing."

Keybra stares back for a long moment. Finally, he nods in agreement. "Very well. I do not wish to perpetuate cruelty. I would rather that cycle fade and die."

"Exactly." Syfaedi pats his shoulder a single time.

"Tell me," Deybau sneers, "how does it feel to be a wanted felon? These slaves have been promised to lords and ladies! You have threatened their treasure, Kysaire—they will burn your ship and rip you to pieces!"

She dips her chin, chuckling softly through her nose. It comes as a quiet puff, tinged with amusement and weary rue. " 'They.' " She locks eyes with Deybau. " 'They' are a passel of cowardly whelps. They lack the courage to defend their spoils, and send churls like you to do it instead. They vilify us, these supposed nobles, when there is only this difference: they rob the poor under cover of law, while we plunder the rich under protection of our own courage. If you have any sense in that wealth-addled brain, you will roll up your sleeves and serve as a pirate."

" 'Serve as a pirate?' " Deybau scoffs. "Woman, have you lost your Nok-damned *mind?* Look around you—" He swivels angrily in place and spreads his arms, "*—the sea is your prison!* You are doomed to sail as a hunted mark, fleeing the slightest whiff of rule or authority! Perhaps you aren't bound by conscience or virtue, but you are still a captive all the same!"

Syfaedi throws her head back and roars with laughter. "I am sorry, Deybau, your mention of conscience is far too much!" She encompasses the sea with a wave of her arm. "This is not my prison, nor my retreat. This is my *choice,* Deybau. I am a sovereign queen—I have just as much authority to make war on the world, as she who has a thousand ships, and a thousand armies at her beck and call. *That* is what my conscience tells me. But there is no arguing with one such as you: a small-minded brute who snivels and panders, who pins their faith on a low-shadow tyrant."

He tries to respond, but Syfaedi keeps going. "Harry me not with your 'conscience' and 'virtue.' Pair those words with your mechanized heart, and you cheapen them to naught but evanescent ash." She sweeps the deck with a steely gaze, her voice rising with force and conviction. "But we who are present in both flesh and spirit, we are the same in what matters most! Our blood runs hot, our dreams shine bright, and *let no one tell you a damn bit different!*"

There's a hanging moment of pin-drop silence.

Then the deck explodes with raucous cheers. Blythe and his mates try and resist—they look on with wide, unrestrained grins—but give into the energy a moment later, chanting, *"Cap-tain SYF! Cap-tain SYF!"* along with the rest of the cacophonous audience.

In a rare display of unfettered passion, Syfaedi strides in an expansive circle, pointing at individuals and shouting, *"Let no one tell you a damn bit different! That is your truth! That is your RIGHT!"* She spreads her arms and thunders, *"Lyderea has divided us, turned us into a horde of low-shadow brutes! No longer, you hear? No longer! You are free princes—ALL OF YOU!"*

The roar grows to a fever pitch, transforming their chants into a wordless howl.

I wasn't expecting an epic speech, but much to my surprise and utter delight, that's exactly what I'm getting. In my opinion, it's as good as the one from *The Return of the King.* Better, in a way, because she's appealing to their desire to live out their dreams, to enjoy their lives to the absolute fullest. This isn't about sacrifice or protecting what's theirs; it's about their personal reason for being, the basis for their joy and drive to exist.

And that's why I'm cheering right along with them.

25

Unfortunately, speeches are just a part of the equation. There's tons of nuance beneath the glamour, and it's a lot more important than bombastic rhetoric. People get angry when promises fizzle, especially if they've invested emotions and trust.

Syfaedi, however, isn't yet ready to address the particulars. Her first priority is an epic feast. As supplies start moving and chefs start cooking, she buzzes between ships and converses with sailors.

"Well?" Erany prompts. "What do you think?"

"I don't know." I warily scan the cliques of deckhands, clustered together and chatting amiably. "A couple hours back, they were trying to kill each other. Now they're ready to share a meal? Doesn't that strike you as a tad bit strange?"

A casual shrug. "During the Wars, hasty pacts became the norm. When Reft-stricken hordes are climbing your gates, 'tis easy to bury your quibbles and spats."

"So this is a cultural thing?" I ask skeptically. "Sorry, I don't buy it. People are slow to forgive, slower to forget."

"True," she allows. "But don't make light of Syfaedi's presence. She's formulated different options for the *Spiral's* crew, and their articles of agreement are halfway drafted."

"Already? Wow. Easy to see why they elected her captain."

"Mm." Erany stares wistfully at Captain Kysaire. She's busy conversing with Tallix and Keybra. "Easy. Yes."

"Wait." I stiffen in shock. "Are you *attracted* to her?"

A quizzical look. "Aren't you?"

Dissonant thoughts clash and collide—*she's into chicks that is HOT no I'M her boyfriend no one else*—rendering me into a stammering mess. "I...I mean...um..."

" 'Tis a passing fancy, nothing more. Why?" She cocks her head. "Does that steal your peace?"

My brain and mouth remain stuck in neutral. "I...what does...do you..."

She howls in mirth and slaps her thigh. (Great. Now I'm flummoxed by her super-hot laugh.) "Adorable." She reaches out and ruffles my hair. "Quell your worry. I lack the patience to cater to a third."

I a-a-*hem* into my fist. "Yep. Smart. I, too, lack the patience to cater to a th—" Then I break into a round of anxiety-induced coughs.

"Good to know. We share the same vantage." Erany pats my back in bemused consolement.

I pound my chest as I finish coughing. " 'Xactly," I wheeze. "You. Me. Same."

Her lips twitch in an almost-chuckle. "Come." She glances at a hatch leading down to the kitchen. "Our food is ready." Seconds later, calls erupt throughout the ships: *Dinner is served! Dinner is served!* (Man, her half-Elf hearing never ceases to amaze me. She heard the cooks finish several holds down).

Folk consolidate aboard the *Knife,* forming a line across the deck. When the first diner emerges with a loaded plate, the line ripples with heartened murmurs. *Blackwidth flank? Haven't had that in a day and an age!* And: *That's elysium pudding! Gods, it smells just like my nan-ma's!* Also: *Would you look at that bread? Not a single weevil—not a single one!* (That one comes from the *Spiral's* sailors. The *Knife,* thankfully, hasn't been plagued by weevil-infested bread.)

I lean close to Erany and murmur, "A big step up from what we were eating."

"Syfaedi knows this is a delicate juncture. It is to her advantage to bring us together."

"And she's going to do it with a tasty meal?"

Erany shrugs. "I wager she's ready to arbitrate terms, but it will be easier after a hearty dinner."

Gyrax approaches with a Wolven-sized platter. "Look—blackwidth flank!" He holds up a piece of sear-glazed meat, then maows it down with doggish aplomb. *"Mmm!"*

I stifle a laugh. "Beats the hell out of Zig Zag Zoomies, eh?"

"Perhaps, but I am loath to deride such an august establishment. Their puppucinos and barking biscuits..." He stares thoughtfully into the night, prompting me into an involuntary chuckle. "What?" He grins faintly at me.

"When it comes to anything related to food...well, heavy contemplation doesn't begin to describe it."

"Food is my *friend!*" he declares. "And it never fails to please or astonish! You're Nok-damned right I'm going to contemplate its merit!"

That makes me straight-up guffaw. Erany joins in, gracing my ears with her gorgeous peals.

He grins again, patting my shoulder as the line shuffles forward. "Enjoy your dinner." He nods at Erany. "Milady." She returns his nod with a slight curtsy.

Minutes later, we're standing in a lower hold passage. As we bustle through the kitchen, servers pile goodies atop our plates.

Once we emerge, I glance questioningly at Erany. "Where should we eat? Stateroom? Cabin?"

"Topside." She jerks her chin at a nearby ladder.

"Yeah, but the climb..." If I try to go up and spill my noms, I will hate this ladder with all my heart.

She looks pointedly at the floor, which hasn't yet suffered a dinner-related accident. "Not a single soul has dropped their food."

"You don't know ladders," I grumble. "Buncha shifty metal dickheads, waiting to trip you up and ruin your meal."

"Oh for the love of—" she rolls her eyes, exasperated. "Give me your plate." She slices a hand at me, displacing my fingers and stealing my dish. (Holy crap—she just pulled off a yank-the-tablecloth-style magic trick, but it was a thousand times cooler 'cause she did it with her *hand*.)

"Watch." She curves her right instep under the second rung, using it as a hook to pull herself in. At the same time, she braces her left heel on the rung below, straightening her leg and pushing away. The pull of her right leg, combined with the push of her left, allows her to stay upright while holding our plates.

"Ready?"

I suddenly realize what she's about to attempt. "Erany, *don't.* You'll lose your bal—"

She switches her feet in a nimble twitch, hooking the next rung up with her left instep, while bracing one rung below with her right heel. I yelp in alarm, but that doesn't stop her from ascending the ladder. Halfway up, I'm struck by wonder—she's climbing the rungs *with just her legs.*

She hops on the deck and throws me a grin. "Coming?"

I return her grin and shake my head. Legolas Greenleaf, you got nothing on Erany.

In a dumbass attempt to match her grace, I go up the ladder as fast as I can. Even though I'm using my arms, I clunk my leg against the topmost rung. "Ow! *Shit!*" I roll off the ladder onto the deck, grabbing my shin with both hands. *"OW!"*

Erany rolls her eyes again. "My hero."

"You love it." I clamber to my feet, hop-skipping twice. "Don't pretend."

"Would you have me kiss it and make it all better?"

"Nah." I reach out and nab my plate. "Food first, then sexy time."

She places a hand on her cocked-out hip, issuing a challenge through her posture. "You would rather eat than enjoy my kiss?"

My fingers, now clutching a piece of glistening meat, freeze six inches in front of my lips. "Uh…I mean…would you like to…should we…"

Erany laughs. "So easy." She pushes my meat-hand toward my mouth. "Eat, Jon. 'Twas merely a jest."

Like the relieved boyfriend I am, I bite down and chew with gusto. "Yeah, I knew that." (My mouth is full, so it comes out as *Yuh, uh nuh thuh.*) "It was just—"

"A test," she finishes. "I know. You like to test me with your masterful wit."

I swallow and gulp. "That's right. Masterful wit. Gotta keep it sharp."

Erany gives an amused scoff—*such a doof*—and pulls a fork out of her carry.

As the night winds on, we lapse into easy conversation, talking about anything and everything under the sun. It's one of those chats that could go on forever, the kind that sometimes come at the expense of romance. *You spent all night chatting? Why didn't you KISS HER?* But that isn't even remotely an issue, because Erany's mine and I'm hers.

Right now I've got it all: tasty noms, a beautiful girl, and a summer night cruise on a moonlit river. The night is warm, the stars are bright, and the food is delicious.

There's nowhere else I'd rather be.

———

The captains and their mates start making the rounds, picking up plates and passing out cigars. By ordering high-ranking folks to help with the cleanup, Syfaedi's sending a subtle message: *there's a hierarchy in place, but we haven't forgotten that it's here to serve everyone.* She truly considers herself part of the crew. Compare that with Deybau, who believes personal worth is dependent on station...yeah, it's easy to see why they made her the boss.

Lucky for us, we get Syfaedi as our dish picker-upper. She stacks our plates on a wooden cart, then offers us both a fat cigar. "These are from Seldas."

"Grace and thanks." Erany plucks a stogie from Syfaedi's grasp.

"Pretty good politicking." I accept the smoke with a dip of my chin. "Pleasure before business, eh?"

"I am no politician," Syfaedi says irritably. "I am trying to effect a harmonious outcome, that is it and that is all. Now hold your cigar above this bowl."

"Wish be done." I flip it around and offer the cap. She positions her finger an inch away, then slices it down in a neat little arc. Her palm-centered loci briefly gleams, channeling energy through her finger and forming a white-cored crescent with a shining blue rind. It expands, intensifies, then cuts through my stogie with laser-like ease. A moment later, she does the same for Erany's.

I jab the air with the end of my smoke. "Not only are you a great politician, you're the rare person who deserves to be one."

"Careful how you speak," she threatens, "or you'll be the rare person I club with my pistol."

"It would be an honor," I intone with mock graveness, "to be clubbed by a captain as esteemed as yourself."

Syfaedi half-scoffs, half-chuckles, then pushes her cart toward the next group of diners.

Erany draws a mouthful of smoke. Her brow furrows as she explores the flavor. "Mm," she mutters. "Lovely."

I light mine up, coax it with a test-draw, then sample the tobacco with a good-sized puff. Flavor crawls across my palate, engulfing my senses in citrus and pine.

"I could definitely get used to these." I hold it out and admire its length.

"During the Bright Age, there were merchant empires built on tobacco," Erany says. "They fell apart when the Reft arose. Fortunately, legions of artisans came to the fore and crafted cigars of their own volition. Luxuries vanished and hardship reigned, but cigars remained handy throughout the Wars." She exhales steadily, lidding her eyes as the smoke flows thick. "A trivial blessing, mayhap, but I am grateful nonetheless."

"You and me both." I watch as Syfaedi confers with Keybra and Tallix. "I think they're about to start talking business."

"I believe you are right," Erany agrees.

"Some night, huh?" I tap a nubbin of ash into the water. "Epic speech, epic dinner. Now we're capping things off with a badass smoke."

"It's not over yet," Erany says. "There are certain matters that require attention."

I throw her a quizzical glance. "What're you—"

She cuts me off with a sly grin.

"Oh. Right." I cackle knowingly. "I'm ready to go, just say when."

Still smiling, she says, "Finish your cigar."

"Race you!" I draw a mouthful of smoke, blow it all out, then suck in another as fast as I can.

"Dolt," she snickers.

Sorry, not sorry. When my super-hot girlfriend wants to get laid, I'm gonna make good and damn sure that I don't keep her waiting.

26

The next morning, our chefs cook up a giant breakfast. There's different kinds of eggs (I'm partial to scrambled with herby cheese), strips of bacon fried in bacon fat (it coats the meat in a crispy shell, giving it a delicious consistency similar to chicharrones), along with biscuits and buttered-grain porridge (chewier than grits, with a little bit of spice). Its simple stuff, but you can't go wrong with melty cheese, fresh-cooked eggs, and big ol' hunks of tastified carbs. As an added bonus, the sun is out and the breeze is mild.

Erany and I linger by the mizzenmast, picking at our noms and engaging in banter. One by one, the rest of the party saunters over. A couple minutes into our casual chat, Lucky shakes his head in disbelief.

"The *Knife* and the *Spiral*. Once enemies, now friends. Who would have thought?"

"That remains to be seen," Ren cautions. "A temporary peace does not mean friendship."

"It does to me." Lucky shovels eggs into his gob.

"Syfaedi knows what she's doing," Gyrax comments. "Her grasp of the psyche is nigh impeccable."

Erany burps and wipes her lips. "Dinner, leisure, and a solid night's rest. Now, a hearty meal in the warm morning light. She's massaging our spirits, opening our minds to civility and compromise."

Gyrax nods. "Did you happen to see what she did last night?"

Lucky snorts. "She helped with the service, like a low-shadow serf."

"After that." Gyrax scans the party, unperturbed by Lucky's doucheyness.

"She held palaver with Elahqua and the mates," Nyanti says.

"She was clarifying details among the leadership," Erany ventures, "so they can pass organized word to their respective crews."

"Exactly." Gyrax points at her. "Instead of risking a chaotic tumult, she is harmonizing the flow of information."

Lucky scoffs. "A futile effort, for any one soul can tumble her efforts. More folk means greater risk."

"Or, perhaps, they each represent a hidden opportunity," Elier counters.

The thief scoffs again. "Turn your back on subordinate workers, and they will bleed you dry in a low-shadow jiff. Before signing on with Gyrax and company, you and I shared the road. It seems you have forgotten the wisdom that kept us hale."

"I wouldn't call it wisdom, so much as necessity born from lack," Elier replies. "I have changed, Lucky. I shan't view life through a transactional lens."

"Then what sort of lens do you wish to apply?" Lucky tilts his head, clearly amused.

"A perception based on hope and trust. Given the chance, I would like to administer the benefit of the doubt."

The thief guffaws. "Hope? *Trust?* There was a time, Elier, when your cavalry sabers were all that you trusted. Are you telling me now that isn't the case?"

Elier turns to Nyanti, who meets his gaze with a heartfelt smile. "Yes." He turns back to Lucky. "Anyone can change."

"Even Lyderea?" Mockery bleeds into Lucky's tone.

"Even you."

The thief expresses a humorless laugh. "Your wits are in shambles. I feel sorry for you, friend."

"Is there truly such a thing, in the world you inhabit?" Elier asks calmly.

Lucky stiffens. After an awkward silence, he clears his throat. "I am trying to protect you. Don't be—"

"—a fool? By your measure, it is far too late." He looks again at Nyanti and takes her hand.

"You…" Lucky stares at him. "Fah." Then flaps an arm and walks away.

Everyone exchanges a brief glance. *Lucky's a tool, but whatever.*

Once we're done eating, Blythe and Tallix call for everyone to gather on the *Spiral*. Syfaedi takes center stage and announces they've finished drafting the articles of agreement. Her next words evoke a round of mutters: anyone who wishes to serve on the *Spiral*—and that includes former slavers—is welcome to do so. Dissenters can leave as soon as we dock.

"If you have any concerns regarding the articles, refer to First Mates Blythe and Tallix. From now until dinner, they shall frequent the state-room in the third-deck hold, where they will avail themselves to suggestions, opinions, and inquiries. This is your chance to speak on any and all matters pertaining to the *Spiral,* now under the command of Captain Elahqua—"

"Captain Elahqua!" a voice cries derisively. *"HA!"*

The crowd parts, making way for Deybau as he stumbles forward. His hair is plastered to his brow, held in place by sweat and grime. The ties on his shirt are all undone, and his breeches and sleeves are dotted with stains.

"That's rich!" he slurs, waving a flask in haphazard arcs. "A captain! A *captain!* Never, you hear me? *Never!* Once a slave, always a slave!"

"Truly?" Syfaedi folds her hands behind her back (I gotta start doing that; I feel like it boosts her charisma by a couple of points), and strides casually toward him, dipping her chin as if deep in thought. "So there is no hope for those in shackles."

"None!" he brays. "The die is cast! Their fate is sealed!"

Syfaedi stops and meets his gaze. "There is always hope for the lowliest soul. Even one as lowly as you."

Deybau glares, swaying drunkenly back and forth. Then he clears his throat like he's about to hawk a loogie. My gut clenches in sudden dread—this might just end with a bullet in his skull—but much to my relief, he turns sideways and spits on the deck.

Deybau gives her a malicious grin. "You call me lowly. I might as well act like it, eh?"

Syfaedi throws a full-power slap, cracking his jaw with vicious force. Two steps into his backward stumble, she slaps him twice with a back-hand-forehand. As he drops to his butt, his flask slides away and tumbles down a hatch.

"If you choose to act lowly, I shall treat you accordingly," Syfaedi says evenly. "Though new to their duties, Keybra and his folk take pride in this vessel. Defile it again and I shall batter you senseless."

Deybau stares at her, his lower lip quivering in rage. "You...*you...*"

"Show me your heels," she hisses. "Before I give you what you deserve."

He scans the crew, an unspoken question in his eyes: *How are you okay with this?* Once he realizes no one is with him, he sulks to the hatch that swallowed his flask, then disappears into its depths.

"Down to the slave hold," Keybra observes. "Ironic. I was dying to escape, yet he seems to enjoy roaming its breadth."

Former slaves burst into guffaws.

"What?" Keybra looks quizzically from side to side. " 'Tis merely the truth."

Deybau's voice rises up from the hold: *"Low-shadow pack of law-dodging bastards! AAAAARGH!"* setting off another round of laughter. This time, Blythe and his crew join in the mirth.

The writer in me finds it strangely appropriate. When you get past the greed and wrenching agony, the idea of owning someone else is downright absurd.

———

Cliques form aboard the *Spiral*, consisting of sailors who want to discuss the articles of agreement. Syfaedi's crew steers clear of the debate. The other two factions (those who served under Captain Deybau, along with the contingent of former slaves) make their case with passion and ardor. A bunch of them wait impatiently in line, ready to ask questions of Tallix or Keybra.

Our party of seven weaves in and out, listening to sailors converse with gusto. Lucky's the exception; he heads back to the *Knife* and stays in his quarters. (Not gonna lie, I'm kinda relieved. If Lucky chimed in, he might start a riot.) Gyrax, on the other hand, eagerly contributes to the spirited dialogue. As always, his words evoke nods and thoughtful stares.

Much to my surprise, Elier starts engaging with sailors. Erany and I exchange an incredulous glance: *do you see what I'm seeing?* It's a giant departure from his usual indifference. He's asking questions, offering factoids, and elaborating deeply on theories and opinions. I'm not sure if it's because of Gyrax, the slaves, or his connection to Lanctom. Probably all three, if I had to guess.

After lunch, impassioned rants give way to contemplative looks and responses along the lines of, *Good point. Hadn't thought of that.* The evening comes with a different vibe: everyone's ready to decide their fate.

For the most part, Tallix and his crew have signed on with Keybra. The remaining deckhands (about twenty percent) will disembark at Lanctom Downs. I'm shocked by how many have chosen to stay. They were, after all, complicit in tyrannizing Keybra and his folk. Slavery is a new phenomenon here on Evermoor, but still—victims and oppressors have decided to work together, now as equals instead of enemies. It's hard to believe, heartening to see.

Near the end of the proceedings, Deybau makes a brief appearance, flinging his arms wide and screaming, *"Who is with me?"* He thrusts a finger at Captain Elahqua. *"You would bow to a low-shadow Daemos? HE'S NOT EVEN HUMAN!"*

There's a long moment of stunned silence.

Then raucous laughter erupts from the assembly. Apparently, Deybau's statement is completely ridiculous. Seconds later, my brain sparks with a long-ago memory: in seventh grade, I was taught there were Black and White slaves, until the bigwigs used racism to turn them against each other.

One of the sailors yells, "Back in your hole!" The others pile on, heckling Deybau with hisses and jeers. Deybau turns red, hollers unintelligibly, then turns on his heel and heads for a hatch leading down to the slave hold.

His departure elicits puzzled remarks: "There he goes, mucking around in the filthy dark. Afíddi know why...it still smells like a yespid's haunches." And: "At least he's there of his own accord. I was shackled to that deck for two damned weeks."

My writerly brain can't help but wonder: is Deybau trapped in a perceptual jail, or is he truly free in his own mind? He's choosing to stay inside a dungeon, without any coercion whatsoever. That begs the question: am I free right now, or am I confined in a manner I can't yet perceive? Would I even know it if I mentally imprisoned myself, or would I retreat unthinkingly into the hold like Captain Deybau?

As dusk falls, the inevitable distills into a pair of queries:

Did I choose this life? Or did it choose me?

————

We arrive at Lanctom six days later, well after night has taken hold. The town is a bulgy circular peninsula, linked to the mainland through a strip of earth called the Midland Brink. Even though it's dark, I can kind of see where the shore curves in, forming a pair of bays that flank the Brink.

Our ships anchor a quarter mile out. Deybau pitches another fit—he wants to debark *RIGHT NOW, NOK DAMMIT*—but no one listens. There's rum to drink, food to eat, and sex to be had (for me and Erany, at least).

The next morning, we pull into port. Unlike Kessreach, Lanctom is in the middle of a serious growth spurt. Kessreach was defined by an even transformation, graduating from large and crowded to small and diffuse. Lanctom, however, is a slapdash mix of old and new, a clashing swell instead of a smooth-running tide.

The departing sailors are issued a severance, along with letters of reference from Syfaedi and her mates. Deybau is the only one we prevent from debarking immediately, because he'll attract attention with his aristocratic credentials. The former crew will eventually talk, but it'll be a while before they're taken seriously. Accordingly, the captains are readying protective measures. A bunch of the mates are forging identifying documents, and the vokers are changing our arcane insignia.

The *Knife* and the *Spiral* are ditching their old papers (and consequently, their history and endorsements), which will drive up exchange rates and make it hard to get loans. Fortunately, Syfaedi has enough money to smooth things over. The ships will lose out on trade, but they can make up the difference as pirate marauders. That, however, comes with a new set of headaches: more obelisks, more crow's nests (mast-affixed baskets for snipers and lookouts), and a way stronger defensive aegis. During our stay, Syfaedi's going to offload her cargo, refit the *Knife,* and help the *Spiral* do the same.

In the meantime, Elier wants to prepare for the coming offensive.

————

We set off towards Elier's old neighborhood, a district called Aswith Lea. Along the way, he questions the locals about recent developments. We come to find out that Aswith's residences were converted to storage depots.

"This is completely different," the Duelist mutters as we bob and weave through crowded streets. "The Downs were always spare and diffuse." He glances at a tavern called Fellows of Gambol. Its walls are coated in a wrap-around mural, depicting intoxicated hordes of humans and Wildlyre.

Lucky, who's been regarding the storefronts with avid interest, discreetly excuses himself. "I'll meet you at the docks."

"Who are we seeking?" Nyanti asks.

"The Lispsys or Garrants," Elier replies. "Those are the folk who gave me haven."

"They can't be at Aswith," Ren ventures. "Unless they decided to live in a granary."

"Here we are." Erany comes to a stop. "Aswith Lea. Or what remains of it, anyway." Rows of warehouses block our way forward, giving no indication of their residential heritage.

Elier heads for a boxy office, attached to a warehouse off to our right. Gyrax accompanies him as he steps through the door, stopping the rest of us with a lift of his hand. (Good call—that office looks tiny and cramped.)

After a minute, they both emerge. "Almost everyone I know has died or left," Elier says testily. "I have a tenuous lead: the northern edge of the Midland Brink. Supposedly, it is home to folk from days of yore."

As we head for the Brink, the boomtown fades into ramshackle pasture. In between lines of dilapidated shacks, neglected tools speckle the grass. Elier cups his mouth and starts hollering out names.

An elderly man pokes out from a shed. "Who's asking?"

The Duelist stops. "Elier Finn."

The old man approaches and scans our party. "Finn, you say? Elier Finn?"

"Aye," he replies. "You seem familiar. Have we—"

A dagger flashes out and flits toward Elier. The Duelist pivots off-line and presses the man's elbow to his body, gluing his weapon-arm to his ribs. At the same time, Elier draws a saber with a cat-quick swipe, resting its point against the old man's throat.

To everyone's surprise, he cackles with glee. "I taught you that move, you low-shadow snip!"

Recognition dawns in Elier's eyes. "Scaddock? Scaddock Reggels?" His saber droops. "You...you're still..."

"Still alive!" Scaddock crows. "Call me Scads. Haven't been Scaddock in o'er a decade."

"The Lispys? The Garrants? Where have they gone?" Elier sheaths his cavalry saber.

"Couldn't say," Scads rasps. "E'en when you were a waist-high sprout, I lived out here all by my lonesome."

"That you did." He turns to the rest of us. "Scads was my teacher in swordplay and knifework. Without his guidance, I wouldn't have lasted a day in the Taires."

"The Taires…" Scads' eyes widen in shock. "You became a Duelist, just like you wanted! An Arbiter, mayhap?"

Elier shakes his head. "High Taire."

"High Taire," Scads murmurs. "Shaddock's breath! Who would have thought?"

" 'Tis nothing compared to the looming threat. Lyderea plans on assaulting the Downs."

"What for?" Scads scoffs. "Lanctom is booming, but not to the point where the Queen would take notice."

Nyanti fills him in on the yet-to-be-formed, slipworld passage. When he responds with skepticism, she tells him she's an Elerican Witch.

"Hold still," he grouses, "let me have a gander at your aura." Seconds into his magical scrutiny, his wrinkled face goes taut with surprise.

"Deliac's Gleam!" he gasps. "A real-life Wise Woman!"

"Indeed." She touches her brow with her index and middle finger, then brings her hand a few inches out. "Wind at your back and sun on your brow. Tell me, Kai Reggels, how did you ken my Wise Woman sigils? They are only apparent to practicing mages. Or, at the very least, a well-traveled soul with experience and knowledge."

"Used to be part of the Wayfarer Advance," Scads says sheepishly.

Ren gapes. "A Wayfarer? Excepting their captain, I thought they all died at the Battle of Sidehelm!"

Scads looks away. "Not all," he mutters. "I was there, back when I was known as Relegant Syvaelis. I…I broke and ran. Been running ever since."

Ren's face contorts with rage. "Why?" he manages.

"I was scared," he whispers. "But if I knew what awaited us after the Wars…" He draws a shuddering breath. "I was sorely tempted to end my life, but I knew I had reason to wait for the Clear. I just couldn't say what it was." His features harden with resolve. "Now I know—I was meant to aid you against the Queen."

"I welcome your steel." Gyrax gives Ren a meaningful glance. "It is never too late for redemption and grace."

"What of Lanctom's village counsel?" Erany asks. "Will they aid us in our defensive efforts?"

Scads shakes his head. "They are driven to act by coin or treasure. Unless a blade is creasing their necks, they will insist the Queen is in favor of peace."

"But you have seen different," Gyrax prods.

"Aye. During my travels, I beheld what Lyderea wrought throughout Evermoor. She must be stopped, before she strangles our dreams and lays us low."

"If only you had stopped her at Sidehelm Pass." Ren's voice is dripping with sarcasm.

Scads reddens and averts his gaze.

"Ren." Erany shoots him a warning look, then turns back to Scads. "If we wished to enlist the aid of your officials, who would we start with?"

"Thab Sefic," he replies overeagerly, keen to move on from Ren's contempt. "Lanctom's Portmaster. The council is slow to listen, slower to act. As the docks are the crux of Lanctom Downs, Portmaster Thab holds the most sway."

"Thab Sefic," Elier repeats. "Our next destination." He gives Scads a once-over. "Are there any you know who will make a stand? Perhaps a few of your swordplay students?"

He scratches his forehead. "Been a day and an age since I had any students. Still...mebbe the Yaedic boy, or the twin girls who live by the Mire..."

Elier lays a hand on his shoulder. "Spread the word. Gather any folk who are willing to fight."

Scads' face wrinkles with doubt. "But—"

"Without your support, I would have been lost. I still trust you, Wayfarer Syvaelis."

At the mention of his former title, Scads stands a little taller. "I'll do what I can."

Elier pats his shoulder. "And so will we."

———

Over the next three days, we try and meet with Portmaster Sefic. After our seventh attempt, Gyrax bribes a clerk and gains us an audience.

Thab Sefic is plump and bald. He's wearing a festive-yet-formal, silk-woven shirt, embroidered with colorful designs that are vaguely reminiscent of a Persian rug. Its neck descends into a trio of buttons that form a line to his sternum. All are open, revealing an unsightly tuft of ginger chest hair.

"Close the door," he orders. "Six of you, eh? I hope you have coin. If not, you're wasting my time."

Gyrax gives him the Evermoor salute. "Wind at your back and sun on your brow. We have come to warn you, Portmas—"

"Warn me?" he snorts. "Of what?"

"Lyderea intends on taking the Downs. She wishes to—"

Thab brays out laughter. "The Protectorate? *Here?* We pay more than our share in tribute and tax. Your jest is—"

" 'Tis not a jest, Kai Sefic," Elier says urgently. "A slipworld passage will form in Lanctom, a portal that can shuttle armies and hordes. It will be of incalculable value to Lyderea Fairdyle, as she has failed to conquer the Deadlocked Strait."

Thab leans forward and stares at the Duelist. "Do I know you? Kai..."

"Finn. Elier Finn."

"Ah." Thab wags a finger, a mean glint shining in his eye. "I was a lowly peasant in days of yore, when you were a talented blade with a promising future. Remember how you cursed and jeered at us bumpkins? But now that steel hangs off your hips, now that you've friended these low-shadow rakes, you wish to lay claim to our growing wealth?"

"That isn't the case," Elier protests. "I have come to—"

"Away with you." Thab waves a five-ringed hand. "I have no time for ingrates and rogues."

"But—"

"Shall I call for the guard?" He steeples his fingers and leans back in his chair.

Elier drops his eyes and clenches his jaw. "The Lispys, the Garrants..."

"Dead or departed."

"Where?"

"I do not know. I do not care. If that is all..."

A cry of pain sounds from outside. The door bangs open, revealing a short, dark-skinned woman (I'd guess Indo-Pakistani if I was back on Earth) holding a clerk in a painful shoulder lock.

"Do not touch me." She kicks him in the butt and releases the hold.

The clerk stumbles back, clutching his arm. "She's plagued our steps for the last two days, demanding to speak with you! We tried to—"

Thab yells, "Summon the guard! *Now!*"

The clerk scurries off as the newcomer enters. Thab raises his hands in reflexive fear, but she doesn't attack. Instead, she touches her brow and offers a greeting.

"Wind at your back and sun on your brow. My name is—"

"Idinia?" Elier edges into her field of view.

"Idinia Skyfold?"

27

Idinia swivels toward him. "How do you know my—" Her mouth drops open. "Elier? Elier Finn?"

They both pull a foot of steel, then just as quickly raise their hands. He blurts, "I am not here to—" right as she says, "This isn't the right—" They both fall quiet, waiting for the other to speak. A second later, Elier offers an upturned palm. *Go ahead.*

She turns back to Thab. "A slipworld passage is forming in Lanctom, large enough to transit an army. Lyderea will be drawn straight to your—"

He rolls his eyes. "Another lunatic!" A handful of guards appear in the doorway. The Portmaster barks, "Stand by!" evoking assent from his armored goons. "Right." Thab gives us a mistrustful stare. "Depart from this bureau or I'll throw you in gaol."

Elier and Idinia try to speak, but Gyrax interrupts with an open hand. "Perhaps we could rent out a parcel of land."

"Whatever for?" Thab growls.

"Earthworks and bulwarks along the Brink."

"You would make the Downs into a military fortress?" The Portmaster snorts. "Our trade would die in the span of a week!"

" 'Twouldn't be the case," Gyrax replies, "as the bulk of your commerce comes from the river."

"Yes, but—"

"I am willing to pay."

Thab hems and haws. Finally, he says, "Ten thousand regals upon inscription. Five thousand more per following month."

Gyrax nods. "I have the sum in notes and gems. Give me a day to convert them to regals."

"Very well," the Portmaster says reluctantly. "There are several exchanges on Sabbock and Fye. Come back tomorrow an hour before noon. I shall have a contract ready for mark."

Nyanti leans in. "Portmaster Sefic, I am an accomplished mage and an arcane scholar. Believe me when I say that a gateway will—"

"We have mages of our own. None of them have mentioned an arcane gateway." Thab's tone is heavy with exasperation.

"Your wizards are lacking in training or skill. As an Elerican Wise Woman, I assure you that—"

Thab flaps a ring-laden hand. "Come back tomorrow and sign the contract. Let that be the end of this Nok-damned folly."

Nyanti opens her mouth to argue. Gyrax stops her with: "We have what we came for. Let us away."

Once we're outside, Elier and Idinia freeze in their tracks. They regard each other with iffy expressions...then draw their weapons in a quicksilver flash. Elier is wielding his cavalry sabers, while Idinia is brandishing a curved shortsword, complemented by a pair of Batman-like vambraces (tri-bladed armor that covers her forearms).

"Hold!" Gyrax steps between them, hands outstretched. "Observe where you are!"

Folk are watching from nearby storefronts, pressed against windows and peeking out doors. Elier and Idinia both look around, then—slowly, reluctantly—re-sheathe their swords.

"This is ridiculous!" Gyrax exclaims. "It has been a day and an age since last you fought!"

"Our duel was cut short!" Elier argues. "Her weapon snapped and I showed her grace! Fate intervened, but now we are—"

"—united by fate once again," Gyrax finishes. "Do you believe it was just so you could brawl in these streets? Or did she happen upon us for a greater reason?"

Ren gives her a wary look. "How do you know of the slipworld passage?"

"The Volant Oracle," Idinia replies.

"You spoke with the Oracle?" Nyanti asks. "Why?"

The swordswoman grimaces. "For several months, I fought beside rebels at the Deadlocked Strait. It was damn slow going; I realized progress would come in years if not decades. So I struck out on my own and asked the Oracle how I could be of more use."

"Great minds think alike," Erany comments.

"Why would you serve with the Freecast army?" Elier asks. "Aren't you concerned with winning and ranking? You're a High Taire Duelist, so—"

"Arbiter, actually. I was invited to attend a Crossed Blades Council. They conveyed the title onto my person." She pulls down her collar, revealing a tattoo on the side of her neck. It's made of four slashes of intertwining color: blue, green, lilac, and black. A pair of gleams travel their length, deepening the hues wherever they shine. "Here is your proof: the Bladeshimmer Flash. I earned the privilege on last autumn's eve."

His eyes widen in surprise and envy. "I don't know what to..." He shakes his head and regains his composure. "Congratulations, Idinia."

"Is that why you wanted to fight on the spot?" I ask. "Because only an Arbiter can sanction a match?"

"No," she chuckles, embarrassed. "It was simply a reflex."

Elier clears his throat, also embarrassed. "For me as well."

"To record a duel, it requires two or more Arbiters," Idinia explains, "one to document, the other to vouch. As that is the case, recording my own duel would be problematic."

Ren glances back and forth between Idinia and Elier. "Then it seems we are blessed. There are better things to do than spill each other's blood."

Idinia gives Elier a curt nod. "I cede you the win. It is as he says: I have better things to do than uphold tradition."

Elier stiffens. "Forgo our duel? But I...you are asking me to..."

"I know what I'm asking of you. I have asked it of myself."

"You are an Arbiter Duelist!" he protests. "An honor I have yet to claim as my own!"

Nyanti touches his arm. "We have traveled together for over a year. In that time, you could have dueled countless opponents, yet you chose to do otherwise. Elier, we are both driven by greater matters—matters that eclipse our personal fancy."

Elier closes his eyes and takes a breath. "Lanctom. The Downs come first."

"Once I became an Arbiter Duelist, I saw I had been on a fruitless road," Idinia says. "Are we truly designed to wallow in combat?" Her eyes search Elier's. "Struggle needn't define our existence."

He stares past the docks, at the long-flowing blue of the Bysajic River. "As a younger man, I was a selfish ingrate, desperate to prove my worth to the world. Then, as I carved out a niche with my cavalry sabers, I claimed the life I had always wanted. Now..."

"Now you can give back some of your bounty," Gyrax says. "And in so doing, you will reap a fortune that defies scales and ledgers."

Elier turns back to Idinia. "Like you, I wish to defeat Lyderea Fairdyle. There are weapons we seek that will aid our quest."

"Aye?" She tilts her head. "What do you speak of?"

"The Rosecraft Blade on Yom Dagur," Erany says.

"And the Veric Glass in Gracelyn Keep," I add.

Idinia gives me a speculative look. " I know my way through its gutted bowels. Three years back, I served as a guard for a professional treasure-hunter. He led an expedition into the Keep."

"Really?" I perk with excitement. "Did he mention the Glass?"

She shakes her head. "No. Never. What is it? How does it function?"

I sigh in disappointment. "It's a magic mirror. As to what it does, that's kind of complicated. Well...at least you can navigate Gracelyn Keep. Maybe you could help us find it."

"If it will stymie Lyderea, I shall gladly assist," she replies. "An enchanted mirror..." She cups her mouth and studies the ground. "I would start with the treasure hall. After that, I would proceed to the tro-phy chamber, then work my way through the reservoir armories."

"You offer much needed guidance," Gyrax remarks. "Would you care to share travels?"

The Arbiter nods. "I would find the company most welcome."

"Very well," Elier affirms.

"Our crossing seems fated."

28

Gyrax wants to bring Syfaedi up to speed. No one objects, so we start heading back to the *Offset Knife*. Lucky intercepts us on the docks, notably more cheerful than when he left (he must have stolen a ton of stuff).

We come to find out Syfaedi isn't aboard, and that she's probably hanging out at the Perilous Junct. When I ask what that is, Idinia replies it's a well-known tavern.

After a winding series of twists and turns, the Perilous Junct comes into view. Golden light shines from its windows, all of which are open to the warm summer breeze. Beer spills from raised steins, tipsy laughter carries through the night.

As we step inside, Idinia looks at us. "If you describe her person, I can help you search for—"

"There." Ren points at a booth tucked into the corner. Syfaedi's sitting with her back to the wall. First Mate Blythe is sitting across from her.

"Damn," I mutter. "That was fast. Gotta get me some Wayfarer training.

"You're too distractible," Ren says. "It would take a day and an age to sharpen your gaze."

Dick. I make a face and mouth his words back to him. No one notices—they're all moving toward Syfaedi. As Blythe gets up and passes us by, he acknowledges our presence with a Bald Guy grunt.

Syfaedi greets us with a nod, then lasers in on Idinia Skyfold. "A Duelist." She pauses. Then: "A beautiful one, at that."

"Your captain, I presume." Idinia examines her just as thoroughly. "She is quite…"

The rest of us glance back and forth. Are they gonna kill, marry, or—

"I wish to spend time with you," Syfaedi says flatly. A bead of sweat forms on her temple, sending a jolt of astonishment up my spine. I've seen her keep cool in high-seas combat, but Idinia is making her straight-up blush.

The Duelist, however, doesn't seem fazed. "I would be honored by your company." A slight smile tugs at her lips.

"Would you?" A hint of excitement creeps into Syfaedi's voice.

Erany dips her head to hide her smirk. *Adorable.* Syfaedi, never one to misread the room, makes her face go blank and surveys the party. "What ah…why are you here? The rest of you, I mean."

"The same reason as her." Ren, impatient with the meet-cute, gives Idinia a terse nod. "We seek to close the slipworld passage."

Syfaedi's eyes abruptly sharpen. "Is that even possible?"

Nyanti asks, "May we sit?"

"Of course." Syfaedi scoots inward, creating room on either side.

Gyrax nudges Lucky and Elier. "We shall find chairs." The trio depart to grab some stools, then come back a moment later. (Gyrax—massive, kingly, yoked—looks pretty funny on a teeny-tiny stool.)

"You've been mulling the issue." Ren looks at Nyanti. "Have you thought of a solution?"

Nyanti clears her throat. "If we acquired the Rosecraft Blade, I could fashion a ritual around its ontology."

"What about…?" I give Ailura a pointed look, careful not to mention her name.

"No." The Witch shakes her head. "The tides balk at mechanical principles. The Blade, unlike Ailura, is formed from the essence of Saedra ValFae, as well as the children she had with Quare Althaelis. Those entities are bound to the natural elements."

"The right key for this particular lock," Lucky muses.

"Exactly," she affirms. "In theory, I could redirect the tides with the Blade's power, then close the portal after it forms."

" 'In theory.' " Elier loads the phrase with deliberate weight.

"Aye. Slipworld magic is hard to control."

"Can you do it or not?" Ren prods.

"I believe I can. But even if it works, I could be incinerated during the spell."

"Unacceptable," Elier says flatly. "There has to be another way."

"To close the passage?" Nyanti shakes her head again. "Not without Circle SyCajister. And even then, if they didn't have the Blade, they would have to soften the ley lines for over a decade."

Elier's voice rises in protest. "Nyanti—"

"You are willing to die in service of Lanctom. How is this different?"

"You think I'm just going to let you—"

She pulls him close and kisses him deeply.

A few seconds later, Ren clears his throat: a-heh-*hem*. Elier and Nyanti don't seem to mind; their eyes are closed, they're lost in the moment. When they finally separate, Nyanti gives Elier a dreamy smile.

The Duelist blinks in mild shock. "Was...was that an answer?"

The table breaks out in hearty laughter. Ren's the exception. (No surprise there.)

"So," the Wayfarer says impatiently, "it seems we are needed on multiple fronts. We must acquire both the Blade and the Glass, and we must also establish Lanctom's defense."

Syfaedi mutters, "Gracelyn Keep is en route to the Pass...the *Prescient Gauge* is at your disposal."

"The *Prescient Gauge?*" Gyrax raises an eyebrow.

"The *Offset Knife* has been retired. We voted on the change of name."

"A fitting title," he replies. "I am good for the cost of future transport."

"I refuse," Syfaedi says adamantly. "We are fighting for each other's hopes and dreams—the right to pursue our highest desires. Do not cheapen it with talk of commerce."

"It does me glad to hear such grace," Gyrax remarks. "Captain Kysaire, we are deeply indebted to you for—"

"Syf," she interjects. "Call me Syf, unless you are addressing me in front of my crew. Until Lyderea is ousted from rule, I stand with you and your rebel friends."

"As do I." Idinia's gaze slides over to Syf. "I too, am in pursuit of my highest desires."

Syf becomes stock still. Her face turns a couple shades redder.

"Enough," Ren grouses. "Who shall stay and who shall leave?"

"I will stay," Elier declares. "My place is on the frontline border."

"Mine as well," Nyanti states. "The portal must be ringed with complex spells. While the Blade is key, the outcome remains wildly uncertain. I shall stack the odds as much as I can."

"I am with Syf," Idinia says. "I alone have been to Gracelyn."

"I am with Syf as well." Erany looks over at me. "And so is Jon, as he must unearth the Glass from Gracelyn's depths."

Ren says, "I shall sail with you both to—"

"No," Gyrax interrupts. "You and I are needed in Lanctom. Our savvy and skill will be in demand." He turns to Lucky. "I assume you are staying?"

"Aye. I do not care for Sidehelm's wraiths." He glances at me. "Or the bones of a gutted castle."

"Then your contract is amended," Gyrax says, "to include the defense of Lanctom Downs."

Lucky rolls his eyes. "Gyrax, I have no skill in battlefield combat."

"You are proficient in the art of garnering trust. Engage with the folk and curry their favor."

"Easy enough." Lucky shrugs. "But keep in mind I am a thief and a liar. I am ill-suited for heroic endeavors."

"We shall see. I have faith in you, Lucky."

The thief shakes his head. *Hopeless.*

"Then it's settled," Syf looks around at us. "Erany, Jon, Idinia and I will set sail on the *Gauge.* We shall claim the Glass at Gracelyn Keep, continue on to Sidehelm Pass, then debark and summit Yom Dagur. After we acquire the Rosecraft Blade, we shall double back and bolster Lanctom's defense."

"Wish be done," Idinia purrs. "Captain Syfaedi."

Syf ducks her head and mumbles, "As I said before, call me Syf, unless we're in front of the *Gauge's* crew."

Idinia grins. "You may call me Dinny. In front of crew, friends, or in the privacy of your quarters."

Syf bursts into coughs and pounds her chest. "If there is nothing further..." (Nice—I'm not the only who suffers from romance-induced anxiety.)

As everyone rises, Gyrax pulls me off to the side. "Remember: you may lose your way, but you're never off the path."

"Alijyar said that before I left Earth." I give him a wary look. "What aren't you telling me?"

He responds with a chuckle and pats my back. "Nothing. Everything. It only makes sense after you live it."

"What am I going to live, exactly?"

"I'm not sure if it will come to pass, but..." His gaze steadies. "You might have to remember who you are, deep down at your core."

"What does that—"

He raises a hand. "If I explain, you could subconsciously guide yourself into the very circumstance I wish to avoid. And in the end, I am not at all certain—I merely have a nagging suspicion."

"What the *hell?*" I blurt. "So instead of obsessing over what you mean, I'm going to obsess over what I *think* you mean?"

"Listen to what I said, not what I didn't."

"That doesn't help!" I snap.

"Then focus on what brings you joy." He glances at Erany, chatting with Nyanti a few yards away. "You needn't articulate the how and the why, so long as they resonate in your soul. And you needn't justify them to any who judge—you have a right to feel however you feel."

I quote Syfaedi's words on the *Spiral:* " 'Our blood runs hot, our dreams shine bright, and let no one tell you a damn bit different.' "

"Exactly. Be true to yourself, Jon. In certain situations, nothing else will do. I hope you won't encounter any such challenge. At the same time...I believe you are destined to."

"Great," I mumble. "Ominous prophecy-speak, right before I embark on a crucial side-quest."

In an effort to distract myself, I watch as Erany belts out a laugh. To my surprise, it works like a charm and shifts my psyche into moderate optimism.

Right here, right now, she's all that matters. Let the rest of it play out however it has to.

————

The party now consists of me, Erany, Idinia, and Syf. It sucks that we lost our high-level Witch, along with our fount of wisdom and coin (Gyrax) but we still have Syf's considerable wealth, and a better Duelist in the form of Idinia (though I would never say that in front of Elier).

Before we shove off, Syf lets Deybau go, and briefs the crew on our new destinations. Most of 'em don't get the magical bits (slipworld passage, Veric Glass, Rosecraft Blade), but they all understand the overarching gist: we're going to be fighting Lyderea Fairdyle. Accordingly, the *Gauge* holds another vote—anyone who has a problem can cut ties and leave. Everyone decides to stay aboard.

Our first stop is Gracelyn Keep. To get there, we're gonna sail west into the Vallic Sea, drop anchor at Blackvesper Isle, and push inland toward the keep. Once we retrieve the Veric Glass, we'll head down the coast for about a month, then turn east onto the Savilant Rush. That will take us to Sidehelm Pass.

We're three weeks out from the Vallic Sea, and I intend to enjoy those weeks to the absolute fullest. That means chilling with the deckhands, sexy time with Erany, and—surprise, surprise—some occasional lessons from Arisse and her seavokers. They've started to trust me because...well, I'm not sure why, but I think it's my demeanor. The vokers are relaxed and super chill. Even if I'm not like that 24/7, I think they can sense that it's how I'd like to be.

This is incredible. I've learned how to fight, cast Primal Magic, and now I'm dabbling in nautical sorcery.

Who would have thought I could end up here?

———

The Bysajic gradually tapers and narrows, to the point where I can tell it's an actual river. In Lanctom and Kessreach, I couldn't have said it wasn't an ocean, due to its massive width and hefty tide. Now, however, land is visible to our north and south.

Two weeks in, ebony forest appears on the shores. When the wind rushes through, bits of purple flash up from the leaves. Their tops are silky vibrant black, while their bottoms are speckled with lush violet patches. Tim Burton would love the vibe.

Erany loves it too. Long before I spot any trees, she leans against the hull and stares into the distance. Thanks to her half-Elven sight, she can see the vegetation before it registers in my vision.

"The Nightriven Forest. When I was a tot, my family stopped here en route to Sydelian. These woods used to house a thriving community, filled with a variety of shadow-natured folk."

"Like Morteri VySade?"

"He's a Wildfae Kinetic." She shakes her head. "Only partway infused with the essence of shade. Nightriven's dwellers were much more pronounced. Umbredi, Veilistics, Duskfarers..." She registers my puzzlement and explains: "Folk whose lives are structured around darkness."

"Ah. Any humans?"

She shakes her head again. "Umbredi and Veilistics are both humanoid, but their features are comprised of mist and shadow."

"And Duskfarers?"

"They appear as bundles of swirling fog, marked by a pair of glowing yellow eyes."

"Is that how they express themselves?" I ask incredulously. "Through a glowing pair of yellow eyes?"

"Partly. They also speak through bodily vibration." Her gaze turns wistful. "In my earlier years, I wanted to be one—I dressed in pitch-black robes and veiled my face."

"Wait," I chuckle. "You went through a goth phase? Did you wear black lipstick?"

"What's wrong with that?" she snaps. "By your own admittance, you were a hapless dork!"

I raise my hands in surrender. "It's just hard to imagine you all emo and glum."

"Hush," she replies, mock annoyed. "I tire of your prattle."

For the next few minutes, we marvel at the expanse of black vegetation, mottled with scatters of lilac flecks. With every breeze, it's like invisible fingers are combing a sleek growth of hair, revealing long-running streaks of velvety lavender.

Eventually I ask, "What happened?"

"Lyderea." Her eyes search the forest. "Nightriven spurned her edicts and levies. Her forces intruded, then claimed the land as Protectorate ground."

"So the woods are filled with Iaetrix Knights?"

"No." She gives a bitter laugh. "The native folk departed in droves. Once they were gone, there wasn't any reason for the Knights to stay. All that is left are faltering ruins, overtaken by the ebony thicket."

"Maybe it's better that way."

"Maybe."

We lapse into silence, drinking in the magnificent black.

"Hey." I turn towards Erany.

"Mm?" She returns my gaze.

"The bottom of the leaves...it's the same shade as the purple in your eyes."

Erany chuckles, curling a lock of hair behind her ear. "They're completely at odds. Your human sight is stunted and choked."

"That so? Then maybe I need a closer look." I snake an arm around her and pull her close.

My girlfriend gives me an ear-to-ear smile, searching my face with her violet pupils. "See the difference?"

"Nope."

I lean in and kiss her, gently sliding my lips against hers. Screw the leaves. And forgive my old-ass taste in movies, but screw you too, Di-Caprio.

Because right here, right now, I'm the king of the world.

———

The estuary leads into the Jadewisp Breaks, named for the emerald coral on the ocean floor. It grows in parallel lines along the coast, which allows it to break up incoming swells. It's also luminescent. Light from its polyps gleams on the water, marking the surface with sparkling green bands. (Jesus, Evermoor, you visually top yourself *every single time.)*

"See those waves?" Syf points outboard. "If not for the coral, they would drown the forest and push everything inland."

I squint into the distance. "Are they really that—" Before I can say *big,* one of them forms into a towering wall.

Holy. *Shit.*

"It's touching the clouds!" I squeak. "That thing is as big as a god-damn skyscraper!"

Syf cocks her head. "An appropriate name, but we call them 'tall breakers.' "

"We're not going through them, are we?"

"We are," Syfaedi answers. "Gracelyn lies beyond their crest."

I nervously eye the rippling liquid. It's like something you'd see in National Geographic, filmed for an extra-large 3D IMAX. There's a primal immensity to its heft and span, a vastness that echoes for miles and fathoms.

Arisse joins us on the forecastle. "Been a day and an age since we skimmed a breaker."

"Aye." Syf agrees. "Make it fun, will you? I'm trying to impress—" She clears her throat. "I mean...Idinia hasn't seen one, so if you could—"

Arisse gives her a lopsided grin. "Relax, Syf. We'll catch us a view."

"If there is anything else..." Syf glances at us. We all shake our heads. "Very well."

As she heads for her cabin, Erany and I exchange a smile. It doesn't matter if you're a badass pirate—a brand new crush is still pretty cute.

The oncoming wave hits the Jadewisp Breaks, bleeding off mass with each line of coral. At the same time, a new wave forms behind it, and...what the hell? I point ahead, at a handful of figures swimming toward the tsunami.

"Who are they?"

"Merfolk," Arisse says. "They're going to surf the barrel."

"Barrel?" Erany wrinkles her brow.

"Under the right conditions, a breaker will spill over and form into a tunnel."

"Ah. Could we sail in its eye?"

Arisse shakes her head. "They are rife with peril. They would also take us far off-course, as the barrels continue for weeks at a time." She pauses, then adds, "At the height of the Bright Age, intrepid mariners rode their breadth. Now it is the province of merfolk alone."

Erany responds with a thoughtful nod. "I believe I have heard of those sailors of yore. Surgerunners, correct?"

"Aye," Arisse affirms. "They were mostly comprised of retired Wayfarers."

The wave ahead of us crests and foams, churning through a bank of sun-dappled cloud. As it picks up steam and sucks the merfolk in, it crashes into a tube and quickly roars sideways.

"That's amazing," I whisper.

Arisse gives us an inquisitive glance. "Would either of you care to join our circle?"

"You want us to join your seavoker coil?" Erany's voice rises in mild surprise.

Arisse replies with exaggerated patience. "That is what I said, is it not?"

"But we're not vokers...we..." I stammer for a second. "I mean, I've had some lessons, but..."

"You needn't haul wind or pull any current. Just relish our magic as we summit the breaker."

Erany and I exchange a glance. She says, "We would be honored," at the same time I blurt, "Abso*lute*ly!"

"Good." Arisse smiles. "I thought you would agree. Come."

I push my sight into medium Shift, then survey the energy rising off the coil. It's predominantly green, with lithe purple threads woven throughout. Even though it's comprised of two main colors, they encompass dozens of gradients and touches of shadow. (I'll never see ships in the same way again. Without the coil, the *Gauge* would feel like an abandoned Disneyland, bereft of costumes and working rides.)

The vokers are limned in glimmering runes, thicker and viscous near their skin, thinner and fluid on their auric borders. Their outer letters are blending with the coil, exchanging characters and glyphs in a mercurial flux.

Arisse indicates where we should stand. The trigger-spark catalyst (the stone that stores their aegis umbrella) lies directly between us, on my right, on Erany's left. Once we're set, she addresses the other five vokers. *[I have invited these two into our coil. If there are no objections, I will link them to our thalassic web.]*

The mages voice their collective assent.

Arisse looks between me and Erany. *[Try and relax.]* She moves her hands in bird-like flickers, joining tendrils of energy to our loci. My awareness of the ship doubles, triples...

Holy. *Crap.*

I can feel the life beneath our hull, along with the wind in our sails and the power-charged coral. As I reach past the sky and sea, I'm hit by a tingle of fluttering body-high. If I follow that tingle, I might be able to merge with Evermoor's continents, then possibly space and the planets beyond...

Arisse telepathically anchors my psyche. *[Stay with me, Jon. Ship and the sea, nothing more.]*

[Right.] I solidify my presence.

Arisse's lieutenant, a lizard-woman named Sekrish, shouts, *[TALL BREAKER!]*

A blue mountain rolls toward us, inhaling the water directly to our front. As it gains in height with breathtaking speed, its trough gains depth and fills with shadow.

[Faster!] Arisse commands.

The currents form into a smooth-running lane, filling my ears with liquid rush. My arms and legs are the sails and the hull. My lungs are the masts, creaking and straining from wind-flooded cloth. My eyes are the *Gauge's* streamlined prow, focused on the ocean rising before us. Everything narrows into a mental absolute, a single word that defines our existence.

And that word is *forward.*

I lean into the slanting deck, gluing myself down with static magic. The vokers beside me blaze and flash as they funnel more energy into the coil. As the crest of the breaker starts to flatten, I turn and glimpse our majestic surroundings. The clouds are rendered in stunning detail, while the sea-level swells are tiny and distant.

And then we're peaking and leveling out, slicing through a bank of crisp-cold fog. The wide world of Evermoor yawns beneath us, stretching for miles in every direction. In that endless span of ocean blue, I spot our destination: a forested island with a castle in its center.

We coast for one second, two...

WHOOMP.

—then angle down onto the back of the wave. Deckhands echo shouted commands, but they barely register in my adrenalized brain. As we scream down a ramp of sun-glazed water, the spray gives birth to glittering rainbows: parallel stripes, single-color bands, and a concentric series of sparkle-dotted circles. Much to my delight and jaw-dropping awe, the ship punches through them as if they were hyperspace portals. At the same time, furious whitewater churns in our wake, accentuating the storm of heavenly color.

In the midst of all that chaos and beauty, I throw Erany a cheese-eating grin. She meets my gaze and throws it right back. Judging by her elated expression, we're both thinking the exact same thing:

I can't believe we get to see this.

29

The ocean beyond is calm and serene, a jarring foil to our tall breaker ride. I feel like I hopped on the mother of all rollercoasters, immediately rode again on its Adderall-powered sister, then shifted gears into an absurdly calm, elevator-music-accompanied, spa-resort glide. My nerves are still zingy from sensory overload, quivering with the echo of full-body jitters.

Against the picturesque water, Blackvesper Isle (a fog-shrouded mass coated in bare twisty trees) looks starkly out of place. Gracelyn Keep is built on its central hill, but it's barely visible due to the gloom.

As soon as we breach the concentrated fog, we're plunged into a world of quiet murk.

Syfaedi issues a new set of orders. The crew is going to stay aboard. They would detract from our stealth, and they don't provide enough bang for the buck to justify the risk. Meanwhile, the onshore party (Syf, Idinia, Erany, and me) will row to the island and retrieve the Glass.

When I ask about the vokers, Syf tells me they're staying on the *Gauge*. Sailing the breaker weakened the coil, and it's going to take dedicated work to bring it back up to snuff. Also, the vokers aren't good at trekking and fighting. They can whoop ass with heavier magic, but having them along would be like lugging a wrecking ball, instead of moving light and easy with a regular-sized hammer. Syf would rather have the *Gauge* ready to haul ass (in case of pirates or Dwellers or something equally unexpected), instead of having to protect (and risk) any of her mages. Nevertheless, the vokers have found a way to contribute: they've boosted Syf's pistols with complex enchantments. It takes a good deal of power, but everyone agrees it's a sensible compromise.

If we're not back in a week's time, Blythe will become captain and set sail for wherever. Blythe, predictably, isn't happy with this. After haranguing Syf for fifteen minutes, he gets her to agree to a magical signal flare.

"Fine," she snaps. "In a day's time, I will cast a flare."

He crosses his arms and shakes his head. "That's too damned long. Every hour you walk that isle, give us a sign you are—"

Syfaedi speaks evenly and forcefully: *"In a day's time, I will cast a flare."* She stares unblinkingly into his eyes. "You overstep your bounds, First Mate Blythe."

He stares back for a couple seconds, then points at a mate with bright red hair. "Erigar. I want snipers on shift, ready to cover them upon their return. Same with the bombards—draw staggered beads along the beach."

Erigar cedes with a dip of his chin. "Wish be done."

Blythe points at a female Daemos. "Elefi. Assemble a quick-launch team, in case they need a hasty rescue. Ensure that—"

"Belay that order," Syfaedi says curtly.

Blythe ignores her. "—all are good with a pistol and blade. Designate leaders according to experience, but make it clear that—"

"Blythe."

He swivels toward her and roars, *"WHAT?"*

"Aside from the four I have already mentioned, not a single soul will debark the *Gauge.*"

He gets right in her face. "This damnfool plan will—"

"I assent to the snipers and bombardier obelisks. No launches. No rescues."

"Fine!" he snarls. *"Let it be known that I did what I could!"* As he storms away, he glares at Erigar. *"Snipers and obelisks—GET ON IT!"* Erigar mutters his assent and slips out of sight.

Idinia sidles up beside Syfaedi. "I can see why he's cross," she murmurs. "I would be too, if I were deprived of your captainly presence."

Syf clears her throat, abruptly flustered. "Idinia! Ah...may I speak with you in private?"

Idinia's smile grows a couple notches wider. "Of course, Syf."

Syfaedi grabs her arm and pulls her close. "Call me *captain* in front of the others!" she hisses.

"Of course. *Captain.*" Idinia searches her eyes with a bemused grin.

Crew members watch from the corners of their eyes, exchanging smirks as they pretend to keep working. Syfaedi looks around, registers the schoolyard vibe, then turns to the Duelist and sputters, "You...why..." before gripping her elbow again and marching her sternward. "Quarters. *Now.*"

Idinia purrs, "Your wish be done," allowing Syf to drag her along.

Halfway across, Syf glowers at a sailor. "What are you looking at? *Get back to work!*" She flashes a glare to either side. *"All of you!"*

A chorus of "Wish be dones" echoes from the crew, followed by a round of knowing grins. Erany and I are no exception; we both lock eyes and share a chuckle.

"Private quarters?" she asks mischievously.

I grab her wrist and head for our room. "Wish be done."

———

After we sate our raging hormones, we make our way back onto the deck. Syfaedi's already out and about, drifting between sailors and wishing them well. They're not goodbyes with hugs and laughter; it's more like a commander checking in with her troops, asking how they're doing and if they have what they need. Idinia trails Syf, watching her (fling? Girlfriend?) chat with the crew.

Blythe, meanwhile, is performing last-minute checks on our launch canoe. Once Syf is finished, she walks over to her sulky First Mate.

"Blythe."

"Hrrm." He tightens a rope inside the canoe.

"Aegelton."

He stops what he's doing and stares straight ahead. "Captain?"

"While your dithers are flattering, they are entirely unnecessary. I shall return hale and whole, as the day is bright and the night is long."

"You can't be sure."

"I know this is hard, but we all took a vote."

He squares up with Syf. "The vote was to oppose the Nok-damned Queen! Not to face peril all by yourself!"

"There are four in our party. I will not be alone."

"You know what I mean!" he explodes.

She lays a hand on his shoulder. "We cannot engage with piecemeal evil. We must venture forth and address the—"

"Your launch is ready." He turns on his heel and storms away.

She follows Blythe with her gaze, a faint smile playing across her lips. "That's his way of showing affection."

"I've seen his like," Idinia remarks. "Good men, rough manners."

Syf pokes through our launch canoe, giving its contents a brusque once-over. "Water, provisions...we're ready to depart."

A team of four begin working the pulleys, lowering the canoe into the water. Two other sailors unfurl a rope ladder. One by one, we make our way to the launch. Erany grabs the first set of oars, Syfaedi nabs the second.

Syf and Erany begin to row, guiding us through the fog-coated water. Halfway between the ship and the shore, Blythe materializes on the deck. He touches his brow with his middle and forefinger, then moves his hand a few inches out. *May light find you in dark places.*

Syf expresses a satisfied smile. "And may it ease your eyes and guide your feet."

————

Once we're ashore, we turn the canoe upside down. (If it rains while we're gone, our supplies will be covered, and we won't have to deal with a boat full of water.)

Syfaedi checks her triple brace of pistols. Then she asks, "Ready to step off?"

The rest of us nod and voice our agreement. (Damn, her six flint-locks look bad *ass*. Their enchantments appear as translucent machinery—elaborate steampunk with a nautical flair—accompanied by glyphs and arcane designs.)

The sand underfoot is crunchy and dark. Up ahead, the tree line stretches to either side, forming a creepy tangle of leafless branches.

"This a preview for Sidehelm?" I mutter. "I could do without it."

Erany peers into the forest. "A fell development."

"What are you talking about?" I ask.

"You'll see." (I really need to get me some half-Elven vision).

Idinia comments, "When last I was here, I encountered an outpost of Nightriven dwellers—they wished to settle the isle and tame its breadth. Now, however...now it feels lost to the unkempt wild. There." She points at a tree and looks at Erany. "Is that what you saw?"

I zero in on a drippy heart, hanging off the end of a spindly branch. Its glistening surface is covered in tumors, bulging with veins and glabrous white tissue.

"Aye," Erany affirms.

As we approach, my lips part in amazement. "What in the..."

It starts to beat with alarming fury, causing everyone to take a quick step back. A moment later, it lurches, throbs, and abruptly stops. The tumors keep going for a couple of seconds—their rhythm isn't synced to their ailing host.

Erany mutters, "If Nyanti were here, she could shed some light on this cursed eyesore."

"Isn't it a result of the arcane tides?" I venture.

"Everything is, in one way or another. That's not what I meant."

"The nuance of it." Syfaedi's gaze remains fixed on the heart. "She could tease out the nuance of the how and the why."

"Correct."

"Should we cut it down?" Idinia asks.

"Leave it," Syf says. "We are here for the Glass, nothing more."

The cancerous hearts appear with increasing frequency. A half mile in, we're surrounded by a mess of nasty red globs. Man, they smell straight-up *disgusting*—a muggy stench that's similar to an overheated dumpster.

"How much longer until we reach Gracelyn?" Syf asks.

"Two more hours," Idinia replies. "Keep in mind that—"

The wind picks up, swirling the fog and clearing the air. A dozen yards ahead, a ramshackle hut comes into view.

————

"Mind your flanks," Syf hisses. She's already drawn her flintlock and cutlass. "Be ready to fight or break for the—"

"No need." A mass of thick gray mist emerges from the trees. It's got the vague hint of arms and legs, along with a pair of shining yellow eyes.

"Whoa!" I snap Weak Sauce up into high-middle guard.

Erany stands tall. "Quell your worry. 'Tis merely a Duskfarer."

Idinia lowers her shortsword. "Where are your kith?"

The Duskfarer's eyes glimmer and pulse. "Departed or dead. Do I know you, swordswoman? You seem familiar." (Man, her voice is *trippy*. Whenever she speaks, her words echo in a series of whispers.)

"I once accompanied a man from Varr. A mouthy rogue named Pelwick Lonce."

"Ah, I remember you now: the treasure hunter's bodyguard. How does he fare?"

"He breathed his last in a dingy tavern, face down in a bowl of stew."

"A shame," the Duskfarer sighs. "A pleasant enough fellow, when he wasn't raving about riches and jewels."

"He tried to con the Black End Harriers." Idinia shrugs. *Should have known better.* "What is your name, Duskfarer?"

"Veldiri Tysídi. Yours?"

"Idinia Skyfold."

We sheathe our weapons and introduce ourselves. The Duskfarer nods with each of our names, then gives us the fingers-against-the-brow,

Evermoor salute (only she doesn't have fingers, it's more of an indistinct arm tentacle.)

"A pleasure to meet you," Veldiri states. "What do you seek upon this isle?"

"The Veric Glass," Erany replies.

"I do not know it, but I assume it lies in Gracelyn Keep."

"Aye."

"Best cry off," she warns. "The keep is brimming with hordes of kehcraw."

Syfaedi's brow wrinkles in puzzlement. "Kehcraw are harmless."

"These have been changed by the arcane tides."

"How so?"

"They have quintupled in size, grown venomous tails, and their claws are as sharp as whickerwisp knives. Lastly, their shells have turned clear and transparent."

I'm hit by a flash of intuition. It prompts me to nudge Erany and whisper, "Is she talking about crabs? Giant crabs with poisonous stingers?"

"There are similarities in general aesthetic," she whispers back, "but kehcraw possess a dozen legs, linked to their thorax via central stalk. They are also much taller—one or two feet, give or take. From what she is saying, I assume the ones on this isle are as tall as us."

"Creepy," I mutter.

Veldiri stares at the ground and expresses a sigh. "We thought we could reclaim this low-shadow isle, but plague and famine routed our folk. The kehcraw scourge was the last straw."

"Why did you stay when your fellows departed?" Idinia asks.

Veldiri meets her gaze. "Why does anyone stay, when hope has withered and turned to ash?" She starts to drift toward the trees.

"Because they're a fool who can't let go."

———

"We are here for the Glass," Idinia mutters. "To Khel with the beasts and that fell-minded shade."

"If the mutant kehcraw are lacking in wit, I can dim our presence with an occlusive spell," Erany suggests.

"How long will it hold?" Syfaedi asks.

"Given the vibration of rot and decay..." Her brow crinkles in thought. "Three or four hours? Five at the most."

The captain examines Gracelyn Keep. "Once we're inside, cast your spell. Conserve your aura unless it is dire."

"Very well." Erany draws her collapsible bow, then punches it open with a spell-powered shake. "If any kehcraw wander close, I shall pierce their shells with haste and aplomb."

"Not unless they catch wind of our presence," Syfaedi warns.

Cancer-hearted forest, creepy-ass castle, unending hordes of gigantic scorpion-crabs...as I fall back in line, my brain echoes with a singular thought:

I can't wait to get back to the ship.

———

The forest thins, revealing a sloping trail leading up to the keep. A half mile in, Idinia sprints off the path and ducks behind a bush. As we hustle behind nearby shrubs, she points at her eyes with her index and forefinger, then directs a knife-hand toward the castle.

I track her gesture with my eyes. My breath catches in my throat.

Red kehcraw are climbing the stone, coating the righthand wall in skittering bodies. On the opposite side, blue kehcraw are doing the same. They're all emitting a glowing haze, highlighting clusters of shell-coated organs. Some of the kehcraw are stunningly vivid—a blue so deep it's almost hypnotic, or a red so lurid it's almost sexual—but there's plenty of others that are faint or moderate.

"Cacophony echoes from deeper within." Erany dips her chin, focusing on her long-range hearing. "Like a child banging pots and pans, only greater in scale by leaps and bounds."

"Their shells and their claws?" Syfaedi asks.

"Aye. Fighting or mating if I had to guess."

"Doesn't necessarily mean they want to hurt us," I venture.

"Like that one, mayhap?" Idinia points at a red that's scuttling down the trail.

Erany takes a knee and nocks an arrow. "Syf?"

"Hold," she orders. "If you fire, don't use magic. They might be keen to auric flux."

"Understood."

Syfaedi adds, "Give it time to—" It squeals and gnashes its needle-like teeth, evoking a sigh of frustration and defeat.

"Kill it."

Erany's arrow thunks into its eye. The kehcraw jerks, shimmies, then resumes its skitter. Three more arrows twang and soar, nailing three more eyes in rapid succession. The kehcraw twitches with each hit, then abruptly halts and slumps in place. Beneath its segmented, barnacled stalk, its legs relax in a lazy spread.

The four of us stare, wary of any last-minute surprises. As its faint red glow dims and fades, inky fluid unfurls through its torso. In the span of a second, its transparent shell turns completely black.

"Hopefully, magic and blades will be more effective." Idinia mutters.

Syf looks at Erany. "After you weave your spell of concealment, we shall each take turns maintaining the runes."

"That will lead to dirty magic!" Erany argues. "The charm will slacken in vigor and reach!"

"We don't know how long this will take," Syfaedi counters. "Sharing the occlusion will prolong its duration. It will also minimize auric consumption, a good deal more than if we casted four separate spells."

"But—"

"We'll compensate by moving quiet and light."

"I..." Erany sighs. "Very well."

Syfaedi glances at the keep. "I believe now would be appropriate. Before any more detect our presence."

"Wish be done." Erany collapses her bow and mounts it onto her quiver. Luminous spheres encircle her hands, painting them with rings of eye-catching glyphs.

"Erany?" I stare at a blue that's broken from the pack. It's shuffling toward us and squealing excitedly. "Think we've been spotted."

Her construct emits an electronic-sounding *BMMM,* then breaks apart into four swirls of light. Each swirl picks a member of the party, integrating smoothly into our auras.

"There." She warily regards the errant kehcraw. It stops, skitters aimlessly around, then begins to edge back up the hill. "I believe we are safe."

Idinia says, "I shall go next."

"I shall be third." Syfaedi gives me a dubious look. "Can Jon hold the spell?"

"Um..." I rub the back of my neck. "Yeah, I think so."

"I know so." Erany assures. "Trust me—Jon is a capable and competent mage."

"Then it's settled." Syf jerks her head at Gracelyn Keep. "Shall we?"

Idinia resumes walking. By the time we're in front of the shattered gate (it's ragged and splintered, as if a giant fist punched it clean off its hinges) my stomach is taut with fear and dread. It's impossible to ignore the streams of kehcraw, clicking and clacking and scuttling about.

Find the Glass. I exhale slowly. *Then get the hell out of here.*

30

The courtyard is littered with armor and weapons. Bones and claws are sprinkled throughout, spotted with mold and fuzzy green moss. All of that's creepy, but it's not what catches my immediate attention.

The kehcraw. They are *everywhere*.

Half are engaged in lazy conflict. The rest are climbing the walls or sitting in the yard. I can hear them fighting in the dungeons below; their screeches and clacks are faint but distinct.

Idinia presses a finger to her lips—*Shhh*—and leads us into the horde of crustaceans.

Each step is deliberate and measured. Heel. Then toe. Heel. Then toe. Sweat trickles down my cheeks, beading on my chin and dripping to the ground. Meanwhile, the kehcraw continue to lazily tussle, or click-walk along the walls and the floor.

From here on out, I'm done eating crab.

A quarter-way across, Idinia holds up a hand and halts our file. The Duelist glides forward, putting a dozen yards between her and us. She stops, takes a couple steps at regular speed, then stops again.

My heart jumps into redline overdrive. I almost hiss, *What are you DOING?*

It's a redundant question. From her demeanor, I can tell she's stretching out with her senses, trying to determine if she disturbed the kehcraw.

Seconds tick by, racking my nerves with jittery worry.

Whew. None of 'em noticed.

I blow out slowly and get ready to move...then Idinia expresses a quiet *Tsst.* Once again, my body goes taut.

Nothing. The crabs are oblivious.

She says "Greetings," at normal volume.

Once again—nothing.

Awesome. This means we can move at normal spee—

She picks up a pebble and flicks it at a red. It stiffens as the rock bounces off its leg, then it launches into a rabid frenzy. Its scorpion tail pistons and whips, stabbing helter-skelter with its venom-globbed barb. At the same time, its claws twitch and snap at imaginary foes.

After a minute of feverish wrath, it abruptly goes back to being placid and calm.

Idinia beckons to us. We bring it in and huddle together.

"The occlusion will conceal our voices and movement," she whispers. "But stay clear of their shells, or we'll rouse their fury."

Everyone assents with murmurs and nods.

We reach the end of the courtyard and filter into a corridor. (Man, walking normally feels hella good. Painstaking steps are freaking *exhausting.)*

The interior is speckled with mold and debris. Sporadic kehcraw give off light, painting the stone in a trickster glow. They're staring blankly into space with their beady little eye-clusters, as if they were deep in a catatonic trance.

The passage feeds into a vaulted hall, capped by a throne on the other end. It's set atop a three-tier dais, decked in the remains of a patchy red rug. There's huge windows on either side, but someone tried to board them over. I say *tried* because all the boards have been ripped and smashed.

"Careful." Idinia points at a cruddy skeleton lying on the floor. Its limbs have been cranked into cringe-inducing twists.

We mosey around it toward a door, off to the right of the tarnished throne. (Some of these skulls definitely aren't human.) Idinia reaches out and turns the knob, revealing a descending spiral of dimly lit stairs.

"These lead to the treasure room. That's where we'll start."

The stairwell is lined with magical torches, all of which are spotty and weak. The dancing shadows and greasy light, the grungy stone and weathered steps...this feels like the buildup to a gory horror scene.

Idinia halts and raises a fist. "Kehcraw."

The rest of us edge forward, curving around the stairs and coming face to face with a hulking crab-monster. It's limned in a halo of rose-colored light, interrupted by globs of puckered barnacles. Viscous organs shift and pulse, shining through its translucent carapace. Whoa...its heart is visible in the center of its torso, beating once every couple of seconds.

For a moment I'm taken by childlike wonder. If I saw this thing in a documentary, I'd be tempted to study marine biology.

"I might have to kill it," Idinia says casually.

Syf hisses, "Dinny, you don't have to—"

"Shut up," Idinia says in that same casual tone. "Time runs thin."

Syf clams up and readies a pistol.

Idinia slowly approaches the crab. Her left arm is raised as if she was holding a shield, and she's brandishing her short sword in her right.

I think she can squeeze past its flank...

The creature lunges, Idinia parries. Before I can register the clack of her sword, she severs its stinger with her right vambrace. As she circles left in a fluid blur, she flips her sword like a color guard rifle and drives it into the predator's heart.

Blood erupts throughout its torso, flooding it with clouds of inky black. The kehcraw squeals, shudders, and dies with a sigh.

"Not bad," Idinia comments offhandedly. "On my heels."

As I pass the darkening corpse, its claws open and close in reflexive jerks. I really, *really* hope I don't have to fight one.

After a minute, Syf looks at Erany. "Hand me the occlusion."

Erany condenses our spell of concealment, holding it in place between her slow-moving hands. As Syf reaches for the top and bottom, the sphere glows a couple shades brighter. Its runes gyre clockwise, then it breaks into four smoky tendrils that weave back into our auras.

"Good," Syf grunts. "Keep going."

The stairs feed into an underground hall, supported by thirty-foot pillars ringed with kingly-looking statues. Their feet are together, their backs are straight, and their hands are stacked on downturned swords. Their weathered faces are blank and implacable, heavy with age and somber judgment.

Below the statue-kings, there's uneven piles of coins and jewels, spilling from chests turned onto their sides. All throughout the discarded treasure, mobs of kehcraw are grappling and tussling. Weird...the conflict is now color-coded. The battles are exclusively between blues and reds.

"Spread out," Syfaedi orders. "Keen your eyes for the Veric Glass."

"A locator spell might be in order," Erany ventures. "Otherwise, it will take a day and an age to find in this hoard."

"Nyanti never taught me that," I mutter.

"Go by feel," she advises. "You are well-versed in Primal enchantments."

I respond with a shrug. "Might as well try."

"We need to maintain our spell of concealment," Syf advises. "So mind your auras and hold some magic in reserve."

They touch their brows with their index and middle fingers, causing two-inch spheres of yellow-orange light—they each contain runes that resemble a gothicized pi—to materialize directly in front of their foreheads. When they look around or move their heads, the spheres and runes flicker and brighten.

"There." Erany meets my gaze. "Can you fashion a simile?"

I close my eyes and relax my aura. Align my emotions, connect with their essence, let the tension fall away and focus on the result. More importantly, focus on the *feeling* of the result...

"Interesting." Syfaedi's voice pierces my reverie.

I open my eyes and marvel at three violet spheres, circling the space around my head. Each sphere contains a blue question mark. They're dotted at the bottom with wide-open eyeballs, wreathed in halos of light green fire.

I can instantly sense my spell is different. Theirs are more like traditional flashlights, while mine is akin to a trained search dog. It's looking anywhere and everywhere with avid fervor.

"Do you sense anything?" I stare at the end of the chamber. "Because I think I know where we're supposed to go."

The others glance at each other.

"Do you feel any pull?" Erany asks. Syf and Idinia shake their heads. "Neither do I." She lifts an arm. "Lead the way, Jon."

"Feel out to either side," Syf orders. "Just in case his magic is off."

I'm uncomfortably aware of a new kind of pressure: the others are depending on me not to get lost. I never thought I would ever take lead. Yet here I am, blazing a trail through a monster-filled dungeon. At least the kehcraw aren't too crabby (pardon the pun).

As we progress, I survey the jumble of gleaming treasure. It's close to what I envisioned in D&D, only a lot grimier and notably stinky (I forgot how bad metal could smell). Nevertheless, it's still pretty cool. There's weapons buried in heaps of coins, interspersed with mounds of colorful gems.

Once we make it to the end of the hall, Idinia nods at an open doorframe, leading into a curving, descending stairwell.

"There? 'Tis the secondary trophy room."

"Hold on." I close my eyes and quest out with my senses. Doubt and certainty nettle my brain, depending on where I'm aiming my focus.

"I think...yeah." I open my eyes. "Definitely."

Down we go, treading deeper into the castle's guts. I wouldn't be surprised if this place had a soul. It feels like I'm being watched by invisible eyes, tracking me with a pair of unblinking pupils.

We file behind Idinia into the trophy room, then take a moment to scan and assess. The walls are lined with enormous heads. Serpents, eels, fish...they're all gargantuan. Every so often, there's a supersize weapon mounted between them.

"Relics of the Bondigo," Syf remarks.

"Bondigo?" I ask.

"A long-dead race of towering folk," Erany explains. "They stood five times as high as a full-grown man. After the Elder Folk vanished, the Bondigo flourished for several eons."

Idinia jerks her chin, directing my attention to the end of the chamber. "Which path would you have us take?"

There's a door on the left and a door on the right. "Let's keep going. I can't tell from way back here."

"Very well," Idinia says. "On my heels."

The kehcraw are everywhere. Maybe it's just my imagination, but I think they're being a little more vicious than—

"Whoa!" I jerk back as a red stings a blue. At the same time, it crunches down with serrated claws, cracking through shell and ripping up organs. Screams erupt from the dying kehcraw, assaulting my ears with high-pitched whistles.

The rose-colored killer doesn't stop; it sucks fluid-coated chunks into its needle-toothed mouth. As it vacuums up its buddy, it expresses a hiss-moan of undisguised pleasure.

"Uh...guys?" My eyes tick back and forth.

"There's another." Idinia points at a blue eating a red.

"This is what we heard while crossing the courtyard," Syf observes. "Jon?"

I force myself to concentrate on the doors. "Um...the one on the left."

"That one leads to the castle well," Idinia says doubtfully. "Are you sure? The other one leads to the reservoir armories."

My attention flicks between the doors, testing them both with magical scrutiny. Door number one is the clear winner.

"Yep. I'm sure."

"Very well." Idinia turns to Syf. "Pass the occlusion. I shall maintain our enchanted concealment."

Syf condenses the charm into a ball. Idinia takes it and re-expands it into our auras. "Ready?" she asks.

We all assent and resume our trek. As we pass by groups of feasting kehcraw, I shiver with revulsion. Thankfully, none of them notice as we enter stairwell number three.

The further down we go, the more it smells like mold and decay. I swear the air has an actual *taste.* It's thick and heavy, like that fuzziness you get when you don't brush your teeth. Only this isn't restricted to just my teeth, it's my entire body. Skin, mouth, nose, eyes...

The stairs open into an expansive chamber, defined by a giant stone circle built into its center. That would be the well. Scores of ropes protrude from its maw, leading into a vertical tunnel that distributes the water. Clusters of buckets are hanging from the lines. Just like the ropes, they're broken and shredded. Their wood is black with age-old rot, their metal bands are green with tarnish.

The kehcraw are entering through holes in the walls. The red ones are coming from a gash on the right, the blue ones are coming from a breach on the left. Once they make it to the well's circular platform (it adds a hundred-plus yards in surrounding diameter), they start gnashing and stabbing with unabashed fury.

Interesting...the conflict is no longer color-coded. They're killing each other without discrimination. And for some weird reason, they're all circling clockwise.

You'd think with an endless supply of dying kehcraw, they'd pile up and block any path to the well. There's a gruesome reason why that isn't the case: as soon as they die, a bunch of their peers hoover up everything—and I mean *everything*—into their needle-toothed mouths.

The locator spell grabs hold of my eyes, directing them onto a goldlink necklace levitating above the well. Its centerpiece is round, maybe six inches across. I can't see into it—there's a dust cover cinched around its surface.

"That's it," I breathe. "The Veric Glass."

"**A**re you certain?" Syf asks.

"Yep. This is like when I healed Nyanti."

"When you healed Nyanti..." Erany's eyes widen in awe. "You mean Laiddinic?"

I respond with a nod. "It's giving off this absolute *rightness*—saturating every thought and hint of feeling."

Idinia and Syf exchange a glance. *Is he for real?*

"Laiddinic powers..." Syf trails off, then cedes with a shrug. "I knew you were the Traveler, but it is one thing to hear it, another to trust it with life and limb."

"No worries," I assure. "You're preaching to the choir. Okay, how do we get it? Erany, you're the best mage here. What do you think?"

Her brow furrows. "It doesn't appear in my auric perception. Syf? Idinia? Has it dawned in your register?"

Syf and Idinia shake their heads.

"Wait a sec..." I search their faces with an incredulous gaze. "Are you *serious?* It's the magic equivalent of a nuclear bomb!"

"I suspect you are sensing it through Laiddinic means," Erany replies. "If the Glass is as strong as we've been led to believe, it may exceed the reach of magic and matter."

"How do we proceed?" Syf prompts.

As soon as she says *proceed,* an invisible hook yanks me forward. Erany grabs my left arm, sparing me from a bone-snapping, fifty-foot plunge. "Jon!"

"*Whoa!*" I teeter precariously, then lurch back from the edge of the stairs. "Whoa." I blow out hard and take a moment to compose myself. "This may sound weird, but I think I can pull it toward me. It just pulled me, so..."

"Can you do it from here?" Syf asks.

"Good question." I extend my hands and flex my will. The Glass twitches and lurches...then white-hot pain erupts in my skull.

"AH!" I drop to a knee and clutch my brow.

Erany crouches beside me. "Jon? *Jon?*"

"I'm fine," I mutter. "I have to get closer, I think."

"You think?" Syfaedi presses. "Or you know?"

My girlfriend helps me push to my feet. "Can't say. I've never mind-yanked an enchanted mirror."

Erany studies the warring crustaceans. "Our spell of concealment will likely fail, given their focus on murder and wrath. However..." She chews her lip. "These creatures operate off the basest of energies. Mayhap their fury could serve as a distraction."

"What does that mean?" Idinia asks.

"I believe I can whip them into a frenzy, so they are utterly preoccupied with killing one another. Hopefully, we can sneak by unnoticed while they are fighting."

" 'Hopefully?' " I scoff in disbelief. "Can you do any better than 'hopefully?' "

"Not in this case."

"Then hasten your aura and cast your spell." Syf eyes the whirl of vicious monsters. "I wish to be free of this cursed isle."

———

Erany begins chanting, moving her arms in smooth-running waves. As her magic thickens into byzantine patterns, it expands and settles on the murderous kehcraw.

A second later, they start to lag. Every so often they falter and hesitate, as if they had just forgotten something important.

Huh. I thought they were about to go buck-nuts crazy. But hey, maybe the spell will calm them down. I much prefer that over—

Suddenly, they start gnashing and stabbing with twice the rage.

Damn it.

Idinia catches our attention with a jerk of her chin. "Be ready to move at a moment's notice. If they pull or trip us, we must drag the imperiled back into file."

"Think it's time for Ailura Qartesi." I reach for my gun, but Erany places a hand on mine.

"Her presence might alert them. Also, keep both hands free. You might need them to summon the Glass."

"All right." I sweep the air with an upturned palm. "After you, ladies."

Down we go. As soon as Idinia breaches the horde, the frenzy around us ratchets up.

The Duelist halts and tenses in place. "Erany?"

"My spell is holding," Erany replies.

Idinia resumes walking, sword at the ready. Her gaze tracks evenly from side to side, processing input from every direction. A few yards right, one of the blues falls to a red. Off to my left, a bunch of them crowd a fresh-slain corpse. Fluid splashes my cheeks and neck. Warmth spatters my fingers and hands. Pretty soon, the four of us are speckled in crab-monster juices, dotted with innards and fragments of shell.

"Jon?" Idinia prompts. "Can you fetch the Glass from where you stand?"

"Trying," I reply. "We need to get closer."

"Very well."

The mirror looms heavy in my mind, filling my brain with its weighty presence. As I coax it with my intention and will, it moves back and forth on its levitative perch. Back on the stairs, it resisted my pull with obstinate strength. Now, there's an elastic quality to its retreat and advance.

When we finally reach the lip of the well, Idinia grabs my shoulders, places me against the rock, then gestures for the others to guard against kehcraw. The crabs are radiating frenzy and hate, triggering something deep in my psyche. An ancient part of me—my vicious lizard-brain—is resonating with their unthinking bloodlust.

Idinia, center blade in the three-sword perimeter, addresses me calmly from over her shoulder. "Let us know if you require assistance."

"Will do."

The Glass resembles an overlarge medallion, covered by a plain brown cloth. Despite its seemingly innocuous appearance, the energy pouring off it is undeniable. After a moment, I realize the word *energy* doesn't do it justice. Energy requires a low and a high, an absence and presence to give it definition. Whatever's up there is beyond duality. It simply *is*, in serene defiance of comparative measures.

I extend my hands, close my eyes, and reach for the Glass with my intention. Even though it's fast asleep, I can feel its awareness at a soul-deep level. I thought holding Ailura was peak surety, but this is so much stronger it's almost laughable. In the face of this much certainty, the idea of free will is almost a joke.

Nice...I can feel it drifting towards my fingers...

The backs of my lids light with color, fractalizing into a languid rhythm. As I'm deluged by their ebb and flow, I lose track of time and wallow in the moment...and then I'm holding the Veric Glass, draping it shakily around my neck. I'm taken by a fit of blinks and shudders. For a wobbly moment, I have to focus on regaining my sense of self.

"Jon?" Idinia whispers. "Are you ready to leave?"

"Yeah," I whisper back. "But why are we whisperi—"

Then it hits me: the kehcraw have stopped. They've all fallen silent.

Idinia starts walking. "On my heels."

We reform our line and inch past the crabs. Every one of them swivels in place, tracking us with legions of beady little eye clusters.

"Guys?" I whisper. "Do you think we—"

"*Shh,*" Idinia hisses.

I desperately want to draw Ailura, but I don't want to risk setting them off. The others are the same—they're holding their swords as still as they can.

Then I hear it: *Click-clack.*

Perspiration stings my eye, forcing me to swallow a vehement curse. Half my vision just went kaput.

Clackety click.

They're moving. Not much, but—

Clickety clack. Click click click.

"The diversionary spell," Idinia whispers. "Erany?"

"Still holding. For some reason, they're drawn to the Glass."

"Clearly. Keep going."

The clicking picks up, steadily increasing in strength and frequency. We're almost to the stairs. If we can—

Suddenly, one of them lunges at Idinia's flank. She severs its claw with a backhanded swipe, then butchers it with strikes from her bladed vambraces. As inky black pours through its torso, it slumps in place and relaxes its legs.

Everyone freezes.

My dilated pupils shift left and right. The kehcraw are watching with expressionless stares.

"Very well." Idinia circles her sword back into guard. "It was just the one. Don't make any sudd—"

Angry squeals pierce the air.

"RUN!"

32

I snap-draw Ailura and start blasting away. In between shots, I fan her hammer like a cowboy gunslinger.

Giant rays pour from her barrel, flooded with chains of fantastical glyphs. The blaze washes over dozens of crabs—they're briefly transformed into glaring silhouettes—then entire lines of them explode and vaporize, misting the air with fragments and gore. Whenever a round hits a wall, it vanishes into a roil of harmless light. Ailura's ensuring we won't be crushed; she's adjusting so the castle doesn't come down on our heads.

Whoa. My gun is *evolving.*

[Jon!] Ailura yells into my mind. *[Dip me to your belt!]*

I try and obey, but a stinger arcs in toward my face. I draw Weak Sauce and parry the barb; my fingers zing with jarring force. A loud **FSSSH** sounds from behind me, evoking a screech from my kehcraw assailant. As it crumples into bloody, magic-scored fissures, I'm hit by a wave of cognitive dissonance—what the hell was *that?* Then I realize it was Syf's enchanted flintlock.

The round doesn't stop at just one crab—it keeps zipping forward, searing the air with laser-blue fire. Her discharge kills a second crab, ricochets off a wall, then hits a third and sets it ablaze. The flames are as bright as a magnesium flare; they incinerate the kehcraw in less than a second.

Nice. That gives me time to lower Ailura and—

[Relax your control!]

—she takes charge of my gun-hand. I dump the casings with a flick of my wrist, then my bottom two fingers hook the grip. The others pop the wheel and shuttle rounds from my belt into the chambers. I'm struck by a flash of panic-threaded awe—*my fingers are moving with stage-magic speed. It would take me a decade to learn how to do this.*

Syf yells, *"Our front, Jon! SHOOT THEM!"*

Ailura fires three more shots—***CHOOM CHOOM CHOOM***—ruffling my hair with gusts of feedback. I jerk right, parry a claw, then ravage our foes with three more bullets.

[Jon! Again!]

I dump the casings, lower the gun, and flick rounds from my belt into her chambers. The wheel snaps shut, a gleam runs up Ailura, then she leaps into action with six more shots. Blackened body parts fly and whirl, engulfing me in char, ozone, and the briny-sweet smell of roasted crustacean.

As I dodge a claw and reload Ailura, Erany runs a few yards past me and screams, *"OUT OF THE WAY!"* while cocking her sword like a one-handed golf club. Her aura flares with runic power—it flows up her torso, into her arm, and imbues her weapon with jade-fire light—then she swings her blade in a rising chop.

Emerald waves jet off its edge, flying up the steps and scorching assailants. In the blink of an eye, the staircase turns into a kehcraw graveyard, glowing with charry-embered corpses and sullen red flames. Most of them die and gutter out, a few cling to the mold and the moss.

Halfway up, my ears pop and suddenly clear. I didn't notice the change in pressure, Erany's spell was strong as *fu*—

Idinia flies into the Bondigo trophy room. *"Kehcraw!"* A loud ***FSSSH*** sounds from behind me, another one of Syf's enchanted flintlocks. As she follows up with a slice from her cutlass, I pile in behind Erany and decimate kehcraw, surfing the recoil from left to right.

"Keep going!" the Duelist yells.

Thankfully, there aren't as many crabs to our front. That isn't gonna last—the ones from below are hot on our heels.

"Jon, mind the van!" Syfaedi screams. *"We'll take the flanks!"* Syf and Erany push out to either side, creating space to my left and right.

"Got it!" I snap Weak Sauce back into his sheath. If the others are gonna brawl, I need to focus on leveraging my range.

The majority of kehcraw are coming from the well, so I swivel in place and blast them apart. Pop the wheel, dump the casings, and snatch up six more bullets. Without intending to, I pull off an impressive feat of prestidigitation: I flick my right hand open, *throwing* the bullets into their chambers. The wheel spins closed and I'm right back at it, murdering crabs with rune-limned force.

"Sorry!" I yell. *"I know you said to watch our front, but—"*

Syf ducks a claw and severs a leg. *"Just make sure we can keep moving forward!"*

"Yep!"

As we dash up the stairs, kehcraw boil toward our rear. Syf reaches in her tailcoat, produces a dark iron ball, and lights its fuse with an auric flicker. (She has grenades? *What?*)

"Cover your ears, open your mouth!" She chucks the explosive down the steps.

The fuse hisses loudly as the bomb clunks once, twice—

BOOM!

Combustive pressure surges past me, roasting my lungs with suffocating heat. As I blink away runnels of smoke-infused tears, Idinia leads us into the treasure hall. We frantically rip through a mob of crabs, then pour into the next flight of stairs.

Halfway up, a glimmer of hope dawns in my mind. *I think we can make it.*

Four of them rush our quick-moving front. Idinia turns into a bladed dervish, killing them all with brutal efficiency. She looks like a hellish D&D serial killer, layered in flesh and chitin-flecked slop.

As soon as we bust into Gracelyn's courtyard, kehcraw swarm us from every direction. My companions surround me in a moving triangle, allowing me to shoot without worrying about blocking or dodging.

Now that Syf is in my field of view, I get to see her pistols in action. Whenever she fires, their sheath of steampunk spells whir and connect, triggering a nifty series of spark-boosted couplings. A moment later, they project a bright web of glyphs before cutting loose with devastating ordnance. Each shot obliterates three or four crabs. Most of them die from concussive implosions, while the third or fourth—whichever is last in the ruinous sequence—is consumed by a flash of ultra-hot flames. Her pistols aren't as strong as Ailura, but their energetic artistry is absolutely stunning.

Once we clear the shattered gate, our kehcraw pursuers abruptly lose focus and start milling about. A few of them charge—Erany and Syf dispatch them with ease—but the majority have lost their psychotic murder-boners.

"Keep going," Syf gasps.

We downshift into a rough trot. Three faires in, Syf calls for a halt. "Face outward," she pants. "Stay keen."

I suddenly realize I have twelve rounds left: six in my gun, six in my belt. As we transition into a fast walk, I reach in my carry, pull out rounds, and start pushing them into my empty belt loops. Unlike before, when Ailura turned my hands into precision machines, my fingers now feel dumb and clumsy. To make matters worse, I'm hit by a case of full-body shivers—it's a visceral reaction to the change in pace.

Branch-grown hearts begin appearing on the trees. When I first saw 'em, I couldn't stop staring. Now, they're a distant afterthought. My focus pings between keeping up, reloading my belt, and turning in a circle to check on our rear.

"Kehcraw." Idinia points at a red, partially concealed by a snarl of branches.

"More up ahead," Erany says tersely.

Syf gestures with her flintlock. "There's another." A sky-blue crab is holding position, tracking us with its pitiless, deadpan eye-clusters.

"Don't sprint." Idinia shifts into a light jog. "Save your breath for the actual rush."

Groups of kehcraw are forming around us, flanking us with pincers and transparent shells. Bioluminescence pours off their torsos, bathing the trees in a muddle of light.

Directly ahead, a slim gap divides the woods, offering a tantalizing glimpse of sandy beach.

"Almost there," Idinia says.

Christ, they're *climbing on top of each other.* At first they tumble and spill to the ground. Then, as their numbers increase, they gain enough purchase to pile up and stack.

"Almost there," Idinia repeats.

I can see the *Gauge* on the foggy swells. All we have to do is get to the canoe, and—

The crabs to our front close the gap.

Idinia screams, *"RUN!"*

An ocean of shells boil toward us. I blast away with Ailura Qartesi, opening lanes to our front and our sides. Trees and kehcraw flatten and vanish, reduced to strips of smoking dirt.

"Swords are nice, but we could really use magic!" I yell.

"Can't!" Erany yells back. *"Spent it on concealment and locator spells!"*

Syf chucks another iron ball. My heart lifts as it explodes and roars. It sinks just as fast when she shouts, *"Last one!"*

I lower my gun, unlock the wheel, and flick more bullets into her chambers. I knew the others were low on aura, but I didn't realize they were magically exhausted. As far as artillery, it's down to me and Ailura.

Un*less...*

I mentally withdraw, giving Ailura control of my body. The sentient weapon is happy to comply. She ripples into my limbs and nerves, flooding me with a rush of energized certainty.

Focus, Jon, focus. All you need is a little distraction, some way to slow them down. There's an opportunity here, isn't there? Of course there is—existence is filled with infinite possibilities. You just have to open your mind and direct your emotions, let them flow through your loci and out your meridians...

As Ailura finishes shooting beneath my right elbow, my right hand contorts in an elegant twist. A foot in front of my sweat-soaked chest, a cobalt glyph materializes in the air.

I throw my arms in a backhand slash, chucking the spell as hard as I can. It uncoils and surges into the forest, causing trunks and branches to glow and shine. The trees immediately come to life, elongating and grabbing dozens of kehcraw. I take advantage of the break by snap-loading Ailura, then blowing apart the crabs between us and the launch.

"MOVE!" Idinia hustles out of the woods.

The air on the beach is expansive and fresh, charged with the promise of imminent safety. Then buried crabs erupt from the sand, turning my hope into gut-clenching panic.

" *'Ware your flanks!"* Syf shouts. She annihilates four with her last pistol. *"They're hiding in the ground!"*

"I'll right the launch!" Idinia sprints toward our downturned canoe.

A dozen yards in, the crack of muskets rattles my ears. I'm thrown for a moment—is someone shooting at us?—then I realize it's the snipers on the *Gauge*. As kehcraw burst from their sandy hides, their bodies spark with iron shot. Half of it fails to pierce their shells, but still—it's ridiculously awesome to get outside help.

"Bombardier obelisks!" Erany yells, directing my attention toward the water.

The *Gauge's* flank glows and brightens, then expels a salvo of naval artillery. I fight the urge to cower as it scorches overhead, eclipsing the sun with breathtaking glare.

The earth behind us erupts with soil, intermingled with bits of atomized kehcraw. Three shots skip off the beach, searing the deck before continuing onward. Two of them ravage the gloomy forest, bulldozing swaths of fog-wreathed trees. The third crashes into Gracelyn Keep, obliterating a parapet and a big chunk of wall.

The *Gauge's* snipers pick up the tempo, harrying crabs with a crackle of shots. Idinia sheathes her sword and grabs hold of the canoe. Before she can right it, Syf pulls her to the deck. A second later, Erany yanks me to the ground.

"INCOMING!"

The ground quakes, the beach explodes. Debris comes down in a choppy rattle, pelting my skin and coating my hair. I cough reflexively as it slips in my throat, then force my eyes open and scan the beach. In between the shattered corpses, patches of seaweed are steaming and hissing. A few are ablaze with reluctant flames.

"Erany! Jon! In the canoe!" Syf yells.

We both hop in. Syf and Idinia push the boat, sloshing us into calf-deep water. Hot damn, we're almost—

The ocean explodes with frothy churn, resolving into a quartet of murderous kehcraw. Ailura fires twice, taking out the leftmost pair with laser-thin beams. Before I can shoot the pair on my right, they lunge forward in scary-fast twitches. A stinger pierces Idinia's thigh, a pincer encircles Syfaedi's torso. They both scream in pain—there's a nasty *CR-CR-CRACK* as Syf's ribs give way—then I dispatch their attackers with two more shots.

"Jon, stand guard!" Erany hauls Syf and Idinia into the launch. "Keep them at bay!" She grabs the oars and starts to row.

"Got it!"

The *Gauge's* obelisks fire again, re-clearing the devastated beach. It was never much to look at, but now it's littered with broken shells and smoldering craters. The forest is the same—it's lined with scores of giant bare patches, riddled with embers and coated in smog.

After we make it past the surf, I swing around and check on our wounded. Idinia's cutting the fabric off her leg. Syf is clutching her chest and breathing in gasps.

"Jon." Erany jerks her chin at the other set of paddles. "Help me row."

"Yep. Sure." I holster Ailura and start working the oars.

Idinia groans and collapses on her side. Her leg wound is now a fist-sized pit, agleam with a crust of lurid green pus. Black lines are creeping out from its edges, thick white boils are forming in their wake.

"Dinny…" Syf reaches for her, then retracts her hand and hisses in pain.

"*Don't,*" Erany warns. "One of your ribs might pierce a lung."

The obelisks hurl another salvo, wracking the beach with riotous thunder. A dozen kehcraw wade into the tide, but the *Gauge's* snipers make short work of them.

"Almost there," Erany says tightly.

As soon as we breach the *Gauge's* shadow, Blythe yells, "Stay in the boat!" and orders his sailors to throw lines in the water. Thankfully, we don't have to tie them; the vokers magically fasten them onto our grommets.

Syf's eyes flutter open. "We might strain the launch. We need to climb out before they pull it aboard."

I look up at Blythe and yell, "She says we need to climb out before—"

"*TELL HER TO SHUT UP!*" he roars.

Syf mumbles under her breath, then closes her eyes and trails off. Idinia passed out a few seconds back.

My gaze drops to her twitching fingers. Inky trails are crawling down her wrists, accented by clusters of glistening boils.

The crew swings us inboard onto the deck. Arisse and a voker—the lizard-woman named Sekrish—huddle over Syf and Idinia, accompanied by a gaggle of anxious sailors.

"Give us space," Arisse snaps. "Back to your posts."

The other vokers try and help, but Arisse tells them to work the coil. Anchors rise, canvas billows, and—after one last round of obelisk fire—the *Gauge* begins to pick up speed.

"Arisse, I can help," I insist.

"No." She's crouched over Syf, engaged in auric whack-a-mole. Every time she aligns a meridian, it snaps out of place or a loci begins dimming. A couple feet away, Sekrish is doing the same for Idinia.

I step forward. "I'm telling you, I'm—"

"*No*, Jon! You don't have the skill!" Without looking up, Arisse asks, "Erany, can you assist with the mend?"

She shakes her head. "My aura is down to the dregs and scraps. But Jon isn't lying when he says he can—"

"Thank you," Arisse says tightly. "That will be all."

"But—"

"That will be all."

A voker on the coil shouts, "Arisse! We need you in circle!"

"Not now!" she roars. *"Can't you see I'm—"*

"Protectorate craft!"

"What?" She stares at four big ships as they cut around the isle. "Why in Khel are they sailing en masse? They're going to rouse a Nok-damned serpent!"

A second later, Blythe yells, "BEAT TO QUARTERS!" triggering a storm of frantic activity.

Arisse curses and gets to her feet.

"Syf and Idinia are nearing the Clear," Sekrish warns.

"We don't have a choice!" Arisse rages. "Those are heavy frigates! If any serpents are drawn by their presence—"

"They've already roused." Erany points at a mob of long-running shadows, swimming briskly towards the frigates. The vessels responds with rune-laden spheres, causing the serpents to break left and right.

"I thought they didn't have enough mages to protect their ships." My eyes tick back and forth across the frigates.

"They don't," Erany replies. "Not all of them. These have been tasked with a specific mission."

"What do you mean? What could—"

A spell-boosted voice booms from the frigates: **"BY ORDER OF THE QUEEN, YOU WILL SUBMIT TO A SEARCH FOR**

CRIMINAL ACTIVITY! DOFF YOUR WIND AND PREPARE TO BE BOARDED!"

"Pirate hunters," I whisper.

Arisse grabs my shoulder. "Heal our wounded."

"Got it," I reply. "I'll do my best."

"I don't care about that," she hisses. *"Heal them."* Before I can answer, she runs into the coil.

"I shall assist." Erany meets my eyes. "I can monitor your aura and give you advice."

I nod curtly and take a knee, looking back and forth between Syf and Idinia. "Relax," Erany urges. "Open your senses. Take stock of their plight."

I close my eyes. Measured inhale, controlled exhale. Back in Elerica, I healed Nyanti after she was in the magical equivalent of a high-speed crash. Same thing here, only I gotta do it for two different people.

I open my eyes and stretch out with my Shift. Their meridians are snarled into toxic knots, but it's not a result of the kehcraw attack—not directly, anyway.

[It's because of their perception.] Erany explains telepathically. *[Their trauma shocked their core beliefs. They're both convinced they're going to die.]*

[Not gonna happen.] I reply. Then I realize I have no idea how to go Laiddinic. *[Uh...you wouldn't know how to—]*

She shakes her head. *[I cannot help when it comes to that.]*

[Right.]

It'll be okay. Just focus on—

Blythe interrupts with a piercing roar: *"SERPENT ON OUR FLANK!"*

33

A giant monster breaches the water, engulfing me in shadow as it soars overhead. It strongly resembles a Chinese dragon, but this isn't a painting you can appreciate and savor—this one here is *right in my face.* Its size and presence have a visceral impact, on par with a brutal sucker-punch or a vicious throw.

My brain claws back some lost composure, easing my prey-freeze and allowing me to process additional details. The serpent is coated in rich green scales. Its belly is armored in thick yellow plates. Serrated spines protrude from its back, bright and orange and wickedly curved. All that pales before its red-glowing pupils—they're blazing with mindless, un-fettered rage, so damn pure that it approaches insanity.

The beast cranes forward and trumpets a roar, dousing me in stench and torrid heat. Our snipers respond with a fragmented volley, lighting its torso with sparks and glints.

[Erany?] My panic bleeds into our mental link.

She's keeping her fear tightly in check. *[The vokers will handle it. Syf and Idinia are depending on your spell.]*

The serpent snarls and lunges at our mizzenmast. Our vokers save us with rune-flooded light, causing it to flinch sharply back. The serpent blinks as if it smelled something foul...then beelines away from the *Gauge's* hull.

Whew.

I focus again on Syf and Idinia, realigning a handful of distorted meridians. It's all Primal, nothing Laiddinic, but at least I'm stopping their trauma from spreading. Then a sniper yells, *"IT'S COMING BACK AROUND!"* dousing me in a wave of electric fear.

Arisse calls for deterrent magic, triggering a round of vehement protests. They've used the contingency stored in the coil—if the vokers tap their personal auras, they'll bleed off speed and the frigates will catch us.

"It's either that or the serpent!" Arisse rages. "Certain death in the maw of that beast, or a fighting chance against those ships! *Now do as I say if you value your life!*"

As the monster towers above our masts, the vokers project another spell. Unlike the last one, they have to craft this one on the spot. It's evident in the blast of unrefined power, accompanied by a surge of jarring feedback.

[Erany!]

[I'm here.] She shores my consciousness with her own.

On the fraying edges of my battered perception, I sense two of the vokers pass out and collapse. My fear gets the best of me—I flail and thrash with my intention and will, trying to reinforce my aura and lessen Erany's burden.

She isn't having it. *[You're making it worse! RELAX!]*

Relax? *Relax?* We're being chased by a *goddamn sea serp*—then I catch myself. She's right. I'm in no condition to weave any magic, much less tap my Laiddinic powers. I need to calm down and restore my perspective.

For a nerve-wracking second, my thoughts spin out and violently clash, then a shaky peace begins to take hold. My emotions unknot and I shift into apathy, allowing me to brush against hope and optimism.

Here we go.

The physical world fades and dims. All that matters is Syf and Idinia. Healing these two isn't a matter of skill, it's a flat-out, unquestionable certainty. I just have to—

[NOT YET.]

The sentiment blares from the core of my soul, evoking a rush of frenzied desperation. Not yet? *Not yet?* What are you *TALKING*

ABOUT? They can't die because of my stupid quest! I'd trade a thousand magic mirrors for—

[Jon!] Erany shouts. *[What happened?]*

I try and articulate my livid frustration, my inability to go Laiddinic, but all I can project is a red wave of anger. I'm not performing at the level I want, and it's preventing me from—

[It doesn't matter!] Erany screams. *[Idinia and Syf are going to die! DO WHAT YOU CAN, BEFORE THEY PASS INTO THE EVENTIDE CLEAR!]*

Her words anchor me back to the present. Do what you can, Jon, do what you can.

Even though I'm using Primal magic, the enchantment is still incredibly difficult. I've been given a crowbar to move a boulder. Unfortunately, the boulder in question is as big as a house, and it might just crack my psyche in two.

Healing. Stability. Healing. Stability. Go past the words, abide in the feeling. Ignore the chaos and imminent danger...

After a minute, the discord in their auras begins to abate, and their meridians begin to ease into place. For a harrowing moment, I'm afraid they'll snarl back up...then they tentatively wobble into alignment.

"It's working!" Erany exclaims. "They're both accepting your auric input!"

Thank. *God.*

Syf's breathing is now even and steady. Idinia's leg is still swollen, but the kehcraw's venom is contained to her wound. It's no longer rampaging through her body.

My triumph gives way to a surge of dizziness—that was the hardest spell I've ever had to cast. As our prow hits a choppy wave, I'm thrown off balance and toppled sideways.

Erany swoops in and hooks my arms. "Easy, Jon."

"Sorry," I mumble. My eyelids twitch as I fight off exhaustion. "Don't know if—"

Blythe roars, *"TARGET THOSE SHIPS!"* drawing my attention to the approaching frigates. They're firing a sequence of bow-mounted obelisks, marking the air with long-running blaze.

"Tall breaker tunnel!" Arisse yells, pointing at a mass of water forming in front of us. *"It's our only chance!"*

"Are you mad?" Blythe screams. *"We'll be dashed to pieces!"*

"We either risk that wave, or we surrender to the Queen!"

"So be it!" he bellows. *"Syf has a chance on those Nok-damned ships! I won't let her—"*

"No," Syf croaks. She props herself onto her left elbow, and levels a finger at First Mate Blythe. "I would rather die here than rot in a dungeon."

Blythe stammers, "But...you..."

Her voice steels. "Helmsman! Direct the *Gauge* into that breaker! *Into,* not onto!"

"Aye, Captain!"

Five shots hit, lighting our aegis with rippling hues. Six more follow, causing our shield to bulge dangerously inward.

"Clear the masts!" Blythe orders. *"Hold fast!"*

As sharpshooters scramble down from the rigging. Erany grabs me and pins me down. Out of the corner of my sleep-hazed vision, I glimpse Syfaedi holding onto Idinia.

Someone screams, *"IT'S SPILLING OVER!"*

Water soars above our masts, slicing through a bank of high-flying cloud. My terror gives way to jaw-dropping awe as we enter a tunnel of spiraling current.

Two of the frigates try and follow. One of them whirls up the side, all the way over, and smashes into its oncoming partner. Our pursuers explode into showers of fragments, then vanish into the ocean churn.

I have to stay awake. If I'm gonna pass into the Eventide Clear, I want this to be the last thing I see: this abundance of light and kinetic energy.

That's my last thought before I pass out.

34

From the dim glaze limning the curtains, I can tell that it's night. I sit up in bed, swing my legs over the side, and—*murggh*—get to my feet. Christ, it feels like I red-lined a workout after a month of doing nothing. Maybe I should do some warmups, just to—

My memory hits like a ton of bricks. Syf. Idinia.

I yank on the door and charge into the hall. I fly up the ladder, burst through the hatch, and almost fall back down as I scramble topside.

Gorgeous scenery floods my perception, glitching my brain and freezing my body.

We're smack in the middle of a tall breaker tunnel, enclosed in a gyre of silky ripples. A pair of moons gild its leftmost edge, limning the water in red-tinged silver. Instead of whirling sunlit gloss, we're trapped in a loop of shadowy flow.

A second later, my panic comes rushing back. "Syf! Idinia!" As I break for the stern, someone grabs me and swings me around.

"Jon!" Erany exclaims. "Thank Shaddock you're—"

I shrug her off and glance wildly around. *"Where are they?"*

She grips my shoulders, forcing me to look her square in the eye. "Alive. Safe."

I slump and sigh in sheer relief. "Thank God. I can't believe..." I survey the liquid swirling above us. "They didn't capture us, did they? If we're inside a breaker, then..." My gaze settles on the seavoker circle. Arisse Eledy is the only one on it. She's enveloped in a flare of weighty-looking magic.

"How long was I out?"

"A week." Erany releases my shoulders.

"A *week?*" I gape dumbly at her. "So is Syf—"

"Resting in her quarters. Idinia as well. Not yet hale, but well on their way."

"Good." I sigh again. *Whew.* "What'd I miss?"

She jerks her chin at a starboard hatch. "Food first. I have been feeding you through a series of iatrical spells. Now that you're finally up and about, I can ease off my aching aura."

We make our way into the ship's kitchen, where I nab some biscuits and a big hunk of cheese. As I eat, she fills me in. The *Gauge* escaped Lyderea's frigates. That's the good news. The not-so-good news is we're trapped inside a tall breaker barrel.

Erany nods at Arisse Eledy, standing alone inside the coil. "The junior vokers cannot help. They are busy healing Syf and Idinia."

"So the wind and the currents...it's all Arisse?"

"Sekrish as well. They eat, sleep, and work the coil. That is it and that is all."

"That sounds exhausting." I rub the back of my neck. "Syf and Idinia...is it okay if I see them?"

"Syf, yes. Idinia, no."

"Why?"

"Idinia's condition is far more severe. She needs to sleep as much as she can."

"Got it." I cede with a nod. "Just Syf, then."

"On my heels." She strides over to the captain's stateroom, and announces our presence with a couple of knocks. "Syf?"

It triggers a series of deliberate steps. The latch snaps back, the door cracks open, and Syfaedi Kysaire—dressed in an oversized shirt and baggy trousers—peers at us through the dim-lit gap.

"Yes?"

"Jon is awake."

"I can see that."

I raise my hands in a *take-it-easy* gesture. "If it hurts to talk, we can do this later."

"No." She winces in pain. "I won't be hale any time soon." She exhales carefully. "Unfortunately, Dinny and I...we cannot venture into Sidehelm Pass."

"Totally understand. You can barely walk."

"Grace and thanks." Syf averts her gaze. "I apologize for Blythe and the rest of the crew."

Erany responds with a disgusted scoff. "We have been over this, Syf. There is nothing to forgive."

"I'm sorry..." I tilt my head, puzzled. "What happened with Baldhead McGrumperson?"

Syf winces again. "He feels responsible for both our injuries. To make up for his imagined wrong, he wished to guard you while crossing the Pass. I ah...I denied him with a tad more vehemence than maybe I should have."

"That's ridiculous," I snort. "Unless he's secretly a fiftieth-level kehcraw slayer, he would have passed into the Clear if he set foot in the keep. And he can't help us through the Pass," I shake my head in firm denial. "Blythe and his guys can fight and sail, but their magical defenses are nonexistent."

"Aye." Syf grunts. "I said as much. He didn't agree."

"What about mages? A couple vokers, maybe?" I glance over at the ship's coil. "No pressure, though. If they don't want to go, they should stay on the *Gauge.* Phantom vampires..." I shudder and wince. "Blech. Yeah."

"None of the vokers will be able to help," Syf rasps. "Unless they rest for at least a month."

I raise an eyebrow. "It's that intense?"

The captain nods. "Who would willingly sail this chaos?" She glances at the water surging around us. " 'Tis a daunting task for Arisse and Sekrish, and they are veteran masters of their craft. The other four vokers are just as tired, as they have been serving as our arcane healers. Now if you'll excuse me, I will take my leave and focus on breathing. It feels like an Ogre is sitting on my chest."

"Of course." Erany pats my arm. "Let us away."

We pass by Arisse but she doesn't notice. Her aura is ridiculously bright and her pupils are blank. She's deeply connected to the ship's energies...I've never seen her this entwined.

Erany tugs on my arm. "Leave her be. She doesn't have time for idle chit-chat."

"I know. It's just..." I blow out a sigh. "How much time are we losing in this breaker?"

She descends into the passage leading to our room. "The tunnel is on a southward heading. If we don't overshoot, we'll arrive at the Pass with little delay."

I climb down behind her. "Really? That's great!" Then I correct myself: "Well...great if you're looking for vampire ghosts."

"Would you cease your dithers?" She throws me an irritable glance. "In all likelihood, we shan't even see them."

"You really believe that?"

"We'll be fine," she says brusquely.

"Yeah," I agree, trying to hide my unease. "It'll all work out."

My self-assurance feel empty and hollow. As a writer, I'm painfully aware the Watchers have been foreshadowed, and that it would be a waste of narrative if we never met 'em. But if this is a story, am I a character, reader, or the author? I know it sounds like philosophical nonsense, but...

She closes the door and clicks the latch. "Get undressed," she orders. "I've been waiting a week for this."

"Yes, ma'am." My unease gives way to a cheese-eating grin. Screw the philosophy—I don't care if I'm the hero, author, or the mustache-twirling villain.

This right here is all that matters.

———

While they're on duty, the deckhands radiate businesslike poise. If we weren't in a breaker, I'd swear it was just another day for 'em. Sekrish and Arisse are a different story. Whenever they're done working the coil, they sag and age into withered crones (they regain their youth over the next couple hours, but it's still pretty freaky.) Nearby sailors try and help, but the vokers wave them off and stagger away.

After a week, Syf and Idinia begin to heal on their own, freeing the junior vokers to assist with the coil. They're not as skilled as Arisse and Sekrish (either one can handle the ship by themselves, while the junior vokers have to work as a team) but it allows them to set up a three-shift rotation: Arisse, Sekrish, and the other four vokers.

Now that we're out of imminent danger, life on the *Gauge* feels quasi-normal. Without exception, Erany and I watch the sunrise and sunset, because those two events are not to be missed. Think of the most beautiful sky ever, then imagine it refracted through a barrel of surf. It's like soaring through a vortex of liquid color, comprised of pink and orange and even some green.

Three weeks into our barrelized journey, Syf calls for a meeting with Erany, me, and Idinia. We file into a second deck stateroom, where she proceeds to give us some much welcome news: the water's slowing down. Pretty soon, we'll be free to sail in any direction.

"How far have we strayed?" Erany leans against the wall and crosses her arms.

"Three days travel, probably less." Syf distractedly leans left and right. It's a reflex she's developed in the last few weeks, a way of testing her healing ribs. Idinia responds by shifting off-crutch, dipping her wounded leg a couple of inches, then straightening up a moment later.

My lips curve into a faint smile. They've grown super close—enough to cue each other's injury-born tics.

"I may be able to traverse the Pass," Idinia ventures. "If my leg keeps healing as fast as it has..."

Erany interjects with a derisive snort. "You're on *crutches,* Idinia!"

The Duelist's features twist in protest. "One more week and I'll be ready to walk!"

"More like a month," I counter, "maybe longer."

Erany adds, "Lyderea would love that, wouldn't she? If we had to care for you while crossing the Pass."

"I…" Idinia registers our dubious stares, then stares at the deck and mutters, "Fine."

Syf reaches out and rubs her back. "You're making good progress."

"Fah." She circles her arm, brushing Syf away. "I'll be in your quarters."

"I won't be long."

As she exits the stateroom, Idinia flings a hand in the air. *Whatever.*

Syf chuckles, then turns back to us and sighs in regret. "I wish I could help, but—"

"For the millionth time, quell your worry," Erany says irritably. "If recent events are any indication, Jon and I are meant to press on by ourselves." She searches my face with her lavender eyes. "We have spoken of this, no?"

"Yeah…" I hiss through my teeth. "When I tried to heal you with Laiddinic powers, it was…well, the word *unthinkable* comes to mind."

"Someone obstructed you?" Syf's brow furrows in concern.

"No." I shake my head. "From what I understand, that isn't even possible. It's more like I wasn't meant to use them. I've only channeled 'em twice before—once in Elerica and once with the Glass—but I know how it feels when they're about to kick in. This was the same level of surety, only in direct opposition to my intention. I wish I could articulate, but words are just a rough approximation."

If I'm slinging lead (or magical blast-rays, to be exact), I'm guided through twitches and subtle pressure. Laiddinic powers, however, are comparable to having a psychedelic breakthrough. My *entire being* is flooded with knowledge: a deep-seated awareness of past, present, and future, and how they're actually a single occurrence. It's frightening in its inescapability—there's no other option aside from success.

"I wouldn't know." Syf shrugs. "The strongest thing I can imagine is love at its peak."

"Yes!" I nod vigorously. "That's it! I mean…" I glance at Erany, suddenly nervous.

The smile on her face is gorgeous and pure. It isn't lost on Syfaedi Kysaire—she regards us both with a knowing grin.

"Well. I suppose for whatever reason, you two are destined to push into Sidehelm, without the addition of myself or my crew. 'Tis a Nok-damned shame, but this twist of fate cannot be shirked."

"Be dust upon your breath." The words spill from my lips without conscious direction.

"Aye," Erany agrees. "The pieces are set and all are in motion."

"You see this as a game?" I ask.

"Only when I'm in the right state of mind. Unfortunately, my dealings with Lucky fall well short of grace. That Nok-damned scoundrel reddens my sight." She scoffs in disgust.

"I suppose that's it." Syf looks back and forth between the two of us. "We have naught to do but enjoy the journey."

"Aye. May light find you in dark places." Erany touches her brow and brings her hand out.

Syf dips her chin and returns the gesture. "And may it ease your eyes and guide your feet."

As Erany and I cross the deck, I glance over at the seavokers' coil. Sekrish is on duty, stabilizing the currents and inter-tunnel winds.

"Jon." Erany nudges me.

"Mm?" I lock eyes with my girlfriend.

"She doesn't need your help. Enjoy the journey, remember?"

"Yeah…yeah, you're right."

Before I follow her down the hatch, I glance up at the watery churn. Our world is defined by a lustrous swirl, aglow with slashes of exquisite luminescence. All we can do is keep moving forward. It would be wasteful and silly if we died in this wave.

It is what it is. I clop down the steps. *You're caught in the flow of existence and fate, but you get to decide if you enjoy it or not. It's the only choice you have at this moment.*

A moment's pause, then: *Maybe it's the only choice you ever really had.*

And, of course: *Be dust upon your breath.*

35

After the tunnel dwindles and fades, Syf confers with Blythe and her mates. Once they're done, she calls me and Erany into her cabin.

"Where's Idinia?" I glance around.

"Practicing in the lower holds, refusing to rest her Nok-damned leg." A dismissive wave. "Dinny will be Dinny. Fortunately, the breaker didn't foul our progress. We lost a day, maybe two."

"How much longer?" Erany asks.

"One week," Syf replies. "Four days south, then three days east on the Savilant Rush."

Erany nods. "Very well."

My body tightens with instinctive dread. When I first heard we were bound for the Pass, the vampire phantoms were comfortably distant. Now they're only a week away.

Easy, Jon. In all likelihood, we won't even see 'em.

But my gut says different—we're going to confront them.

I'm all but sure of it.

———

Plain-jane forest crawls by the hull, morphing into an expanse of rocky flats. Three days into our eastward glide, we anchor a hundred yards out from the riverine shore. As we get ready to disembark, Syf informs us the launch has been stocked with provisions.

"Come danger or hardship, give us a signal," Idinia says. "We shall assemble a party and—"

"Idinia," Erany chides. "We have discussed this at length. If the crew runs afoul of a predatory haunt, their auric demise is all but assured."

"But—"

"Can any of them fend off spectral wiles?"

"I..." Idinia looks conflicted, then hangs her head. "Damn it," she mutters.

Blythe glances up as we approach. "We've finished our checks. The ladder is set."

"Thank you," Erany says.

"Your brain has gone slack," he grouses. "Take a handful of crew so you can at least—"

"Blythe." Erany holds up a hand. "I have given you my reasons. More times than I care to count."

Blythe glares at her, subjecting her to a full dose of Bald Guy Fury. My badass girlfriend isn't fazed. She raises an eyebrow as if to ask, *Are we done here?*

He flings up his arms and tromps away. "If you wish to pass into the Eventide Clear, *be my guest!*" The outburst evokes grins from Syf and Idinia.

"Ready?" Erany prods me with her lavender gaze.

"Yep. Let's do this."

———

We paddle to the shore and invert our canoe. The beach is coated in gravel and shale. Further inland, it graduates into clusters of moss-coated hills. Some have grass, a couple have bushes, but the predominant feature is austere stone.

"Great," I mutter. "Nothing but rocks for miles around."

As we start walking, Erany glances to either side. "I suspect it is because of the lesser haunts. Hardier life can persevere. Weaker auras, however..."

"Where do I land on the hardy-frail spectrum?" I ask. Before she can answer, I grumble, "Forget it, I'd rather not know. My saving throw versus specters is probably horrible."

"Jon," she says patiently. "Magically speaking, how strong do you think you are?"

"Is this a trick question? Because—"

"You are easily my equal. Likely my better."

"What?" I regard her suspiciously. "What are you talking about?"

"I doubt I could match you spell for spell."

I'm surprised into laughter. "Are you...wait, you're messing with me, right?"

She shakes her head. "You might even best Nyanti Eldara. She would lay you low nine out of ten, but you would still enjoy a fighting chance."

I probe her eyes with a half-formed grin—*come on, I know you're kidding*—then it falls away as I realize she's being completely serious. "No way! No *way! Nyanti*? Erany, she's been casting magic since before she could *talk!* I've only been—"

"It doesn't matter. When someone embraces their inherent purpose, their potential and promise are greatly accelerated. Conversely, when they choose to spurn their True-born calling..." She shrugs. "Well, you already know. Your life before Evermoor—it was stale and maudlin, was it not?"

"So we each have a calling?" I ask doubtfully. "What about free will?"

She shrugs again. "That depends on which of your aspects you happen to be referencing. From what I was taught, our greater aspect cannot directly enjoy free will."

"What?" My brow wrinkles in confusion. "Isn't it omnipotent? It can enjoy anything it wants."

"In its native form, it is omnipotent, omnipresent, and omniscient. Consequently, it has nothing to overcome, nowhere to go, nothing to learn, and nothing to choose between. So in order to revel in progress, motion, and choice, it has saddled its fragments with time, space, and individuality. We have other constraints, but 'tis the long and short of it."

"That's us," I clarify. "We're the fragments. How does any of that relate to spellcraft?"

"Some of our constraints manifest as proclivities, which are tied to our innate True-born callings. It's not just magic—your prowess in swordplay has blossomed and grown."

I contemplate the hills. "So this is all by design...a story that springs from my greater self."

She gives a nod. "The best I can describe it is in terms of a lesser and greater self. That, however, doesn't encapsulate the overall truth, as scholars will say they are one and the same. But in order to apply causality and logic, there needs to be a separation. Our greater aspects create the game, our lesser aspects explore its breadth."

"Wish I could skip all the lesser aspect stuff," I grumble, "and let my greater aspect handle our problems."

"If it intervened on every issue, it would trap itself again in omnipotence, omnipresence, and omniscience. How could you write stories without linear time? There would be no beginning, middle, or end. Similarly, how could you travel when you're everywhere at once? And how could you become anything, when you're already everything? To be truly unlimited, it must express itself through finite perspectives."

"Interesting. Where do Laiddinic powers fit in?"

"They're a result of harmonizing with our greater aspect. Our innate potential flows through our aura, free of obstruction or singular doubt. But as I understand it, they cannot sustain continuous omnipotence."

"Huh? Why?"

"If you could change anything at any moment, you would defeat the purpose of a finite perspective. You would simply revert to an omnipotent—and consequently limited—state."

"Hmm...does that mean there are things I can't change?"

"I believe so," she hedges. "According to my tutors, our creative power flows from our greater aspect, as we are mirrors of its creative essence. But it has to stop short of unfettered omnipotence—and the accompanying omniscience and omnipresence—to preserve its ability to continuously surprise itself. Without constraining its power and knowledge, novelty would ultimately cease to exist, and it would end up rotting in a prison of certainty."

I think back to when I was trying to heal Syf and Idinia. I was unable to do it through Laiddinic means, but it wasn't for lack of desire or effort. It was as if I knew at a soul-deep level that it wasn't part of our collective fate. But what does that mean? *Fate.* I guess fate is relevant to the lesser aspect (because within the constraints of time/space/individuality, choice and fate become an issue) though not so much from the whole-being perspective. From the whole-being perspective, everything is fated—everything is already chosen and expressed—because you're already everything manifested at once. There's no way to choose what to be next, because you are that thing at this very moment. And there's also no "next" because Capital You—or everything—is happening at the exact same time.

I can't prove it, but my gut is telling me that some things are fated (I'm guessing you could file those under "constraints") while the rest is up for free-will grabs. For some reason, having it one way or the other—where all of it's scripted, or where it's a constant free-for-all—doesn't feel right to me.

Hmm...when I played D&D, I always chose to be a fighter/mage/thief. Now...well, that's what I am. Is there anything to that? There must be, right? If I had to frame it in my own words, I would say my life is like an open-world game, where I have bounds and parameters (stuff like breathing and sleeping, obviously), but certain decisions enhance my access and options.

"Take my advice with a grain of salt," Erany cautions. "I am not a sage. If I was, I would tolerate Lucky with far more grace." Her brow crinkles in thought. "Ever since we came back from Earth, he's rustled my ire with maddening ease. For the life of me, I cannot see the reason behind it..." She shakes her head. "No matter. I am not a thinker, nor a teacher. That is my point."

"I don't know..." I muse. "You're pretty damn smart. Also, the stuff you're talking about...it seems like it organically escapes definition. At least in the long-term, anyway. The labels degrade with time and culture, or if you try and apply them to every individual. You gotta keep adjusting for context and perspective."

She searches my face with her lavender eyes.

"What?" I ask irritably. "Do I have something on my—"

"No, it's just..."

"Just what?" My irritation gives way to curiosity.

"Swordplay, thievery, magic...those aren't your only talents. You are starting to grasp the nature of existence. It is all too evident in your conjecture."

I'm taken aback. "Erany, I wasn't trying to be enlightened or wise. I said the first thing that came to mind."

"That only serves to prove my point—your response to my premise was authentic and pure. During my studies, I encountered gobs of tutors and scholars. By and large, they were disconnected folk wedded to rhetoric and formula, desperate to convince others they had mastered reality. You, however, naturally expressed what they tried to subdue."

My face reddens—I'm flattered and embarrassed. "I mean...they'd probably own me if we ever debated. I dabbled in philosophy for the sake of writing, but I'm by no means an expert."

She shakes her head. "Do not shortchange your own perception. Your statement about adjusting for context and perspective...like I said, I have encountered teachers who mauled me with proofs, yet failed to convey an ounce of truth." She pauses for a second, then says, "Perhaps it cannot be grasped through others' insistence."

Her next words send a chill up my spine.

"Maybe you just have to live it and be it."

36

The haunts resemble people or Wildlyre, but they're all transparent and limned in wan gray haze. Their expressions are blank, their posture sucks, and they drift around in aimless circles, about two or three feet off the stony ground. I thought I'd be scared, but I kinda feel sorry for 'em.

"Wow." I scan the muddle of dejected souls. "They're not what I imagined. Not at all."

"Lesser haunts are like bothersome insects. Still dangerous, but only if you lack intermediary magic." Erany nods at Weak Sauce. "Draw your blade."

I pull a foot of steel and examine the metal (almost forgot it could sense nearby spirits). "It's barely glowing." My forehead crinkles in puzzlement. "The Watchers of Erendor...they've gotta be stronger, right?"

"I believe so," she says. "Haunts are anchored by emotional resonance, and Erendor's kings are legendary traitors. When it comes to anything concerning the negative, betrayal exacerbates by orders of magnitude. As that is the case, I assume the Watchers are far more formidable."

"What the hell," I mutter. "How hard is it to lay off the backstabbing?"

In seventh grade, I toured the prison on Alcatraz Island. Everything felt quiet and unassuming, the exact opposite of what I had expected. That's what radiates off these haunts: not the oogy-boogy I first imagined, but a glum muddle of vague unease. I can feel it tugging at the edges of my brain, trying to develop into a forlorn conclusion. *You shouldn't even try, don't make waves, what makes you think you deserve to* *be happy, when there are so many people worse off than you...*the list goes on, needling my psyche with quiet futility.

"Guard your aura," Erany cautions. "If they worm their way into your orphic body, they will slowly gray out your personal vantage."

"Yep, got it." They're easy to fend off but it's low-key annoying, like brushing away an invisible spiderweb. "Do they ever pass on?" I stare at a desiccated Goblin-spirit. It stares back for a couple of seconds, then its jaw hangs open in a wordless yawn.

"From what I have heard, they eventually fade." As we pass by a ten-foot boulder, Erany points at a blob atop its crest. Its eyes are a couple of blacked-out circles, its mouth is an expressionless horizontal line. "That one, I wager, isn't long for the Clear."

"I hope so." I track it with my gaze. "No one deserves to be stuck in limbo."

———

One of 'em is sneaky—it latches on to my aura and drains a little juice. I flick it off before it causes any damage; it's the magical equivalent of popping a pimple. (Weirdly enough, the sense of satisfaction is almost the same.)

They're ghoulish embodiments of cautionary tales, but they're also a lesson in Primal awareness. Whenever I'm stuck in anger or fear, I've used futility as a reliable go-to. Now I realize that if I indulged in hopelessness for an extended stretch, I'd probably start resembling one of these haunts. They don't use apathy as a mental stepping stone, these poor bastards live and wallow in it.

As night falls, the wind picks up into a whistling howl. Thanks to a repellent spell we add to our nighttime wards, the haunts give us a wide berth. Unfortunately, sexy time is off the table. The rugged ground is bad enough. Throw in the ghosts and shrieking drafts...yeah, there's no way.

Four days later, Sidehelm Fortress comes into view. The castle is wreathed in eddies of fog, its ramparts and battlements are in severe disrepair. Everything is built around a north-south path—it runs straight through the multi-peaked structure.

"Wow," I murmur. "You weren't kidding. That path is *huge.* You could stuff it with thousands of wagons and soldiers."

"Aye." Erany starts up a bank of loose-piled rock. " 'Tis why it was coveted by nobles and generals." She pauses, then says, "At the peak of the Bright Age, Sidehelm was known for its welcome and cheer; 'twas a haven flowing with drink and festivities. Towns sprouted around these vales, then shrank and dwindled throughout the Decline. When the Reft spread wide, they vanished altogether."

"Damn," I huff. "Wish they'd kept a couple of those taverns—I could definitely use a festive drink. This feels like leg day times a thousand." These damn rocks keep slipping out from under me. My feet are getting a hell of a workout.

"There." Erany points ahead, where the incline leads into a flat gully. "That will take us past the castle, then we'll arrive at Skytooth Ridge."

"Sounds good," I pant. "Gotta be better than this Nok-damned hike."

After a final bit of lung-busting effort, we transition into the flat-running gully. For the next half hour, we trek along in amiable silence. My ears are drawn to our crunchy steps, grinding and compressing the fragmented rock. *CrrRK. CrrRK.*

Suddenly, my hip starts tingling, cuing me to pull Weak Sauce halfway out. Uh oh. He's glowing as bright as a magnesium flare.

"Erany?"

She doesn't respond. She just keeps moving forward.

"Erany?" I walk up behind her and grab her shoulder.

She turns around, causing me to stumble back in shock. Her face has gone completely blank. It's a smooth, featureless oval.

[I am not Erany.] the Watcher projects.

37

After they ensorcelled Eralindíany, the Watchers mazed Jon's mind and aura. But as he plodded into their castle, a wordless part of him remembered who he was (along with all he had done and all he would do) and held to that knowledge with steadfast resolve. If he allowed It to speak through his heart, It would help him break free of the Watchers' spell. (A part of him knew that was humorous and ironic, because he was It and It was him.)

There wasn't any way to think his way out of this. As always, however, he could feel his way into It.

————

In some ill-defined fistula of time (the eighties and nineties had bled together, mixing with the twenty-first century in a mishmash of culture) Jon Dough pondered his future. He couldn't shake the feeling that he was destined for something more. Something different and strange, drawn from the stuff of dreams and fantasy. He knew it was crazy—the path before him made absolute sense. He would earn a degree, work a few jobs, and eventually retire.

But there was still that *something...*

"Hey. Stranger guy. You gonna order or just stare at the menu?" the barista prodded.

"Huh?" Jon shook his head, snapping himself out of his self-induced haze. "Sorry."

"Just messing with you. As you can see, there isn't any rush." She glanced around at the muted cafe. The only other patron was a dreadlocked Black man, seated in the far-back corner. He was sipping a cup of steaming coffee, perusing a book titled *Simulacra and Simulation*.

She followed Jon's gaze. "That's Al. He's a permanent fixture here at the Wakeup."

Al raised his cup. "Wind at your back and sun on your brow. Don't scare him off, Erin—your last boyfriend is still in recovery."

"Shut up," she said good-naturedly. She leaned toward Jon with conspiratorial cheer. "We all love him, even though he's partial to old-timey phrases."

"You would be too, if you'd been playing D&D for as long as I have!" Al crowed. "I've rolled twenty-sided dice for a day and an age!"

Erin rolled her eyes. "Weird flex." She focused on Jon. "He's more than an offbeat tabletop gamer. I know how to code, but it would take lifetimes of study to get to his level."

"He's that good, huh?" Jon's voice was tinged with respect.

"Yep. His nickname's The Wizard. You know what you want?"

Jon's breath caught in his throat. He'd been lost in thought, and that had kept him from noticing Erin's beauty. Now it was blasting him right in the soul. She looked remarkably like a young Taylor Swift, before Jake and Kanye and the sexual harassment.

The light glanced off her sky-blue eyes. For a tantalizing second, he could have sworn they were purple.

Irritation crept into her features. "You gonna order or what?"

"Oh. Right." Jon gulped. "I'll have a..." *Say something cool ask for her number GOD she's pretty...* "I'll have a..."

She raised a brow. "You'll have a..."

"I'll have a coffee."

She threw up her hands in sarcastic frustration. "Oh I'm sorry—I thought you wanted the steak tartare. *Which* coffee, genius?"

Jon's cheeks turned bright red. "Uh...I...plain."

"Plain *what?*"

"Wh-what?"

"Say *what* again!" she demanded in a surprisingly good Samuel L. Jackson/Jules Winnfield impression. (Jon instantly recognized it. His taste in movies was pretty retro).

"What? I mean—sorry!" Jon blurted. "Plain! Plain coffee! Small!"

Erin smiled. "You're blushing. Cute."

"Wh—really?" (He silently offered a prayer of thanks. Right at that moment, his only goal in life was to avoid saying *what.)*

"Really." She rung up his purchase. "Anything else?"

This is it. Don't screw it up. He took a breath and met her eyes. "Erin, right?"

"Yeah?"

"I'm Jon. Do you...would you..." His mouth worked silently, failing to verbalize the all-important question. Finally, he managed, "Date?"

"Are you asking me out?" Before he could reply, she said, "I know that you are—I can tell by your sweat-stache." She gave him a once-over. "You're not married, are you?"

"Why would you—no! I'm *eighteen!*"

"Relax." Her grin returned. "Creepy married guys like to hit on me, so I promised myself I would always ask. And to answer your question, yes—I'll go on a date with you. Lemme see if I can clock out early."

"Don't get in trouble on my account," Jon blustered. "I can wait for—" Before he could finish, she disappeared into the breakroom.

After a bit, she came skipping back. "Yep, I'm good. Can we hang out here? I'm feeling kinda lazy."

"Wherever you want."

"Great. I'll meet you by the sofas."

He muttered his agreement, then headed over to the window-side chairs. As he sat on a cushion, he struggled to process his newfound attraction. Erin was hot, but this went deeper than physical allure.

She plopped down beside him. "Jon, right? Jon what?"

"Dough."

She almost did a spit-take. "Jon *Dough?* Like a *dead frickin' body?*"

"Yeah." His bright red cheeks turned a few shades redder.

"Your parents—what were they *thinking?* Sorry." She shook her head. "I shouldn't give you crap. You must have caught hell."

"Not really. It comes up occasionally, but…" He rubbed the back of his neck. "For the most part, people don't notice. I'm doing my best to live up to my name." He followed up with an awkward laugh.

"Pfff," Erin scoffed. "That's a terrible joke. You'll have to do better or we're gonna have problems. What are you into?"

"Um…I like to write stories?" he ventured. "And I'm registered for classes at San Francisco State. That's pretty much it. I'm kinda basic."

"Way to sell yourself," Erin replied sarcastically. Then she sighed. "Though it's not like I have any room to talk. I too, am destined for San Francisco State. I'm in the same boat as you, only I don't write stories."

"You're hot," Jon offered. "That's something."

Erin gave him a lopsided smile. "Never imply hotness is a defining quality. Especially if you happen to be talking to a girl."

"That's not what I meant!" he protested. "I—"

"I know what you meant. Just messing with you."

"I should get used to that," Jon chuckled. "Seems like your thing."

"It absolutely is." Her expression turned distant. "I just graduated, I've signed up for classes….the world is my oyster, but a part of me feels like I'm still missing out." She cleared her throat. "Random tangent: I've been listening to this guy named Alan Watts. Half the time, I have no idea what he's saying, but I can't stop listening to him. You know when your *entire being* responds to an idea? Like when it hits you on a Primal level?"

"Total resonance." Jon nodded. "Like a key fitting into a well-oiled lock."

"Exactly. I feel like I'm destined for adventure and travel, with something extra I can't define. I dunno. In the meantime, I was thinking of studying psychedelic therapy."

Jon laughed. "Life is psychedelic as it is. Think about it: billions of years ago, something triggered an expansion of energy, and it crystallized into matter and sentient life. We have no idea why, no idea how."

"I'm with you," Erin agreed. "I mean, who even knows if I'm a brain in a jar, or a simulation crafted by alien gods?"

"Speaking my language!" Alijyar exclaimed without looking up from his treatise.

"Anyways," Erany continued. "I'm not even sure if this is my story. Maybe I'm a character in someone else's book."

"What? Come on," Jon argued. "Of *course* it's your story! Are you saying you're helpless? That you're at the mercy of someone's random-ass narrative?"

"Nothing like that," she replied hesitantly. "I think we co-star in each other's productions, while simultaneously playing the first-person hero." She laughed self-consciously. "You think I'm crazy, don't you." It was phrased as a statement, not a question.

"No. Never." He took her hand and gave it a squeeze.

She took a moment to savor the contact, then searched his face with her rich-colored gaze. "Want to get out of here?"

Jon stared back at her. He could easily get lost in those full blue eyes, taunting him with flashes of not-quite purple.

"Absolutely."

———

They strolled past rows of storefront windows, lost in a maze of ataxic desire. An hour into their meandering journey, they made their way over to the fog-coated beach. Jon and Erin were the only ones there. No one else wanted to brave the gloom.

"Ordered this fog up just for you," he joked.

"Thanks," she said dryly. "Making me feel like a fairytale princess."

A hundred yards north, the clouds began parting. The sand below shone bright and warm.

"That's our sign," Jon declared. "Come on."

They started walking toward the radiance. On any other day, Jon would have complained about the weather, but right at that moment, he couldn't have cared less. This beautiful girl was all that mattered. Her animated laugh, her entrancing blue (purple?) eyes, the way she grinned with impish delight...

"We're here," she said.

"Huh?" Jon was startled; he'd been admiring her out of the corner of his eye.

"Creeper," Erin teased. "Just be glad that I take it as a compliment. If you were a sex pest, I'd take you down and choke you out."

Jon flushed with pleasure and embarrassment. "I'm sorry, I..."

"Too late. You let the cat out of the bag when you said I was hot. It's all right—you're not so bad yourself." She looked around at the sunny beach, ringed with a perimeter of heavy fog. "Nice. Our own patch of heaven. What do you think?" Her almost-purple eyes locked onto his.

"What do I..." Jon trailed off, lost in her gaze.

Something inside him sparked and ignited, prompting him to curl her hair behind her ear. She pressed her cheek against his palm, closed her eyes, and sighed with pleasure and soul-deep warmth.

He leaned in, relishing her surrender and heart-stopping beauty, and met her lips with a perfect kiss.

Everything around him suddenly deepened. The sun on his skin, the crisp sea breeze, the sweet-summer scent of her long blond hair...

As soon as they parted, his anxiety came rushing back. "I'm sorry," he stammered. "I should've—"

Erin chuckled. "Relax. If you cross the line, I'll twist you into a funny-looking pretzel. I've been training jiu-jitsu since I was eight."

"Oh." He laughed awkwardly. "Maybe you could teach me."

"It'd be my pleasure." She draped her arms around his neck. "But first things first..."

This time, she was the one who initiated the kiss. Once again, every-thing intensified, filling him with elation, yearning, and an undeniable sense of flat-out rightness. After that moment of absolute heaven, she pulled away with a dreamy smile.

Jon blinked and struggled to compose himself. "Not my first...defi-nitely my best."

She laid her head against his chest. "It is written."

"What?"

"Oh." She laughed and straightened. "It's from a movie. Didn't mean to say it out loud."

Recognition flickered in his brain. *"Slumdog Millionaire,* right? One of my favorites."

"Mine too." She pecked his cheek. "Let's keep going. Plenty of time to make out later."

"Sure." He was already falling for her. He knew it was crazy (they'd only just met, after all) but it was the truest thing he'd ever felt.

As they walked up the stairs on the beach-side cliff, the clouds parted even further. The incline flattened into level grass, revealing a decaying, timeworn house. The awning on its porch was broken and rotted, sagging dangerously low in several places. Mold and grime coated its walls, marring the paint with sickly green-gray. The windows were all dusty and shattered, offering fragmented glimpses of its busted interior.

"The Sidelman house." Erin put her hands on her hips. "Creepy, huh?"

"Super creepy," Jon agreed.

"Let's go in," she said mischievously. "Perfect makeout spot."

"I don't know," Jon hedged. "There's something about it that..." He trailed off and stared at the house. Even in the light of the afternoon sun, it gave off an aura of ruin and doom.

"Yeah." Her mischief gave way to hesitant doubt. "Maybe we shouldn't. This feels like the start of a cheesy horror movie."

"No." Jon shook his head. "We're not victims."

"Not yet." She threw him a glance. "But if we go inside that creepy-ass house..."

"We have to. Both of us."

"What? *Why?*" she demanded. "If you're trying to impress me, then—"

"That's not it," he said quietly. "This house...it's part of my story. I can't explain it any better than that."

"Part of your *story?*" she fumed. "Do you realize how *stupid* that sounds?"

"I do." He chuckled ruefully. "This whole thing is stupid, when you stop and think about it. I mean, I just met you, right? But I'm already—" He stopped himself before he could say the words.

"You're already what?" Her eyes ticked across his face. "Jon?"

"I think you know." He stared calmly back at her. "Just like you know we have to go in."

After a second, she muttered, *"Simulacra and Simulation."*

"What?"

"Nothing," she said. "I just...for some reason, I thought of Al. Okay, I trust you. There's no good reason for it, but...yeah."

He squeezed her hand, charging her with a jolt of surety and faith. "Thank you. I couldn't do this without your help." His statement didn't make a damn bit of sense, but they both felt the truth of it deep in their bones.

Erin swept the air with an upturned palm. "After you."

38

A decrepit living room bordered their left. It was furnished with a sofa and a battered pair of dressers. Off to their right, the foyer merged with an open-plan kitchen. Its counters were heavy with broken debris, mostly junk from the 1950s. Rotary phones, record players, pastel clocks...it all reeked of outdated cheer. Lastly (as an oddly beautiful cherry on top), particulate dust hung in the air, highlighting a mesh of radiant sunbeams.

"What now?" Erin asked.

"Um..." Jon looked around. "I think..."

"Second floor?" A set of stairs loomed before them, defining the middle of the ramshackle house.

He thought it over. "No. Basement."

"Where do you see a—"

"This way."

A hot/cold flicker grew in his mind, blooming into surges of conviction or misgiving. They told him to ignore the grime-streaked bathroom, to go around the steps to their paint-chipped rear...

He stopped in front of a rickety door, directly beneath the staircase's peak. Its surface was dotted with cruddy black, rife with a web of splintery cracks.

As he grasped the tarnished knob, Erin's hand settled on his. "Be careful." Then she gave him a mischievous grin. "Hey, I just realized: I'm Sam to your Frodo, only ten times hotter."

He raised an eyebrow. "Try a *billion* times hotter."

"Facts," she said gleefully.

He opened the door and they began their descent.

———

He maxed out the flashlight on his phone, but the walls remained immutably dark. As crazy as it seemed, they seemed to be stuck in a pitch-black vacuum.

After what felt like a lifetime, Erin asked, "Jon? How long have we been on this stairwell?"

He checked his display. "We're coming up on our third hour. I know—there isn't a basement on Earth that goes this deep."

"Where do you think it leads?"

"No clue. But I can feel the end somewhere ahead. Trust me?"

"Yes." She had no reason to believe in this tousle-haired boy. A nameless part of her, however, had unquestioning faith in him. They were treading through what felt like the start of a horror movie, but she knew in her heart that wasn't true.

No, she thought. *This isn't a horror movie.*

It's an adventure, *goddammit.*

"See that?" Jon pointed directly ahead.

"Light," she whispered.

A tentative glimmer shone to their front. It slowly grew in size and strength, resolving from a far-off dot into a plain-looking door. Eventually, they halted before the dubious portal. Its edges flickered with pallid gleams. Muted voices drifted out from behind it.

"Whoever's in there is watching a movie." Jon looked at Erin. "Want to go in?"

"I think we have to." She glanced over her shoulder.

He followed her gaze and stifled a flinch. The entrance they'd used was gone from view, lost in a sea of impenetrable gloom. The fact that he couldn't see the walls, even with his phone right up against them...

No. He shook his head. *Stay focused.*

"Jon?" Erin prompted.

"You're right. We can't go back."

He took a breath and turned the knob.

———

It wasn't a movie. It was a video game.

They were greeted by the sight of an HD monitor, glowing with a scene from the latest *Fallout*. Jon had played it, but it wasn't his thing. (To no one's surprise, he preferred open-world fantasies). The walls were slathered in '50s wallpaper, clusters of flowers and pastel blah. Dark green carpet coated the floor, choking it in knots of dreary curls.

"Hey." A teenage boy was sitting before them, dressed in jeans and a dirty t-shirt. He was facing away, legs crossed, surrounded by a ring of junk food wrappers. "I'm Norm. You guys want to eat?" He didn't turn around; he kept staring at the screen and clicking his controller.

"We came down the stairs," Jon said. "Is there another way out?"

"Nah. Make yourself comfy. This right here is your final stop."

Erin strode forward and grabbed Norm's shoulder. "We're not just gonna—" As he swung around, she stepped back in shock.

Both his eyes were completely black.

"Starting to get it?" he asked. "This is it. There's nothing else." He resumed playing and shook his head in annoyance. "You ruined my shot."

"This can't be real," Erin whispered.

"I know," Jon whispered back. "Maybe we're—"

"Dreaming?" Norm interjected. "Nope. This place is haunted." His onscreen character dropped into a sewer. "Those stairs took you, what—three, four hours? We're not underground, we're in a different world altogether."

"Your eyes," Erin ventured. "They weren't always like that."

Norm nodded. "Happened during my seventh year here. I'm not sure why...I wouldn't worry. Didn't feel a thing."

You're lying, Jon thought. *You know* exactly *what caused it.* "There's gotta be a way out."

"Nope. I tried to escape for over a decade. Without these games, I would have gone nuts."

Who says you haven't? Jon wondered. But even as he thought it, he knew it wasn't true. Norm wasn't crazy. If anything, he was tragically rational.

Erin pointed at the doors bordering the television. "Where do they lead?"

"Bathroom's on the left, kitchen's on the right," Norm answered. "Got everything you need. Food, shower, games..."

"Where do you sleep?" Jon asked.

Norm glanced over his shoulder, flashing them a glimpse of his blacked-out eyes. "Sleep?" A cynical chuckle. "I haven't slept in over a century."

Jon and Erin exchanged a look. *We* have *to get out of here.*

He took her hand and headed for the bathroom, evoking a chuckle from the basement-dwelling spirit. "You gonna have sex? Enjoy it while you can—the urge will vanish soon enough. All of it goes. Hunger, lust...everything except these goddamn games."

"Why do you still eat?" Erin looked at the wrappers.

Norm shrugged. "Same reason I play these games: I'm bored."

Jon opened the door and looked around. The floor was coated in checkered tile, painted in shades of asylum green. There was a tub and a shower, a toilet and sink...he straightened in surprise.

"The mirror."

Arganti Knifelock was staring back at them.

"We're both transparent," Erin said.

"What are you—" Jon threw her a puzzled look. "No, there's a guy with a blindfold in the middle of the..."

The stranger was gone. And Erin and Jon were indeed transparent.

Norm paused the game and made his way over. "What are you talking about?" He studied the glass with his blacked-out gaze, causing their reflections to abruptly sharpen. "It's just us. And we're not transparent." He walked back to his controller and resumed playing *Fallout*.

"I'm not crazy," Jon whispered.

"Me neither," she whispered back. "The door...I think it's how you trigger the mirror. Let's try it again."

"Let's try it again," Norm mocked. "I spent over a decade trying to escape, and you figure it out on your first day here?"

Jon ignored him and closed the door. Erin counted, "1...2...3..."

As he swung it wide, Arganti Knifelock shone in the mirror. A second later, the Nightkeeper vanished.

"See?" Norm called. "We're stuck." Their reflections cohered in time with his words, then faded back into inconstant transparency.

"Can you play online?" Erin asked.

"What?" His brow wrinkled. "Yeah. Why?"

"This place is linked to the outside world. Otherwise, you wouldn't be able to access the internet. Also—who stocks the kitchen? And how does water get to the bathroom?"

Norm snorted. "You're stuck. Get used to it."

Erin nudged Jon. "Do it again."

Once again, the door opened and shut. Once again, Knifelock appeared and vanished.

"Keep going," Erin urged.

The door opened and shut, opened and shut, striking up a relentless tempo. For some reason, it kindled hope within the teens. Existence seemed to be pulsing with the door, giving rise to a transcendent cadence.

In less than a minute, the bathroom fixtures began to fade, giving way to a different backdrop altogether.

"How did you do that?" Norm rushed up beside them. "It's...it's..." The spirit trailed off, overcome by wonder.

"A ballroom." Erin examined a dirty banner, hung in the center of the dilapidated room. Some of the letters were torn off and missing. "For senior prom, it looks like."

"What the..." Norm was flabbergasted. "How did you do that?" he repeated.

Jon struggled to catch his breath. While the Shift in his perception felt natural and right, it still took physical effort. "Followed my gut." He almost said *Followed my heart,* but somehow he knew that would infuriate Norm. "Come on." He took Erin's hand and they both stepped through.

Norm tried to protest. "Wait, what if it's worse than—" As soon as they entered, his voice went mute.

"Same vibe," Erin hedged.

"Pretty much," Jon agreed. The carpet was ratty. And the wallpaper was thick with mold and grime.

Behind them, the portal echoed with a metallic *chunk,* much like a padlock unhitching its shackle. Norm stepped through midphrase—"both *crazy*"—then stopped and gaped at their decrepit surroundings.

"I never went to prom," Erin stared at the banner.

"Me neither," Jon replied.

"Who cares?" Norm muttered.

The teens spread out and explored the room. After a bit, they met back in its center.

"No way out," Norm observed. "This place is a bust."

"There's something here…" Jon's brow wrinkled in thought. "You hear that?" He glanced at Erany. "It sounds like…"

"Music," she marveled. "It sounds like music."

"I can't hear a thing," Norm complained.

Jon and Erany didn't acknowledge him. As they smiled and bobbed along to the song, it strengthened into "Here's to the Night" by Eve 6.

"Not my favorite." Jon grimaced.

"Nor mine." She grinned wryly.

"Care to dance?" He extended an arm.

"Enchanté." She mimed a curtsy with an imaginary dress.

They clasped hands and swayed together, exchanging eyerolls, sighs, and rueful chuckles. The song was annoying and hopelessly maudlin.

Thankfully, an upbeat guitar took its place, infusing them both with a fresh burst of energy.

" 'Lucky Love!' " Erin exclaimed. "The acoustic version!" She chuckled self-consciously. "We're about to dance to Ace of Base."

"It's a big step up," Jon opined.

"I'm not complaining."

The song was corny and cheerful, light and pretty. Jon felt a hint of protest as the lyrics crystallized—Ace of Base was crooning that a lucky romance belonged in heaven for teens—because even though he was still a teenager, he felt a hell of a lot older. Not geriatric...ancient, somehow.

Norm yelled and gestured in frustration. I can't hear him—he's been put back on mute. That doesn't strike me as the least bit odd, because this is *my* story, not his. As I sync to the beat and beam at my girl, I realize I'm perfectly willing to dance the night away. What's the alternative? Playing predictable games in a blocked-off basement? God, her eyes and her smile...she's so damn *beautiful*. I know we just met, but it feels like we're destined to be together.

The music transitioned into a melancholic fade—*"I'm a prisoner of hope, I know"*—as Norm's voice strengthened and clarified. "—need to go back before it's too late." He stared at the portal leading into the basement. It was shimmering and hazing with sullen light.

Jon's intuition came to the fore. "Erin..."

"Yeah?"

His brow crinkled. "I think I can..." He could feel possibility blooming and shifting, pulling at his soul with steady insistence. "What do you want to hear?"

She pondered the ceiling. "Um...oh! You know Walk the Moon? They wrote a song called—"

" 'Shut Up and Dance.' You got it." He reached for the vibration of potential and play, then manifested her request into physical reality.

Norm shouted in protest, but he faded again into a background drone. Jon and Erany, meanwhile, went from a muted shuffle into an animated boogie. We aren't that good, but we make up for it with our delight and enthusiasm. I'm fully immersed in Erany's joy, the whirl of her hair and her ear-to-ear grin. For a resplendent moment, I remember all that I am and all I could be. It isn't a thought so much as a feeling—a full-being knowing that doesn't just erase my doubts and my fears, it makes them into ridiculous jokes.

"Jon." Erany studied the ballroom with growing astonishment. "Look."

Threadbare carpet shrunk and vanished, replaced by tracts of glossy wood floor. Tattered wallpaper curled and withered, giving way to a fresh coat of paint. Darkened chandeliers sparked to life, flooding the room with bright gold light.

"Erany." Jon nodded at Norm.

She stiffened in shock. "What the…"

Norm had split into nine distinct figures. Whenever he moved, the motion echoed throughout his clones.

"Norm?" Jon asked uncertainly.

The multiple Norms raved and ranted. Nothing came out—they were still on mute. After a minute of silent fury, they crossed their arms and glared at the couple.

"What *is* this place?" Erin muttered.

Jon canvassed the room with a thoughtful stare. "I think we know, somewhere deep in our collective unconscious."

"Yeah…if I had to guess…I…" She shook her head in wordless frustration.

"Don't," he advised. "Trying to define it makes it…" This time, he was the one at a loss for words.

"Slower," Erany finished. "You can't stop it. You can only slow it down."

"Yeah." He nodded. "Exactly."

Erany gave him a quizzical look. "Do you feel that?"

"What?" he asked.

She tilted her head, as if she was trying to hear something in the far-off distance. A second later, warmth bloomed inside his chest, lighting his nerves with budding elation.

They were going to dance to another song.

"This is it," he murmured. "The last one before we remember who we are."

"There's never a last one." She gave him a haunted smile, deeply profound and somehow ecstatic.

" 'All Through the Night.' " he chuckled. "Just the instrumental, though, and…it's a slow-dance version. I never knew that was even a thing."

"*So* cheesy." Erany sighed in mock exasperation.

"Shall we?"

"We shall."

As they swayed together, he snuck a glance at the multiple Norms. The spirits were nursing plastic red cups, bobbing along and trying to look natural. Upon closer inspection, they seemed to be stuck on eternal repeat. It was subtle as hell—you really had to focus in order to catch it—but once you saw it, it was blindingly obvious.

"Are they even real?" Jon muttered.

"I think so. I think they did this to themselves."

He raised an eyebrow. "So it's their fault? 'Pull yourself up by your own bootstraps?' "

She scoffed in disgust. "Don't be gross. I go out of my way to expose self-righteous victim-blamers—they're insecure tyrants who project their need for control. That's not what I'm getting at. I'm trying to determine if existence is benevolent, cruel, or random." After a brief pause, she added, "I'd say random is arguably cruel, because there would be instances where you would be rewarded with atrocity and horror, no matter how hard you worked or how good you were." Her face turned contemplative. "Think about it: what if perspective determines reality? What if it determines coincidence and circumstance? You would have the power to shape your own life, and everyone else would have that exact same power."

"Republican and Democrat all at once. Egalitarian because everyone has it, individualist because you have total say in how it's used." His expression softened and became reflective. "You couldn't ask for anything too specific, or you would run into scarcity and technical obstacles."

"What do you mean?"

"Barring implications from quantum physics, there's only so much of this or that in any given place, at any given time. So in order to leverage hidden potential, It would need a creative license to grant the essence of your desire, perhaps in a better way than when you first imagined."

Erin nodded. "Makes sense."

"But what if you screw up?" His gaze turned pensive. "Or never accept your inherent potential? That's where it stops being fair and impartial. Especially since we start out ignorant, with different stats and disparate resources."

She pursed her lips and thought it over. "You would have to incorporate reincarnation. When you play a game and things go south, you need to be able to reset the board."

"Or respawn and try something different," Jon mused. "But you can't tell your avatar how to win, or it would end up spoiling the immersive experience."

"Still, you can't let past-game knowledge go to waste..." She chewed her lip. "You would have to communicate it. Not overtly, or it wouldn't be a game; it would just be a set of technical instructions. So how would you communicate with your in-game avatar, and offer yourself clues without ruining the play?"

His eyes ticked back and forth. "Through indirect hints, I imagine. I would lean on personal experience: anecdotal events that impact our lives. Also, you would need some form of private guidance—cues that applied to your unique perspective."

The epiphany struck them at the exact same time. They both declared, "Emotions." and chuckled together.

After a second, he asked, "What about addicts, or people who are compelled to be destructive and unhealthy? You can't just tell 'em to follow their gut."

She pondered the ceiling. "Maybe it requires a unified perspective. I'm just spitballing, but I'm guessing you would first have to feel your way into existential integrity. A soul-deep harmony only you can confirm, transcending judgment and societal measures. Then, once you're aligned, Capital You—"

" 'Capital You?' "

"The one that can dictate synchronicity. Once you're aligned, Capital You can guide lowercase you into a desirable outcome." She laughed self-consciously. "Silly, I know."

"Not at all," Jon said firmly. "I would just add that maybe It's our natural state, and it's not so much a matter of working towards It, as remembering who we are and relaxing back into It."

Erany nodded in thoughtful agreement. "I've done a lot of research on psychedelics. Some people say they change your life, but a lot of people take 'em and don't change at all. When you think about it, that's how it should be, right? How ridiculous would it be if enlightenment depended on an external trigger, and it was subject to control through scarcity and force? You'd be at risk of being damned by default. Like people who are excluded from religious salvation, because they live in a culture without the 'correct' theology. I think psychedelics are more like a brief reminder. And while that can be useful and provide us with clues, it can never replace our personal guidance."

"A reminder? Of what?"

"I..." She shrugged. "I think it's better off if you leave It unnamed."

"Voldemort in reverse," Jon chuckled. "I think you're on to something. People go astray when they try and define It. It's always expanding and taking new forms, so It'll defy any attempt to confine or restrict It." He glanced at the Norms. "I wonder what they're thinking."

"We can't really know. All we've got are impressions of their thoughts, not the actual thoughts themselves. We might guess correctly, but at the same time..." She shrugged again.

"No, I get it," Jon assured. "I think that's part of why politics gets so dysfunctional. Folks pretend to know what others are thinking and feeling, then try and force-correct those thoughts and feelings."

"Sounds about right," Erany remarked. Then: "The song's ending." They stepped away from each other.

"That was disappointing," Jon commented. " 'Not with a bang, but with a whimper.' Wish we could have danced to the regular version."

She put her hands on her hips and stared at the floor. "You can still kind of hear it..."

"It's getting louder." They exchanged a grin. " 'All Through the Night!' " he declared. "The faster one!" Sure enough, the tune was straight from the eighties, heavily flavored with pop-music synth.

"Ask and you shall receive," Erany quipped.

Jon drew her close. They swayed together through the slow-paced intro. The tempo picked up, cuing them to unclasp their hands and grin a bit wider. As soon as the beat kicked into gear, both of them fused with the heartfelt music, riding the cadence with body and soul.

After a minute, the music slowed. Jon and Erin followed suit.

The Norms had faded into bare transparency. It registers in the back of my mind, but only in the faintest sense. Ultimately, it's not like I can save him without his consent. If I argue him into a healthier state, it'll only last if he's willing to shift his perspective. I can't do it for him—the best I can do is shine my own light and hint at what's possible. Whenever he's ready, my door will be open and I'll gladly help out. But if I'm not around for whatever reason, he'll find a way to claim his potential. And even if he doesn't, that's all right, because we're all stuck in a no-lose game. We all eventually return to the True.

In the meantime, it's up to me to enjoy the journey. So when the refrain kicks in, I dance with everything I've got. I don't care if I look dorky or stupid or cringey as hell; I beam at Erany and give it my all.

The synth grows louder, blossoming into full 80s glory. I twirl her, she twirls me, we go back-to-back...Evermoor's gone and so are the Watchers (which I knew were the Norms all along, somewhere deep in my untrammeled soul). It's just me and her, dancing without a care in the world.

A moment later, the synth drops off and gives way to the lyrics. Cyndi voices our unspoken thoughts, asking to linger in a half-awake dream...and then we're channeling the upbeat refrain, part and parcel of its dynamic energy.

As the outro dwindles, we regard each other with bone-deep appreciation and overwhelming gratitude. Not the kind that requires justification—*be grateful you're not starving, be grateful you're employed, be grateful you have it better than everyone who suffers*—but the kind that comes without any words. I'm thankful it's possible to feel this much joy. There's no rationalizing, no comparing it to this or that, no need to explain or validate.

That is your truth. That is your right.

"I love you." I say it without transactional pretense, as a pure expression of my unfettered self.

Her lips crook up. "I know."

Hearty laughter bursts from my mouth. "Did you just pull a Han Solo on me? It's okay, you don't have to—"

"I love you too."

The words are simply a manifestation, a natural follow-on to what we're both feeling. Now that they're out, there's nothing more to say.

So I lean in and kiss her.

We melt together, adrift in a sea of utter belonging. After we part, I drink in her half-lidded eyes, her dreamy smile and heady warmth.

"I can't believe I'm about to say this..." I dip my chin and chuckle softly.

"What?"

I meet her gaze and smile again. "I'm glad we came to Sidehelm Pass. This isn't a horror movie—"

"It's an adventure," she finishes.

She palms my cheeks and tilts her head, prompting me for a follow-on kiss. I catch a glimpse of her eyes falling closed, then I'm lost again in her sweet embrace. A moment later, we touch foreheads and she bites her lip. The sight of it triggers a fresh wave of lust, devoid of shame or any remorse.

"You are blessed beyond measure," a voice says.

We both step apart, regarding the Watcher who just addressed us. He's adopted his true form—that of a withered old man, adorned with jewels and stuffy robes—along with his eight other cohorts. They're all transparent, flickering with patches of fleeting detail. Jags of solidity dart across them, bringing clothing and flesh into short-lived relief.

Unsurprisingly, their eyes are pools of unseeing black.

"Jon." Erany glances to either side. The ballroom's dissolving—the walls and the floor are morphing into stone.

"Long have we idled," the Watcher rasps. "We prayed for an end, but it never came. And so we have languished for countless millennia, waiting for someone to show us the way. I beg of you: free us from this torturous ennui."

"It has not been millennia," Erany corrects, "but decades since you were cursed to linger."

The Watcher flaps a dismissive hand. "I have wandered this fortress for untold eons."

"She's telling the truth," I affirm. "You once lived as kings and generals. When you were called upon to—"

"Lies!" the Watcher bellows. His eyes briefly assume their original humanity. I can see the definition between pupils and whites, and even a bit of blue in the iris.

"I think you know," I say quietly. "I think you know how long you've been stuck. If you shift your perspective—"

The forgotten king drops to his knees. "Free us from this mournful lack!" The other Watchers begin wailing and moaning.

I hold up a hand and cut them off. "I'm the Prophesied Traveler. You know this, don't you?"

"Yes. Otherwise, you couldn't have escaped our stygian glamour."

"You can escape the exact same way—you have the capacity to see that you were never really trapped. But I want you to know: if you decide to stay, you will eventually pass into the Clear, and you will eventually find your way to the True. You can't lose, not in the long run."

I feel like I'm channeling Gyrax, Alijyar, and every quote I've ever resonated with. At the same time, I'm not parroting them. My speech has a power all its own.

The Watchers turn to each other, muttering and whispering with newfound urgency.

"You remember," Erany says gently. "Despite your refusal, the knowledge cannot pass into shadow and void."

The lead Watcher gets to his feet. "We cannot follow in your steps. But one day...one day, we might be able to forge our own way out."

"I look forward to that day." I step toward him and offer an arm. "May light find you in dark places."

"And may it ease your eyes and guide your feet." The Watcher grasps my forearm. For a couple of seconds, his body coheres, and I feel solid flesh beneath my fingers.

Then he offers an Evermoor salute, touching his brow and bringing his hand a few inches out. "We thank you for your clear-souled wisdom. More importantly, we thank you for living it. Go with our blessing."

I nod respectfully and return his salute.

"Stay here with mine."

39

The haunts aren't as gloomy, the sun is out, and the general vibe is...I wouldn't say *cheerful,* but the air is infused with mild positivity. Kind of like a bright summer morning, when the dew is still wet and there's an overall sense of easygoing optimism.

"Jon." Erany points at the ground. Stalks are emerging and blooming into flowers.

"Wow." I marvel at the sped-up growth. "What are they responding to? Us or the Watchers?"

"I don't believe it is an either-or."

I take a moment to appreciate their color. Then I ask, "How much do you remember? It's already starting to feel like a dream. Something about *Simulacra and Simulation,* and how we voluntarily constrain our omnipotence..." I scratch my head, struggling to shore up my fading memory. "Huh. Weird."

"I remember our prom." Her lips curve into a radiant grin.

I duck my head in a joyful smile. "Me too." I'll never forget dancing with Eralindíany, even when I'm old and gray. "Anything else?"

"I remember what you said." She looks me in the eye. "You said that you love me."

"And you said it back."

"I knew it before, but it wasn't until then that it felt right to say it."

"In the grip of the True."

"Even that feels..." She searches the horizon with her gaze. "It doesn't..."

"I'm with you," I remark. "Trying to define It with thoughts and words...it's like trying to grab a handful of ocean. Best to enjoy It and leave It be."

"Aye," she agrees. "We'll inevitably forget the minutiae and details. That will allow us to perceive It without any hindrance, in unexpected forms and novel occurrence."

"Couldn't have said it better myself."

I also know, soon enough, we'll have to find some other way to describe Its breadth. And that after a bit, our descriptions will become dull and obsolete.

And that's okay, because I know I'll be able to feel my way back to It.

———

Erany taps her gold-weave brace, activating its dormant locator spell. It spreads into a hologram of the Rosecraft Blade, surrounded by arrows and fluxing glyphs. She swipes through a bunch of glowing designs, then nods to herself in self-assurance. We're going the right way, according to her bevy of direction-finding charms.

The cliffs are adorned with dark purple fronds, roughly as thick as a stereotypical cactus, with a wide base and a thin tip. They poke four or five feet from the austere rock, then curl downward and inward, like fingers forming into a fist. Erany says they're called pockleaves or bouncefoles. They're hallucinogenic if you boil them with mint, and you can build a shelter with 'em if you know what you're doing.

The pockleaves are accompanied by reptilian fauna: pitbull-sized lizards (wyrecks) that are jumping, climbing, or just hanging out. They've got bright red frills, prehensile tails, and a stretchy quartet of six-jointed limbs. It wouldn't be right to say they have paws, 'cause these guys have legitimate fingers. Each foot (hand?) ends in seven digits, scaly and taloned and as long as E.T's. Occasionally, one of them will bleat a nerdy-sounding honk, then bounce off a pockleaf like a springy trampoline. At first, I find 'em intimidating (they're big, athletic, and super lizardy), but after a bit I start to relax. They're actually kind of funny and endearing—a bunch of awkward dorks that happen to be master climbers.

Midway across the second peak, the pockleaves and wyrecks disappear. Everything here is gray and sterile. It's just stones and dust, stones and dust. One moment we're hiking past lizards and fronds, the next we're trudging through a lunar vacuum.

"We're close, aren't we?" I ask. "You said the Blade nuked the surrounding terrain. This is the aftermath, right?"

"Aye," Erany answers. "It used to reach dozens of faires past Sidehelm Pass. Over the years, animals and plants have crept back in."

I'm not sure how to feel about what comes next. For the longest time, I was preoccupied with confronting the Watchers of Erendor; I gave little thought to how Erany was gonna win the Blade. I plan on helping however I can, but my gut tells me this is her journey.

Two days later, we step foot on the base of Yom Dagur.

———

Erany stops and points at the summit. "There lies the Blade."

I shade my eyes and study the peak. "Is it flatter up top?"

She cranes forward and squints at the mountain. "The tides are moving in a downward flow...if I had to guess, I'd say there's a crater."

"Makes sense—the Blade was forged in a massive explosion. Ready?"

She takes a breath and gives a nod. "Yes." Followed by a grin. "And if not, well...I don't have a choice, do I?"

"You always have a choice."

"Then it's an obvious one: return with the Blade, or allow the Queen to lay waste to our efforts."

"Set aside logic and duty. What does your heart say?"

"I..." Erany falls quiet. Then: "I am destined for the Blade. Beyond any qualm or shadow of a doubt."

"I wasn't trying to question your commitment, it's just—"

"No, I am grateful," she assures. "I had to know the Blade was mine, free of rationale or imagined obligation. Sometimes, only our soul will reveal our needs, in full defiance of sense and reason."

"Amen to that."

" 'Amen?' "

I chuckle ruefully. "It's a religious saying that means I agree. Not transcendental, I know—"

"Transcendence surpasses words and phrases. 'Tis a function of your inward state—how aligned you are to the present-moment True."

"Well...maybe it is transcendent, then."

"What does your heart tell you?" She raises an amused eyebrow.

"Throwing my own question back at me, eh?" I chuckle again. "Um...it's not telling me anything." Sudden resolve floods my brain. "You know what? It doesn't matter. I'm here to support you. That is it and that is all."

Erany smiles and doesn't say a thing.

Which, I dare say, is the most transcendent response she could have given.

————

The slope descends into a striated crater, about twenty feet deep and a hundred yards long. Halfway down, a blocky figure—around nine feet tall, comprised of rough-hewn rock—is walking in an expansive circle, tromping around three green figures. They're seated around a bright patch of glass, growing from the middle of the desolate crater. All three are naked, and they seem to be meditating.

"Their golem protector." I track the stone-man with my gaze.

Erany nods. "And the Blade."

In the patch of grass between the dryads, a lush rose protrudes from the ground. Its petals lighten and dim in an alternating rhythm, exchanging hues and tones in slow-winking flashes. Its elegant stem is simple and exquisite, defined by arresting slants and tilts. This may sound weird, but it's giving off the vibe of an expert supermodel, right as they strike a flawless pose.

"Wow," I breathe. "That thing is *beautiful.*"

Erany glances at me, amused. "Should I be jealous?"

A self-conscious laugh. "I know, I know; I've been handling Ailura for months on end. I shouldn't be thrown by the sight of a—"

"Nonsense," she says. "All Great Weapons are worthy of awe."

"Right." I sweep the air with a hand. "Your show, Princess. I have your back through thick and thin."

She places a hand on my cheek, holds my gaze, and gives me a kiss.

Then she turns and heads for the Blade.

———

The golem's face is a stony oval. Its arms and legs are columns of rock, bound by a series of burly enchantments. Its hands are made from smaller chunks, giving it the semblance of jointed fingers. Each movement is paired with a creak, a result of its parts rubbing together. It keeps walking in a wide-ranging circle, seemingly oblivious to our approaching presence.

That changes when we enter its orbit.

The golem halts, foot in the air...then tromps toward us with frightening speed. It's one thing to watch it from a good ways away, entirely another to have it charging toward you. Have you ever been inside an unstable building, or a dicey situation with heavy machinery? That's what this feels like. The golem embodies natural disaster, on par with an avalanche or a devastating earthquake.

Erany shoots an arm across my chest, stopping me from drawing Ailura Qartesi. "Don't." As I ease off Ailura, the golem stops before us. In the gap between its thighs, I can see the dryads getting to their feet.

Erany leans sideways, poking out from the rock-man's bulk. "I have come for the Blade."

"Your name." The dryad's voice is clear and strong, accompanied by a series of low-volume sounds. The rustle of leaves, the trickle of water, grass hissing in the brisk autumn wind...I'm sure there's more, but my ears are too dumb sort it all out.

"Eralindíany Ailahdi. Heir to Delán and blood of ValFae."

"Meaningless," the center dryad scoffs. "Ogbosh, move your rump. I wish to gauge our foolish arrivals."

The golem cants its head. *Are you sure?*

The rightmost dryad snaps, *"Move."*

Ogbosh complies, resuming his circuit around the Blade. (I might be imagining it, but I think he's sulking.)

The three dryads are tall, willowy, and green. Their faces are thin, home to expressive eyes and full sets of lips. Tiny leaves dot their skin, speckling their bodies with occasional sprouts. All three all nude, but they don't have naughty bits. There's no way to tell if they're a he or a she; if they were wearing clothes, they would be able to pass for either one.

The dryad on the left says, "My name is—" before voicing a series of outdoor sounds: the pop and whoosh of burning wood, the harsh thunk of rock on rock, and the crackle of branches snapping underfoot. "—but you may call me Numiné."

The middle dryad offers a nod, expresses a different combination of outdoor sounds, and concludes with, "I am Aesmotí."

The dryad on the right crosses their arms, states their real name, and says, "I am Dyneckta."

Erany offers a courtier's bow—her left leg assumes a jaunty diagonal, her right arm traces an elegant flourish, and her left hand angles close to her chest. "I have come for what's mine."

"Temper your claim," Aesmotí cautions. "The Blade must be won through a contest of riddles." (Like in *The Hobbit?* Cool.)

Dynecta adds, "If you fail to answer, Ogbosh will send you into the Clear." (Wait—*what?)*

Erany dips her chin and mutters, "That is what happened to the other seekers..." Then she nods. "Very well. I trust in my savvy."

"Ha!" Dyneckta barks. "We have challenged over a hundred souls, and not a single one has passed our test! Below this crater's western edge, there lies a plateau heaped with their scoured bones!"

"No matter. I accept."

Numiné gestures at the circle of grass. "Sit." The dryads face the Rose/Blade, then take a seat and cross their legs.

Erany doffs her cloak, sword, quiver, and carry. "Here." She holds them out to me. "Care for my things while I spar with these faeries."

"Can't we talk about this?" I sputter. "You're about to put your life on the line!"

"Riddling was popular back in Delán. I am intimately familiar with verbal enigmas."

My heart kicks into overdrive. *"Plateau heaped with bones,* remember? Erany, you don't have to—"

"Jon." She puts a hand on my shoulder. "What is the alternative? To skulk away and abandon our plans? We are here for a reason."

"I..." My face twists in frustration. "How do you know—"

"This is my story now. Let me write it as I see fit."

Her words strike a chord. "I...okay. I love you." (Yes it's lame, but it's all I can think of.)

"I know." She throws me a lopsided grin.

Son of a bitch—that's the second time she pulled a Han Solo on me. "Fine. Let's do this." I blow out hard, trying to calm my frazzled nerves.

And remember, Jon: this is her story, not yours.

40

As soon as Erany takes a seat, Ogbosh tromps back over. He stops behind her and spreads his arms, ready to pop her skull with a single clap.

"Before we begin, we must shackle your aura," Aesmotí says.

Erany closes her eyes and starts to chant. Her arcane meridians brighten and pulse, then gradually fade into muted opacity.

The dryads respond with a low-toned hum, summoning transparent glyphs from the rose's cup. They snake upward, outward, then hook tightly into Erany's loci. I'm no expert, but I get the gist: she can't access her magical energy. If she fails to answer, she'll be easy to kill.

"You have first right of query," Dyneckta states. "Refuse to speak, and you will pass directly into the Clear."

"Understood," Erany replies. "I'm tall when I'm young and I'm short when I'm old. What am I?"

"A candle," Numiné answers. "What month has twenty-eight days?"

"All of them. What is always in front but cannot be seen?"

"The future," Dynecta replies. "What has teeth but cannot bite?"

"A comb. What part of roads do ghosts love to travel?"

Under other circumstances, I would find this cool. The similarity to *The Hobbit* (which, despite my issues with *The Lord of the Rings,* happens to be a book I truly enjoy) is undeniable. But the love of my life is in mortal danger—that's all I can think about as the duel goes on.

An hour becomes two. Two becomes three. As the clouds glow rich with sundown color, I begin to settle down. Neither Erany nor the dryads have shown any doubt. It's just question-answer, question-answer.

I think she's got this.

The sun disappears below the horizon, giving way to Evermoor's lunar quadrivium. Usually, only one or two moons are out and about. Tonight is different—all four orbs are stunningly full. One is pink, the second is red, the third is green, and the fourth is violet. They've risen equidistant from Yom Dagur (north, south, east, west), imbuing the night sky with a ritualistic vibe.

As crazy as it sounds, I'm starting to get bored.

I explore the crater, stare down at the plateau littered with the remains of challengers (most of their clothes have blown away, but there's still a handful of carries and weapons), then wander back over. As long as they don't try a Bilbo-style *What's in my pocket,* I think we're good. My girlfriend seems to have an endless supply of—

"Why are you worthy of the Rosecraft Blade?" Dyneckta asks.

Erany stiffens, taken aback.

"That's not *fair!*" I scream, gripping Ailura. Ogbosh's arms twitch a bit wider, coaxing a ghastly scrape from his rocky joints. "That's not a riddle! That's—"

"Jon." Erany raises a hand and cuts me off. "Please."

"But—"

"Don't." Her gaze holds me in place. *This is my story. Let me write it as I see fit.*

I slide Ailura back in her holster. In my hot-blooded panic, I drew her halfway out. "Fine." The word comes out choked. "I just…"

"Jon."

"Yeah," I manage. "Sorry."

"Shall we continue?" Numiné asks.

Erany nods. "Yes."

"Very well. Respond with the truth and we shall cede you the Blade."

"Three chances!" I blurt. "Make it fair, goddammit!"

Dyneckta glares at me, then addresses Erany: "You have one chance, Princess. But you may cry off now, if you so wish. Renounce the Blade, and you can depart with your life."

Erany shakes her head. "No."

"Then you are bound," Aesmotí declares. "Four have arrived at this critical juncture. All fell short and passed into the Clear. We acknowledge your courage, blood of ValFae."

Erany waves a dismissive hand—*doesn't matter*—and studies the ground, lips moving in silent inquiry. *Why am I worthy of the Rosecraft Blade?*

After a minute, her questioning ceases. Understanding dawns in her eyes, tinging her face with a hint of a smile. She dips her chin, shakes her head in amusement—*good one*—and reaches out for the magic rose.

My body clenches in shock and horror. *"Erany, you didn't answer the—"*

Too late. Her fingers tighten around the stem.

41

Elongating thorns gore through her palm, piercing her wrist and weaving into her forearm. As spears of light erupt from the rose, I snap Ailura out of her holster. The radiance grows twice as bright, and—

BOOM!

—I fly backward ass over teakettle, landing on my belly and rolling onto my side. It's a bad angle, but I need to make the shot or—

Holy. *Shit.*

The rose has morphed into a full-on sword, thrust point-down into the patch of grass. Light-woven tendrils blaze from its edge, encompassing Erany in an orbit of colors. They're paired with a rush of dust-streaked eddies that flutter her hair into golden twists.

"Erany…" I rise to a knee, gaping at the torrent of She-ra-esque brilliance.

Blue jags of energy materialize around her. They flare, sizzle, and leave fierce-glowing prints hanging in the air. Lightning crackles down from the storm-torn sky, so damn wide that it fully encompasses Erany and the dryads. They're reduced to a clutch of glaring silhouettes, awash in a barrage of dancing incandescence.

Colored bolts strike with breakneck speed—black, green, red, pink—then converge on Erany all at once, triggering an eruption and throwing me off my feet.

I prop myself up and spit out dust. *"Ptt. Ptt."*

My sight resolves. My lips part in amazement.

Erany is wielding a green-tinged rapier. Its guard is adorned with a rough-hewn ruby, which, much like the rose, is trading gradients of red across its slow-winking facets. She's also wearing armor, sleek and silver with a sylvan aesthetic. Instead of concealing her athletic figure, it accentuates the flow of her arms and legs, along with the line of her neck and jaw. Around her joints and throughout her core, the plating gives way to bare skin. Each interruption shines with runes—those gaps are filled with protective magic.

She stares at the back of her non-sword hand (her other hand is healed, thank God), now adorned with triangular metal. "Deliac's Gleam…" She turns it slowly back and forth, then examines the sword with a wonderstruck gaze.

The three dryads rise to their feet. "Congratulations, Princess," Numiné says. "The Blade is yours."

"Hmpf," Dyneckta mutters. "Dumb luck is all it was."

"You know that's not true," Aesmotí chides. "She saw past the riddle's cognitive artifice."

Erany lowers the Rosecraft Blade. "It wasn't a riddle…'twas a simple affirmation."

"Aye." Numiné smiles. "Though you knew that before you started the contest."

Erany gives a thoughtful nod. "In my heart of hearts, there was never any doubt."

Aesmotí gestures at the Blade. "Upon receiving your channeled intent, it will summon golems and nature-born constructs. Also, it will consistently project the Trividian Slash."

Erany tilts her head. "Is that an attack?"

Dyneckta barks, "Ogbosh! Assume high guard!"

The golem raises his hands like an orthodox boxer.

"Deliver three slashes unto the air," Numiné instructs. "At the same time, imagine Ogbosh is an enemy combatant."

Erany whirls into a three-stroke attack, leaving three separate gleams hanging in the air. The blue-green crescents pulse a single time, then hurtle toward Ogbosh and strike his arms. Consecutive flashes erupt from his skin, inching him back with each magic missile. *(Damn* that's cool. See that, Weak Sauce? Now *that* is a magic sword.)

"The Trividian Slash," Aesmotí declares. "Against multiple opponents, it will serve you well, though you will have to employ a sweeping technique."

"I shall adjust." Erany marvels at the Blade, now flickering with lingering energy. "Does it pair with a sheath?"

"No," Numiné replies. "But if you wish, it can revert back to its original state."

Erany's brow crinkles in puzzlement. "How do I—"

Before she can finish, the Blade shrinks down and morphs into the Rose. At the same time, her armor fades and gives way to her clothes.

"Amazing," she whispers. She affixes the weapon to her non-sword hip. "It slides in my belt without catching or snagging....also, its aura is almost completely hidden. Why, though? I have beheld Ailura Qartesi," she jerks her chin at my holstered revolver, "and her magic outshines the high-noon sun."

Dyneckta barks a contemptuous laugh. *"Ailura Qartesi?* Of course she would bray out her Nok-damned presence!" The dryad flings a hand at my gun. " 'Tis a crude machine, meant for naught but ruin! The Blade, on the other hand, is born of clime and terrain and the wild heart of Evermoor. Keep that in mind, lest she ravage your flesh with another ream of thorns."

Erany dips her chin. "I will not forget."

Dyneckta grumbles something under their breath. While I can't hear the words, the gist is clear: *That's right. You better not.*

"We are done with this world," Numiné states. "If you wish, you may accompany us to Lanádrhiel Quendessir."

Erany's face goes blank with amazement. "The Radiant Forest? I..." She glances over at me. "We..."

"What are they talking about?" I ask.

"A sylvan plane. I used to revel in its lore, hoping I could one day visit its fabled reaches."

"You would live eons longer, as Lanádrhiel softens the passage of time," Aesmotí says gently. " 'Twould be a charmed life, one of whimsy and dreams and carefree ease."

"Too bad we can't, right?" I chuckle nervously. "I mean, maybe after we beat Lyderea…"

Erany shakes her head as if she's clearing her senses. "You're right. We can't. It would make a lie of all I have done."

Aesmotí nods. "Then, if you wish, we can send you back to Sidehelm Pass."

"Can you send us further? To the shore that borders its gullies and vales?"

Aesmotí nods again. "Very well."

"Lazy and greedy," Dyneckta grumbles. "We've already ceded the Rosecraft Blade, yet still you pine for additional favor."

"Ignore the griping," Numiné says affectionately. "On the platform below, there lies a tract of arcane rimples. With a couple of tweaks, they should be easy to collapse into a slipworld passage."

With that pronouncement, we set off for the plateau. The dryads take lead, then it's me and Erany, and finally Ogbosh in the rear. I sneak a glance at him every few seconds. I can't help it—he was ready to kill Erany with his giant stone hands.

The path is crimped by zigzag switchbacks. As we navigate the turns, I study the dryads out of the corner of my eye. It's kind of disorienting; they alternately appear male or female, depending on the light or the angle of view. Their physical attractiveness is just as erratic. Sometimes they're ugly, sometimes they're plain, and sometimes they're drop-dead, Fair Folk gorgeous.

Halfway down, I turn to Erany. "I'm still confused…how'd you solve that Nok-damned riddle? I know you took what was rightfully yours, but—"

"I refused to answer. That's why I won."

"What do you mean?"

"If I had given a verbal response—if I had acknowledged the premise that I need to justify my inherent worth—I would have cut myself off from the objective truth: that I am inherently worthy no matter what. Whenever you rationalize or justify why, you agree to the implication that another must validate you, and that you aren't worthy unless scrutinized and approved. So I didn't respond at all. I made the same statement I would have made if the dryads had been absent."

"Okay," I nod slowly, digesting her words. "You're speaking from an existential sense. If we're parts of an omnipotence that manifested into fragments, a singular fragment needn't justify its worth to any other fragment. If it does, it's perpetuating the illusion that—once again, in an existential sense—certain fragments are better than others. And if it commits to that illusion, it's cutting itself off from its whole-being perception, and that's what gives rise to the power of the True."

"Exactly. I knew in my heart that the Blade was mine. I merely had to reach out and claim it. Much like your abilities, I imagine—you needn't justify why you need them, you simply let them flow into being."

"Yeah..." I rub the back of my neck. "When I go Laiddinic, I'm so damn sure of whatever I'm doing, it feels like it's straight-up destined to happen, and there's nothing I can do to change the outcome."

She gives a nod. "The True is the same in that it lacks any say. In omnipresence and omnitemporality, everything has been said, every choice has been made. During a Laiddinic event, it makes sense you would feel that same lack of choice, as you are channeling your omnipresent and omnitemporal self."

"Ugh." I wince. "I kind of like my finite perception, even if it means I'm not using God-mode."

"Ultimately, that may be our only option," Erany muses. "To view reality through a narrow lens, or allow a richer connection with our greater aspect."

I rub my eyes with a thumb and forefinger. "Let's change the subject. I feel like I smoked too much weed and ate a buttload of shrooms."

"Very well," Erany glances at the mountain plateau, heaped with the bones of ill-fated seekers. "Maybe Ogbosh did them a favor. It's hard to go crazy when your brains have been smashed."

I make a face. "Not funny."

She throws me a smirk. "It's a little funny."

I open my mouth, about to chide her for being disrespectful, then acquiesce with an easy chuckle. "Yeah, I suppose." After I die, I hope I'm honored with a joke and a smile, instead of tears or anger or righteous indignation.

As we step on the plateau, Aesmoti points at its cliff-wall border, speckled with bones and piecemeal remains. "That is where the passage will form. Keep your distance. If you touch it before it is stable, it will throw you into mantic chaos."

"Yep. Got it. Mantic chaos sounds like dog poop." We move back to the edge of the plateau, placing mounds of skeletons between us and the dryads.

The dryads face inward and begin to chant. At first, the rocky cliff remains obstinately still. Then, as poetry washes over its surface, its cracks and crevices crawl and squirm, pulsing and breathing with liquid movement.

Slowly but surely, an ornate door forms on the stone.

Dyneckta glares at us. "Our offer still stands. You can leave this cursed world behind, and fashion a life in yonder lands."

Erany shakes her head. "Thank you, but no."

"Very well," Dyneckta grumbles. "Your loss."

"We shall go first, then it will shut," Numiné says. "After that, you are free to enter."

"Understood," Erany replies.

Aesmotí reaches out and opens the door. Color pours from its scintillant depths, evoking excitement and soul-deep yearning.

"Jon." The dryad beams at me. "It was good to see you again."

"Again?" I point at my chest, look dumbly around, and meet (Her? His?) gaze. "Me?"

Dyneckta passes into the spill of hues. Numiné's next, then it's Og-bosh (due to his bulk, he has to bend down).

"Yes, you." Aesmotí's eyes shine with nostalgia. "In other lives, we were lovers and heartmates."

I straighten in shock. "Wait, how is that possible? I'm a guy and you're a...well I'm not sure what as far as gender, but are you even human? Is there some way for us to..." I make a hole with my thumb and forefinger, then jab its center with a couple of pokes.

Erany covers her eyes in second-hand embarrassment. "Jon."

"Crap! Sorry!" I raise my hands. "Right—other lives. We could have been anything. Forget I—"

"Quell your worry," Aesmotí chuckles. "In this incarnation, I exist as an embodiment of the natural world. As that is the case, I can express myself through a spectrum of gender." They throw me a wink, appearing feminine and coquettish, then clear their throat, turning undeniably masculine.

"Whoa," I whisper. "I've heard of that in frogs, but..."

"Not just frogs," Aesmotí corrects. "Plants, fish, mollusks...humans as well, arguably."

"So does that mean..." My brows knit together. "In that other life..."

"Other lives."

"In those other lives, what were you?" Then it strikes me: I could have been the woman. Or the man. Or a novel mixture of both.

"We loved each other. Through thick and thin, through light and dark." Aesmotí steps in the luminous doorway, turning sideways and catching my gaze. "That was our principal reason for being, and we lived that reason to our absolute fullest. As for the rest..."

Their lips crook up in a knowing smile.

"I couldn't care less."

And then they're gone, surfing an infinity of boundless potential.

The door claps shut. Its edges twinkle with prismatic light.

"Other lives...I never thought I would..." I trail off in wonder.

Erany gives me an amused look. "Sooner or later, you must embrace the infinity that forms our existence. It is, after all, the very foundation of the Unbound Realm."

"The Unbound Realm..." I scratch my temple. "When I first arrived, Ren said it was a definitive endpoint for all of reality. But what if there isn't a definitive end? Or a beginning, or a middle? What if we're already there and we choose to ignore it? That seems to fit with everything I've heard. I dunno..." I probe her eyes with a speculative gaze. "What do you think?

"I cannot say. I can somewhat understand through logic and thought, but..." She shrugs in defeat.

"I get it." A knowing nod. "Understanding it and feeling it aren't the same thing."

"Aye."

A bunch of the pieces have fallen into place, enough for me to guess at the underlying picture. But along with that clarity, I feel a scary sense of inevitability, the same thing I feel when I go Laiddinic.

"Jon? Why are you wincing?"

"Oh!" I blink and straighten. "Nothing, it's just...time to cry off. I'm starting to overthink it."

"Moment by moment, step by step." She looks at the door. "Shall we?"

"After you."

My senses peak with wonder and delight. There's nowhere to go, nothing that needs doing...then we're standing in front of our launch canoe.

As we push it into the river, Erany shoots me a knowing grin. "Now that I have claimed the Rosecraft Blade, I am firmly established in my role as the sailor."

I give her a puzzled look. "Sailor? What are you—oh! You mean the one who kisses the nurse in the photo. You know, I just remembered: he was actually pretty sketchy. Decades later, they interviewed the nurse and discovered he forced the kiss. She said it wasn't assault, but it absolutely wasn't by choice."

"Truly?" Her face twists in disgust. "When you first told me, it seemed quite fetching."

I hop in the boat and grab the nearest set of oars. "Sorry. I forgot the postscript."

"No matter. 'Tis their tale, it needn't be ours. We can write our own and fashion it just for us." Our paddles sync up as we match our strokes.

"I'm with you." I smile. "New chapters. Exotic characters."

Erany smiles back. "A joyous end. And a fresh beginning."

For the first time in a long while, I feel at peace with my expansive destiny. I'm the Prophesied Traveler, through and through, and I don't need to prove it to anyone else. When Erany claimed the Rosecraft Blade, she embodied that truth with spectacular clarity. There isn't any reason that I can't do the same.

In my own way, of course.

————

"Steady!" Blythe yells. "Smooth on the ropes or I'll blacken your gams!"

The sailors pulling up the canoe chant, *Aye, First Mate Blythe!*

"Where lies the Blade?" Syfaedi hurries over. "Dinny and I are almost healed. If you give us a week, we can accompany you back into Sidehelm Pass—"

"Here." Erany lifts her cloak, revealing the rose sticking out from her belt.

"If this is a jest, it is in poor taste." Idinia's brow furrows in reproach. "The bloom on your hip is barely enchanted, much less—"

Arisse Eledy walks up beside her. "That is the Blade, as steel is sure and water is wet."

Erany cocks her head. "How did you know?"

"Along its stem, there are four striations of dryadic influence, mingled with runes from nymphs and sprites. Near its cup, there are several archaic Evermoor glyphs, typically associated with Elder Folk magic. Lastly, its orphic vibration is mellow and even, and shifts in time with the wind and the waves. In the forest or desert, I imagine it would adjust to reflect the clime."

"Truly?" Syf peers at the Great Weapon. "I can't see a thing." She cranes her neck and squints a bit harder. "A faint shine, mayhap..."

"My orphic senses are unusually sharp," Arisse explains. "Unfortunately, my arcane strength pales before my Shift—plenty of mages are stronger in craft."

"Your words bring solace," Erany says, mildly relieved. "I worried a stranger might ken its nature."

"Not unless they were as touchy as I," Arisse assures. "For much of my youth, I was fascinated with Great Weapons; I perused legions of tomes that mentioned their lore. Nevertheless, if I hadn't known of your recent quest, I might have failed to identify its aura. 'Twas a lucky conflux—my sensitivity, education, and the fact that I knew exactly what you were seeking—that allowed me to confirm it was indeed the Blade."

Idinia crosses her arms. "I can barely tell the thing is ensorcelled, and that is only if I am employing all-out focus." Her and Syf have the same *I'm-not-sure-about-this* facial expression.

Erany draws it and holds it out. Its petals begin glowing, assuming different shades of vibrant red. A second later, blue-purple motes shimmer into existence and circle the rose in a leisurely orbit.

Syf and Idinia take a step back, staring at the Blade in wonder and awe.

Erany slides it into her belt. "If there is any further doubt…"

Idinia shakes her head. "None here."

Syfaedi says, "Nor here."

"Good." Erany clears her throat. "Are we still bound for Lanctom?"

"Aye," Syf confirms, "our plan is the same."

"How long?" I ask.

"A couple of months," she answers. "We have ample time to prepare for the battle." She gazes west, down the river toward the ocean.

"I have a feeling it won't be easy."

———

Over the next few weeks, I brush up on basics. Swordplay, magic, thievery…everything besides marksmanship. When I ask Ailura if she wants to practice, she brusquely informs me she's got it covered, and to let her snooze before the fracas. (She doesn't like being up and about, unless there's something that needs to be shot). Meanwhile, Erany trains with the Blade and her plain-steel rapier. In order to maximize the Trividian Slash, she's going to adopt a two-sword style that emphasizes sweeping cuts.

It makes zero sense, but I find myself drawn to sleight of hand. The weirdness continues—as I practice with the medallion I got from Ren, I increasingly mistake it for the Veric Glass. Over the course of our adventures, the Glass has shrunk down to match the medallion: same weight, same shape, and—just like the medallion—its gold-link chain has morphed into a tattered strip of hide. With the dust cover on, it could pass as a duplicate.

When I ask Arisse what's going on, the voker responds with a clueless shrug. The Veric Glass is Laiddinic in nature, which is like the magical version of quantum physics. It's so far beyond anything traditional or Primal, it's almost impossible to suss out the why and how.

On a whim, I start practicing with the Glass, causing the spirit inside it to stir and rustle. For the next two days, I go down a sleight of hand rabbit hole, trying to wake the Glass with incessant prestidigitation. Much to my dismay, it doesn't work. Guess I shouldn't be surprised (Raef said that it could only be woken by its one true love) but still, the fact that it stirred…well, at least I'm sharpening my sleight of hand. Nevertheless, I think I'll stick with my traveler's medallion. If I lose the Glass in a sleight of hand fail, I could doom everyone in Evermoor to unending poop.

The crew is somewhat informed as to what's going on. Most are skeptical (they regard the portal-to-be in the same way that scientists think about ghosts) but their trust in Syfaedi (and hate for Lyderea) trumps any doubt. If the captain says we're defending Lanctom, then that's what we're doing, come flood or fire or Khel-spawned demons. Part of it comes from their personal frustration—they're pissed that Syf got hurt in Gracelyn, and they're itching to compensate with physical action. As far as the Glass, they're glad that we found it, but they're not really sure why it's important, especially since it doesn't register in anyone's Shift. Our vokers do their best to explain, but the deckhands aren't in the headspace to get it. They're here to live that high-seas life, not delve into arcane philosophy.

Four weeks in, as we're passing by the Nightriven Forest, Erany catches me spacing out on the forecastle. "Jon?"

"Oh, hey. Just uh…" I glance back and forth between her and the river. "I was, you know…"

A knowing smile. "It won't help to fret or worry. Things will pick up soon enough."

I force a nod. "Yeah…you're right."

And with a conviction I don't feel, I mutter, "Be dust upon your breath."

———

I spend the next few days plagued by disquiet. I know, I know—I'm not supposed to fight negativity, it's better to distract myself or focus on something positive. But this time, for some reason, my emotional go-tos fail to work. Whenever I reach for apathy or ease, my thoughts slide back into low-key turmoil.

Why, though? What am I not embracing? I don't have a problem with Shifting my senses, so that means I'm in sync with my personal destiny. (According to the Sygress, anyway.) Is this all in my head?

Easy, Jon. Be dust upon your breath.

I pillow my head on my hands and stare up at the ceiling. Erany's out and about, so it's just me by myself hanging out in our cabin.

Be dust upon your breath. Be dust upon your breath.

I mentally repeat it over and over, trying to relax into calm and serenity. It doesn't work. The lap of water against the hull (which I typically find soothing and peaceful) sounds discordant and jarring, like the tick of a clock in a timeless prison.

Be dust upon your breath. Be dust upon your breath.

Eventually, I give up and fall asleep.

————

A dozen faires out, we're intercepted by a pair of Lanctom's schooners. They know who we are, thanks to the efforts of our stay-behind friends. After Syf and their crews exchange greetings and courtesies, they proceed to escort us back to the docks, staying far enough away so they don't attract serpents.

The town is now lined with bunkers and barriers, along with a battery of bombardier obelisks. Archers dot the fortified shore, watching suspiciously as we pull into port.

Unlike the townsfolk, Gyrax, Nyanti, and Lucky meet us with cheer. We debark the *Gauge,* then share a round of hugs and hellos.

Nyanti asks, "The Glass? The Blade?"

"Here." I tap my sternum.

"And here." Erany flares her cloak.

"Incredible," Nyanti murmurs. "Its aura is nearly undetectable."

"Elier? Ren?" I look around with mild concern. "They're not hurt, are they?"

"No," Gyrax assures. "They're busy on the Midland Brink, guarding our lines from obtrusive Knights."

"They're here?" Idinia's brows knit together. "Already?"

"For the last two weeks. After we captured some wayward raiders, the Protectorate decided to entrench their forces." He glances at Lucky. "Thankfully, we have someone who knows how to charm the locals."

The thief shrugs. "Without your purse, I would not have succeeded." He grips his jaw and works his mouth, as if he was trying to relieve a muscular tweak. "Though my tongue has been exhausted as of late. Certain folk have greater demands, when it comes to their desire between the sheets."

"You sold yourself?" Syf asks incredulously.

Lucky looks puzzled. "Of course. Wouldn't you?"

"No!" she blurts. Idinia, who usually takes pleasure in Syf's agitation, appears just as shocked.

The thief shrugs again. "We all have a price. Sometimes, it isn't written in coin or credit."

Erany and I exchange a glance. Part of me admires his open-mindedness, but it's still rooted in his cutthroat worldview. Judging by her perplexed expression, my girlfriend shares my confliction/confusion.

Syf asks, "The Portmaster?"

"Gone," Gyrax answers. "Once the Knights began to arrive, Sefic took to his low-shadow heels. We urged most of Lanctom to evacuate with him, but three-quarters decided to stay. While some are gray and some are young, everyone here is stout of heart."

Idinia clicks her tongue and hisses through her teeth. It's not ideal, but she knows it's ultimately their decision.

"Different souls have come to the fore," Gyrax continues. "Most notably Relegant Syvaelis."

My eyes crinkle in puzzlement. "Scads Reggels?"

"Aye. He reclaimed his name from days of yore. Ren convinced him to reassume it."

"Wretched Ren?" Erany mutters. "I never would have thought."

"And the slipworld passage?" Idinia asks. "How much longer until it opens?"

"Hard to say," Nyanti replies. "In all likelihood, it will blossom in a month, though it could be as long as two or three."

"So what's next?" I ask.

The Witch glances at Erany's hip, where the Rosecraft Blade is lying dormant. "Follow me."

43

The buildings are coated in metal panels, imbued with no-frills wards that are designed to quench fire. There's also a change in general demeanor—folk are speaking in clipped phrases, and they're all carrying some sort of weapon.

Nyanti guides us into an alley, between a couple of three-story townhomes. "There." She points at a swath of distorted air.

The portal-to-be is a wavy glob. Its undulant edges are shimmering and hazing, dappled with glints of striking clarity. When I Shift my perception, the distortion resolves into an oval-shaped nexus. Shining lines are materializing around it, crawling slowly toward its convex center. Before they can touch its prismatic core, they're pulled into a drifting clockwise gyre, surrounding it in an orbit of letters and glyphs.

Erany pulls the rose from her belt. "Should I..."

The Witch shakes her head. "Not until it is fully open. Only then will it assume a polarity. At that point, I can use the Blade to negate its bloom."

"In the meantime, can I fight with the townsfolk on the Brink?" Erany perks with hope.

"Absolutely not," Nyanti says firmly. "I need you here, in case the portal unexpectedly quickens. Lyderea and her sorcerers are already aware of it—I can sense them probing its runes and patterns."

Gyrax clears his throat. "If you were to craft a short-range teleport, Erany could assist with the frontline defense, then join you when the rift is nigh."

Nyanti looks torn. " 'Tis within my power, but she would be at risk upon the field."

"Is it really that bad?" I ask. "Are there that many Knights?"

"Their numbers increase with each new dawn." Lucky says. "Judging by their fast-growing presence, I'd say the Queen is amassing her northern forces, and directing them to Lanctom's edges and borders. Yesterday, they were joined by wyverns and battlefield mages. There have also been sightings of Protectorate ships, which means we might have to adjust our defensive heft. Right now, it is weighted towards the Midland Brink. But if Lyderea chooses to blitz the shore..."

Erany and Gyrax, both familiar with big army strategy, exchange a knowing look. "Then it is settled," Erany declares. "I need to bulwark the Nok-damned field."

Nyanti sighs in resignation. "This was not unforeseen. Accordingly, I called in some favors from my extraplanar colleagues: Demiurges, the Mind's Eye Fated, Nocteral Adzerai..." She registers our clueless expressions and produces five amulets (seven-sided, with blue-green eyes and silver-link chains) from the depths of her robe. "During your absence, I wove exotic energies into Kalsaedian armor, stored and projected through these enchanted fetishes. Once they are triggered, they will grant you a boost in protection and strength. In between clashes, reweave the runes as best you can. They can heal themselves, but your efforts will speed the arcane mend."

"Grace and thanks." Gyrax accepts the amulets from the Witch. "These will allow us to establish a buffer. The five who bear them will push onto the field, so they can doff all restraint and wreak maximal havoc."

"Why not just fight on the primary line?" I ask.

"If we fought alongside green-bladed villagers, we would have to hold back for their bodily safety. Now that we have this Kalesaedian armor, we can venture forth and leverage our wrath."

"I was hoping the villagers could help out more," I mutter. "Like in *The Two Towers,* you know? But this sounds closer to *Thirteen Assassins.*"

"How is their morale?" Idinia asks. "It can't be good, considering they're outnumbered by..." She trails off and raises an eyebrow.

"Three-to-one," Gyrax answers, "although as Lucky said, the odds worsen by the day. As far as morale, it's surprisingly good. Seizing handfuls of raiders has emboldened our folk."

"A decent start," Syf remarks. "May we visit the front?"

Gyrax nods. "On my heels."

————

We're greeted by the sight of a long-running berm, dotted with batches of shielded arrow ports. Behind the berm, offset trenches furrow the soil. Just like the ports, they're fitted with a series of enchanted steel canopies.

Elier and Scads (sorry, Relegant) are making the rounds and checking on soldiers. Ren is conversing with a grim-set woman, explaining how a layered defense is best for the archers—it'll discourage the wyverns from punching straight through.

As we come into view, he stiffens in shock. "You're back!" His exclamation alerts Elier and Relegant. "Did you—"

Erany flares her cloak. "The Rosecraft Blade."

"Amazing." He cranes forward and squints at the weapon. "It barely has an aura."

"That is the Blade, as the day is bright and the night is long," Nyanti assures.

"I wouldn't believe it if you hadn't said it." Elier walks up and gives it a doubtful look. "But your word is enough. More than enough."

The Witch responds with a sweetheart smile, triggering a twang inside my heart. Erany's given me that exact same smile, and it's better than cold Mountain Dew on a hot muggy day.

"Very well." Relegant is dressed in hodgepodge armor. Even though it's outwardly ratty, it still comes off as dashing and cool, a fantasy-world version of *Star Wars* grunge. "I trust your judgment, Wise Woman."

Ren glances at the soldier he was talking with. "Arthia, if you would give us a moment..." She cedes with a mutter and begins walking the line, two trenches back from the arrow-ported berm. He turns back to Erany. "A demonstration, mayhap?"

Erany holds out the weapon. Its petals blaze into a She-ra-esque dazzle, evoking shouts of surprise from nearby villagers. As the rose elongates into a sword, her clothes give way to sleek-fitting armor.

"Battle-ready." She smiles and salutes with the rune-scriven blade.

Ren shakes his head in undisguised envy. "I claim rights to the next Great Weapon."

Erany starts up the berm, cuing the rest of us to follow. We halt at the top and study the Protectorate camp. Packs of wyverns are circling their tents. They're interspersed with catapults, and...ballistae, I think? They look like giant crossbows, angled at a skyward cant.

As I deepen my Shift, the haze around the camp brightens and flares. Glyph-heavy patterns morph and twist, trading safeguards and buffers in a complicated flux.

Damn...they've got pretty good shields against incoming magic.

Erany drops to a knee and thrusts the Blade in the berm. A ring of blue-white light jets from its edge, followed by energized arcs that bound onto the field. Halfway across, they narrow into spell-crafted tentacles that pour into the encampment, lighting patches of grass with magic green ovals. Each one draws inward and upward, forming eight-foot hulks made of roots and flora.

Holy. *Magoobers.* My girlfriend just summoned an army of Swamp Things.

Half-armored Knights run to and fro, clashing with mobs of lumbering plant golems. One of 'em throws a backhanded swat, sending a trio of bodies soaring through the air. Another vomits a tangle of thorns, wrapping dozens of Knights in sharp-needled vines. A minute into the frenzied brawl, wyverns swoop in and roast the Swamp Things. They erupt into fiery, apocalyptic silhouettes, then wither into mounds of ember-threaded char.

The villager-defenders (all of whom have run up the berm to watch) burst into a series of hearty cheers.

"That's enough," Nyanti says.

Erany pulls the Blade from the magic-webbed ground. "I could have kept going," she grumbles.

"So could they." The Witch nods at the Knights. "They'll recover their numbers before the moons rise."

Erany looks crestfallen. "Once a day, maybe?"

Nyanti crosses her arms. "I believe that is safe, but remain wary of your arcane reserves. Closing the portal will take a great deal of power, as much as half the Blade's organic magic."

"I shall only drain it a quarter way," Erany assures.

Gyrax clears his throat. "If wyverns attack, take shelter beneath the enchanted cover." He points at the canopies lining the trenches. "They'll hold up for hours against Rainfire Knights. Your main concern will be—"

"Rainfire Knights?" I ask.

"The wyverns' pilots. Trained to dismantle protective wards."

"Gotcha."

"The canopies will shield you from single-breath streams, and fare decently well under a pair of drakes. Unfortunately, they won't last long with three or more wyverns. And if one of them hovers and sustains their fire, all bets are off, although that is not how they typically engage."

"Swoops and dives," Lucky elaborates. "They like to establish an alternating rhythm. That way, they can pin you down and minimize their exposure."

"The wyverns can't break through our layered defense," Elier adds. " 'Tis stronger here on the Midland Brink, though it stretches around the entire peninsula."

"You've got boatloads of archers." I scan the trenches. "More than skirmishers, it seems."

"They form the backbone of our force," Gyrax acknowledges. "It is by necessity—a drake could wreak havoc if it slips past our lines. Hopefully, we can soon expand our potential for melee, as I have dispatched missives through my trio of aviads."

"Anyone I know?"

"Wolven tribes, Yire Anon, and various other sympathetic leaders." He crosses his arms. "The aviads returned after each report. That doesn't guarantee physical receipt, but it is a highly favorable indication."

"They couldn't have just sent a letter back with an aviad?" I ask.

Gyrax shakes his head. "I started with five, two have vanished. To curtail the risk, I adjusted them to drop their missives in flight."

"That sucks. Those things are a work of steampunk art." I point at a makeshift catapult behind our third-line trench. "What about artillery?"

"Ours reach the last quarter-stretch," Ren says. "Theirs are the same—they can hit the quartile in front of our berm. If anyone ventures across the field, they will suffer bombardment from siege engine batteries. While that can be factored into a push, it prevents the instatement of closer entrenchments. Consequently, each garrison remains in its bounds."

"Everyone's staying exactly where they are, 'cause they're afraid of getting hit by the other side's guns. Seems kinda pointless," I hedge.

The Wayfarer shrugs. " 'Tis the nature of war. It is the same with our arrows; their charms nullify Rainfire armor, but our mages cannot afford to do anything more. Between our spells and the pilots' wards, it's as if they didn't have shields and we didn't have magic."

"Fine by me." Elier shrugs. "Duelist magic is similar in nature—it passively nullifies arcane protection, allowing combat to progress in its truest form."

"What about our flanks?" Erany glances at either end of the long-running berm. "The water on the sides will inconvenience Lyderea. Inconvenience, however, does not equate to physical deterrence."

"The town is circled by archers and lookouts," Ren assures. "As for the water flanking the Brink, it is guarded by teams of skiffs and obelisks, along with Seavash Tarrick and his Merfolk renegades."

Syf raises an eyebrow. "Seavash? How did he come to Lanctom's shore?"

"He wished to trade in abber and kret. Lucky intercepted him at the exchange, and convinced him to bulwark the river with corsairs. Why? Is he an acquaintance?"

"Aye," she chuckles. "Three years back, I partnered with Vash on a nautical seizure. His fins are swift and his trident is sharp. If I was in search of a Merfolk commander, Tarrick would be at the top of my list."

I peer at the camp. "Man, all those wyverns, but zero cavalry…"

"Beasts of burden are logistical assets," Ren says. "Lyderea isn't short on swords and Knights. Her struggle lies in their large-scale maneuver."

"Yeah, I know. It's just weird to see it in the flesh. So that's it?" I ask. "We're gonna bunker down here until they attack?"

"Aye," Gyrax says. "And remember: we are here to prevent the portal from opening. Felling the Knights is an unfortunate consequence."

Elier scoffs. " 'Unfortunate?' Gyrax, *they're trying to kill us.*"

"And they've spared no expense," Lucky adds. "Sorcerers, ballistae, Protectorate drakes and their Rainfire pilots…"

"We serve a greater end than mere survival," Ren chides. "Keep that in mind, or we risk devolving into a mob."

Everyone stops and stares at the Wayfarer. I did *not* expect that from the Master of Dickish Negativity. Judging by their collective response, neither did the others.

After a pause, Idinia shoots Syf a weighted glance. " 'Our blood runs hot, our dreams shine bright, and let no one tell you a damn bit different.' "

Ren nods. "Exactly. Now if we're done with the chaff, find a spot in these Nok-damned trenches."

My lips crook up in a knowing smile. There's the Ren we know and love.

———

When I'm not standing watch in a canopied trench, I help the others train Lanctom's villager-defenders. Lucky abstains (thieves gonna thieve) and so does Nyanti. The Blade is key to closing the portal, but it'll need all the help it can possibly get. To that end, she's gonna be working some arcane overtime.

The townsfolk are psyched about the upcoming battle. Can't say I blame 'em—they've been spoiled by victory. I think they've a lost a total of three (when they were still emplacing enchanted cover, a wyvern broke through and toasted some villagers).

The Rosecraft Blade is a cause for celebration. Every day, Erany thrusts it in the ground and summons a horde of constructs (water folk, plant creatures, mud golems, etcetera). Occasionally, she'll blast the Knights with lightning or frost, both of which go several steps beyond what you'd expect. The lightning twists, curves, and forms into balls that project fast-moving tendrils of thrashing electricity. The frost is similar; it traverses their camp in serpentine flourishes, lashing and snaking around nearby targets. (I feel kinda bad for Lyderea's Knights. Imagine going about your day, then suddenly fighting off monsters and weather rays.)

Day ten comes with a nasty surprise. Right after breakfast, the Velic Tessellate takes root in their camp, bolstering their defense by leaps and bounds. This is the first time I've been in Lyderea's presence. Even though it's indirect (she's projecting her intent through an arcane supercloud), it's deeply unsettling. Also: it is *ugly*. Magically speaking, it's akin to a zombie infested with eggs, agleam with larvae and ready to burst. Jagged runes mar its red-black miasma, sickly yellow infects its breadth. The worst thing about it, however, is its undeniably malevolent vibe. I can't help but feel tense and rattled, as if I'm being stalked by a deranged predator.

As it gathers and settles over the Knights, everyone walks up the berm and stares into its depths.

"It's hard to believe...the Tessellate once stood for alliance and synergy," Gyrax says quietly.

"I'm not surprised," Lucky mutters. "Given time, all turns to ash and rot."

"Don't be so sure," Ren counters.

"Aye," Elier agrees. "If we let go of decay and focus on—"

"You two have lost your Nok-damned minds." The thief scoffs at Ren. "We might have fought in earlier times, but you at least saw the world for what it is."

"Perhaps he has gained some healthy perspective," Syf comments. "And perhaps you have lost it."

Lucky responds with a caustic laugh. "My vantage has been proven time and again; 'tis bound in fact and etched in history. All that we do—all that we *are*—is determined by greed and physical function. As that is the case, 'tis damnably easy to condemn you and your ilk."

I freeze in place, all too aware of what he's referring to.

"My ilk?" Syfaedi raises a casual eyebrow. Despite her seeming nonchalance, I can tell she's dangerously close to pulling her gun.

Lucky responds with a Joker-like grin. "I lay with any and all for favor and coin, but you...you rut with women for no good reason. Your body has a specific design, and to scorn it for naught makes you foolish beyond measure."

Idinia grips the hilt of her sword. "Careful, thief. For I too, am a foolish woman. Who knows what carnage I'll wreak, if you rankle me or my foolish mate?"

His face twists into a venomous sneer. "You are doubling down on—"

Gyrax barks a single word. *"Lucky."*

It almost doesn't work—his mouth opens and closes. After a second, he scoffs again and storms off the berm.

Idinia turns to Syf. "Are you—"

"I'm fine," she says brusquely. Her hand is clutching the grip of her pistol. When she uncurls her fingers, I notice they're shaking. She sees me looking, clenches them into a fist, and holds my gaze without blinking or moving.

I quickly look away. I'm not sure why I'm embarrassed. Probably because that was intensely personal, and also because it was none of my business.

Idinia clears her throat. "Erany. You owe us a show."

My girlfriend, who's been observing the spat with a blank expression (I can see right past it—she's insanely pissed) answers with a nod. "Very well." She triggers her nature-princess glow-up, then thrusts the Blade into the ground.

Villager-defenders mutter excitedly, eager for their fill of Knight-blasting mayhem. A minute later, it becomes depressingly clear the Knights are safe. When Erany's spell reaches the Tessellate, it grows nasty wrinkled puckers that devour her magic.

The townsfolk begin to murmur and fret. Conversely, the Knights know the tide has turned; they're hurling taunts and insults in our direction. Dozens of yards above their camp, wyverns break out in triumphant roars. Their Rainfire pilots brandish lances and swords.

Erany stands up and deactivates the Blade. As her armor disappears, she sighs in disappointment. "It's to be expected."

"It's all right." I force reassurance into my tone. "We'll find a way."

She flings a hand at the Protectorate camp. "We are stuck in a hold, awaiting relief that may or may not come. To add snarl upon snag, we are staking our lives on an iffy hope: Nyanti believes she can close the portal, but slipworld magic is notoriously fickle." Resignation darkens her face. "Perhaps Lucky's right."

"Princess." Gyrax's voice cracks with reproach. "Those words are beneath you. Steel your gaze and rally your will, or cry off this front and take up with the thief."

Her features twist with sudden rage. *"Who are you to—"* Then she stops and exhales deliberately. "You are right. I plead thy grace, Kai Aclasian."

He waves a hand. "All is forgiven. Have faith in Nyanti's expertise. And do not forget: we have acquired both the Blade and the Glass, which means fate has been working in our favor."

"I dunno..." I hedge. "Right now, the Glass is kind of useless. I still have to wake it, remember? I'm supposed to find it's 'one true love,' but I haven't figured out who—or what—that is."

"Trust in our fortune," he urges. "If Lanctom was destined to fall to the Queen, we wouldn't have acquired such powerful items."

"You gotta admit that's flimsy logic. There's millions of stories where someone almost made it—where they had what they needed and it all fell apart."

"If this is such a tale, then so be it," Ren declares. "I would rather die here, upon this berm, then suffer beneath Lyderea's rule."

"Aye," Elier agrees. "Under the Queen, our spirits would die an inch at a time."

"Really?" I raise an eyebrow. "Not to be rude, but I haven't seen any widespread oppression, except for the slavers and those are a recent development. I'm not trying to be a reflexive contrarian, but—"

Erany interrupts with quiet gravitas. "Jon. You don't know what it's like in the Southern Reach. And even here, further north, you don't know what it means to surrender much-needed coin, simply to glut the Queen and her nobles. You led a privileged life back on Earth—I saw your home and well-made goods. And on the way to your affluent dwelling, I saw paupers rotting upon the streets."

"I..." My cheeks redden with guilt. "You're right," I mutter. "I'm sorry, I just..."

"You lost your perspective," Gyrax says. " 'Tisn't a crime—it happens to us all." He puts a hand on my shoulder. "Jon, look at me."

I struggle to meet his eyes. "I didn't mean to judge."

"Yes you did." His voice is simultaneously kind and merciless. "Don't try and convince yourself otherwise, and don't punish yourself for your mistake. More importantly, don't renounce whatever you are feeling. You have experienced love and pain, just the same as anyone else. The hardest thing that someone has been through, whether slight or horrendous by anyone's standards...is still the hardest thing that person has been through."

"Not sure I follow. I feel like you answered me, but it went over my head." I laugh shakily. "Where does that leave me?"

"I cannot say," he replies. "Search your heart with an open mind, free of judgment and comparative worth. What does it say? What is important right at this moment?"

I look around at my expectant friends. They're committed to helping me, but not because someone told them to do so. They're each following their own design, the calling within their True-born souls. It just so happens that our goals overlap. Enough to travel together, fight together, and—if necessary—to die together.

My gaze shifts to Lanctom's villagers, all of whom are ready to hold the line. Right here, right now, they're stepping up to fulfill their destiny. My knowledge is more than a hunch or opinion, it goes so far beyond that it's...

Yep. Definitely Laiddinic.

"We can't lose..." I marvel. Folk edge closer, drawn by our exchange. (Much to my surprise, Lucky's among them.) "Lyderea could kill us and burn us to ashes, but we'd just come back in a different form. I used to regard her as something inevitable, as irresistible as the wind or the tide. But that's not true. She's not the tide...we are." I nod slowly, relishing the optimism growing within me. It's completely unsupported, yet undeniable in its True-forged surety. "We're the tide." My gaze drifts across the villagers. "And if we fall, we shall rise again and claim our peace."

I draw Ailura, hold her high, and roar my next words with conviction and passion: *"As the day is bright and the night is long, WE SHALL RISE AGAIN AND CLAIM OUR PEACE!"* (Not the most alpha of lines, I know, but it comes straight from the depths of my goddamn heart.)

Erany flashes the Blade and shouts, *"Lanctom! Delán! For any and all who dream of better!"*

Everyone else joins in the cry, brandishing their weapons and declaring their truth. Amid the outpouring of hope and resolve, Gyrax leans in, a twinkle in his eye. "Yet another reason I continue to believe in you."

"What are you talking abou—" As my intuition comes to the fore, I catch myself and grin. "Because at the end of the day, I believe in myself. Gotcha."

A second later, a voice sounds from our lines:

"THEY'RE CHARGING THE FIELD!"

44

Enchanted boulders ravage the earth, flinging crud and debris up in the air. It all comes down in a choppy rattle, slipping in my clothes and clinking off canopies.

I kick-slide my way into the nearest hide, shoo away the attendant archer, and start blasting away with Ailura Qartesi. My rounds decimate oncoming Knights, not just slowing them, but pushing them back toward their camp.

Before I know it, they're retreating from the field.

"CEASE FIRE!" The call ripples down our lines. *"CEASE FIRE!"*

I snap-load Ailura and climb out of the hide. "The hell was *that?* Gyrax?"

"They're testing our mettle." He brushes dirt off his furry arms. "Lyderea sees Knights as an expendable resource. Her generals are willing to throw some away, if it will help them gauge our strength and response."

Relegant Syvaelis crawls out of a hide. "Made 'em think twice!" he cackles. He nods at the Great Weapon on my hip. "Thanks to you and that Nok-damned canno—"

He's interrupted by a frantic shout: "They're fighting on the water!" A villager points toward Lanctom's skyline. It's pulsing with a layer of magical haze, courtesy of our ships and their bombardier obelisks.

"Quickly!" Gyrax breaks for the docks. "Relegant, stay on the front and neaten our defense!"

He's answered by an *Aye, Wolven,* but I barely hear it—I'm sprinting with the others toward the shore. After a blur of shops and homes, Lanctom's docks come into view. Standing atop the central pier, there's an unmistakably distinguished-looking figure.

"Raefingham!" Elier exclaims.

"Wind at your back and sun on your brow." Raef touches his forehead and brings his hand out. "As promised, I have returned to participate in Lanctom's defiance." He nods at a carrack moored to a lefthand dock. "Not just me—I have allies in tow."

"Those are no mere soldiers." Syf watches them as they file off the gangplank. They're older folk (not sure about the Wildlyre, it's hard to guess their age) who are all exuding a capable vibe, low-key rugged and brimming with confidence.

"Clandestine Inspectors," Elier ventures. "Your warrior-spies from days of yore."

"Aye."

Idinia perks up. "Can you spare a detachment?"

The Detective shrugs. "Make your case and try your hand. It has been a day and an age since they served as my agents. I have no say in what they do."

The Arbiter breaks into a spirited jog. Elier follows, yelling, "Idinia, wait—you can't have them all!"

The rest of us exchange a knowing grin. *Duelists—amirite?*

"I brought close to a hundred," Raef says. "Each one is worth a company of Knights."

"You also brought ships." Syf glances at the water, dotted with an assortment of motley vessels.

"Not I. 'Twas Keybra Elahqua, captain of the *Empyrean Reckoning.*"

"Keybra?" Syf dips her head and chuckles softly. "Who would have thought he could do so much, in the short while since we met on the *Spiral?*"

"The *Reckoning,*" Raef corrects. "The *Spiral* caught fire and sunk in the Vallic. According to a set of well-forged documents, anyway."

"Fitting." Syfaedi scans the spread-out fleet. "Their scatter should deter any wayward serpents. I am concerned, however, as to how that will affect their combat response. If a wedge of frigates tries to drive through..."

"Before you arrived, that is exactly what happened. They are all lying at the bottom of the river."

"The Queen will send more," Syf counters. "These craft must respond with precision measures. While fortune and chance can win a clash, they shan't endure in a protracted war."

"Keybra has issued an order of battle," he assures. "The first in contact will retreat towards center, drawing in foes while signaling allies. Our vessels will form a concave line, then proceed to envelop Lyderea's forces."

Syf purses her lips. "Dozens of factors could foul that maneuver. Winds, tides, the timing and rhythm of signal and echo...you would need gobbets of practice to—"

" 'Tis all they have done for the past two months." Raef gestures at the ships. "Even now, they are absorbing the lay of the currents and shore, preparing to use it to their advantage."

"Very well," she cedes grudgingly. "It appears that Elahqua has risen to the occasion."

Raef moves on with a brisk nod. "How goes it on land?"

"Surprisingly well," Gyrax replies. "Although our odds look grimmer by the day. If Lyderea strikes with the Velic Tessellate..."

"I understand. Nyanti..." The Ogre looks around, noting her absence. "I assume she is working on closing the portal."

"Aye," Erany says. "If you scan my aura, you will see she has crafted a short-range teleport. When the hour is nigh, I will appear by her side."

"Why would she need to access your presence?"

"In order to shift the arcane tides, she must channel power from the Rosecraft Blade." Erany lifts her cloak, briefly revealing the rose on her hip.

Raef plucks his monocle from his right breast pocket, affixes it to his eye, then leans in and studies the Blade. "I've honed my Shift for a day and an age, yet I can barely detect this storied weapon. You are certain that's the Blade?"

"Ask the dryads from Yom Dagur," I say.

"Or the Knights I felled with Elder Folk magic," Erany adds.

"If you say it is so, I shan't raise doubt." His gaze tracks left and settles on my fingers—they've been absentmindedly performing sleight of hand. "What are you doing?"

"Oh, uh...getting in some practice." I rub the back of my neck, embarrassed. "Sorry, it's become a habit."

"Too much time with our larcenous friend Lucky," he chuckles.

"Not really. It's just..." My eyes flick over to Gyrax. "I've been doing it on a hunch. I can't explain it any better than that."

"You needn't elaborate," Raef assures. "On many an occasion, my heart and my gut have spared me from ruin."

Gyrax asks, "Will you buttress the coast or bolster the field?"

"The field," the Ogre answers. "For someone my size, much can go wrong atop the water."

"Now that Lyderea is attacking with ships, the shore is where I am needed most," Syf declares. She glances at Idinia, who's in animated conversation with a gray-haired Inspector. "Dinny will insist on guarding my flanks. Count us as part of the coastal defense."

"Very well." Gyrax nods. "If that is all, then—"

"Ho!" Lucky strolls into view (to no one's surprise, he didn't run with us toward obelisk fire; he made good and damn sure it was safe beforehand). "Ships and swords and Raefingham Bask! What news, Detective?"

"Naught but what you have likely heard. Lyderea will press us as hard as she can. On land, obviously, but also from the river."

The thief joins our loose-formed circle. "That's to be expected."

Gyrax's face wrinkles in puzzlement. "You don't seem concerned."

"The peril is still at a leisurely simmer." He watches me complete a sleight of hand flourish. "Your time is better spent on swordplay or magic."

"Yeah, it's just..." The medallion flips through each of my fingers, then I pop it into the crook of my elbow. "It's kind of relaxing, you know?"

Lucky scoffs. "Indulging your heart at the expense of your head. Should you persist, yonder Knights will cut it from your neck."

Erany gives me a dubious look. "It pains me to say it, but Lucky is right. I don't see how thievery can aid our cause."

"Leave him be," Gyrax chides. "If anyone here should trust their instincts, it is first and foremost the Prophesied Traveler."

"Aye," Raef agrees. "If he is intuiting something we haven't yet thought of..." He prompts me with an inquisitively raised eyebrow.

"I don't know." I slip the medallion up my sleeve. "I can't say for sure."

Lucky surveys the ships with a thoughtful expression. "I am not long for this low-shadow city. Whether I flee on foot or upon a vessel..."

"I don't understand." Erany's voice is tinged with irritation. "Why stay at all?"

Lucky shrugs. "Something in my gut. I trust its veracity."

"Then we are gathered here on the premise of faith," Syfaedi observes. "An unexpected twist from our resident thief."

"We all converge," Gyrax comments, "somewhere along our winding journeys. Even if it is not within this life, we find each other in the Eventide Clear."

"You truly believe that." Syfaedi examines the Wolven's face.

"Of course." He gives her a radiant smile.

"Fah." Lucky waves dismissively. "Your faith and mine are vastly different."

"Outwardly, perhaps. But if you account for the long-term flow of events—"

"All that matters is the coin in my purse," Lucky says brusquely. "Save your bunk for gullible folk."

Gyrax shrugs. "My view is practical. The *most* practical, I'd argue, as it fosters a sense of soul-deep peace. That, in turn, calms and opens my perception and thought, leading to strategy and honed intuition."

"I believe it," Erany states.

Ren says, "I as well."

I stare down at my fingers, which are busy manipulating the traveler's medallion. It vanishes and appears time and again, catching the high-noon sun along its surface.

"Yeah...I'm with you."

45

The Knights charge again. We easily repel them. They don't seem to care about retrieving their fallen—mounds of corpses lay rotting on the field.

The next day, we find out why.

Cries of alarm sound in the trench, snapping me out of my late-morning snooze. I open my berm-port and watch as the Tessellate crawls across bodies. Bones snap, joints pop, then they all start twisting and curling together.

The masses resolve into eight-legged hulks, ten feet tall and twenty feet wide. Their limbs are speckled with armor and bone, bound by skin and pulsing wet organs. Their auras match their physical appearance; each one is stuffed with broken runes, throbbing and bulging like greedy tumors. Finally, as an extra disgusting cherry on top, their footprints brim with gory slop.

"Necrotic Shambles," Erany murmurs, "woven from a series of Malefic enchantments."

"Malefic enchantments?" I whisper.

"Banned since olden days of yore."

Lyderea's army is using them as cover; they've settled into files behind their legs. Our archers fire several volleys, but most of it thuds into decaying meat. The biggest threat is the Rainfire Knights. They're flying low and slow on their fire-breathing wyverns, directly behind the Shambles' torsos. We need to intercept them before they get close, or they'll suppress our archers with a cadence of fire.

Elier gives voice to our collective concern: "Deadlier folk must thin their press, or the weight of their numbers will shatter these lines."

Gyrax calls, "Ren and Elier, harry their left! Raef and I will assail the center! Jon and Erany, strike from the right!"

Erany replies, "Hold," and goes full-on She-ra. As the Rose lengthens into a green-tinged sword, gleaming armor replaces her clothes. Once she's ready, she walks up the berm and thrusts the Blade in the ground, drawing a groan from the surrounding terrain. A battalion of rock golems (not as big as Ogbosh, though similar in appearance) rise from the earth, breaking through soil in ponderous lurches.

Erany pulls out the Blade, flips it right-side up, and draws her non-enchanted rapier with her other hand. (Dual-wielding princess. Bad. *Ass.)* She cants her head, meeting our gaze from over her shoulder, and raises an eyebrow.

"Shall we?"

The five of us tap our Nyanti-crafted amulets, activating sheaths of light-woven armor. They appear as networks of blue-white plates, bound with flickering, crisp-angled shimmer.

Elier's the first to rush down the berm. Ren mutters "Finally," and accompanies the Duelist into the fray. Erany's rock-golems charge alongside us, chucking pieces of themselves at Shambles and Knights. A second later, Gyrax drops to all fours and sprints up the middle. Raefingham Bask runs halfway across, takes a knee, and levels his cane at the nearest zom-spider. As I draw Ailura and veer right with Erany, the Detective ratchets his cane and primes an arcane slug. *Click-clack, BLAM! Click-clack, BLAM!* Apparently, he boosted his cane's magical capacity; it used to hold four shots max, but he's already fired six.

"I'll stymie their front!" Erany yells. "Jon, target the Shambles!"

"Got it!" I level Ailura and blast a pair of corpse-spiders. Erany runs between them and whirls her rapiers, pummeling Knights with the Trividian Slash. Every time she spins and cuts, she leaves three glowing slices hanging in the air. After a fleeting pause, they briskly fly outward, breaking through armor and ravaging flesh. She quickly strikes up a lively tempo, felling assailants in rapid-fire time.

I run sideways and gun down a Shambles, causing the wyverns behind it to swoop in toward me. Easy pickings—I tear them apart with a runic death-ray. I kill another Shambles, a couple more wyverns, then Lyderea's forces start to retreat. To cover their withdrawal, the Knights unleash hellish artillery. Most of it misses, but our amulet-armor absorbs the stuff that doesn't.

"Break off, or keep pushing?" I have to yell it extra loud. My ears are ringing from the din of battle.

"Back!" Gyrax waves his massive axe, signaling us all to about-face. *"Back to the berm!"*

As we run for our lines, I glimpse some Knights that bypassed our six-person vanguard. They've dropped their swords and raised their hands. Villager-warriors brandish their weapons, ready to skewer the would-be invaders, but Relegant tells them to stand the hell down—we don't execute unarmed soldiers.

A bunch of defenders grumble and mutter, galvanizing Ren into a heated stride. He walks tall on the berm, snarling, *"Curb your tongue and honor your code! I've heard you praise mercy in peace and lull, but it is here and now, when swords are drawn and tempers are hot, that your words are put to a test of heart!"*

The villagers exchange weighty looks. *Guy's got a point.*

I sidle up to Ren and give him a nudge. "Never thought that would ever come from you. I mean that as a compliment."

The Wayfarer, much to my delight, begins to redden. "We need to maintain a battlefield standard. Otherwise, these soldiers will devolve into a weaponized mob."

Erany almost laughs, but she covers her mouth and turns it into a snort. "I'm sorry. I didn't mean to—"

"Didn't mean to *what?*" Ren snaps. "You were taught the same under Terrelly's wing!"

She lowers her hand and grins. "I'm not laughing *at* you, Ren. I'm laughing because...well, if you had asked me earlier, I would have said that Ren might think it but he would never speak it—that he would grumble and pout and curl his lip."

His eyes flash with irritation. "I do not 'grumble and pout.' Nor do I 'curl my lip.' "

"You kinda do, actually," I offer.

"Fah." He turns on his heel and storms away. As he departs, I catch him trying to hide a smile.

"You see that?" I look incredulously at Erany.

"I did," she chuckles. "If Wretched Ren can lighten and buoy, I daresay we might just emerge victorious."

Maybe it's petty, but seeing Ren break out of his dickhead shell...

Yeah, anything's possible.

———

Lanctom's defense turns into a slog. Every time the Knights attack, they leave more corpses on the field, which translates into more Shambles for their next offensive. In a progressively ominous chain of developments, it takes more effort to drive them back. They're growing in size, strength, and durability. We try and collect the abandoned bodies, but Lyderea's artillery makes it way too dangerous.

It's not just us. Whenever we repel a wave of Knights, our shoreline armada gets hit by frigates. Thus far, we've lost a tenth of our ships. A fifth have been sidelined due to repairs.

Two weeks in, they attack us at night. It's the scariest thing I've ever experienced. The world narrows down into shadows and screams, a torrent of boulders and eruptive wyvern fire. I'm sure the Knights hate it as much as I do, because they mostly stick to daytime combat.

When I'm not sleeping or stuffing my face, I check my amulet-armor for mangled runes. Occasionally, there's nothing I can do, and I have to let it self-repair. Most of the time, I can untangle some glyphs and reweave my shields.

As time goes by, I start to normalize the fighting. That's good and bad. I'm not as prone to fear and despair, but it's easier to slide on stuff like food, sleep, or shoring up my arcane protection. Sleep, eat, fight.

Sleep, eat, fight. Turn everything off, stay in the groove. It's been three weeks, but it feels like years. So when Lucky interrupts as I'm counting my ammo (I have about seven hundred rounds), I'm grateful for the distraction.

"You seem well."

"Mm." I finish pushing bullets into my belt, then I start fiddling with my traveler's medallion. Sleight of hand has become a must, a crucial tool to keep me occupied.

A voice sounds from down the line: *"They're mounting a push!"*

I jump to my feet, drawing Ailura in a reflexive twitch. Lucky hunches in place, ready to flee...then a following cry echoes through our trench: *"Quell your worry, false alarm!"*

"That was vexing." Lucky offers a grin.

"You get used to it." I holster Ailura and resume my sleight of hand.

He glances at my fingers. "As I said before, other pursuits would serve you better."

"For some reason, this feels important." I laugh self-consciously. "Weird, huh? Speaking of things that don't make sense, why are you still here?"

He gives a shrug. "The same reason you're trifling with that bauble."

"Lanctom's a fortress. It's slim pickings, isn't it?"

"Indeed. There is nothing left for me to steal. I'm staying because—"

"Of a gut feeling," I finish.

"That's right."

We share a chuckle over our unexpected bond. I was never woo-woo before I came to Evermoor, but my perspective has gradually shifted over time. Lucky, though...I never thought he would listen to his gut. Thus far, his decisions have sprung from an ethics-free balance sheet.

"Well I'm glad you're here." I mean it too.

"Grace and thanks."

A comfortable silence grows between us. When I first arrived, he was quick to joke or goof around. Then, after my Earth-side trip, he became increasingly darker and depressingly paranoid. Now he seems to be lightening up. It isn't much, but I'm grateful nonetheless.

After a minute, I say, "Never thought I would end up here."

"Nor I." He studies the berm. "How often do they strike?"

"Once a day. Sometimes twice."

"And your gun will hold? You have sufficient ammunition?"

"Over seven hundred rounds, plus the ones in my belt and the chamber. Lucky..." I tilt my head and throw him a grin. "Are you concerned for me?"

"Keep it mum," he chuckles. "I wish to maintain my unsavory standing."

"Absolutely." Then, without knowing why, I mutter, " 'Be dust upon your breath.' "

"Aye." He gives a nod, which is mildly surprising. Typically, he rolls his eyes and scoffs at that phrase.

I stop messing with my traveler's medallion. "You seem different. Anything I should know?"

For a second he looks torn. "I doubt that fate will take your side, but..." He looks me in the eye. "I hope it does. You deserve it."

"Lucknar Hap." My grin returns. "Was Gyrax right about you?"

He chuckles again. "Mayhap. I have surprised even myself by lingering in this Khel-hole."

"Khel for us, not for you." I cock an eyebrow. "*Unless*...are you planning to fight?"

"Please." He snorts. "I have done plenty of fighting. It hasn't been with my aura or blade, but I have tendered my effort nonetheless."

"That's true," I acknowledge. "It's just easy to forget, when you're accusing me of being a bundle of 'arcane shot.' Or an idiot kid instead of the Traveler."

A wry smile. "I plead thy grace. You have proven your worth time and again."

"My personal worth was never in question. Neither was yours."

"Fah." He flaps a hand in mock annoyance, then snaps his fingers and produces a pair of cigarettes. "Care for a loken? Nyanti's best."

"You didn't steal 'em, did you?" I accept a smoke from his outstretched hand. "How's she been?"

He lights his cig with a magic-fired thumb. "Mm." He takes a drag, closes his eyes, and blows out a stream of winding gray. "Busy. I don't understand what she is doing. It seems rather—"

"Softening the connotation of interconnectivity," I reply distractedly. "When the portal opens, she wants it inclined toward disunion and rupture."

He raises a brow, clearly impressed. "I must confess—your explanation exceeds my grasp."

"Oh, uh...right." A puff of air blows through my nose. Not quite a laugh, but almost. "I could elaborate, but I'm pretty sure you don't want to hear about arcane philosophy."

"You are correct," he affirms. "Nevertheless, I am glad you have acquired skill and knowledge. 'Tis a marked change from days of yore."

" 'Days of yore?' Has it really been that..."

I suddenly realize Lucky's right. I haven't kept track, but the months have been steadily adding up. My interdimensional trip didn't help—everyone aged a year during my two days on Earth.

"Man, I think I'm twenty..." I contemplate the sky. "I might be twenty-one. Trippy. Every so often, I find myself wondering if any of this is real. Did I fall asleep and dream it all up?" I look at Lucky again. "Sometimes it feels like time has flown by, sometimes it feels like I'm stuck in a loop."

The thief shrugs. "In any case, I wish you happiness for your birthday, late though it may be."

"Where I come from, we say 'happy belated birthday.' " I click my jaw forward and blow out a smoke ring.

"It has been a day and an age since I heard the equivalent," he muses. "In many ways, time froze when I turned ten—when I fled the wrath of my avaricious brother."

"I'm sorry." The words come naturally, without excess sentiment or a hint of insecurity.

Lucky responds with an appreciative nod, conveying recognition of my nuanced sincerity. "Thank you. We both appear to be adrift in time. Perhaps we are due for a collective rebirth."

"Perhaps."

I inhale smoke and bask in the silence. While I appreciate Lucky's approval, I'm more pleased with my internal response: I don't care if he approves of me or not. I know that I'm worthy through and through, regardless of what Lucky or anyone else thinks.

I take another drag. "We could definitely use you here on the front."

"It would be paltry and wasteful."

"Yeah," I cede, "you're more of a behind-the-scenes guy. Even if we tasked you with a crucial heist, it probably wouldn't be a smart play; every time you steal from a badass, they catch you in the act and smack you around."

The thief laughs. "Indeed. My attempts to pickpocket Ren and Syfaedi..." A rueful smile. "You would think I was incompetent by the result."

I throw a good-natured scoff. "Whatever. I've seen you pick hundreds of pockets. I'm sure you've picked more when I wasn't looking."

His smile turns a notch slyer. "Flattery won't help you into my carry."

"I'm not trying to steal from you." I shake my head in bafflement—he never lets up on his damn paranoia.

A long pause. Then: "I believe you. Aside from Gyrax, you might be the only person that..." He taps some ash off the end of his loken. "No matter. You are honorable and decent." Before I can thank him, he adds, " 'Tis a double-edged sword—it distracts you from guarding against this gods-cursed world."

My smoke is done, so I drop it to the ground and stamp it out. "I'll take precautions. But I'd rather focus on solutions instead of the problem."

"Focusing on problems *is* the solution."

"Agree to disagree."

He sighs in defeat. "Ware your flanks, Jon. Life is filled with tyrants and predators."

"I've got you on the ropes." I flash him a grin. "That sigh sounded like you're softening up. As for your warning, I'll say this: tyrants and predators are a bump on the road, a pause between beats. There's something greater beneath it all. It may cast shadows here and there, but only to add depth to the light and the color."

"If anything, it is the opposite," he replies. "We may enjoy an occasional reprieve, but existence is rife with shadow and night."

"You just admitted to the occasional bright spot, free and clear of any dark conspiracies. There's hope for you yet, Lucky."

His mouth opens and closes. Then he concedes, "Perhaps."

My eyes widen in mock surprise. "What did you say? Could you repeat it for the recor—"

I'm interrupted by a shout: *"GET IN POSITION!"*

"THEY'RE COMING!

46

I race onto the field alongside the others, into a record-breaking swarm of Knights and drakes. As I struggle to process the massive horde, an unwelcome thought comes to the fore:

This might be our last stand.

———

In previous battles, they were gauging our response and building up Shambles. This is different. This is meant to overwhelm and destroy. They've sent ten times the Knights and four times the wyverns. The sky is *thick* with 'em—legions of fliers are blotting the sun.

The Knights roll past our six-person vanguard, wracking the berm with fire and chaos. We have medium-level troops on the primary lines (sand/dirt golems and Clandestine Inspectors) but it won't be long before they fold.

Seconds into the raging brawl, I snap out Weak Sauce. Typically, I fan Ailura's hammer with my right hand, but we're ridiculously outnumbered, so I need a blade to parry and block. Thankfully, Ailura commandeers my fine motor functions. Whenever the loops on my belt run dry, I flip her into her holster, reach in my carry for a handful of bullets, then push-drop them efficiently into my belt. I also grab rounds and literally throw them, seating them in the loops with preposterous accuracy.

This is *insane.* I've never had to load my belt on the field, and I'm about to do it a second time. If they keep this up, there's no way we can—

Someone to my rear screams, *"SHAMBLES ON THE LINE!"*

I swing around and hit it with a bullet. Due to my jacked-up senses, I can see the discharge flowing into the wreck. It digs a hole in the gore-formed spider, then blows it apart into a rain of filth.

I turn on my heel, block a slash, and muzzle-jab a Knight with my hot-glowing barrel. I ride the momentum of my strike, cracking another on the nose with the butt of my gun. Thrust-kick the guy directly behind him, snarling up his buddies and forcing a gap. Level my pistol, and—

"BACK TO THE LINE!" Gyrax roars. *"FALL BACK TO THE LINE!"*

—fire one last shot into their midst. After a panicked sprint, I crest the berm and bullseye a wyvern. This is it. Unless Gandalf and Eomer come over the ridge, we're—

"LOOK TO THE RIGHT!" Elier screams. *"FREECAST ALLIES!"*

I fail to register why that's important; I'm preoccupied with Knights, wyverns, and a trio of Shambles attacking the trench. Then someone else repeats the cry. Then someone else.

Pretty soon, the whole line is shouting.

The wyverns have set up a cadence of fire, raking our lines with stream after stream of lung-searing heat. Now they're starting to fail and stutter, allowing our archers to respond with arrows. As I swivel and shoot, swivel and shoot, I catch sight of the reason behind our reprieve: there's Felinx and Wolven on our right, Elerican Witches on our left. (Whoa, the Felinx are dressed in feline armor). Lyderea's forces are caught in a pincer, stuck between Wildlyre and Elerican spells.

Hell yeah. *Hell* yeah.

Supercats and Wolven rip into the Knights, breaking their press and killing them en masse. The Witches, meanwhile, soak the field in uncoiling brilliance. It's simple stuff—force and lightning and violent detonation—but none of that matters. I don't give a shit about magical elegance. All I care about is holding the berm.

Suddenly, Lyderea's troops start falling back.

Villager-defenders run up the berm, brandishing their weapons and cheering themselves hoarse. They were probably thinking the same thing as me: there's no way in hell we'd live through the day.

I'd like to join in, but I need to make sure the Knights are driven all the way back. So I sheathe Weak Sauce and stride onto the field, fanning Ailura's hammer with my newly freed hand. I feel like Eastwood in *The Good, the Bad, and the Ugly,* when he's walking beside Tuco and gunning down bad guys (once again, yes—I have a boomer's taste in movies.) Only I'd say I have the edge on Clint. Eastwood shot a couple of mercs, while I'm out here blowing through corpse-spiders, Knights, and fire-breathing squadrons of mounted wyverns. While .45 Colt is pretty impressive, it doesn't hold a candle to Avalonian ammo.

During her fifth or sixth salvo, Ailura Qartesi levels up again. She used to be a souped-up pistol that could take out demons (I even missed, the first time I shot her). Then, in Gracelyn Keep, she adjusted her blasts so she didn't bring the castle down on our heads. Now, our bond has pushed us to a new level: after pummeling a target, her death rays continue across the field, hunting down additional prey. Sometimes they even split or explode, adding a welcome dose of random lethality.

Once the Knights are back in their camp, I retreat behind the smoking berm. A minute ago, the villagers were cheering our Hail Mary save. Now, however, they're regarding our saviors with cautious apprehension. Relegant Syvalis is the one exception—he's yelling at soldiers, telling them to sheathe their weapons and relax their guard. *These are our friends, Nok dammit!* Some of them listen, but a fair amount stay exactly as they are.

I understand—it's not every day you meet supercats, Witches, and gigantimous dog-warriors.

"Yire Anon!" Gyrax strides over to the Hunter Prince. "You brought your milk-lapping tabbies! Deliac's gleam, I could kiss you!"

Yire flicks his protective visor, causing it to retract with a heavy-sounding CLANK. (Damn, his armor is *bad ass.* A mix of Black Panther cool and Sauron-edged layers). " 'Milk-lapping?' Tread soft and speak light—Wolven smell like sodden fabric! And next time, use a better messenger device. I almost devoured your aviad before I realized it wasn't a bir—"

Gyrax whacks him square on the mug. Yire reacts with a snarl and a swipe, then they're both rolling across the ground, roughhousing with aggressive schoolyard energy. Nearby villagers raise their weapons, alarmed by the wanton brawn and speed, but I just chuckle and shake my head. Gyrax usually has to restrain himself. It's nice to see him cut loose and have fun.

After a brief tussle, the Wolven gets up and dusts himself off. Yire performs a full body shake (it's super loud, thanks to his clanky-clank armor) and glances around. "It appears we have saved you just in time. These small-bodied humans were bound for the Clear."

Relegant tromps forward, pointing indignantly at the Hunter Prince. "Careful, Felinx! My kith may be new to the blade and the bow, but their hearts and souls are stout and bold!"

Yire chuckles. "I plead thy grace." He peers closely at Relegant. "You seem familiar..." His slit-pupiled eyes light with recognition. "You fought at the Battle of Sidehelm Pass."

It takes the wind out of Relegant's sails. "No," he whispers, staring at the ground in shame and regret. "I cut and ran like a low-shadow churl."

Yire growls, "Lift your gaze and stiffen your spine! Honor your title, Wayfarer, and stow your regret until the battle is won! Better yet, do away with it altogether!"

Relegant's eyes widen in shock. Then he offers a bashful smile. "Thank you, Felinx. Long have I endured the burden of—"

"And now you wish to renew its weight, and bear it ever longer into your dotage!" Yire roars. "Look to your front, ranger! Claim who you are meant to be, instead of dwelling as a shadow of your incomplete self!"

Ren clasps his shoulder from behind. "All stumble in darkness and chaos. But those who can hold their mettle in dusk...they reap the grace of an honest dawn."

Relegant's eyes shine with moisture. He clears his throat to regain his composure, then reaches up and pats Ren's hand. I'm astounded and touched—it's crazy to see Ren being this supportive.

A Wolven named Ripfang (I recognize him as the were-shepherd who gave me crap at Hafferly Crossing, back when I was still a level zero noob) walks up with Lyné Anir, Sygress of the Witchcraft City. She's still in a robe (kind of like what Neo wore in the second *Matrix*), rocking a pair of cut-off sleeves that show off her muscled-up tatts (she's got the Ninja Turtle cuts between her shoulders, biceps, and triceps. I've been working out for months and I *still* don't have those). Back in Elerica, her clothing was black with golden trim. This time, it's vibrant blue with rich green streaks. Ripfang, meanwhile, is decked out in basic wanderer gear: cross-slung carry, a pair of scimitars on his hips, and a worn gray cloak hanging down to his knees.

Gyrax steps up as our diplomat-leader, running everyone through a round of introductions. When he gets to Raef—"Before you stands the Detective Savant"—Ripfang and Lyné recoil in surprise.

"Morteri Vysade has been wreaking havoc," the Sygress says. "Your reemergence warms my heart."

The Ogre tips his stylish bowler hat. "Morteri and I have unfinished business. Rest assured, he will know my wrath."

"He has tightened his grip on a range of folk," Ripfang growls. "Sydelian hunters, Asídí wardens...he even tried to poison us Wolven, but our spymasters caught his perfidious agents. They are now tilling our hottest fields, up to their elbows in smelly fertilizer."

"What?" I ask incredulously. "Did anyone die?"

"A handful of pups turned sick and feeble, but that was the extent of their low-shadow crime. Thank Fenrus, Bao, and every deity in between."

I sigh in relief. *Whew.* "Wolven pups dead of poison...I imagine that would constitute an act of war." (What kind of sicko poisons Wolven babies? I could never, *ever* hurt a cute-faced doggo).

"Our Rex would unleash the fires of Khel, most likely through our clandestine operatives." He directs a nod at the Wolven king. "Thanks to the foresight of Gyrax Aclasian, they have swelled in numbers and capability. In these uncertain times, the Shrouded Fang has proven invaluable."

Gyrax waves him off. " 'Twas common sense, nothing more."

Ripfang jiggles his thumb at Gyrax. *This guy.* "Does he always shuck praise?" Our party issues a resounding *"Yes,"* drawing chuckles from everyone present. "In that respect, he is utterly predictable. All of our jesters poke fun at his modesty."

"Enough." Gyrax throws a good-natured swat.

A full-grown man would be knocked on his ass, but Ripfang just shakes his head and snickers impishly. Then he gives me an inquisitive once-over, and his mirth transforms into thoughtful appraisal. "You were a clueless boy when I saw you in Hafferly. Now, however..."

"He is the Prophesied Traveler," the Sygress states. "It seems he has embraced his True-born design, which has bolstered his power by leaps and bounds." Her colorful pupils—blue-green-indigo with night-black swoops—switch directions and gyre clockwise.

"Mm," Ripfang grunts. "Well it suits you, human. You are still smelly, but no longer puny." Then he corrects himself: "Not as much, anyway.

"Thanks, Ripfang," I reply dryly. "You're pretty smelly yourself."

"Ha!" He leans back and guffaws. "I cannot deny it. Even among Wolven, I have been deemed malodorous. Careful." He wags a finger. "I can break your valor through stench alone."

"Bring it," I retort, shooting a playful look at Gyrax. "I've handled my share of wet stinky dog."

Everyone laughs, causing subtle joy to bloom in my heart. Outwardly, it may appear to be nothing more than good-natured teasing. Inwardly, it's an important marker of who I used to be and who I am now. I've grown into someone who can stand his ground, make hard calls, and banter with others who can do the same.

"We should pay a visit to Nyanti Eldara," Gyrax looks at Sygress Anir. "You may be able to help with the portal."

"Will your defenses hold?" She glances around at Lanctom's earthworks.

"Without a doubt," Raef assures. "Especially now that we have Witches and Wildlyre."

"Very well," the Sygress says. "To Nyanti, then."

"With pleasure." Elier turns and heads for the Downs, a noticeable pep enlivening his step. (Can't blame him—he hasn't seen her in several weeks.)

I fall in beside Ren and throw him a smile. "This is what you wanted, right? After all this time, we're in open conflict with Lyderea Fairdyle."

The Wayfarer snorts. "We're fighting her forces, not the actual White Veiled Queen." His eyes light with an eager gleam. "Though I ken the meaning behind your words. It feels Nok-damned good to bloody my sword."

I'm taken aback. I've been framing this conflict as a series of tasks, not an interaction between thinking folk. Ren's giving off a more personal vibe—he's embracing the individuality of each of our foes, and he's more than fine with their pain and destruction.

That leads me to wonder: how would it feel to fight for the Queen? She wouldn't care if I lived, died, or spent the rest of my life as a mutilated cripple.

Ren searches my face with his gaze. "The world is cruel, Jon. We must rival its cruelty if we hope to claim victory."

A sideways glance. "You sound like Lucky."

"He's not always wrong."

"So your recent positivity...it was all just an act?" Anger and frustration creep into my voice.

"No." His lips curl into a tired smile. "Lucky and I agree on the need to be vigilant, but we differ on the amount of malice in the world. Nevertheless, you must always keep your sword at the ready."

"You believe in balance," I venture, "whereas Lucky believes the game is rigged."

"Aye." He shrugs. "Fortune will eventually collect its due."

"That's a change. You used to be a hell of a lot darker. When I first arrived, I thought you were going to end up as cynical as Lucky."

" 'Tis why we fought." He gives a rueful laugh. "I was damnably close to sharing his view, but I was afraid to acknowledge it even to myself. So I bowed to my fear and turned it outward, spewing it onto all and sundry." His tone becomes solemn. "Jon, it would ease my heart if you would embrace the truth: for every joy, there must be sorrow. For every gain, there must be a loss."

"Not gonna happen, not when I've seen you change and grow. You used to be a moody dick. Now...well, you're slightly less moody."

Ren guffaws. "Who am I to challenge such praise?"

"Yeah," I chuckle. "Keep your challenge to your Nok-damned self."

"I'm glad we met. I'm glad I met everyone in our party." He dips his chin and murmurs, "Even Lucky."

"Don't get all mushy on me."

The Wayfarer looks puzzled. "What does that mean?"

I clear my throat, slightly embarrassed. "On my world, this guy named Han Solo—" I register his faint grin and indulgent nod: *Nerd.* "Forget it. It basically means don't be sentimental."

"Wish be done." He cocks his head and his grin widens. "You would think it would be the other way around—who would have thought you would say that to me? Strange, no?"

"Yeah. Definitely." I chuckle again.

As we stride into town, doubt takes root in the pit of my stomach. Which of us is right? Ren, me, or Lucky? It has to be me. It *has* to be. After everything I've seen, everything I've done...still, I can't shake the feeling that I'm missing something big.

Then it hits me—there's something in my palm.

I halt in my tracks and look down at my fingers. My medallion is dancing across their tips.

For the last two weeks, I've had on-and-off spurts of runaway hands, where they've done sleight of hand without conscious direction. I blamed it on the stress of battle, and wrote it off as a trifling matter.

But this time, for some reason, it shakes me to my very core.

47

The townsfolk have armored more of their buildings. There's also a scatter of standalone booths, reinforced to withstand magical fire. To the casual observer, it might seem excessive, but if a wyvern gets through and strafes the city, it could burn everything down to cinders and ash. Accordingly, Relegant has formed teams of firefighting archers, designed to neutralize fliers and minimize damage. There's a bunch of 'em drilling on Lanctom's streets, echoing commands and working through imaginary scenarios.

After a series of twists and turns (during which Lucky slips unobtrusively into our ranks) we arrive at the alleyway containing the portal. Nyanti's standing in front of the rift, manipulating designs with her outstretched hands.

Through unShifted sight, it used to appear as a distorted blob. Now it's a sphere of white-cored blue. That's not all—glimmering cracks have formed around it, as if reality itself was breaking and gapping.

The Sygress strides up to her fellow Witch. "Nyanti Eldara. How do you fare?"

"My flesh is worn, my spirit is hale." Nyanti favors us all with a brief glance. "Pardon the brevity. I have much to do and time runs thin."

Elier reaches for her, but she stops him with a shake of her purple-skinned head. "No. I need to focus on these Nok-damned spells."

The Duelist's arm hangs in the air. His face, typically stoic or nonchalant, morphs into the epitome of the word *crestfallen*. I'm struck by the desire to laugh out loud, but I smother the urge in a fair-weather jiff.

"Nyanti..." His hand wavers.

"No," she repeats. "I need to prime this Nok-damned portal. We'll have our time, my love."

As the Duelist sighs and shuffles away, Erany catches my attention with a lift of her brow. *Did you hear that? 'My love?'* I respond with a nod. *Oh yeah—definitely heard it.*

"Do you require assistance?" the Sygress asks.

The Witch shakes her head again. "I am aurically bound to the primary locus. If someone added their arcane perception, it would downgrade the spells I have woven in place."

"As I suspected," the Sygress replies. "Very well. I shall tend to the berm along with your friends."

Nyanti looks around, registering the presence of Yire and Ripfang. "Wind at your back and sun on your brow. Have you brought any kith?"

"Aye," Yire growls. "Six prides of my deadliest Felinx."

"Five packs of veteran Wolven," Ripfang adds.

"And several dozen Wise Woman coteries," the Sygress concludes.

"We'll need them all," Nyanti states, "as I believe our plight is about to worsen. Lyderea is countering my spells with her own. The ensuing overflow does not bode well—when the portal opens, it will give birth to a chain of subordinate gateways."

"What?" Gyrax's features sharpen with concern. "Where?"

She continues fiddling with runes and designs. "I cannot say, exactly, but they will be relatively close, six faires distant at the most. The good news is they won't be as large, so they won't be of interest to Lyderea and her generals."

"The smaller portals are due to the overflow?" I ask. "How does that work?"

"She's using the Tessellate as an arcane prybar, jamming it in the tides and applying maximal force. When the portal opens, the resultant bloom of slipworld energy will funnel through the clash between my spells and the Tessellate, and transcribe into an array of lesser rifts."

The Sygress cups her mouth, studying the ground with a furrowed brow. "She could bridge our world with another plane...invite untold horrors onto the field."

The Witch nods. "She is willing to risk it to further her plans."

"You shouldn't be doing this all by yourself!" Elier protests. "You need ample time to sup and rest!"

"Elier, I know my craft, *and I shan't brook any Nok-damned—*" Nyanti falls silent and regards the Duelist with narrowed eyes. Her hands continue twisting and curling, kneading the portal with nonstop enchantments.

"Come here."

I almost snicker at his response. Elier Finn, one of the most badass fighters in all of Evermoor, glances fearfully from side to side, like a little kid who's been caught red-handed.

"Ah...what about your spells? I wouldn't want to upend your efforts..."

"Come. *Here.*"

His mouth opens and closes. Then he creeps forward with hesitant steps. (This time, I have to clear my throat to keep from laughing.) He stops six feet away, almost wrings his hands, then lets his arms dangle by his sides.

"Closer," she orders. He takes a half-step forward. *"Closer,"* she demands. Another half-step. Once he's within arm's reach, she tilts her chin and parts her lips. "Kiss me."

The Duelist's jaw drops in surprise, then a cheese-eating grin blooms on his face. He leans in, closes his eyes, and presses his lips firmly against hers.

Still working her bevy of spells, Nyanti holds the kiss for a lingering moment. Seconds later, she draws away with a knowing smile. "There. Something to remember me by, when you're busy fighting Knights and wyverns."

He touches his lips, face shining with wide-eyed wonder. It's pretty adorable—they've been together for over a year, but he's acting like that was their very first kiss.

"As far as rest and victuals, quell your worry," the Witch assures. "I enjoy intermittent sleep, while the villagers provide food and water. For the moment, it can't be helped. 'Tis far too late to add another mage."

Sygress Anir, who's been circling the portal and peering into its depths, grunts in agreement. "These patterns are Nyanti's, through and through. Additional sorcerers would only hinder her efforts." She scrutinizes the gyre of runes and glyphs. "Telic variations of SyCajister coils, a small touch of Raiesa's Cry, and..." She straightens in surprise. "You wove in a trio of seavoker charms."

"I learned them during my time on the water."

The Sygress nods, conveying professional approval. "Impressive." She looks around at us. "All is well in regard to the portal. My next concern is your placement of assets. I wish to speak with your various leaders, along with whoever is in charge of runners and supplies. Also, if you have assigned rotations, I wish to check them for redundancy and—"

"Thank you, Sygress," Ren interrupts. "But we have the minutiae well in hand." He crosses his arms and stares her down.

Nyanti shoots him a horrified look. *"Ren!* You are speaking with the Sygress of Elerica City! You would do well to—"

The Sygress interjects with an easygoing chuckle. "I stand corrected, Wayfarer. My Witches and I are at your service."

Ren uncrosses his arms and scratches his temple, mollified by her casual response. "Ah...thank you. You honor me with your well-tempered stance." He closes his eyes and swallows hard, as if what he's about to say is causing him physical discomfort. "If you have a suggestion, I welcome your advice. Also..." He ducks his head and mutters, "I was pert without reason. I plead thy grace."

The Sygress's lips twitch up in amusement. "All is forgiven. You have made strides and bounds, Rennarean—when last we met, the tact you are showing would have been far out of reach."

Ren looks away, a hint of a smile playing across his face. Erany and I exchange another grin. Grumpy McGrumperson is softening up, and I am one hundred percent here for it.

Then a thought comes to the fore, prompting me to raise a loose-fingered hand. "Back in Elerica, you portaled me to Earth without any prep. This one is different—it's taking months to form. Why, though? Is it just because it's bigger?"

"That's the main reason, yes," the Sygress replies. "However, there were other factors in the Witchcraft City. One, we were standing in the hexflow spring—'tis a powerful nexus, an amalgam of Evermoor's oldest ley lines. Two, the arcane tides will occasionally surge, in a burst of power known as an eldritch billow. I took advantage of three such billows, and channeled them into an acausal shift. With the temporary release of cause and effect, I was able to bridge your world with ours."

" 'Temporary release of cause and effect?' That sounds Laiddinic."

"Everything is, if you look past the illusion of mental separation."

"Wait a second..." Wonder builds at the edges of my mind. "Could anyone become the Prophesied Traveler?"

The Sygress smiles at me. "The outcome is based on personal belief."

"That's not an answer!" I blurt. "If others can help, they need to step up and—"

She holds up a hand. "We must each discover our path for ourselves, free of the compulsion for external validation. What do *you* believe, Jon? Relax your mind, abide in the moment, and let yourself merge with your personal truth."

Something in her voice tells me that isn't just a casual recommendation. So I take a breath, close my eyes, and let it all out.

I'm here for a reason, aren't I? I must be. It'd be straight-up ridiculous if I didn't have a purpose. I went from being a freshman in college to learning magic and swordplay. I've fought Nightkeeper assassins, survived horror-movie kehcraw, and managed to break free of the Watchers of Erendor. I asked for adventure, and boy did I get it.

A half-buried memory comes to the fore: dancing with Erany at our existential prom, musing about how everyone gets a chance to star and co-star, and how we go from rationalizing the answer to actually living it. I can advocate for others to do the same, but the best way to do that is to embody my beliefs. I can't force anyone to share my convictions, or people wouldn't find their own unique truth; they'd be a muddled reflection of what I thought they should be.

I open my eyes, reveling in a wash of soul-deep certainty. It must show on my face, because the Sygress is regarding me with knowing amusement.

"There you have it. That answer was for you and you alone. You posed the question in days of yore, then permitted the solution to come into being. You will do so again, if you continually allow it into your life."

"And how do I allow it to into my—" Then I stop myself. "You can't tell me." I say it slowly, exploring the idea with my heart and my mind. "If you could, it would make a lie out of my personal guidance."

She gives a nod. "Even if I told you what to do, you would have to express it through your own perception. You are not a machine, Jon." She glances toward the inland border. "Lyderea does not share that view. She sees us all as soulless cogs, designed to cater specifically to her. The irony is clear: she denies her subjects their innate purpose, while making a mockery of her own."

"That doesn't help her victims," Lucky counters.

The Sygress squares up with him. "I could elaborate further with arcane philosophy, but it would only sound like sly rationale. In the end, you must live your truth. There is no substitute."

"This reverie is fine in a cozy sitting, not in the face of strife and death!" Lucky snaps.

The Sygress gives him a cool stare. "As fragments of an omnipotent benevolence, how else could we structure our lives? Our purpose is to craft our own narrative. 'Tis the driving principle behind magic and creatio—"

"Spare me!" Lucky screams. He thrusts a finger at the gore-strewn Brink. "Magic gave rise to that Nok-damned boneyard! And as far as your notion we are born from omnipotence, that is foolish beyond any measure or scale! Our lives are a churn of chaos and spite, where all must watch their imperiled backs! That is it and *THAT IS ALL!"*

The Sygress cedes with a dip of her chin. "So you have said, so shall it be. I cannot force you into your power, for the Truest power is a personal choice."

"You are rife with folly and lowest deceit," he hisses. "You and your kith are destined for woe."

"I disagree," she replies. "Through perspective and focus, I can open a door into serendipity, and shape my future for the better. If you are ever interested in doing the same, I will gladly join you in—"

"You are just as fell as the White Veiled Queen." He gives her a venomous sneer. "She plied my kin with similar lies, then twisted their hearts with a wink and a smile."

She closes her eyes in muted pain. "In another life and a different plane, Lyderea was once known as Enthimy Nilena. It saddens me to see her perpetuate vice. But you, Lucky..." The Sygress opens her mesmeric eyes. "You needn't be a hapless cog."

"You have described yourself, not I," he scoffs. "I choose to eke out what I can, in a senseless world defined by malice. I would say you are harmless, but you hold sweeping authority—you are prone to infecting others with folly."

Her voice remains calm. "You must strive to release your venom and hate, or—"

"Or *what?*"

"Or they will wrack you to your dying day, and you will wait incarnations to feel your True-born reality."

"I know my reality," he jeers. "And it is not at the mercy of an invisible force."

"You are correct," she agrees. "It is you and you are It. Right at this moment—and for much of your life, it seems—you have cut yourself off from the whole of your being. I advise you to choose a more congru-ent perspective."

"My time here is short. I would rather not waste it on fools and pat-sies." He flaps a hand—*away with you*—and departs from our midst.

The Sygress trails him with her gaze. "His story is young and there is much to write. But the consequent chapter...he is bound for sorrow, as the day is bright and the night is long."

Her words land heavy on my ears. My hands, however, are in a world of their own.

This whole time, they've been fiddling with the Veric Glass.

48

I'm not gonna mention my runaway hands. The important thing is they aren't messing with my aim or my swordplay. If anything, they feel surer and smarter than ever before. *That,* ironically, is what makes me uneasy—they're giving off a Laiddinic vibe. It's a gradual build instead of a rabbit-hole plunge, but the low-key certainty is still disconcerting.

"Back to the front," Gyrax declares. "I'll meet you there soon enough. I wish to palaver with Syf and Idinia."

"Wise," Erany remarks. "With the addition of Witches and martial Wildlyre, there's a good chance we'll hold the Brink. The shore may soon be our primary worry."

"Curb your zest," Ren warns. "Lyderea has employed but a fraction of the Tessellate. If she presses our lines with its full capacity, the Downs will fall in a fair-weather jiff."

She rolls her eyes in exasperation. "Wretched Ren comes to the fore—of *course* we can't stand against the Nok-damned Tessellate! Does that preclude us from counting our blessings?"

To everyone's surprise, Ren chuckles agreeably. "I plead thy grace, Eralindíany. I did not intend to douse your light."

For a brief moment, she's taken aback (an apology from Ren is like spotting Banksy on a unicorn during a blue moon eclipse). After giving him a suspicious once-over, she grudgingly says, "All is forgiven. You seem to have sworn off the shade in favor of shine, and I shan't discourage a good turn of heart."

"We must hold to the belief that things can improve," he says. "You and I, in particular. Terrelly deserves nothing less."

At the mention of their embittered mentor, Erany nods and swallows thickly. "Aye," she whispers. "At the very least, we owe him that."

Elier, meanwhile, has been staring into space, processing variables and possible strategies. "If the Tessellate is busy here in Lanctom, it won't be as strong on other fronts."

"Correct." Nyanti stays focused on her portal-meshed spells. "Unfortunately, we cannot determine if it's flagging or keen, unless we observe its multilocal nodes."

" 'Multilocal...' " My brow wrinkles in thought. "I'm guessing that means it can appear in different locations, making it impossible to assess unless we can monitor all of Evermoor."

"Aye," she affirms. "So be prepared for misdirection, and assume Lyderea is holding wild."

"I wish I could say the same for us," Yire mutters. "Unless we stumble upon a miracle, we have been dealt our hand as far as battlefield capital."

"Quell your worry," Ripfang growls. "When a miracle is needed, one shall arise."

"I was at Sidehelm," Yire rumbles. "On that day, the Juric Unity experienced no such miracle."

"We are not the Juric Unity," Raef counters. "Nurture your hope, lest you follow in my steps and rot in a self-made prison."

The Hunter Prince gives a reluctant nod. "Very well, Detective. If nothing else, 'twould be low to discourage the stalwart townsfolk."

"Remain open and light," Gyrax advises. "If there's a glint in your eye and a spring in your step, you shall help ward their minds against woe and despair."

Yire looks at me. "Why not, eh? Fate has summoned the Prophesied Traveler. Who can say what else is in store?"

I stop in the middle of a sleight-of-hand twist. After a second, I meet his gaze.

"I share your vantage, Hunter Prince. Life has a way of defying expectations."

"Indeed, little human. I pray to Shou that it will be to our gain."

———

Over the last two weeks, the villagers have constructed a chain of shelters, about a hundred yards back from the berm-side trenches. They're neat rows of wooden huts, a couple steps up from a dirt-floor lean-to.

I was offered a spot, but I promptly ceded it back to the defenders. I've gotten used to sleeping in the dirt. Also, I feel more secure when I'm right on the line, ready to fight at a moment's notice.

After the arrivals settle in, they emerge from their huts and start to commingle. The Felinx and Wolven strike up a friendly rivalry (it involves a lot of smack-talk and cat-dog wrestling), while the Witches kick off some magical games (the arcane equivalent of hackey sack and frisbee). The Clandestine Inspectors are the least outgoing. They're super courteous, but they're also casual and unobtrusive (probably because of their spycraft training). As the shindig progresses, villager-defenders filter through the crowd, exchanging nods and wary greetings.

Dinner's informal: rough-cut sandwiches and lukewarm tea. Everyone digs in except for the Felinx. A dozen scoff in haughty refusal, prompting the friendlier ones to explain that they stick to a warrior-cat diet. They elaborate by reaching in their armor-slung pouches, and producing an array of colorful meatballs.

Yire observes with narrowed eyes, then quietly stalks through the motley assembly, nudging any cats that came off as snooty. They follow him behind an out-of-the-way hut, where he proceeds to give them a royal ass-chewing (he sounds like a growly, half-tiger drill instructor). Once he's done, they slink back into the fold, noticeably humble and way less conceited.

Not gonna lie, I like the fact that he set 'em straight. Maybe it's petty, but so are dickheads, right? This might rank low on the dickhead scale (which, in my mind, goes from slightly standoffish to Ren on a Monday), but it's cool to see Yire keeping things healthy.

Soon enough, Lanctom's villagers are chatting and laughing. I guess I shouldn't be surprised—life is too short to be nasty and mean. Especially here on the primary line, where it's all but guaranteed that some of them will die. At the same time, it could have easily gone the other way. The villagers could choose to be distant and aloof, afraid to bond with the others out of fear they might perish. That's probably what's happening in Lyderea's encampment. I would do the same, if my peers were getting assimilated into gigantic corpse-spiders.

As dinner winds down, Relegant Syvaelis climbs onto a hut, raising his hands and calling for quiet. "Townsfolk and Witches, Wolven and Felinx! If you could all indulge me for a brief moment…"

We all bring it in.

The former Wayfarer clears his throat. "I have palavered with your respective leaders, and we have crafted a plan that will play to our strengths. Certain folk will provide a base of destruction, enabling the others to harry and press. Jon is one such person," he gives me a nod, "along with the Sygress and some of her Witches. The rest of us will flank if given the chance. Your leaders have been given the relevant details—refer to their aides for calls and signals."

He pauses, gathers his thoughts, then downshifts into a more personal gear. "May your deities guard your body and aura. And if you happen to believe in naught but this world, I would have you remember: Lyderea craves your unthinking worship, and ceding to her will is a fate worse than death. If you see her on the field, fell her if you can. But in her absence, *send her low-shadow Knights to the depths of Khel!*"

A spirited roar erupts from the crowd.

I have no idea if we'll win or lose. At the end of the day, that isn't my call. The important thing is we're coming together and making a stand. None of us want to drown in lack, just so Lyderea can glut herself with riches. Everyone here is hoping for better.

And while our future might be wildly uncertain, I'll gladly die to uphold that hope.

———

The next morning, fog settles across the field, stoking my fear and paranoia. What if Lyderea recruited a Balrog? What if her mages summoned a Demagorgon? What if—

The Tessellate begins to filter outward, infusing maggot-ridden corpses with nasty-ass runes. Rotten bodies squeeze together, sliding and shlooping and mashing into Shambles. As warnings echo across our lines, I reach down and unholster Ailura.

"Disgusting."

"Lucky!" I spin around in my hide. "What are you doing here?"

"Following my heart." He responds to my stare with mock-annoyance. "Gawk at someone else, will you?"

"You're here...to *fight?*" My brow wrinkles in confusion.

"Those monoliths seem a tad bit angry." He directs a nod at the rising eyesores. "Unless we check their unsightly advance, the townsfolk behind us will suffer greatly."

A lump of emotion grows in my throat. I never admitted it, even to myself, but I had given up on him a long time ago.

"Thank you," I manage.

"Fah." He throws a good-natured wave. "I am charging you for each second I am on the field."

I laugh in relief. "I'm good for the money. Every damned cent."

He snorts in derision. "What is a 'cent?' Pay me in coin, dundernonce, or I'll rack you with fees that beggar your carry."

"Coin it is." I exit the hide and start up the berm. "You should find an arrow-port and fire your bow. I'm part of the heavy-hitter front."

"Nonsense." He follows behind me. "I have stayed on the sidelines long enough."

The others are gathered atop the berm. Erany, who's just transformed the Rose into the Blade, registers his presence with incredulous shock.

"*Lucky?* What are you—"

"Standing with those who stood with me." He casts his gaze across the field, at the ponderous Shambles wreathed in fog.

"The risk will be dire," Gyrax warns. "We cannot spare a Kalsaedian amulet, and we cannot afford to imbue you with shields."

"Quell your worry." Lucky pulls up his sleeve, revealing a bracelet comprised of silver-white twists, capped by a lucent blue gem above his wrist. "I enjoy the protection of this magical armor. 'Tis a physical instantiation of Threshwind's Barrier."

He slaps the jewel with his right hand, activating it with energy from his palm-centered loci. Slashes of light project from the gem, cutting diagonally across his body before sinking into his aura. For a couple of seconds, the spell expands and solidifies, then it settles into a network of disembodied plates.

"There," he announces. "Not as strong as Kalsaedian shields, but I believe it will serve reasonably well."

"So I would think," Ren says dryly, "as it was intended for use by an Elerican Witch. Tell me: did you switch it with a twin? Or did you filch it while she was fast asleep?"

"He bought it fair," Raef offers. "I saw the exchange with my own eyes."

Lucky shrugs. "Her name is Kinsé Faejewel. She had this spare, and ceded it to me for an equitable sum."

We stare in amazement at the nimble-fingered rogue. *Who are you, and what did you do with Lucknar Hap?*

He shrugs again. "People change. I am no exception." He snaps his fingers, producing a figurine shaped like a gargoyle in flight. "I did, however, liberate this bauble from her carry. As a matter of principle, of course."

We break out in groans and rueful laughter. *That's Lucky.*

The thief shifts from playful to thoughtful. "You know of what befell my kith and kin. If Lyderea wins, it will continue to happen." He scans the party with a steadfast gaze. "I need to be on that Nok-damned field."

"Very well," Gyrax replies. "You have earned your place by our side. With your aid and your skill...and also your heart."

A flash of complicated emotion—sadness, amusement, regret—passes across Lucky's face. "I'm still the same thief."

"We shall see," the Wolven replies.

Suddenly, the Sygress's voice coheres in our brains: *[I have connected us through a telepathic plexus, grouped into thoughtways and apposite buffers. Mind-to-mind speech will be sorted for relevance, directed toward the intended recipients, then clarified for intent without emotional overflow. Express yourself freely—it will auto-regulate so it doesn't overwhelm.]*

All across our trenches, folk regard each other with muted astonishment. I can mentally intuit their wonderstruck mutters.

[Fitting.] Nyanti projects. *[United in heart and now in cognition.]*

Relegant jumps in. *[All are set. Waiting on the van.]* (That's how they refer to our six-person—sorry, seven, with the addition of Lucky—vanguard.)

Ren unsheathes his blue-steel longsword. *[Very well. Let us wreak havoc upon these Knights.]* Thousands of minds exchange a grin, infusing the plexus with aggressive cheer.

I'm not sure why (could be adrenaline or my deepening Shift), but my perception slows as we crest the berm. Wind ruffles our hair and cloaks, adding a dramatic flair to our battlefield entry.

I'm hit by a surge of absolute clarity. I'll remember this moment for the rest of my life—this perfect instant of shared resolve, of our desire to fight for a better world.

And then I'm thrown into violence and chaos.

49

Siege engine missiles crater the ground, smashing the battlefield quartile closest to the berm. The Necrotic Shambles—momentarily obscured by eruptions of soil—are now so damn big that six Knights can stand shoulder-to-shoulder behind one of their legs. Dozens of feet up, mounted wyverns fly low and slow, moving in tandem with the ground-side hulks. Their Rainfire pilots are using the Shambles as cover, just like their counterparts down below.

When the Shambles are roughly halfway across, the ballistae and catapults abruptly stop firing. That's my cue.

I run down the berm and start blasting away, gauging a mess of angles and vectors. There's mages commingled with oncoming Knights, which means this is an all-out, full-force attack. If it was just another probe, they wouldn't have risked any precious sorcerers.

[I'm targeting the Shambles.] I project.

[My Witches and I shall deal with the mages.] the Sygress assures. *[It will curb our support in other matters, but it is better than inviting an arcane barrage.]*

[Agreed.] Raef ratchets his enchanted cane. *[If anyone suffers an arcane barrage, let it be these Nok-damned Knights.]*

[I have spillover.] Elier projects. Clusters of Knights are streaming around him, dying in droves to his cavalry sabers. *[All to my rear—ready on the berm. Erany, if you could funnel more constructs into my lane...]*

[Done.] She's summoned a mix of elementals: sentient dust devils, eagles made of char and ember, as well as wormlike waves of earth and vines. She commands their attention with Deláni Elvish, then urges a horde of them toward the Duelist.

Gyrax twirls his massive axe, felling a pair of Knights with a single stroke. *[Felinx and Wolven, get ready to charge. As soon as their fliers are in range of our bows—]*

[We KNOW, dog-brain!] Yire rages.

I blow apart a trio of Shambles, exposing a clutch of Knight-mounted wyverns. Our bowfolk respond with a heavy volley, riddling the lizards with steel-tipped shafts. Five die while still in the air, the other two fly behind adjacent Shambles. Our berm-side archers don't miss a beat—they shift their fire onto the newly exposed soldiers below.

[I have spillover.] Ren emotes. His longsword is working in quicksilver flashes, complemented by spells from his half-gloved free hand. *[All in my lane, ready your weapons.]*

[Not yet!] Yire booms. *[Wolven and Felinx, savage their ranks!]*

[WITH PLEASURE!] Ripfang charges over the berm, leading a mass of giant dog-warriors. Full-armored Felinx join the rush, leaping and sprinting onto the field.

Their physicality hits like a brutal sucker-punch—legions of Knights freeze in place, overcome by instinctive terror. I don't blame them. If I was attacked by Sauron-armored tigers and beast-mode were-dogs, I'd pee my pants and fill 'em with brown.

Beleaguered Knights sprint for nearby Shambles, but the Wolven and Felinx are insanely agile. They flow into graceful spins and reversals, yanking Knights off their feet, throwing 'em in the air, or smashing them together with sickening force.

Nyanti warns, *[The dominant portal is starting to open! Subordinate rifts are forming en masse!]*

All around us, liminal gateways crackle into existence. Judging by the imagery within their bounds, most of them lead somewhere into Evermoor. A few, however, offer disturbing glimpses into other dimensions. Eye-speckled tentacles, gnashing teeth, hazy blotches of soul-draining color... they're all faded and rife with static, coated in a mess of fractures and breaks.

[Ready to assist.] Erany declares. *[Nyanti?]*

She gathers Erany in the folds of her mind, activating their pre-built, short-range teleport. I perceive my girlfriend as a steady presence, then—after a startling instant where she's gone from my perception—she reappears beside Nyanti.

[Sword in the portal?] Erany asks.

Nyanti nods. *[As hard as you can.]*

She thrusts the Blade into the rift, causing violent feedback to pour from its center. Erany and Nyanti squint and grimace, their hair and clothes whip and flutter. All around them, magical curlicues blaze into existence, searing the air with lightning-threaded power. Out of the corner of my eye, I spot dome-shaped radiance limning the skyline, marking where they're struggling to close the portal.

The Sygress projects, *[Nyanti, how do you fare? Is Lyderea—]*

The Witch's response is wire tight. *[She's blitzing me as hard as an Asterdei rip, but my spells and the Blade are holding for now.]*

[Let me know if you need support.] The Sygress refocuses on battlefield magic.

Nice. It seems like the odds are on our side. Just gotta hold off these goons until Nyanti and Erany can finish with the—

[Lyderea has projected her orphic simulacra!] the Sygress thunders. *[Evade its wrath unless you are van, or you count yourself as a member of my Wise Woman coterie!]*

She beams a plexus-wide image into our brains: a black-and-crimson, female-shaped figure, spawned from the Tessellate's noxious magic. It's strolling through the raging battle, clutching a blood-red whip in her right hand. The undulant weapon is impossibly long; it surrounds her in wide, serpentine loops, before splitting into nine, snake-headed tips. Each one is hissing and weaving, displaying a set of gleaming white fangs.

[The Redmordent Scourge!] Nyanti exclaims. *[Stay clear of its bite!]*

[Redmordent Scourge?] Alarm slips into my telepathic query. *[As in Great Weapon?]*

[Aye.] Gyrax affirms. *['Tis a projected simile, but it is strong enough.]*

[She's coming down the center, right? I'll move inward and see if I can—]

[She's already here!] Yire warns. *[She crossed the field in a low-shadow jiff!]*

Lyderea's simulacra slashes downward, causing the Scourge to elongate with terrifying speed. As it zigs and zags throughout the chaos, it binds a dozen Wolven and seventeen Felinx. The nine at the end get it the worst—they're bitten by the weapon's snakeheaded tips. Malignant rot pours through their auras, causing them to crumble into desiccated husks. Meanwhile, the whip-bound defenders scream as the Scourge constricts, cracking their bones and ripping their flesh with its scales.

She just took out thirty-eight badasses. Without even breaking a goddamn sweat.

A hefty torso charges beneath me, flinging my legs into a wide V. My heart lurches with reflexive panic, then—as I land on a mass of galloping muscle—I realize Ripfang's decided to give me a ride.

[If you ever recount this, I shall deny it to my dying day!] he thunders.

The significance isn't lost on me. Using a Wolven as a mount (or any Wildlyre, for that matter) is considered degrading. But Lyderea's simulacra is way too dangerous to quibble over niceties.

[Thanks! I know this is—]

[Just keep her from using that Nok-damned Scourge!]

I sheathe Weak Sauce and shout *[Incoming!]* at the allies to my front.

Wolven and Felinx dive and scatter, granting me a momentary field of fire. I'm jouncing around like a rodeo cowboy, but Ailura guides me with absolute surety, allowing me to shoot and reload without hesitation. All across the field, broad rays of force maul Shambles and Knights.

That was just a set-up—I had to open a path toward the simulacra. I dump my casings, load the wheel, then flick it back in with a snap of my wrist. Another six blasts roar from Ailura, directly into Lyderea's avatar. With each insanely destructive hit, it stumbles back and sprouts a see-through hole. A second later, they slowly but steadily start to close.

[Let me off!]

[As you wish!] Ripfang curves into a sharp turn, dumping me off his back and onto the ground. I tumble across grass, come up on a knee, and fire six more times. Nice—the simulacra hasn't recovered from my previous salvo. All I have to do is hurt it faster than it can heal.

[Converge on Jon!] Ripfang smashes into the Knights on my left. *[Guard his flanks!]*

I stride forward, dumping casings and loading the wheel. A trio of wyverns try and attack, but our Witches blast 'em out of the sky. One moment they're flying directly toward me, the next they're spiraling across the horizon, leaving smoky trails in their crumple-bodied wake.

Six more shots roar from Ailura, blowing six more holes in Lyderea's simulacra. Its posture matches its battered appearance: its knees are bowed in and it's hunched at the waist.

I dump my casings and lower Ailura. When I try and snatch up six more bullets, my fingers whisper across empty cartridge-loops.

What the—*shit.* My belt's run dry. I reach in my carry for my sack of ammo, but it...what the hell? Where did it go? Where the hell could it have—

"I'm sorry." Lucky's voice sounds from behind me.

"For what?" I rifle through my carry, glancing briefly at Lyderea's simulacra. It's flat on its back, struggling to prop itself onto its elbows. "You haven't..."

And then it hits me.

I slowly turn and lock eyes with the thief, knowing exactly what I'm going to see.

My ammo is dangling from his hand.

The battle fades into a background drone. "Lucky..." I try and speak. Nothing comes out.

"I'm sorry, Jon."

He kicks me in the gut, shoving me toward Lyderea's simulacra. Its nine-headed whip wraps around me, pulling me toward a subordinate rift.

[Guys, she's trying to drag me into a portal! I can't—]
Before I can finish, Lucky rushes me and clinches my waist.
"Lucky, *NO!*"
And then our momentum takes us into the gateway.

50

Everything dissolves into color and sound, swirling and merging into synesthetic harmony. I don't want any damn part of it.

Lucky has to *pay.*

We emerge on a stretch of rocky turf, tumbling and spinning and scrabbling for purchase. I end up on top, press my chest onto his, and spread my bent-kneed legs in a heavy side-pin. As he reaches down and draws a dagger, I channel half my aura into a wild blast of magic, ripping his Elerican armor into useless wisps.

Before he can stab me, I seize his arm in a two-handed keylock. After a split-second's pause to make sure it's secure, I yank it inward, snapping a ligament and drawing a scream. I flip his arm toward his waist, inverting my keylock and entangling it again. This time, I crank violently upward, tearing his shoulder with a loud *POP.* He screams even louder. It barely registers. I slide-mount his belly and shift to the side, trapping his head and shoulders with my knee and my calf. Hook his unguarded wrist, and—

CRACK

—arch back and dislocate his elbow. I adjust my weight, ready to start in on his fingers and wrist, when someone kicks me off his torso. My response is instinctive: I shoot to my feet and grip my rapier. A trio of longswords track with my neck, slowly forcing me down to my knees.

These aren't your typical Knights. Their auras are stronger, riddled with deep-colored runes and exotic designs. But that isn't what makes me stiffen in shock.

Arganti Knifelock is standing behind them.

Between the Glass and the Blade and Lanctom's defense, I almost forgot about the Nightkeeper Captain. He's on our side…I think.

A woman orders, "Justicers, lower your weapons."

I turn toward her, and I get my first look at Lyderea Fairdyle.

The Queen is dressed in flowing white robes. Her exposed skin is unnaturally pale, aglow with ethereal luminescence. There's no denying her physical beauty, but it doesn't resonate at any level—it's cold, impersonal, and dishearteningly mechanistic. Her features are simply a check in the box, instead of a source of true allure.

My eyes drop to her right hip, where the Redmordent Scourge is wound into coils. Against the sheen of her alabaster clothes, its blood-red scales are strikingly vivid.

I'm no longer blind with murderous rage. That allows me to scan and assess. We've teleported onto a soaring mesa, dotted with a mess of slate-gray platforms. A wide stone bridge (ten, maybe twenty yards across) connects us to another butte, where Lyderea is standing atop a plateau. Behind her, wyverns are flying in and out of the towering stone. Its Swiss-cheese network of militarized caves is fitted with ropes, catwalks, and supply-laden perches.

Similar mesas stretch into the distance, forming an expanse of austere scenery. A hundred yards down, thick fog obscures the ground, adding to the sense of mind-boggling height. If someone fell, I would have no idea when they'd eventually stop.

"This used to be known as Aerie DeBaric." She surveys the range of garrisoned mesas. "Now it is home to my skyborne cavalry. Beautiful, is it not?"

"I'm going to kill you." I can't help it—the words are reflexive.

Her lips curl in amusement. "Charming. Lucky?"

A Knight hauls him up, triggering a cry of reflexive pain. His mangled right arm hangs limply by his side.

"Jon, I'm sorr—"

My hand flashes down to my sword. Just as quickly, the Knights level their weapons and spin up their loci. Once again, I find myself staring at a trio of blades. Only this time, they're all glowing with destructive magic.

Knifelock gives an almost imperceptible shake of his head. *Don't.*

"These are not ordinary Knights," Lyderea states. "They have cut their teeth in the Argent Regiment, the most elite of my—"

"I don't care," I snarl. Then I fix Lucky with a burning stare. "You're not sorry—not yet. But I swear to you, Lucky: I will personally show you what it means to be sorry."

He averts his gaze. "Regardless of what happened, I wish you the best. Jon, I—"

"You have the bullets?" Lyderea asks.

"Yes, my Queen." He lifts the sack of enchanted ammo.

"Bring them to me."

Lucky begins walking across the bridge. She holds up a hand, halting him five yards in.

"Did he manage to acquire the Veric Glass?"

"I do not know."

"Search him."

"I have never seen it, my Queen. What does it—"

" 'Tis a magic mirror on a length of chain, most likely hanging from his neck."

Trumpets sound from various bluffs, causing Lyderea to look wildly around. "Who would *dare?* Arganti?"

The Nightkeeper Captain tilts his head. Simultaneously, his aura expands with violet-black runes. He just connected with a telepathic plexus, a lot like the one I was using in Lanctom.

A second later, his aura condenses. "Winged raiders are assaulting our peaks. From the cut of their foil, I believe they hail from Aerie Denir."

A note of concern tinges her voice. "Adraeka? Kyvanxir?"

He shakes his head. "No reports of any dragons, nor any mention of their electric breath."

She visibly relaxes. "Continue, thief. Bring me the Glass."

"Yes, my Queen."

As he doubles back toward me, I stifle a roil of animalistic fury. He's ruined everything, and for what? He could have fled or stood idly by, instead of giving us up to Lyderea Faird—

Then it hits me: he's trained me for this. All those drills in sleight of hand, the interplay between the Glass and the medallion...it's not a solution, but if the dynamic changes and I can take advantage...

The sky above us erupts with fire.

Lyderea curses and draws the Scourge. It surges open into serpentine coils, hovering several yards out from her ghost-pale body. "How did they get here so damn *fast?* They couldn't have evaded our sentry observers unless..."

Realization dawns in her eyes.

"Unless someone told them where to fly."

Mounted drakes swoop and dive, engaging with gliders and their wand-wielding pilots. There's two pilots for every glider—one on the left, one on the right—allowing them to divvy their field of fire. Typically, I would be straight-up enthralled by the aerial battle, but I'm totally focused on what comes next.

"I will find the traitor," she says calmly. "And I will make them into a low-shadow haunt."

Lucky blanches in reflexive terror. The Knights who are guarding me exchange uneasy glances.

She beckons again. "The Glass. Now."

Here we go.

While everyone was focused on the airborne drama, I switched out the Glass with Ren's medallion. For good measure, I threw a layer of illusions onto the dust cover. They wouldn't deceive Nyanti Eldara, but Lucky's no Elerican Witch.

The thief winces as he lifts it off me. As he turns around, the Queen curls her hand in quick succession. "My agents said you were eager to serve me. I would never know it by your lagging gait."

Lucky picks up the pace, limp-hitching toward Lyderea Fairdyle. Halfway across, a pair of combatants fly dangerously low, causing the Queen to flinch back from wand-light and drake-fire.

"Churls!" She flings her whip in a long-running slash, entangling the glider, wyvern, and their respective pilots in loops of razor sharp scales. She follows up with a vicious yank, shredding flesh and armor into spurting gore. As their corpses vanish into the mist below, Lucky steps onto the opposite mesa.

"My Queen." He sinks to a knee and offers the fake.

The whip's leftmost snake bites the medallion, then brings it in toward Lyderea. For a brief moment, I glimpse the insanity behind the facade—her eyes shine with piggish glee, her mouth widens into a Joker-like rictus.

"Finally," she breathes. The Velic Tessellate blooms around her, surrounding her in miasmic red and black glyphs. "I can finally rest easy, now that—" Her brow wrinkles in puzzlement. "This isn't the Glass." She fixes Lucky with a dangerous stare. "You think I'm a fool. A low-shadow mark you can ply with a con."

Lucky straightens in panic. "No, I swear! That was the only—"

"Traitor!" She cracks her whip, binding him in a mess of lurid red coils. As they lift him up and begin to gyre, their scales flex out and ravage his body. Runnels of blood ooze from the twists, streaking his hands with bright crimson streaks.

"My Queen!" he gasps, dropping my sack of enchanted ammo. (If I can grab it, I might be able to turn the tables.) "It wasn't me, I—"

"Quiet." Her whip compresses, causing three of his ribs to break and pop.

Lucky screams, expelling a mist of pink-flecked spittle. At the same time, the Scourge lurches grotesquely inward, devouring the slack and cutting deeper into his flesh.

Her cruelty flips a switch in my psyche, transforming my anger into pity and horror—it's the emotional equivalent of an ice-water plunge. I wasn't using a magic whip, but I was torturing Lucky nonetheless. She undoubtedly thinks he deserves the agony, just like I did a few minutes prior. Now I realize that I didn't hate him because he's weak or evil, it was because I fooled myself into thinking he'd truly changed. I desperately wanted him to conform to my standards, and I couldn't accept that he'd sided against us. But regardless of his deceit and betrayal, it's stunningly clear that he doesn't deserve this.

No one does.

"I will keep my promise." The Scourge tightens, drawing a moan from his red-brimming lips. "You will persist as a shiftless haunt, burdened by the same curse that I levied on the Watchers."

"No." Lucky winces. *"Please..."*

Lyderea cants her head. *"Khazion! Come and feast!"*

I scan the towering mesa behind her. All I see are wyverns and gliders. Who was she talking t—

Midway up, a humongous leg emerges from a cave. It's followed by seven spine-coated limbs. They're all connected to a bulbous torso, agleam with eyes and snapping pincers.

Jesus Christ. It's a giant spider. Maybe eight feet high and twenty feet across.

Lyderea smiles at my shock. "A Qhybát Crawler. It took me a day and an age to enhance his stature and weapons. Beautiful, isn't he? He will pick you apart bit by bit, staunching your blood with his bladed silk. Then, when you are nothing but nerves and glistening organs, he will finally grace you with his venom. Come, Khazion! Come and enjoy your midday snack!"

Instinctive fear grips my brain, triggering shivers and flashes of heat. That thing is going to eat me a piece at a time.

This can't be happening.

Khazion stops beside Lyderea, fangs shining with yellow-green venom. My stomach drops, my skin goes cold. Even the Knights are visibly unsettled.

"Remember, love," Lyderea reminds him. "Fingers, toes, limbs...save your poison for last."

Khazion chitters and goes utterly still. The venom on his fangs goes from a dribble to a drip, then cuts off altogether.

"Good Kozzy," Lyderea purrs. "Now. The boy on his knees...doesn't he look tasty?"

The spider replies with scraping whispers. Lyderea nods in supportive assent. "He's *very* tender."

Khazion responds with an ear-piercing shriek.

"Aye," Lyderea agrees. "Go on—your morsel awaits."

The spider rears back, pawing the air with its lead pair of legs. Each one is coated with devilish quills; they look more than capable of maiming or killing. As he starts to click-walk forward, his disgusting eye clusters bulge and throb, radiating a carnal mania that approaches insanity.

Deep breath, Jon. Don't panic. Maybe I can tap my Laiddinic powers...nope, nada. I'm not resisting, it's more like there's nothing's there. I can logically understand I've used them before, but right now they seem like a ridiculous joke.

Screw it. At least I can throw some Primal Magic. I can't just stand by and—

"What are you *doing?*" Lyderea blurts.

Knifelock strides confidently past me. A quarter-way across the windswept bridge, he draws a pair of violet-bladed daggers.

"Knifelock!" she sputters. "Have you lost your Nok-damned *mind?*"

The tails of his blindfold lash and flutter. I'm staring at his back so I can't see him smile, but I can absolutely hear it in his voice. "My name is Dake Harkness. I knew you as Enthimy in another life."

"Other *lives?* That is a *myth,* Knifelock! This is all there is, and—" She regains her composure and shakes her head. "Something has taken control of your mind."

"Close but not quite." His aura begins to flare and intensify.

"Remember who you are!" she yells. "You're a Nok-damned *Night-keeper!*"

"That I am." He halts and sinks into a mid-level cat stance, extending his arms and crossing them deliberately—almost ceremoniously—in front of his chest. His violet knives, both held in an angled reverse grip, strike a pair of opposing diagonals. Most of his weight is on his right leg. His left is bent and planted a shoulder's width forward.

"But there are still some of us…" As he settles into place, he finishes reiterating the Nightkeeper motto:

"…who keep the night at bay."

51

"**Y**ou," she hisses. "You brought the gliders to our door. You told them how to elude our sentries."

"Cry off, Enthimy. This needn't—"

"*Don't call me that!*" she shrieks. "*I don't know who that is!*"

"Then we're done with the banter." And with damn-near egregious, brass-balled calm, he asks, "Shall we?"

"*Kill him!*" Lyderea screams. "*Rip his Nok-damned head off his Nok-damned neck!*"

As Khazion charges, I glimpse a proboscis-like tube within his maw. It's lined with rows of saliva-strung incisors, a horror movie mouth-within-a-mouth. I've seen similar stuff in tv and games, but it's one thing to see it contained on a screen, entirely another to see it bolting toward you.

Knifelock flows into an angled spin, paired with a series of violet-bladed slashes. Khazion responds with front leg swipes, followed by a flurry of mid-leg stomps. The Nightkeeper dodges with fluid grace, rolling sideways before surging into a back-rising handstand, then snapping to his feet with nimble alacrity. With every evasion, he scores a thrust or a long-running slice, ensuring Khazion pays for each of his misses.

After nearly a minute of spectacular violence, Knifelock transitions into a brutal combination: he stitches a leg with icepick stabs, then arcs his knives wide in a double arm slice, leaping ten yards back while still facing Khazion.

"*What are you doing?*" Lyderea screams at the Knights who are guarding me. "*KILL THE BOY!*"

One of them manages, "Yes, my Queen!" before a glider swoops in, blasting him with a fork of electric green magic. In the blink of an eye, his face and helmet fuse into smoky black gunk. His rudderless body, confused by the absence of a working brain, stumbles and falls into the mist-laden chasm.

Knifelock gestures at the other two Knights, casting double corded streams of rune-whorled spells. My captors fly into the rocky cliff wall. Blue-purple sparkles hang in the air, fading as they plop unconscious to the ground.

"Soft. Weak," Lyderea sneers. "The Knifelock I know would have split them apart."

"He would have," the Nightkeeper agrees. " 'Tis good for your men I'm a marked improvement. You, however, have only gotten worse since your last incarnation."

The Redmordent Scourge tightens around Lucky, evoking a gargle and fresh streams of blood. "A foreign demon, that's what you are. I promise you, spirit: I will bottle you inside a Khavrizite crux, then undo your mind with soul-wracking horror."

"Boring. Trite," Knifelock retorts.

Her alabaster face contorts with rage. *"Khazion!"*

The monstrous arachnid charges again. Knifelock reacts by punching his knives forward, expelling violet tendrils from their lavender edges. The magic blooms into hundreds of curls, blasting the spider from a seeming infinity of unexpected angles. As his thorax is blitzed by pops and flares, he stumbles sideways and struggles for balance.

That was just a setup. Knifelock is casting a follow-on spell, with a lot more buildup and concussive force. In between a chain of knife-limned passes, a ball of eye-searing red begins to form. Lyderea is screaming at the top of her lungs, but Knifelock's magic is snapping and sizzling, emitting a high-pitched keen that's drowning her out.

Khazion yowls and staggers, still under assault from the previous spell. After the last discharge erupts and vanishes, he shimmies in place like a dog shedding water, then gallops forward in multi-legged twitches. He makes it a couple of yards before Knifelock shoots his arms forward, and—

BOOM!

—hurls a thirty-foot helix of red-orange energy directly into the spider's thorax. For a heartstopping second, arcane blaze whites out my vision. It resolves as Khazion lands on his back, twitching and smoking in a roach-leg crumple.

Arganti Knifelock doesn't miss a beat; he rushes forward in a smooth-running blur.

"NO!" Lyderea screeches. *"Kozzy, get up! Kozzy, he's COMING!"*

At first I'm confused—why isn't she helping? Then my intuition comes to the fore: she sees others as lesser and wants them to serve her. It's rooted in the core of her psyche; she's deeply averse to getting her hands dirty.

Khazion attacks with legs and fangs, combined with threads of bladed silk. Knifelock evades with gymnastic ease, slashing them apart into feathery drifts. If they weren't so cruel, I would find them entrancing. The air is blooming with ethereal fiber, some of it's opening into angular webs.

"Stifle your hope," Lyderea snarls at Lucky. "Your death and damnation are still in the cards."

Shit. I was distracted by Khazion's terrifying presence, then amazement at Knifelock's last minute save. I have to free Lucky before he bleeds out.

Can't go Laiddinic, so I gotta try Primal. I extend a downturned hand, tracing a small circle as I activate the loci in the center of my palm. Beneath my gesture, runes form into a loop of destructive magic. I flex my aura a couple of times, filling it with crackling blue-purple-green, and—

"LUCKY! GET READY!"

—fling the blast at the White Veiled Queen. It veers to the side, flying briskly around Arganti and Khazion, then spirals inward and hits Lyderea's shoulder. The Queen takes a quick step back, shock and anger playing across her features. I didn't hurt her, but I caught her by surprise. More importantly, Lucky took advantage and retrieved an item from his pocket. I can't see what he grabbed, but I hope to God it's some sort of weapon.

"How dare you?" Lyderea looks between her shoulder and me. *"How DARE YOU?"*

I cast another spell, a slap-dash mix of traditional and Primal. Lyderea smacks it away, causing it to fly right and gutter out. "Do you honestly think that—"

Before she can finish, Knifelock throws a *Tekken*-style blitz, hitting Khazion with ice, fire, and lightning. Three of his legs freeze winter-blue solid, burn to a flaky, ember-laden crisp, then black electricity rips them clean off his thorax.

"NO!" Lyderea screams. *"Stop!"*

Knifelock dodges a leftover leg, cutting it several times with machine-gun speed. As it retracts, it twitches and spasms—it's hanging by a thread in three different places. The Nightkeeper severs a glistening fang, then another leg rockets toward his neck. He intercepts it with a violet-bladed dagger, halting it a foot from his blindfolded face.

The spider leans in, saliva-strung fangs spread wide in triumph, but Knifelock's weapon emits an aura-charged flash. The next thing I see is Khazion's blown-off limb, pouring thick green blood as it falls into the chasm.

Lyderea shrieks, *"Arganti!"* The heads on her whip surge toward him.

His knives work in a busy rhythm, parrying the snakes with spark-lit strikes. For a breathtaking moment, he's ringed by deflections—violet-edged gleams and rapid-fire glints. Then two of the serpents yank him off his feet. Four stand by, weaving and hissing, while three dart in and tear at his aura.

He stabs two of his attackers, pinning their heads onto the stone bridge. Then he releases his daggers and grabs the third with his hands.

His aura accelerates into a roiling churn, sizzling with power as he wrestles with the serpent.

"Your last moments, traitor," Lyderea hisses. "If you beg, I might just—"

"Rrrr*rrrRRR!*" He tears the snakehead off the Scourge, hurls it into the misty chasm, and channels the bulk of his aura into the pair on his legs. Both of his captors let go and writhe, blackening into shriveled husks. The other two—the serpents pinned onto the bridge's surface—rip free of his enchanted knives, thrashing ghoulishly about with their dagger-riven skulls.

The Nightkeeper scrambles up to his feet, only to be caught in Khazion's silk. It wraps around his armored torso, cracking his plates and gashing his skin.

"Come, then," he growls. He spreads his legs, roots his weight, and grabs alternating handfuls of bladed fiber. Khazion lurches and tries to escape, but for some reason—I think it's because of his crippling injuries—he can't let go. As Knifelock continues reeling him in, the weaponized threads cut deep and long, mutilating flesh as they gyre and wind. The Nightkeeper, however, doesn't seem to care.

"I welcome the Clear."

With that declaration, he hooks Khazion's incisor in the crook of his elbow, then yanks them both off the side of bridge. As they fall, Knifelock rips off chitin with his spell-charged fingers. He intersperses the butchery with devastating strikes, lighting the mist with arcane feedback.

"*Kozzy!*" Lyderea stares into the foggy crevasse. "*KOZZY!*" She fixes me with a spiteful glare. "Do you realize what it took to raise him? You have no idea. *None.*" The heads on her Scourge—the remaining four that are still intact—begin twisting and hissing.

"Jon..." Lucky gurgles and coughs.

"*Quiet.*" Her whip tightens, cracking another rib.

I turn away and shut my eyes. I wish to God he would just pass out.

He coughs again. "*Jon.*"

Then it hits me: he's trying to tell me something.

I spot his hand, slick with blood and trembling with effort, manipulating something between his thumb and forefinger. It's clumsy and ugly and obvious as hell, but none of that matters. The only thing that matters is that Lyderea doesn't see it.

"I shall get to you soon," Lyderea promises. "First, Jon will die a bit at a time."

His fingers stop shaking and I see what's between them: a single jade bullet. Ready to be chambered in Ailura Qartesi.

I shot her once without any rounds, back in Elerica when she was only half a revolver. Now that I've leveled up as a mage, I have a better grasp of magical nuance, and I understand why that isn't an option here. She couldn't have fired without the Demon Blood Moon, specifically its outflow of combative energy. Also, even if Ailura could do it again, it wouldn't be strong enough to hurt Lyderea.

There's no way around it. I need that bullet.

Lucky's arm is bound to his side, which means he can't throw it. He's going to flick it as far as he can, but I'm still going to have to close the distance.

"Savor these moments," Lyderea warns, "these precious moments when you can still form—"

I sprint onto the bridge. Everything around me hazes and blurs, rendered trivial by Lucky and the bullet. No more chasms, no more peaks, no more dogfighting gliders and wyverns...if I don't pull this off, I'm going to die in horrible agony. Even if I succeed, I'll still probably die, so I might as well give it everything I've got.

Lyderea barks a disbelieving laugh. It's comically sluggish due to my heightened perception. Doesn't matter—just keep her distracted. I flare my hands in matching arcs, throwing wild streams of artless magic. The Redmordent Scourge curls and weaves, protecting her with a gyre of serpentine coils. As color flashes off its scales, her laughter transitions into a wicked grin.

She's glad I'm fighting back. She wants to crush me and make me beg.

I don't care. I'm not afraid. Lucky and I have come together. Everything we've experienced—hope, betrayal, countless hours of sleight of hand—has led us to this very moment, this culmination of our friendship and discord. As unlikely as it is, fate has made us allies once again, and we have one last con to pull on Lyderea.

The thief fixes me with an unblinking stare. He's deep in the grip of his entire being, taken by a conviction beyond faith or knowledge. He's nothing but the moment. He's dust upon his breath.

Then he flicks the jade-green bullet.

Up it goes, backlit by wand-light and billowing fire. At the same time, a snake slices toward me in a horizontal arc. I collapse my legs and relax my spine, bending backward in a double-knee slide. Keen-edged scales graze my chin, evoking a sliver of transient pain. I barely notice. It's a distant sensation.

Because just like Lucky, I'm fully in the moment.

Ailura is already in my hand. Her chamber opens and spins into a whirl, a blur of metal and arcane voltage. I muscle into a single-kneed crouch, and—

Click.

The bullet drops home, the wheel snaps closed. The chamber flares with brilliant dazzle, then I level the barrel and pull the trigger. A weave of light erupts from my gun, slipping between the coiled-snake shield protecting Lyderea, and—

"AAHHH!!"

—explodes dead center in her face.

She clutches her eyes and stumbles back. The Redmordent Scourge spasms and writhes, loosening into a series of frantic waves. Lucky falls and crumples on the deck, shrieking as he lands on his injured arm.

I dart in, throw my ammo-sack into my carry, and start hauling him back across the bridge. He breaks into coughs, spraying a puff of crimson droplets. I wish I could stop and tend to his wounds, but if we don't get out of here—

The Scourge knocks me onto my belly, shredding my amulet-armor with a spate of bites. I roll away, onto my back, and catch a glimpse of its four remaining heads.

"Here," Lucky gasps, shoving another bullet into my hand. I pop it in Ailura and jerk her shut. The angle's bad and the whip is a Great Weapon, so it doesn't surprise me when most of the serpents dodge my shot. One of them, however, gets caught in the blast and yowls in pain.

"More!" I yell.

Lucky reaches in my carry, snatches out rounds, and pushes a bunch of them into my palm. I snap-load six, drop the rest, and graze a snake with a wide-spanning ray. The other three brutalize Lucky's aura, blitzing him with a storm of lightning quick bites. He screams and spasms in violent twitches, contorting and grimacing with each toxic strike.

I rise to a knee, level Ailura, and cut loose with my remaining five bullets. The Queen disappears in a wash of energy, filling me with a surge of desperate hope. As soon as it clears, cold dread unfurls in my belly.

She's extended her hand and caught the discharges. They're hovering about a foot in front of her.

"Different when you're ready for it." She grins and casts her arm to the side, causing the blaze to fade and vanish. "You should be flattered—I've pulled a good deal of energy away from the Strait, just so I could tend to your forthcoming pain. Shoot all you want. It won't save you." Her Tessellate-patched aura is thick around her eyes. I might have damaged her physical sight, but she's making up for it with her noxious magic.

"Jon," Lucky whispers. "You can't let her take you." Blood spills from his parted lips, interspersed with bits of mangled tissue.

"He's right, you know." Lyderea says casually. "Better to turn that gun on yourself. Otherwise, I will show you how revolting you truly are. When organs slop from your fresh-riven gut, you will realize you are merely a vulgar machine, a concoction of meat and unsightly flesh." The snakes on her whip meander and hiss. "Let's play a game, shall we? I will allow you a single shot. Whoever it kills is up to you, but the survivor will be tortured and wracked beyond thought."

I snatch up the rounds lying on the deck, snap-load Ailura, and aim her at the White Veiled Queen.

"And what if I send you into the Clear?"

Lyderea guffaws. "Did you not see what became of your volley? Your clapfire pales before the Velic Tessellate."

"Kill yourself, Jon," Lucky rasps. "I'll follow soon in your wake."

"Sound advice," Lyderea agrees. "Though short of the truth. When I savaged his aura, I infected his loci with multiple curses. Once he dies, his essence will persist as an oblivious haunt." Her grin widens. "I know what you're thinking: he's going to die anyway, so what does it matter? But if you leave him with me, I will keep him alive for at least a month. It might take a good deal of magic, but..." A giggle slips out. "I will gorge upon his pleas and screams. Before I am done, he will beg me to let him fade into a specter."

"Spare yourself," Lucky whispers.

My eyes tick desperately back and forth. There has to be a way out of this. Everything I've done, all I've endured...it wasn't just so I could end my own life. Is this all there is? Prolonged torture or merciful suicide?

"One shot," Lyderea purrs. "Do as he says and claim your peace. There are no miracles lying in wait."

"Jon." Lucky bores into me with his bloodshot eyes. "Do it."

"One shot," Lyderea repeats. "Choose who suffers."

Ailura projects, *[I will make it quick.]*

Her words land like a kick to the gut. Back on Earth, I was pining for something exciting and new. Then I made it to another dimension, only to be caught between damnation and agony.

It all seems like a tasteless joke.

"Leave me," Lucky croaks. "We are doomed to compete for the scraps and the dregs, and I no longer want any part of the struggle. Take what you can, before she takes it from you."

There are no miracles lying in wait.

Lucky's trying to spare me from torture. He's finally showing some bravery and altruism. Does that count as a miracle? If it does, it's bitter and joyless.

"One minute," Lyderea warns. "Choose in that span, or I shall seize your weapon and wrack you both."

"Do it," Lucky hisses.

It's the logical choice but...I stare at the thief, trying to articulate what I'm thinking and feeling.

He stares back up at me. A second later, his eyes widen in horror.

He knows.

He knows I won't kill either one of us.

I flick Ailura up at Lyderea. I pull the trigger, the gun roars, and the Queen bursts into shrieking laughter.

Then I grab Lucky and roll off the bridge.

52

"*I* *won!*" she howls. "*I WON, you hear me?*"

As we fall, I catch a glimpse of Lucky's face. Judging by his slack expression, I don't think he's conscious.

Given his condition, that's probably for the best.

Everything around us is shrouded in fog. Despite that, I can still sense our rate of descent. We've stopped accelerating, which means we've hit terminal velocity. It's kind of peaceful, actually. Between the low visibility and our fixed rate of speed, I almost feel like we're in a cocoon. We're moving through space, but that's a relative concept, isn't it? If everything is constant, we might as well be standing still.

Until we hit the ground, anyway.

I close my eyes and release my fear. It wasn't a bad run. I made some friends, I fell in love, and I got to live as the Prophesied Traveler. We lost to the Queen, but that's all right. Someone else will eventually step up. Even if they don't, things will be fine—Evermoor is a single world in an infinite multiverse.

Peace washes through me, followed by a swell of bone-deep contentment. I open my eyes and smile in surprise. I've felt this before, but I forgot its depth and unquestioning vibrance—the absolute certainty that I'm fine where I am, paired with the inviolable knowledge that it will all work out.

A moment later, something inside me opens and shifts, clearing the way for a surge of energy. My loci and meridians blaze and quicken, evoking a rise of wonder and awe.

Whatever happens next is going to be Laiddinic.

My serenity is replaced by curiosity. This isn't supposed to happen. The only thing left is to check out and—

That's when I see the portal below me.

———

It appears in a crackle of rune-threaded lightning, dissolving fog with its forceful rotation. I hope to God we ditch our momentum, because if we're moving this fast after we emerge—

Magic blaze eclipses my sight.

———

I saw fractalized colors that had no name. They were also sounds and undiluted feeling...it's all fading into an indistinct haze.

"Jon! Lucky!"

Where am I? Looks like some kind of D&D city...

A giant Wolven runs toward me, followed by a bunch of vaguely familiar people. Wow, one of them looks like Taylor Swift...

"Jon?"

My memory comes rushing back. Erany. Gyrax. Lanctom.

"Help him." I force out the words in a choked sob. Lucky's on the ground, limbs splayed in a grotesque tangle.

"Lucky?" Blood drains from Elier's face.

Sygress Anír crouches by the thief. "He's been saddled with a chain of toxic curses. Drainfire bane, blanchvenom woe, along with dozens of other pestilent charms." She shakes her head. "Even if I heal his physical wounds, he will still transform into a vacant haunt."

I stare desperately into her night-swirled pupils. "He deserves better, goddammit! He saved me from Lyderea!"

"Jon." Ren's voice is gentle but firm. "I saw what he did on yonder field. He stole your bullets and gave you to the Queen."

"You didn't see what happened after!" I shout. *"He redeemed himself, Ren!"*

"I haven't," Lucky croaks. "I still owe a debt. Let me pay it."

"Don't." I look at the thief through blurry tears. "Believe in your worth and potential to heal, and—"

"My belief means nothing." He wheezes out a blood-garbled breath. "The world devours without conscience or grace. And we do the same, for we are part and parcel of this Nok-damned world." Crimson trickles from his mouth. "For most of my life, I have stolen from others, striving to reclaim what was stolen from me. Now, finally, it is my turn to give."

"Give *what?*" I shout. "What are you giving? You're volunteering for pointless misery, that is it and that is *all!* Let go of your judgment and tap your—"

"I am not the Traveler. That's you, Jon. My spirit is rotten to the core, and so it has been for a day and an age. Soon, my outer appearance will reflect that rot. As strange as it sounds, that brings me relief—life makes sense in its cruelty and malice."

"That isn't—"

"Enough." His voice gains strength. "Grace my ears with fairer words."

"I..." Part of me wants to keep arguing with Lucky. But even if I manage to go Laiddinic, I can't force him into his True-born power.

So I take a breath and gather my composure.

" 'Our blood runs hot, our dreams shine bright...' "

Lucky gives me a beatific smile. " 'And let no one tell you a damn bit different.' Poetic and touching, but I prefer your declaration upon the field."

"My declaration? What are you—"

" 'We shall rise again and claim our peace.' "

As he utters those words, his eyes slide closed.

53

Erany dips her chin and clenches her fists. "Part of me knew this would come to pass. It was why he angered me with such maddening ease."

My body constricts with sudden rage. You knew? You *knew?* This whole time, I've been honing my intuition and fleshing it out. The fact that she couldn't be bothered to do the same...

Before I can rail at her, the Sygress states, "He belongs in Sidehelm. The portals have closed, but their residual energies are still in play. If I act with haste, I can fashion them into a short-lived passage."

"A sensible course," Nyanti agrees. "His spirit is whittling as we speak. Aurically speaking, he will be as light as a feather or a drift of smoke. It shouldn't be a difficul—"

I shoot to my feet and glare at the Witch. "He's a *person!* Not a feather or a drift of smoke!"

"Jon." Elier steps in and touches my shoulder. "He was my friend too. But you have to understand that—"

I smack his hand away. "Was he, Elier? Was he your *friend?* Because you're acting like *he's already dead!*" My loci and meridians flare with anger. "We can still save him! We can—"

"He is too far gone," Gyrax says quietly. "And that is by choice."

"I...that's..." Fury and heartache snarl in my chest, choking me with a sense of absolute helplessness.

"He will come back around," the Sygress says. "Perceiving the future is a tricky endeavor, but..." Her aura expands, enlivening with a layer of quick-switching runes. "He will exist as a haunt for several eons. Eventually, he will fade away and reincarnate." Her aura shrinks down. "His anima will rise on an alternate Earth, where he will fashion himself into an astral detective. He is gone from our lives, but much of his tale has yet to be told."

"Remember, Jon, we exist inside a no-lose game," Gyrax says. "Regardless of what happens, he will remember infinity and merge with the True."

I drop my gaze and clench my teeth. "That's just an empty platitude. All I feel is…" As the tears begin flowing, he draws me in and holds me close.

"You will come to accept he is writing his own story. But right here, right now, feel whatever you need to, lest you dishonor the narrative you spin for yourself."

I don't care if he chose his fate. All I care about is killing Lyderea, and making her feel the same pain she inflicted on Lucky. It's the only thought that brings me relief.

And I have to let that bloom and flow, because it's just as damn True as anything else.

———

While I was sobbing, someone closed Lucky's eyes. When they were open, he was focused on something distant and invisible. It wasn't an expression of dread or horror, but it was dreadful and horrible nonetheless. Closing his eyes makes it better, but not by much. His expression is still empty and devoid of feeling.

"Nyanti?" The Sygress prompts her with a glance.

"Ready."

The Sygress waves her palm above Lucky's brow. His coal-black aura stirs and thickens, resolving into a sheath of miasmic energy. I recognize some designs from when he was alive. Most of it, however, is a dismal swirl of nasty-looking gloom.

Nyanti extends her arms, fingers spread. Her loci and meridians blaze and rotate, causing Lucky's aura to do the same. As the Witch brings her hands together, dingy energy condenses around him.

The Sygress lifts her arm to the side, clutching the air with clawed fingers. A dozen feet away, space and time wrinkle and brighten, forming into the beginnings of a slipworld portal. It quickly gels into a circular flow, heavy with patterns and pulsing glyphs. A second later, its center shines with familiar scenery.

"Sidehelm," I whisper.

"In all likelihood, he would go there on his own," the Sygress says, "as he will be attracted to the stench of despair and shortage. Sidehelm is a cache of those particular vibrations."

"Couldn't we just—"

"Jon," Nyanti chides gently. "If we leave him be, he will drain a passerby whilst he roams."

Above his body, his aura forms into a shadowy version of his old self. Its face is a mass of expressionless fog, lit by a pair of sallow yellow eyes. Dark gritty smoke weaves and swells, forming the semblance of a torso and limbs. As Lucky solidifies into a haunt, his physical body withers and crumbles, then blows away into vanishing ash.

What remains of my friend silently moans. Its jaw stretches impossibly wide, its gaze pulses with glabrous light. I reach out with my senses, trying to connect with its True-deep essence. Lucky's still there, somewhere inside it. If I could just—

Suddenly, Alijyar's long-ago words come rushing back to me: *When someone's ready, they'll find a way to level up. Whether it's through an app or a book or even a song...*

"Do it." I palm the corner of my eye and wipe away a tear.

Nyanti snaps her purple-tinged fingers. A black flicker appears before Lucky-as-haunt, immediately capturing its full attention.

The flicker beelines into the gateway. The haunt follows and disappears from view.

———

"The portals are closed and the tides are re-channeled," the Sygress declares. "Nevertheless, it is a stopgap measure. The ley lines will build in strength and power, then bend again into their old polarities."

"What does that mean?" Elier asks.

"Lanctom's portal will reappear," Nyanti explains. "And it will be harder to shut with each iteration. Eventually, it will become outright impossible."

While I was defending the Midland Brink, I was driven by the hope we could get some closure, or at least achieve some permanent gains. Now they're saying it was a temporary reprieve, and that Lucky and Knifelock died in vain.

Because everything that's happened...it will happen *again*.

They all start discussing what to do next. Gyrax will call in a contingent of Wolven. The Sygress is going to contribute some coteries. Yire can spare a hundred Felinx, a couple hundred more over the next few months. While Syf and Raef shore up the coast, Relegant is going to formalize training, hit up nearby villages, and start a recruiting and logistics network that will extend beyond Lanctom.

I stare blankly ahead, trying to conceal my disgust and bafflement. How can they be so goddamn calm? I'm supposed to beat Lyderea Fairdyle. I'm supposed to awaken the Glass, shove it in her face, and ride off into the sunset and live happily ever after. Big fun adventure, good guys win, everybody celebrates. But no one told me about this part. The part where life rips your heart from your chest, then stomps it into the muddy ground.

"Most will remain." The Sygress looks at Erany, me, and Gyrax. "Excepting you three. You must travel west to Aerie Denir."

"Go on without me," Gyrax says to me and Erany. "I shall break trail for the Tameless Ursine. After I speak with their Ferine Chief, I will journey to the peaks of Aerie Denir. The delay will be trivial—I will lose a few days, maybe a week. If all goes well, I will enlist the aid of their forest warlords, and perhaps a cadre of their Ragged Shaman."

"My lieutenants and I will guard your flanks," Ripfang says.

Gyrax nods. "After I establish a solid rapport, you can stay with their Chief and offer—"

"Why?" My voice comes out dead and wooden. "Why are we going to Aerie Denir?"

"I have conversed with Alijyar through interplanar means," the Sygress explains. "He foresaw the need for your presence on Earth. I shan't elaborate as time is fluid, and things fall apart if you exert too much control. So. The nearest crossing is in Aerie Denir. It is there, according to my Wise Women, that the tides will form into a Solgraediac Spiral."

"What does that *mean?*" I snap.

"Jon," Nyanti warns.

"Solgraediac magic leans acausal—it lends itself to piercing the dimensional veil. The three of you will enter the Spiral's breadth, and it will transport you back to San Francisco. Gyrax will help you locate Atriya, who will help you awaken the Veric Glass. After you return—"

"I don't care!" I fix her with a livid glare. "You're sending us out on another quest? For *what?* So more people can die or get hurt? As long as it isn't you, right?" My face twists into a bitter sneer. "All you care about is beating Lyderea. The rest of us are—"

"I am just like you," the Sygress snarls. She locks onto me with her swirling pupils. "Every day I wrack my soul, agonizing over the best course of action. Curb your verdict of shadow and malice, lest you paint the world in stifling gloom."

"I don't have to paint it!" My eyes widen in anger. "That's just *how it is!* Lucky did the right thing, but—"

"Debatable," Ren comments.

I swing toward him and grip Ailura. "Say that again." My voice quivers with held-back rage. "Say that again."

He dips his head and raises his hands. "I have been where you are, Jon, more times than I care to count. Believe me when I say that nothing good will come of your fury. Feel it, honor it, but don't let it shape your actions or soul."

"Jon." Erany touches my arm.

"I..." Everything feels hypersensitized.

"Lucky will ultimately write his own story, just as you will author yours," Gyrax says gently. "Will you pen the same chapter of lack and woe, simply because you shared in his tale? You have the chance to live something different."

I let go of Ailura and sag in defeat. "I...yeah. Okay...yeah."

Erany rubs my back and tries to soothe me. I catch bits and pieces of what Gyrax is saying—something about keep the faith and things will get better—but it's like the volume's been lowered and the color's been muted.

Things will get better. Yeah, I know that.

But for the goddamn life of me, *I can't feel it.*

54

Epilogue

The premonition I had after my Earth-side trip—that things wouldn't work out—has now come true. Lyderea is still Queen, Lucky is gone, and most of my friends are stuck in Lanctom.

I barely recognize pre-Evermoor Jon. I've learned how to fight and cast magic spells, but I'm also angry. Like *deep down* angry, to the point where I'm filled with simmering rage. It surges up at random times, snarling my thoughts into sharp little knots. One moment I'm walking or doing whatever, then my jaw will clench, my breath will shorten, and my temples will throb with maddening pressure.

Eventually, exhaustion creeps in and I settle back into numbness.

Erany understands. When she was a kid, she trusted her elders and they sat on their hands. The Queen lulled them with empty promises, then slaughtered her kin and razed Delán. Just thinking about it...it's a good thing those elders aren't here. I'd be tempted to kill them a piece at a time.

As we cross through hills and rustic prairie, I stumble onto moments of spaced-out calm. Fine by me—I just want relief from depression and anger. To that end, I start distracting myself with far-out thought experiments. I'll pretend I'm the only person alive, and that everyone else is an NPC. Or that I'm a brain in a vat, and that this is all an elaborate simulation. Solipsism, I know, but for some reason, it takes a bit of the edge off. For most of my life, I've blindly obsessed over how others saw me. Family, friends, society at large...I've never indulged in a me-first perspective.

Why am I here? Why am I the Traveler? Who, exactly, am I doing all this for? I wanted adventure, got what I asked for, and then it devolved into heartache and sorrow. I'm angry as hell, but I don't know who to blame. Initially, I was pissed at Erany for not speaking up, but after I chewed on it, I realized that—at the absolute worst—it came down to a simple mistake. She wasn't purposefully withholding information. We had a lot on our plate, and she didn't want to complicate it with a divisive hunch.

Knifelock, maybe? Try as I might, I can't formulate a solid condemnation. He stood idly by while Lucky was dying, but he ended up sacrificing himself, and he's also connected to superdimensional forces. It's hard to assign him motives and drive, when his perspective is so far out there that he might as well be an extraterrestrial. He's in the same league as Alijyar, the Oracle, and maybe the Sygress.

Lyderea's the obvious choice for bad guy. But now that I've met her, I see her as more of a reactive animal, not some cunning sinister genius. And from what Knifelock was saying, she's been a tyrant for several lifetimes, so maybe it's ingrained in her. Maybe it's compulsive—maybe she's addicted to transmitting her abuse. (That doesn't excuse it, but right now I'm just trying to let go of my rage, and I'll entertain any speculation that will help me to do so.)

Lucky, on the other hand...I went from liking him to fearing him (when I asked about his past), then supporting him to hating him. Ultimately, I invested my heart and soul in trying to save him. It's been a rollercoaster, to say the least. In a weird way, he's kind of like the Queen. She isn't a ghost, obviously, but she's still trapped in a lack-filled existence. We're not meant to be agents of oppression, just like we're not meant to be directionless haunts.

As I trek through marsh and tundra and forest, my emotions gradually begin to unlock. I start asking myself what I want, rather than what I want to avoid. It all feels eerily familiar. I never thought much about reincarnation, but now I wonder...have I already lived as a tyrant and traitor? Have I borne the same burden as my friend and his killer?

It wouldn't surprise me if I had.

Slowly but surely, my anguish abates. I know it sounds wonky—I just got hit with a crap-ton of trauma—but after months on the road, my perspective is starting to reconfigure. It no longer generates bitter thoughts, red and inflamed and clawing at my brain. When I reflect on what happened, all I can muster are logical rebukes. All brain, no soul.

My heart just isn't in it anymore.

Erany senses it. Thus far, our chats have been limited to physical necessities, stuff like fire, water, and shelter. Now she's guiding them toward past adventures and casual whimsy.

As we emerge from a moss-filled gully, it suddenly hits me: I'm almost back to my old self. If you had asked me a month ago, I would have said that was flat-out impossible—that I would never get over what happened to Lucky. But with time and distance, the darkness within me has lessened and faded. While it isn't dramatic—nothing Laiddinic or dazzlingly arcane—it's low-key astonishing nonetheless. It's not supposed to resolve this quickly. It's supposed to linger for years on end.

Maybe I'm done with that particular narrative. Now that I've lived it, maybe I'm ready to write something different. Or maybe I'm being too optimistic. Maybe it'll come back around, in some way shape or form. But my gut says that I've explored those paths, and that I'm ready to move on to greener pastures.

Traditionally, I'm supposed to turn all grim and dark. Screw tradition. I'm not a template, doomed to fulfill conventional expectations. The choice is mine and mine alone. And right now, I choose to laugh with Erany. I choose to love her without rhyme or reason. And I choose to live a full and joyous life. (Crap—I just touched on the Karen trifecta: live, laugh, love. I need to make good and damn sure I don't ask for the manager.)

Talk leads to smiles, smiles lead to mirth, then we're embracing and kissing once again. I'm not denying that what I went through sucked, but there's only so long I can stay mad and depressed. My tolerance for my own negativity (while it may have been greater in other lives) has dwindled and waned. What's all this for, anyway? I was born into the limitations of time and space, saddled with a mess of biological needs, then poked and cajoled by societal norms. Is life just a game of Simon Says, with random interjections of stress and pain? It can't be, right? Even if it is, I refuse to play. I'm here to engage. I'm here to have *fun.*

As we hit a stretch of sunlit valley, I marvel at streams of ethereal mist, capped by vaguely humanoid faces. According to Erany, they're called *effedia,* and despite appearances, they aren't sentient. There's other stuff too. Potbellied lizards as big as Corgis (jardomets), fist-sized rodents with bisected tails (gopiax), but what amazes me most are the slidefruit trees.

Their leaves are black with bright green bursts. Vivid blue vines grow from their trunks, draping onto neighboring branches. While all of that's cool, it's their namesake fruit that catches my eye.

The trees are coated in footlong berries, shielded by segmented shells lit by an internal radiance. Their ever-shifting light alternates colors, lulling my brain with its slow-fluxing shine. True to their name, the fruits move in snail-like contractions, crawling across branches and gnarly bark.

Erany plucks one off a tree. It responds by curling into an armadillo-like ball. She unsheathes a knife, pops off a crescent of bark-like shell, then cuts out some flesh and maows it down.

"Mm." She raises her eyebrows in appreciation. "Delicious." She extracts another glowing slice and extends it toward me. "Try it."

"You sure they won't mind?" I glance hesitantly at the trees. "I mean...aren't they alive?"

"So is everything you happen to ingest," she replies irritably. "Certain plants appear static and fixed, but that doesn't mean they are exempt from life. Eat." She pushes the glob at me.

I reluctantly accept and give it a chew. It has the punch of sugary Kool-aid, leavened by spritzes of natural fizz.

"Mmm!" I straighten in delight. "Just as good as a Gomptown biscuit!"

Erany gulps another piece of fruit. "If we angered these trees, their berries would turn grayish white, and they would all taste as foul as sun-rotted dung. I've seen it in person, when I was breaking trail with Terrelly and Ren."

"Yeah? What happened?"

"Terrelly fell into drunken spite. At the time, we weren't as savvy in ranging the wilds, so we didn't know the trees were responding to his mood. It was only later, after he recovered from his inebriety, that he explained the reason behind their flavor. He was sheepish at the time, as the poison in his soul had not yet bloomed." She looks away and lets out a sigh.

"Hey, the fruit is gonna hear you," I warn half-jokingly.

"Ha." A faint smile. "Eat all you want. They will simply transcribe into another existence. The same as Lucky, the same as Terrelly."

"The same as us," I add softly.

"Aye. In the future, the tide may turn, and our bodies might feed their roots and leaves. Although..." Her lips curl into a wry grin. "I hope that won't be for a good long while."

"You and me both." I stride to a tree, pluck off a berry, and pop off a section with the tip of my knife. Each bite is better than the last. There's constant variations of layered fruit flavor, combined with the perfect amount of bubbly fizziness.

A couple faires in, Erany mentions I have juice on my lips. As I raise a hand to clean it off, she leans in with a smile, murmurs, "Allow me," and melts my brain with a languorous kiss. (You can guess where that leads—*heh* heh heh!)

After a week, the grove transforms into mesas and valleys. Half of it's rocky, while the rest is lush and strikingly green. We're surrounded by an expanse of sweeping beauty, the kind that makes you stand up straight and stare into the yonder.

"After this slope—" Erany points ahead at a chain of switchbacks. "—we'll climb those bends. It will take four days to cross their breadth."

"And then we'll be in Aerie Denir?"

"Aye," she confirms. "Their scouts have been watching." She studies the sky, shading her eyes with the flat of her hand.

I zero in on a handful of specks, maneuvering around a pair of cloud-wreathed mesas. "Hang-gliders?" I immediately catch myself: "I mean skyfoils?"

"Indeed," she confirms. "More advanced than we have yet to encounter. These are equipped with wands, auras, and an intricate web of steampipe mechanics."

"I've seen those before," I remind her, "when I was fighting Lyderea."

"Ah. Right."

Halfway up the sharp-angled trail, one of the gliders slants toward us, expanding its wings and bleeding off speed. The pilot works some levers and pedals, causing the machine to lower gently to the ground. He's a powerfully built, older Hispanic man, with proud white hair and a luxuriant beard.

Erany's mouth opens in surprise. "Terrelly?"

I'm hit by a wave of cognitive dissonance. When I met him in Naversé, Terrelly Jindow was wasted and sallow. Now he looks rugged and sure, every inch the Wayfarer Captain.

"Wind at your back and sun on your brow." He cranks a rough-hewn dial, causing his glider's skeleton—an artful network of rods and gears—to neatly compress into a tight-wrinkled shell.

Erany rushes into his arms. "I thought you were lost."

He strokes her hair and holds her close. "I could not end life on a despairing note."

"How did you recover?" She breaks away and searches his eyes.

"Ren administered an Elerican remedy. While it boosted my soul for a temporary span, it failed to vanquish my inner lack. I took advantage of the reprieve by journeying into the Revenant Bogs. After a spate of combative trials, I gained an audience with the Shrouded Hag."

"Terrelly!" Erany lurches back in shock. "You put your aura in grievous danger!"

"No more than I was already in." The Wayfarer shrugs. "Ironically, my indifference was helpful in my quest for the Hag. When you have nothing to lose, 'tis a damn sight easier to risk it all." His lips curl up in mild amusement. "Her true form is quite beautiful, contrary to what most folk seem to think."

"If you say so." Erany regards him with overt skepticism. "How did she help?"

"She plunged me into a Cryptic Volution. I wandered my mind for three full days, confronting my beliefs and basal convictions. To regain my health, I had to break and reshape from the inside out."

"Sounds painful," I say quietly.

"Aye." He grimaces. "My anguish had long since run its course, but I kept it alive within my heart. Over the years, it grew from a boil into a festering sore."

"I suppose it's good that you found the Hag," Erany says reluctantly.

" 'Twould have been better if I forgave Lyderea. The irony mounts: I could have opposed her sooner, had I not maintained my toxic hate." He throws me a sheepish grin. "The Prophesied Traveler, correct? I plead thy grace—my tongue was uncouth when last we met."

"It's all right. You weren't yourself."

He nods in agreement. "You seem steadier. Surer. I hope the cost was not too high."

"High enough." I close my eyes, briefly taken by a gruesome memory: Lucky in the coil of the Redmordent Scourge, screaming as its scales rip through his flesh.

I sigh, open my eyes, and regard Terrelly with muted sorrow. "But we have to move on, if we wish to remain free of a self-made prison. You know this as well as I. Better, mayhap."

" 'Mayhap.' " Erany crooks her head in amusement. "Evermoor has made its mark on your speech."

"You're one to talk," I retort. "You've called me a nerd on multiple occasions."

"It's the Nok-damned *best!*" she explodes. "Don't tell me you dislike the word!"

I burst into laughter. "Not at all. Call me a nerd all you want."

Terrelly glances between us. Judging by his face, he's just now realizing we're in a relationship. A moment later, he confirms it with a smile. "I am happy for you, Erany."

Erany beams at him. "And I for you." She gestures at the looming peak. "We are on our way to Aerie Denir. A portal is forming within its bounds, and we have business on the other side."

"If the two of you are willing, I can expand my foil into a three-body glider."

Erany and I share an excited glance. "You want us—" My finger dances between us. "—to *fly?*"

Terrelly shrugs. "If you'd rather not, we can take the long way up."

We both speak at the same time: "No, that's not—" Then we glance at each other again. "If you want to—"

She cedes the floor with an upturned palm. "Speak."

"We'd *love to,*" I gush.

"Very well." Terrelly walks to his glider and flips a lever, re-expanding its metal skeleton. As it clicks and clacks and lurches into place, rune-chained circles blaze into existence, forming a semicircular, holographic layout.

"At your say."

Erany and I share another glance, exchanging a deluge of meaning in the blink of an eye. My arrival, Lucky's demise, Terrelly's recovery...it all led to this exact moment.

A thought bubbles up from the depths of my soul: *Our crossing seems fated.*

And, of course:

Be dust upon your breath.

And there you have it: Jon's sprawling trek across the wide world of Evermoor!

While the break in his fellowship isn't as strict as Frodo's (Jon and Erany weave in and out of different groups, and they aren't stuck with a murderous cave-dweller in full-on Ring withdrawal), it's still a break nonetheless. But regardless of any passing similarity, it's important for me to listen to my heart and tell the story the way it wants to be told. I gotta honor the way it organically unfolds, and, in so doing, honor the originality and energy that flowed through Tolkien.

No one—him, me, or the world at large—wants to see a soulless spinoff of what he wrote.

Lucky will return as an astral detective, but it'll be in a different book(s?), set between a mishmash of dimensions, using modern lingo with a noire twist. I've been playing with this idea since 2016. As cool as that sounds (to me, anyway) I gotta get busy with volume three of *The Unbound Realm,* which I'm pretty sure I'll call *The Laiddinic Return.* I have a rough idea as to what it will include. Lightning-breathing drag-ons. A trip back to Earth. Aerie Denir and its cocky-as-hell, aerobatic pilots. The awakening of the Veric Glass. Yandire Fain, and a tribe of time-skipping nomads who brave the Stillfae and its temporal badlands (which, as of now, I'm inclined to call the Stop Wastes). And, of course, the inevitable ending.

For those of you who've read *The Lord of the Rings,* you know that Frodo eventually ditches the Ring, comes home to the Shire, and expe-riences a big ol' helping of additional trauma. War and oppression have re-emerged (albeit on a smaller scale), and he cycles through them once again. I have no such plans for Jon or Erany. This isn't about a sequence of oppression and conflict that serves to highlight the bliss of peace. It's about how a once-ordinary kid realizes he's writing his own story. (And, by implication, how I'm writing mine and you're writing yours, and how we revel and agonize over our chosen narrative.)

Is any of that true? I can't decide for anyone but myself. Same goes for you—you're entitled to your thoughts and metaphysical beliefs. So I'll let you get back to telling your story, and I'll get back to telling mine. And even though it may sound crazy, a part of me believes that somewhere out there in the infinity of possibility, Jon is hard at work doing the same, and that he/you/I are connected through some wonderful twist of transcendent coevality.

In the meantime, while we're all trying to make sense of our crazy existence, I'll do my best to enjoy the moment, and follow the age-old maxim that weaves its way through my yarn:

Be dust upon your breath.

Kent Wayne

September 24, 2022

At the time of this writing, I have authored a four-book science fiction series called *Echo,* a high school absurdical (yes—that's a made-up word) called *Kor'Thank: Barbarian Valley Girl,* and I am currently in the process of writing the third and final volume of *The Unbound Realm.*

If you like pew-pew warrior stuff with cybernetics, psychic powers, and existential spiritual implications, check out *Echo.* If you like an R-rated version of Calvin and Hobbes where a psychotic cheerleader and a barbarian king switch bodies, all while an angry teen-genius and his master strategist friend race to save the world from an extradimensional horror, check out *Kor'Thank.*

My website is dirtyscifibuddha.com.
Thanks for reading!